The end of the world
was never so hilarious!

The Alien Manifesto

Marv Lincoln

Thunder Mountain Productions

This book is a work of fiction. The characters, incidents, and dialogue are drawn from the author's imagination and are not to be construed as real. Any resemblance to actual events or persons, living or dead, is entirely coincidental.

THE ALIEN MANIFESTO

A Thunder Mountain Productions book

Printed in the United States of America

ISBN: 978-0-9799208-1-3
Library of Congress Control Number: 2010942110

Thunder Mountain Productions
P.O. Box 3804
Sedona, AZ 86340

Contact information:

marv@vortex23.com

www.Vortex23.com (books by Marv Lincoln)

For all the psi people on Planet Earth who tried to warn us…until it was too late to turn back.

Intelligence Briefing

TOP SECRET

The information contained herein is to be viewed ONLY by authorized personnel. If you are not authorized to view this document, you are hereby ordered, under penalty of criminal prosecution for the crime of espionage, to immediately deliver this document, unread, to the Office of the President of the United States of America, Washington, D.C.

TOP SECRET

OVERVIEW

A crisis of unprecedented magnitude confronts the United States of America and Planet Earth. At this moment an ecological collapse has spread worldwide, creating political and economic instability, social unrest, and threats to international security.

This steadily worsening situation has been exacerbated by the destructive criminal activities of an international cartel whose identity is suspected but not confirmed. Further compounding the crisis is the alleged appearance in the USA of extraterrestrial (ET) entities, whose agenda is unknown at this time.

The following Intelligence Briefing explores the background of the ET situation and spotlights several of the major players in the unfolding scenario.

TO: President of the United States; Vice-President of the United States; Secretary, Department of State; Director, Central Intelligence Agency; Director, National Security Agency; Director, Federal Bureau of Investigation

FROM: Secretary, Department of Defense

SUBJECTS: Martin (Marty) Powers, spouse LeAnn (Leela) Powers; Jillian (Jill) Appleton; John (Hacker) Hack, Jr.; Alexis (Aura) Adelstein aka Goddess Kali. All subjects are residents of Sedona, Arizona, a popular tourist destination located two hours north of Phoenix, AZ.

Sedona is known as a hotbed of UFO activity. Military records indicate several direct encounters with extraterrestrials, especially in zones of alleged "vortex energy" within the city. Several of these encounters took place in the vicinity of a natural formation called Bell Rock, which lends credence to the alleged alien presence described in the report below. Several mili-

tary investigators have described Sedona as a "trans-dimensional gateway."

MARTIN POWERS: Writer, journalist. Founded and operated a website called Sedona Confidential, controversial site featuring exposé articles on local issues, politicians, corruption, etc. Also ran website called Soulmates4You, an online dating service, later sold to Yahoo. Subject closed Sedona Confidential after numerous threats from anonymous sources, plus pressure from spouse.

LEANN POWERS: Professional psychic. Worked as psychic reader in Sedona for several years. Employed by major NYC advertising agencies as corporate spy. Important State Department asset now assigned to present crisis. Previous assignment: Stop international cabal seeking to destroy China's financial infrastructure by creating a non-nuclear electromagnetic pulse (EMP). Subject disrupted plot using advanced psychic techniques. Controller: Agent R. Anderson.

JOHN HACK, JR.: Website designer, computer programmer, "hacker." Close friend of Martin Powers, designed his websites. Known as technological genius. Admitted foot fetishist. Arrested by FBI for various cybercrimes and hacker mischief, late 1990's and 2003-2005. Served 30 days prison time, 2005. Plea bargain: Helped government agencies defend against cybercrime and cyber attacks from foreign states in exchange for probation.

ALEXIS ADELSTEIN: Former waitress and part-time psychic. Friend of Mrs. Powers. Former lover of Mr. Powers. Radically transformed after bizarre lightning storm incident (see police interview, below). Later called herself Goddess Kali, founded Tantra Temple in Sedona area. Arrest record: Petty theft, malicious mischief (10 incidents) before age of 16. Served six months in juvenile detention facility.

JILLIAN APPLETON: Former assistant to Mr. Powers. Psychic and channeler. Discovered psychic link to Mrs. Powers during China crisis. Now employed by U.S. State Department as conduit to Mrs. Powers. Controller: Secretary, U.S. State Department.

INCIDENT ON BELL ROCK: THE ORBS

Interview of first responder Emerson Wade, Paramedic, Sedona Fire Department:

Police: What did you first encounter on Bell Rock?
Emerson Wade: There was a tremendous storm, rain and lightning and thunder, in April, like a monsoon storm but totally unseasonable. It only happened around the Bell Rock area. Like a rogue storm cell. I found the victim, Ms. Adelstein, flat on her back on a rock ledge. It appeared that she had been struck by lightning, but there were no outward signs of burns or other injury.
Police: Then why did you think she had been struck by lightning?

EW: Because she was lying very still on her back with her eyes wide open, as if she was in shock. And because a witness, Mr. Powers, told me he had seen a lightning bolt strike Ms. Adelstein.

Police: Was anyone else present at the scene when you arrived?

EW: Yes, the wife of Mr. Powers, who emerged from behind a rock just after our arrival on scene. She was completely naked. She had no clothes on.

Police: This woman was nude?

EW: Yes, stark raving naked. And dancing around in the rain, shouting and screaming. Until Mr. Powers wrapped his jacket around her.

Police: What did Mrs. Powers say to you about the lightning strikes?

EW: She said she didn't see the lightning hit Ms. Adelstein, but that the lightning had brought the orbs. She said there were orbs all around, that these orbs were alien life forms from another dimension come to visit the earth.

Police: Did you personally see any orbs at the location?

EW: No, not personally.

Police: What did Mr. Powers say about the orbs?

EW: He said he had seen the orbs floating around Bell Rock, and that one of them seemed to have entered the body of Ms. Adelstein together with a lightning bolt. Mr. Powers began rambling incoherently, so I asked an officer to remove him from the scene.

Police: What course of action did the paramedics take?

EW: We transported Ms. Adelstein to Cottonwood Hospital, where she was placed under observation. I understand that she was held for three days and that no signs of injury or impairment were reported.

Submitted by Sgt. Wallace Gunderson,
Sedona Police Department
Officer in Charge (OIC) on Bell Rock Incident

ORBS: a Paranormal Phenomenon

Orbs are spheres of light that certain groups of people believe are ghosts, spirits, or life forms that travel inter-dimensionally. Some say that orbs are advanced beings from other realms, dimensions or frequencies who are watching us and sometimes make contact with humans. Orbs are usually invisible to the naked eye. They appear only in images captured with digital or film-based cameras. Skeptics say these images are most likely due to reflections caused by a flash camera or from foreign material such as dust, pollen, or water droplets, especially rain, within the camera lens.

CONCLUSION

Surveillance of above group of subjects (Powers & Powers, et al) will continue until further notice. This will include electronic eavesdropping, e-mail monitoring, satellite tracking of movements, and all other surveillance deemed necessary by Defense Department. Subjects are not considered a threat to the security of the homeland at this time.

Mrs. Powers and Ms. Appleton are considered valuable assets by the State Department because of their psychic abilities. It is because of Mrs. Powers' status and high credibility rating within the Department that the alien scenario is being taken seriously.

We have concluded that the evidence of an alien visitation during the Bell Rock Incident is inconclusive, despite the claims of two eyewitnesses, Mr. and Mrs. Powers. If, however, further evidence of a visitation does arise and becomes public knowledge, the US policy of plausible deniability and disinformation regarding ET visitations remains in place. It is essential that this policy position be maintained in order to prevent further social unrest and panic among the masses.

(signed) Hugo J. Ramírez
Secretary, Department of Defense
United States of America

PART I

Six Months Later

.

"It's global blackmail, Marty.
Nothing like this has ever happened
in human history. We could all be
headed for the trash heap unless
something happens to turn this around."

—Hacker

CHAPTER ONE

The Age of Certain Catastrophe

Unseen forces ruled my world. I was as clueless as a mime in a house of mirrors, a question mark looking for an answer. My chakras were out of alignment, and my karma needed a tuneup. This was Sedona, after all, home of paranormal mysteries and powerful energies that seemed to influence everything in our high desert paradise, even the stale jokes of the tour guides.

Tourists by the millions flock to this cozy little village to gaze upon mind-bending red rock formations, to soak up the powerful vibrations from alleged energy vortexes, to bask in the mysterious milieu of unexplained incidents and fateful meetings too whacky to write off as mere coincidence. Sedona is ground zero for New Age pilgrims and practitioners. Stories of UFO sightings are common and acceptable in ordinary conversation. Hairless, large-headed gray aliens supposedly lurk around hiking trails. Psychics, healers, and channelers roam freely among the town's permanent population.

Maybe that was my problem: I had been in Sedona too long. Maybe I had been contaminated by random particles of cosmic dust, runoff from overheated vortexes.

It was all too much. Strange days and crazy nights, haunted by bizarre dreams; and yet I believed that my brilliant mind could sort it all out and keep my fragile relationships together. Yes, there was a lot on my mind on that ominous day. Indeed.

Orbs, orbs, and more orbs, for openers. Dreams of orbs, flashbacks of orbs. Alien presence. I know what I saw out there on Bell Rock. It wasn't right, it didn't fit my Reality template. I thought of my wife, who was more like a stranger every day. I thought of my ex-girlfriend, a close friend of my wife, who had lit my fire not too long ago.

But it wasn't just me, it was a case of collective anxiety. The ongoing environmental crisis, worse every day, was affecting every conscious being on the planet. And, yeah: I had the feeling that somehow the whole freakin' circus was spinning madly out of control. The natural order of things seemed crazily unnatural.

We all were living in, let's face it, the Age of Certain Catastrophe. We had gone too far in our quest for eternity. There were too many of us. We had soiled our nest. Mother Nature seemed poised to bite us all in the butt and rid herself of the human virus that was poisoning her party.

And so it was on such a day, a bright and strangely brilliant kind of day, a day heavy with anticipation and dread, that the wife and I decided to take a trip to the higher elevations of Flagstaff, twenty-six miles distant, twenty degrees lower in temperature, and a world away in terms of attitude and ambience. We had been arguing most of the morning, although arguing is not the right word. One does not argue with a telepath. She knows what you are thinking before the thought materializes. It is like arguing with yourself—it's a no-win situation.

The wife is one Leela Powers, famous psychic and clairvoyant, occasional covert ops agent for the U.S. government, a ravishing and slender beauty with long dark hair and penetrating green eyes. She had just returned from an assignment for the State Department in god-knows-where Eurasia, some kind of enviro-conference. Of course my wife can't tell me about her work for the government. It's rated Top Secret.

None of my beeswax, right?

Yes and no. That's what our "discussion" had been about that morning, as in, where do we draw the line? I don't pry into her private business. Leela is the telepath in our family. Not me, I'm square: non-psi. My wife can read my thoughts, but I can't read hers. *C'est la vie.*

But I was concerned for her safety. I had the creepy feeling that Leela was in over her head and had grown a little cocky with her string of successes. Plus I had a sinking feeling that she was having a fling with her State Department controller, a dude she called only "Mr. Anderson."

"It's not that at all, Marty," she said as I dried the breakfast dishes and put them away, my mind running at full speed, as usual. "It's strictly business with him. Oops!"

"Damn it, Leela!" I exploded. "Can't a man have any privacy inside his own head?" Not really, I thought, when a man is married to a very gifted psychic.

"I'm sorry, Marty, I didn't mean to invade your privacy. Sometimes I forget and scan you out of habit." She snuggled up to me from behind, thrusting those solid, perfect breasts into my back and encircling my waist with powerful arms. I turned around, pulled her into me, and kissed her so passionately that we were both breathing heavily when I finally released her.

My erotic thought forms must have set off alarms throughout the astral plane. "Not now, dear," she said, gently pushing me away and escaping to her bathroom. That was another issue: our sex life, which had ranged from hot to hotter over our many years together, had cooled considerably in the past few months.

We met in a Tantra workshop at a commune in India years ago, and I've been hooked on her ever since. We hung out for years, lived together, traveled the world, got married on a lark, saved the planet from economic collapse (Leela's work), and settled in the mystical environs of Sedona, where, supposedly, there was a psychic or a healer on every corner. It has been a mad, mad love affair, based on trust, respect, and, you know, yin-yang. Female-male stuff.

But things have changed, as the world has changed. Leela has taken a leap into another dimension. I felt like she had left me behind. Me? I'm just plain ol' Marty Powers, a forty-something retired Internet millionaire with not a whole lot to do—just watching the planet's downward spiral while I put my search for enlightenment on hold.

So we decided that contentious morning to escape our irreconcilable differences as well as the stifling August heat of Sedona, to take a hike in Flagstaff on one of those cool, inviting trails around the San Francisco Peaks, at about eight thousand feet. The higher the better, I thought. Something had gone sour in our relationship, and we both wanted to blow out the negative energy.

Our vehicle for the Flagstaff run, twenty-seven miles of nearly unspeakable grandeur via Oak Creek Canyon, was my souped-up, turbocharged 1200 cc Harley Sportster. Leela loves riding on the back of a motorcycle, digs speed and danger, but usually keeps her eyes tightly closed. Maybe she keeps her third eye open, I'm not sure. For this ride we were wearing lightweight helmets with built-in comm sets so we could talk to each other. On the Harley, we communicate the old-fashioned way.

We zipped out of overheated Sedona as quickly as possible, creeping through the tourist-infested Uptown shopping ghetto, across the Midgley Bridge (a popular venue for suicides), and into the canyon itself.

It is always an adrenaline rush to enter the winding, twisting, deliciously dangerous two-lane road that whisks you through an incredible wonderland into the high country. To the left, the red rocks stay with us for about eight miles—steep, swooping columns of sandstone, etched and sculpted for three hundred million years by the skillful hands of Mother Nature.

To the right, Oak Creek meanders lazily along, a narrow, burbling, silver stream riding a garden of rocks. And above: the canopy of thirsty cottonwood and sturdy oak trees, dappling and shaping the view from the driver's seat.

Our bickering energy seemed to dissolve in a deluge of beauty so profound that it triggers endorphins. Near the entrance to Slide Rock State Park, about five miles into the canyon, two things happened almost simultaneously:

First I got a whiff, then a visual, in the middle of the road, of the first dead skunk on our journey; and a millisecond later I noticed that we were being followed by two bike riders on foreign-looking machines; behind the mysterious pair was a huge black Mercedes, the car that S.S. officers drove back in the 20th Century. Not a familiar sight in the canyon.

I clicked on my comm set by blowing hard on the sensor. "Yo, Leela," I said, "got your ears on?"

"Roger that, Marty," she said, giving me a squeeze. "Got my ears on and all three eyes. And I have a very strong feeling that some people are following us."

"I've got the same strong feeling," I said, as my hand twisted the throttle and pumped the bike up to seventy mph, swerving around two turtle-like SUV drivers blocking our path. "Hang on, honeybuns!" I shouted into the comm. "Let's see if we can lose these jokers."

Silence from Leela, but a tighter grip around my belly. Sailing around the curves of Oak Creek Canyon at high speeds, weaving in and out of cars, is not my idea of a good time, and probably not hers either. But something in my blood caught fire and I felt like a little excitement on this stifling Sedona day.

At about sixteen miles out of Uptown, a transitional zone where the tall Ponderosa pines have taken over the landscape, the bikes were still right behind us, way too close for comfort.

I looked in the rear view mirror. "Ducatis," I said.

"Do what?" answered my wife.

"Ducatis. Italian bikes. Pretty rare in these parts. Racing bikes. Monsters. They could have most Japanese bikes for lunch. Not my Harley. And the two dudes riding the things look pretty sinister." The pair tailing us wore the giant-size helmets that completely obscure the face and create the appearance of giant mutant insects. They wore black leather from neck to toe. Their heads were bent forward as they pursued us.

"Leela," I said suspiciously, "any idea who our friends might be? You've been hanging out with some pretty suspicious characters lately."

"Who, me?" she said, pseudo-innocently "Don't know what you're talking about, Marty." Sometimes my dear wife likes to run little mind games, playing coy, and at this point in time, very annoying.

The winding canyon road suddenly becomes the dreaded switchbacks—two miles of extreme hairpin curves—with a posted speed limit of 20 mph. I downshifted just as we leaned into the first sharp curve; the two Ducatis caught up with our bike and tried to force us off the road. "Leela," I gasped, "hang on real tight. This could get hairy!"

I kicked up the rpm and our speed to about sixty as we zipped around the tight curves, nearly laying the bike down a couple of times. At the top of the switchbacks you come to a plateau where you can look over the side into a canyon that is more than two thousand feet to the bottom. There is a guardrail, but it's flimsy.

The two Ducatis had us sandwiched, boxed in. A look behind, and…what! The big black Mercedes was right behind us, half a foot from the rear tire of the Harley, close enough to send shock waves through my heart chambers.

"Leela, Leela! I shouted. I was freaking out and pissed off, simultaneously. "They're trying to push us over the cliff! It's a long way down, damnit!"

Over the comm I could hear Leela's deep breathing for about three seconds. "Just relax, Marty. I know what they're trying to do. I think I know who they are."

"Great. *I* know what they're trying to do, and I don't give a shit *who* they are," I snapped. "We're almost to the edge and they've got us completely hemmed in! We are up shit creek, Leela!"

"No, we're up Oak Creek, dear," she cooed. "Just leave it to me, Marty. Maybe you should close your eyes and let me take over."

"What?" I screeched. "Look out, we're going over the—"

I must have blacked out for a few seconds, because all I remember is this: We were headed right for the lip of the canyon and the flimsy guardrail, being nudged in that direction by two sleek Italian motorcycles from the sides and a huge black Mercedes from the rear. Suddenly I felt the bike take flight—literally—and float up and away from the guardrail.

I opened my eyes as the Harley gently touched down, then jerked my head to the right just in time to see this: The two Ducatis crashing through the guardrail and plunging over the side of the cliff, followed by the Mercedes! I heard screaming. Then, a few seconds later, the eerie sound of metal objects falling through trees, then hitting the ground with a soft crash. Then the even stranger sound of a large metal object banging into rocks as it tumbled to the canyon bottom.

I braked the Harley to a halt.

Leela dismounted and so did I. We both ripped off our helmets.

"Marty, quick, look down in the canyon. In just a second or two...."

I jacked up the bike and hustled to the broken guardrail. Just in time to see the black Mercedes hit the bottom on its roof and explode with a huge pop. In an instant it was engulfed in a giant fireball. The Ducatis and their occupants were nowhere in sight. A fire suddenly erupted among the towering Ponderosa pine trees on the canyon floor.

"Fire!" I yelled. "Leela, the goddamn forest is on fire!"

"Don't worry about it, Marty," said Leela, soothingly. "Just leave it to me. Let's get back on the bike and finish our adventure."

She was amazingly calm. I shrugged and kick-started the Harley. Nearby I heard the whirring sound of helicopter blades. I turned around quickly as we sped off and saw two black choppers hovering over the fire.

Later, as we snacked silently on our PB&J sandwiches, sitting on a huge granite boulder about two miles into the easy dirt trail, enjoying the cool air at eight thousand feet, the silence was palpable. Leela avoided my gaze. Finally I had to speak up.

"Leela, two things I'd like to discuss with you? One, those thugs just tried to kill us. You know, fucking run us off the edge of the canyon? And now *they're* toast. What's up with that?

"And two, would you care to tell me what happened back there? We were headed right for that guard rail and my bike suddenly sprouted wings! Can you move objects with your mind now? I know, I know, you teleported from Tibet to India once, big deal. But can you really do, what, telekinesis or psychokinesis?"

"They're the same thing, Marty, and yeah, I can do that and a lot of other stuff that may surprise you. But forget that for now. We are really—and I mean it, all of us—are in serious danger."

"I knew you were into some serious shit, sweetheart," I said, "this is just what I was afraid of!"

"Marty, listen to me now. I know who those guys are… or were. I did meet some sinister characters at that environmental summit in Moscow last month, mainly guys from Georgia or Ukraine, thugs with Russian roots. Organized crime. There were these four who were into what I call eco-blackmail. Never mind the details. I saw through their scheme and had 'em busted. All four were arrested and locked away by Interpol. These guys tailing us could have been related to that bunch."

"Oh," I muttered, humbled by my lowly status in the superhero rankings. I looked over at my wife as we set out again on the trail, surrounded by aspens and Ponderosa pines, squirrels chattering endlessly, birds calling secret messages to each other.

She was wearing denim shorts and her Reebok cross-trainers, topped off by a skimpy tank top with one of my blue denim shirts over it. Damn, she was still sexy as hell. Slim but curvy, great ass, shapely long legs, champagne shoulders....And seemingly unavailable, on the physical plane. I reached for her shoulders and spun her around so we were eye to eye. We stopped walking, temporarily frozen in time.

"What about that explosion, Leela! And the freakin' fire! Who's gonna put out the fire?"

"Don't worry, the fire's already out," she said confidently. "Just call it an intervention. I took care of it." She wriggled away from my grasp.

There wasn't anything more to say. Or do. Except proceed down the well-trod dirt trail, breathing in the delicious, highly oxygenated forest air.

I was wondering who—or what—I was married to.

In the distance I could hear the rumble of thunder.

CHAPTER TWO

The Third Eye Coffee House

My favorite place to hang out in Sedona is the Third Eye Coffee House, located just off the main drag in West Sedona. I'm not really into hanging out, per se, in public places where other people can tune in to your private conversations. I'm all for tuning in to *their* private conversations. As a former investigative reporter, snooping comes naturally to me.

The Third Eye had a kind of New Agey orientation. The décor was definitely Late Woo-Woo, starting with the tasteful third eye sign outside the building. Inside you'd find a huge mural covering one wall depicting the cosmos, with a special magnified section emphasizing the Pleiades constellation. On other walls there were framed photos of orbs—those freakin' orbs again!—taken by customers over the years; an acrylic painting of a psychedelic vortex; a framed photo of moonwalker astronaut Edwin Mitchell, he of the UFO advocacy; and a clay figure of the sitting Buddha with an iPod in his hand and headphones covering his ears.

The place smelled richly of coffee, incense, stale flowers, sweat, and human methane gas. It had Wi-Fi with free Internet access, so a parade of Sedonans with nothing else to do sat around all day sipping their beverages and looking for soulmates, I suppose, on the Internet, or updating their Facebook pages. There were about a dozen small tables in the place, a comfortable couch, a large round oak table with six wooden chairs around it, a vase of plastic roses in the middle. The walls were painted a sort of plum color, apparently representing the purple hues of the sixth chakra, aka the third eye.

A lot of my pals hung out at the Third Eye: it was a great place to catch up on the gossip of the day and spread a little of your own.

The morning after the Oak Creek Canyon incident I cruised into the coffee house around ten a.m., expecting a couple of friends to be there and maybe a little buzz about The Event, if word had even filtered into the city yet. What I found was a packed house, about two dozen people excitedly chattering away. When I walked in, all eyes turned toward me.

The place got very quiet. I walked over to the big round table, where I occasionally held court.

John C. Hack, alias Hacker, my best friend and fellow mischief-maker, immediately thrust a newspaper under my nose.

"Marty!" he nearly shouted. "Did you see this? Know anything about it?"

The paper's big banner headline on page one fairly screamed: "FOUR KILLED IN FIERY CANYON CRASH NEAR SEDONA." And the subhead: "Canyon fire squelched by mysterious black helicopters." There was a huge color photo of a badly burned car on its roof, surrounded by charred Ponderosa pine trees. Nearby, two motorcycles lay in a heap of twisted metal.

"Golly, folks," I said modestly, coyly, "I'm afraid there's nothing I can tell you about this— this terrible accident!" I wasn't lying.

Around the table sat the usual members of my posse: Benny Bravo, my former editorial assistant at my Sedona Confidential website and the town's only Jewish Mexican; "Past Life" Penelope, a local psychic and infamous gossipmonger; Claude "Picasso" Imperioli, starving artist and endless pontificator; and Dan Strange, a Jeep tour driver and obsessive government conspiracy theorist.

"What exactly happened?" I asked innocently, flashing Hacker our secret signal—a quick movement upward of the eyes, signaling that something else entirely is going on—and he acknowledged the signal by tugging on his left ear twice.

Penelope jumped in, talking fast. "Two foreign-make bikes went through the guardrail and over the side up by the overlook, just after the switchbacks," she spurted, "quickly followed by a Mercedes. The car had diplomatic license plates, Marty, isn't that a kick in the head? And there were four bodies, all burned beyond recognition. So nobody knows who these people were, or why they went over the side, or—and this is even weirder—how those black choppers happened to be there to put out the fire!"

"How *did* the helicopters put out the fire?" I asked, because I had no idea and wanted to know.

"Says here they just *happened* to be in the area," said Dan Strange, a huge hulk of a man, gentle as a lamb. "Doesn't say they were military, but I figure they had to be. You know, black military choppers been buzzin' Sedona for years, lookin' for alien encampments and UFO evidence in the canyons. Anyway, they used these huge buckets to scoop up water from the creek and put out the fire in three or four trips. Cool, huh?"

"Pretty amazing story," I mused. "Something like this happening in our own back yard. Were there any, uh, witnesses?" I crossed my fingers behind my back.

"Nope," said Benny Bravo. "Choppers did their job, then left, and a few minutes later four fire trucks showed up to make sure the whole canyon didn't go up in flames."

"Verrrrry interesting," I said. "Why near Sedona, I wonder? What were those people doing here?—you know, the diplomatic plates." I was fishing for info, hoping I wasn't too obvious.

Hacker leaned over and half-whispered, "Marty, I gotta talk to you, and soon. Can I drop over to your house maybe this a.m.?"

"Maybe later," I said quietly. "But let's wait a while. Leela will be here in a few. She had to make some phone calls. She's going to D.C. later this afternoon, you know, for a meeting with some bigwigs in the State Department."

"Hmmmm, right," nodded Hacker. "Seems like she's been spending a lot of time out of town lately. Something going on that I don't know about?"

"Hacker, I really don't think that's any of your—"
I stopped in mid-sentence. The room had suddenly
gone silent, as if all the air had been sucked out of it. I
looked around, and froze.

Three young women flounced into the Third Eye,
giggling and laughing, their voices like ethereal music.
They were impossibly cute, looking like clones of each
other: blond hair tied up in ponytails, blue eyes flashing, miniskirts and tank tops, tattoos and piercings
everywhere.

"What the fu—" started Dan, then stopped.

"Hi, folks!" said the three in unison, sounding
strangely like the Dixie Chicks in close harmony. "Don't
let us stop the fun! We're just here for our lattés,"
chimed one of the three, as they headed for the coffee
counter.

"It's the Dakinis," whispered Penelope loudly. "The
recruiters for that bitch Kali's Tantric Temple."

"Recruiters?" asked a guy from the next table who
had been eavesdropping on our conversation. I had
never seen him before. "For a tantric temple? Where
is this place?"

The psychic looked the dude up and down, dis-
missed him with a sneer, and turned back to our little
clique. "Recruiters, right. These little hotties recruit
people for Goddess Kali. But be careful. People say
they have some kind of mystical sex power. They say if
one of them even touches you, you are hooked on her
forever and you become some kind of sex slave."

"That's some kind of bullshit," I said to the folks at our table. "In Tibetan Buddhism, Dakinis are like benign spirits. "I don't think these hussies—"

"Hold it right there, pardner," said Dan Strange. "I have heard that there is some very weird shit going on at that woman's spread out by the creek, that Goddess Kali. And I know there's a lot of tourists coming to Sedona to see her."

The conversational level in the Third Eye returned to normal, although most of the patrons in the place kept a wary eye on the bubbly trio at the coffee bar. Suddenly the three walked to our table and stood directly in front of me.

"Helloooooo, girls," I said cautiously, "something I can do for you?" They looked about fourteen at first glance, high school cheerleader vibes, but up close they showed a little wear and tear. One of them stepped out and looked me right in the eye.

"Marty Powers, right? Goddess Kali said we'd probably find you here. She wishes to send you her special personal invitation to visit our Tantra Temple." I gulped, as the memories of my sorta sordid (and very brief) affair with "Goddess Kali," the former psychic known as Aura, leaked obscenely from my memory bank.

"I'd like you all to meet my sisters," said my new friend, indicating the other two Dakinis, "Karma and Satori. My name is Chakra." Without warning, she plopped herself into my lap, her left arm circling my neck and shoulders. I could feel the energy immediately. Her long, slim legs were now exposed, revealing tattoos that looked like bejeweled snakes enjoined in coitus.

Her two friends moved around our table, Karma connecting with Penelope by placing her hands on my friend's shoulders; Penelope, who is gay and kind of butch, at first resisted, then gradually relaxed into the touch. The one called Satori seduced Benny Bravo immediately, laying hands on the top of his shaved head.

Chakra showed me her ring, which seemed to glow and change colors, the colors of the rainbow, as she spoke. "This is my chakra ring," she whispered in my ear. "It's like a mood ring. It shows what chakra I'm in from moment to moment. Red, the root chakra; orange, the sex center; yellow, the hara, or power center; green, for the heart; blue, the throat chakra; purple, the third eye; and white, the crown chakra."

I took a long look at the ring as the colors shifted hypnotically from one to the next. "Very interesting," I managed. She definitely had my full attention. "And what color is it in now? Which chakra?"

"Sitting physically close to you, look, the ring is bright orange—the second chakra, the sex center."

Sex center indeed. I put my hand on her exposed thigh. I felt myself slide into the second chakra. My shorts began to swell.

Then my wife walked into the Third Eye.

"Leela's here," whispered Hacker.

I stood halfway up, dumping Chakra onto her feet, then sat down and placed a napkin over my telltale lap. Chakra leaned over and whispered in my ear, "Will you come?"

"No...y-yes...m-maybe," I sputtered, as I pushed the young woman in Hacker's direction.

Leela found her way to our table as the three Dakinis moved away and gradually out the door. My wife kissed me gently on the cheek, then sat down with a big smile on her face.

"Wasn't that the three Dakinis? The high priestesses from Kali's temple?" asked Leela. "Did they bring an invitation from Kali?" She was grinning from ear to ear now.

"Well, uh..." I stammered, but Hacker did an intervention.

"They were just flirting with everybody," said my friend. "You know how they work."

"Right," said my psychic wife. "And you know what they say: one touch and it's all over for you. A lifetime of sexual slavery."

"I'll take my chances, sweetheart," I tweaked back. "You know I'm a gambler."

"Leela," interjected Dan Strange, breaking the growing tension at our table, "do you know anything about this accident up in the canyon yesterday? Does your psychic sense tell you anything?"

"All I know is what I read in the papers," she lied with a broad smile and a wink. "You know how these foolish people drive through the canyon: follow too close, drive too fast….So this doesn't surprise me."

"I just channeled a message from one of my spirit guides," said Past Life Penelope, her eyes tightly closed. "The people who crashed were aliens trying to escape from the black helicopters, which were sent from the secret military base in Boynton Canyon to destroy them. The aliens were on their way to the Lowell Observatory in Flagstaff to make contact with their mothership and—"

"Excuse me," I interrupted, and stood up. I can't stand this kind of New Age blather anymore; it drives me nuts. "Sorry, Penelope, but I have to run to the bathroom." I started off, but then turned around with a closing comment:

"Y'know, I have never heard of aliens riding around on Ducati motorcycles. That's a new one!"

Leela reached out and pinched the back of my thigh, hard. In a millisecond I realized what I had said.

"Yo, dawg," spoke up Benny Bravo, "who said anything about the bikes being Dukatis? The paper said the bikes couldn't be I.D.'d. D'ya know something we should know?"

"No," I said, and my face must have started to turn red because I could feel it burning. "I must be psychic too." And I stumbled to the men's room, where I spent about five minutes trying to recover my composure.

When I returned to our table the conversation had turned to other matters, like the crumbling economy, the many business closures in Sedona, and the number of people now living in their cars.

"Leela, let's go home. I've got a little good-bye present for you," I said, squeezing her bare shoulder. "A surprise, kind of." The surprise was in my pants, waiting impatiently for the presentation.

"And I've got a little surprise for you, dear," she said. "Let's go now while I'm still in the mood."

Everyone at the table understood our not-so-subtle coital code, including Hacker, who looked a little exasperated. "I guess our meeting today is off, huh Marty?" he said.

"No, let's just postpone it until later and talk over dinner. If I have any energy left."

My seemingly oversexed wife grabbed me by the arm and hustled me out of the Third Eye Coffee House, into the scorching oven of a Sedona August morning.

CHAPTER THREE

Free Bird

Leela and I had what amounted to a quickie after we got home to our air conditioned love nest. In the past we had enjoyed long, luxurious lovemaking sessions with generous foreplay, and either meditative, Tantra-style couplings or explorations of arcane Kama Sutra acrobatics. This tryst was a bit hurried, because my beloved had to pack and get ready for her helicopter trip from the Sedona airport to Sky Harbor Airport in Phoenix and thence to Washington, D.C.

Leela wasn't talking much about her business with the State Department, and I wasn't asking any questions. She had a Secret clearance and that was that. Case closed. But I knew instinctively, and from overhearing the occasional phone conversation, that something big was brewing on the international scene. Something to do with eco-terrorism. Something frightening. And my wife seemed to be right in the middle of it.

I took Leela to the Sedona airport to meet the waiting helicopter at five o'clock, and by six I was having dinner with Hacker at Sushi Town in West Sedona. We liked to sit in the funky outdoor patio, where we had our most private conversations. As a precaution,

Hacker always scanned the place for bugs, using Microsoft's Bug Cleaner software, an app on his iPad.

"Clean," he said, then cleared his throat. I knew this was going to be serious. Hacker and I had an agreement to be totally honest and up-front with each other. I met my good friend at our local microbrewery years ago when Leela and I first moved to Sedona, and we hit it off right away.

Later he would design my awesome website, Sedona Confidential, and also its Web spinoff, the highly successful Soulmates4U. After I sold Soulmates for five large, I gave two mil to Hacker and a mil to a lovely lady named Jill, who was my former office assistant, a good friend of Leela's, and also a former girlfriend of Hacker's.

"Marty, my main man, don't keep me in suspense," said Hacker. I knew this meeting was not for purposes of gossip, but out of his genuine concern for my relationship with Leela. He is like a member of our family; thus he has access to the most intimate details of my marriage. "What's going on? What's up with you and Leela?"

"Okay, okay, dude," I said, "I will tell all. As much as I know, that is. It's almost as if Leela is leading a second life apart from our life together. Which, come to think of it, she is."

"Let's start with yesterday, okay? I know you two took a trip up the canyon to Flagstaff on your souped-up Harley. Now, I do believe in coincidence, but I figure you two were somehow in the vicinity of the nasty business that occurred up there. Right?"

"You are correct, my dear Hacker. Allow me to explain. Leela is involved in some stuff with the State Department that took her to a big conference in Moscow where some thugs from Eastern Europe also happened to be. She read their minds or something and saw dirty deeds written all over them. So she got 'em busted and locked away.

"Then the friends of said thugs must have put out a contract on her pretty ass. They tracked her here. And yesterday, her pretty ass happened to be on the back of my Harley. So they, said thugs, tried to kill us by running my bike off the road." I smiled weakly.

Hacker looked at me with disbelief. "What? Okay, fine. These people tried to bump you off, literally. But how did two fancy bikes and a big Mercedes and four charbroiled humans wind up at the bottom of Oak Creek Canyon in a heap of twisted metal not to mention a huge fireball?

"And one more thing, Marty," continued Hacker. "I know your tongue was wagging overtime this morning at the Third Eye when you spilled the beans about the Ducati bikes. How would you know the make of the bikes unless you were there? C'mon, brother, don't bullshit your old pal."

I sighed, then patiently explained to my friend how it had all happened: the thrilling chase up the canyon at high speeds, the Dukati bikes, the attempted bump-off, the miracle of my Harley heading off the cliff and suddenly taking to the air and landing safely a few feet away.

Hacker closed his eyes, took several deep breaths, opened them, and looked at me in a curious way.

"Marty, I know your wife has amazing psychic powers now. I know she can move objects with her mind. I know she can read people's minds; she's a freakin' telepath, for chrissake. I know she can teleport her body when she is near the right power source, like what happened in Tibet, when she 'jumped'—quote, unquote—from the top of that mountain all the way to India. But, but—"

(My friend was referring to Leela's most recent heroic exploit, whereby she put the kibosh on a plot to send China back to the Stone Age by some creeps who had wired up a bunch of energy vortexes to create an electromagnetic pulse. It's a long story; I guess you had to be there.)

"I know where you're going, old buddy," I said gently, knowing my friend was having trouble speaking his mind. "How can I live with a woman like that? The answer is: I don't know if I can anymore. Though I'm still crazy about her. She's beautiful, she's brilliant, she's sexy as hell, and we've been through a lot of stuff together. And I know we still love each other, whatever that means. But she's on a mission now.

"Also," I went on, "I'm pretty sure that some very heavy shit is about to come down, and soon, regarding the planet and the environmental crisis. Leela says there's going to be some real catastrophes if some serious action isn't taken. She says it's already too late for many places, like parts of Africa, where there just isn't any more water. She says we're all gonna have to pay the price for ignoring the warnings."

"Marty," Hacker interrupted, "let's get local. Did you know the county just approved that huge development near Prescott? And another monster project between Cottonwood and Sedona got approved too? Thousands and thousands of homes, three or four new golf courses, and we're running out of water right here?"

"That's exactly the point, dude," I said sadly. "Pretty soon we're gonna turn on our water taps and nothing but brown sludge is gonna come out. Damn! The madness is spreading. Leela says she can help the world situation by using her psychic powers. It looks like the State Department agrees."

"I hate to say this, Marty, but I think that geek from the State Department—what's his name, Anderson—also agrees. You told me she's been hanging out with him in D.C. and that he was also on that trip to Moscow. Are you thinking what I'm thinking?"

"Damn straight I am. I've always been suspicious of Mr. Anderson and his connection with Leela. But you know what, Hacker? She's a free bird. I don't own her, and she don't own me. She can do what she wants. Jealousy has never been part of our relationship. Still...."

"Still...what?"

"Still, I've been thinking that it would be good to make sure she's okay, you know? Kind of like tracking her electronically. To kind of keep track of her. Just audio would be enough so I know what's goin' on. Know what I'm sayin'?"

Hacker couldn't suppress a grin. "You mean a bug."

"Yeah, that's it. A bug. Something she couldn't suss out even with her great powers."

"I'm way ahead of you, my man. I must be psychic too. I started working on a bug to plant on Leela, then I stopped. I said to myself, you know what, Leela is a good friend of mine too. I don't think I could do that to her. Plus, she would know immediately if there was a bug anywhere near her. Best if you just accept the 'what is, is' of the situation, ol' buddy. Go with the flow and all that. You know the drill."

"Okay," I said, "I can handle it; no *problema*." Knowing full well that there was a *problema*. My marriage, for one thing. Was it really winding down? I had started to question the assumed integrity of our relationship. Was Leela getting it on with other guys? I had stayed faithful since the brief affair with Aura. Maybe it was time for me to reach out and touch someone...else.

I downed the rest of my Chinese beer and poked at the remains of my California roll with a chopstick. "I've got another bright idea, Hacker. How about you and I pay a little visit to Ms. Kali's erotic emporium in the next day or two? I'm kinda curious about what goes on out there. I've been hearing some pretty weird stories. And those Dakinis definitely rattle my chakras."

Hacker drained his beer and stood up, flapping his arms as if they were wings. He threw back his head and started singing:

"'Cause I'm free as a bird now
And this bird you cannot change."
"Lynyrd Skynyrd?" I said. "Free Bird?"
"You got it, brother," said Hacker. "Free bird indeed. Make the call and we'll head out to Kali's tomorrow."

CHAPTER FOUR

Goddess Kali's Tantric Temple

It turned out that you couldn't just drop in to Kali's temple, like you might drop into Walgreens or the local Catholic church. You had to call ahead, give a full accounting of who you were and why you wanted to visit, and make a reservation for the next available tour.

Hacker and I were having dinner at Moby's, a hip new vegan restaurant in West Sedona. I told him I had already made the call, had thoroughly debased myself and agreed to all of their rules and regs, and made a reservation for the next available tour, which was the following day at one p.m.

"Tour?!" thundered my friend. "What is this, a time-share temple or something? Do they want a blood sample too? I thought this was just a bunch of ex-sex workers who had discovered Eastern religion. Or escort service girls going legit."

I calmed him down and tried to tell him more. He was angry about the whole adventure anyway; he never liked Goddess Kali in her earlier incarnations, and he thought Tantra was just another word for paying for sex, which was against his principles.

"Their main deal is, look but don't touch. Be respectful toward the Dakinis and Goddess Kali, and if you should happen to see her, which you probably won't, but if you do, be sure to kneel down and kiss her feet. Don't touch the sculptures of lingams and yonis, and—"

"Whoa, whoa, hold it right there, dude," said Hacker, pushing aside the remains of his black bean and tofu burger. "Kiss Kali's feet? No way. I wasn't impressed by the lady's feet when she was known as Aura and even then her toes were too fat. Now I hear that she has put on about thirty pounds so those fat toes are probably even fatter. I don't care if she's become a goddess. I loathe and despise fat toes. These lips shall never meet those feet, I can assure you, my friend."

Case closed. For the time being.

It is only fair to tell you that my friend John Hack is a dedicated, unapologetic, and incurable foot fetishist. He loves women's feet the way most men love and admire—and obsess over—other female body parts: legs, eyes, hair, asses, ta-ta's. He makes it clear that he loves feet, not shoes or other inanimate objects. Technically, Hacker is a podophiliac—a person who is sexually obsessed with feet. Romantically, he is the Don Juan of women's feet.

Hacker is a real ladies man anyway. Tall, good-looking and muscular, intelligent and witty, with finely-chiseled cheek bones, a strong, commanding jaw, curly silver-gray hair and penetrating gray eyes, my good buddy exudes an air of confidence without being obnoxiously "male." He loves the ladies, and they love him. He keeps his love for their feet under wraps, but women say he gives the best foot massage in Northern Arizona. He is forty-five years old and always seems to be up and ready for a sexual encounter.

Next day, under a killer blue sky, Hacker and I headed to Kali's Tantric Temple. Excitement was in the air, which registered around 105 Fahrenheit at noon. He brought his stunning Porsche 911 Turbo to an abrupt stop at a red light at the intersection of State Route 89A (Sedona's main drag) and Dry Creek Road.

The subject of feet was still at the forefront of his mind, and he started rambling about his absolute refusal to kiss the feet of the goddess. "Are we clear on that, Marty?" he said. "I don't want any misunderstandings when we get to this place, okay?"

The light changed to green and Hacker floored it though the intersection and speed-shifted up the highway to punctuate his point.

"Hacker, the odds are really against you having to kiss the fat feet of Goddess Kali today. So please relax. And turn left here." His tires squealed as we turned left at Upper Red Rock Loop Road, zipped past the upscale Red Rock High School, and slammed around the tight and deadly curves of the narrow road that would take us to Kali's temple.

Another mile and we reached the gravel road which led to our destination. "Turn left here," I said, my heart not surprisingly pounding with anticipation.

"Hey, isn't this where that cult—er, that religious community used to have their ashram?" asked Hacker.

"Right on," I said. "They were always controversial. Kind of a combination of Jesus and UFOs. Jesus was an alien, or something. The local newspaper wrote a bunch of scandalous articles, and they were basically driven out of town. They sold everything and left. Too bad. The disciples looked like retro hippies. The women were gorgeous with long hair and no makeup. Kali and friends must have bought their property. Fourteen acres, and most of it is right on Oak Creek. Look!"

Straight ahead was what appeared to be the main building. Hacker and I gasped as we approached. "It looks like the freakin' Taj Mahal!" my friend exclaimed.

"Migawd," I screeched. "No, to me it's a cross between the Golden Temple in India and the Sacred Mosque in Mecca! Oh, wait, it kind of resembles the Kremlin. No, check that, Hacker, this must be some kind of hallucination, or perhaps a hologram created by the goddess. Drive on, my man, and we shall investigate Kali's new digs."

What made us gasp and gawk was a gorgeous white marble structure, capped with domes, cupolas, soaring spires, gargoyles, and other symbols of the world's great religions—minus the cross, of course—reaching at least three stories into the sky in utter defiance of Sedona's height limits. (But this property lay in the county, safely out of the reach of Sedona's bungling bureaucrats.)

On either side of the temple were several low-lying wooden buildings, painted a bright burnt orange. Green grass was everywhere, rare in this high desert, plus clusters of familiar cactus and trees such as junipers, cottonwoods, various pines, oaks, maples, and weeping willows. A real Garden of Eden feel to the place. Construction workers scrambled over the facility with tools in hand, the whine of high-tech machinery ever-present.

Hacker planted the Porsche in the paved parking lot and we moved toward the huge oak door of the temple. "Cameras," said Hacker.

"No doubt we are being watched, my friend," I said.

"Cameras in the sculptures," he answered. "Check out their eyes: lenses."

The walkway was lined with marble sculptures of lingams and yonis, of buddhas and goddesses and Socrates and Lao Tzu and Chiang Tzu, and Shiva feeling up Shakti, plus many I didn't recognize. The eyes in the sculptures followed us as we moved down the walkway. Inoffensive New Age music wafted from hidden speakers. The front door was locked, so I banged loudly with the knocker, a somewhat crude representation of the male genitalia, featuring, naturally, an erect member, cast in bronze.

The door was opened slowly by another of the lovely Dakinis, this one wearing a flowing golden robe that just kissed the marble floor of the entryway. "I am Sundar," she purred. "I will be your guide. Please remove your shoes, remain silent, and follow me."

Hacker and I exchanged a furtive glance. He shrugged; I rolled my eyes, wondering where all the money had come from to finance this enterprise. The ceilings in this joint were thirty feet high. First class all the way. The whole place bespoke of big bucks. We followed our guide down a long hallway with wooden doors on either side. The doors had no signs or labels as to what went on inside, but Sundar was helpful.

"This room is for private Tantra sessions," she indicated. "That room is for sensuous massage. And that room is for counseling. That room on the left is group Tantra." And so on. The place was still a work in progress, with workers painting the walls and hanging artworks of goddesses. Hacker and I seemed to be the only civilians in the place.

Our guide pointed upward, from whence issued a cacophony of construction noise. "The whole second level will be an auditorium for Goddess Kali's darshans and other sacred events," she said quietly. "The auditorium will eventually have space for five thousand seekers."

Hacker and I rolled our eyes and made choking sounds—five thousand seekers? That's half the population of Sedona!—but Sundar ignored us and pointed with long, graceful fingers to another room nearby.

"We will see a video in this room," said Sundar (pronounced SOON-dhar, she had politely informed us). "My name is a Sanskrit word. Goddess Kali gave it to me. Means beautiful," she had said. She was tall and wispy and smelled of jasmine, spoke in a sort of southern accent that sounded vaguely like Texas. She opened a double door and ushered us into a small theater that held about thirty seats and had a large screen in front. There were about twenty people already in the seats, mostly white men, looking like refugees from a timeshare presentation.

The video was professionally made, with soaring New Age-type music and lavish attention paid to Sedona's famous red rocks, but the most attention was paid to Goddess Kali herself—described as an "advanced consciousness" and "the ultimate embodiment of positive karma" and a "goddess among earth-bound deities." Pretty extravagant praise for a former waitress and threadbare psychic. Oh, and she did look to have gained at least thirty pounds since the last time I had, uh, seen her.

But let's start at the beginning of the video. A female narrator described what Tantra is and isn't, behind sexy graphics from the Kama Sutra. "A great misunderstanding has arisen over just what Tantra is all about," she said. "To many people, it just means sex—different ways of having sex, with different kinds of partners, usually based around some kind of ritual.

"To Goddess Kali," she continued, "Tantra means expansion of consciousness. Transformation. Opening to life in all of its totality. To be present to the moment. To..."

She went on like that for a good two minutes, spouting all of the New Age clichés of the day about chakras and sharing energy and opening our hearts and living our truth and moving toward the light. I was getting bored and Hacker was squirming in his seat, although the narrator herself was now on the screen, a real doll in flowing robes with mucho cleavage and blond hair spilling over her shoulders.

Tight close-up on the lady as she revealed the good stuff: "You *will* work with partners here. You *will* have orgasmic experiences here. Yes. And more. Once you transcend the barriers of your busy mind and surrender to Goddess Kali, you will learn to perform amazing feats. *Unimaginable* feats." I nudged Hacker with an elbow and he banged his knee into mine. We sat forward in our seats.

Video: Three women and one man sitting in meditation in a beautiful desert garden and slowly levitating skyward a good twenty-five feet, then hovering there for a full thirty seconds before floating back to the earth.

Voiceover: "You will quickly learn the secrets of levitation."

Video: Dissolve to: A series of quick cuts of various locations in the world. The Taj Mahal, the Beijing skyline, the Grand Canyon, crop circles in England, a slum in Rio de Janeiro, a look down at the Earth from a satellite, a beach on some exotic island, and more, and more.

Voiceover: "Imagine being able to travel anywhere you want to go...with remote viewing. No muss, no fuss, no airport security. Enjoy total freedom with Goddess Kali's secret technique. Also, you will learn how to perform lucid dreaming and create beautiful, unlimited dreams."

There was more: The secrets of telepathy, of teleportation, of moving objects with the mind, of healing others as well as oneself. Some wild promises that it was possible to learn and experience all of this through Goddess Kali. And all of this narration delivered in a soft, non-aggressive manner, almost like a TV commercial for a new drug to help you sleep.

The video ended; the lights went up. The entire audience sat silent and stunned for several seconds. "Where do we sign up?" I whispered jokingly to my friend. Hacker gave me a hard, ugly look.

The tour was over. Our guide gave us two colorful brochures on the Tantric Temple's various programs, and ushered us out the front door.

On the way back to West Sedona, as we sailed down 89A, Hacker seemed tense and angry.

"What's up, brother?" I asked innocently.

"It's all a bunch of bullshit," he grumbled. "You know it's too good to be true. There's something…sinister about the whole thing. What's up with this Kali? Your ex-girlfriend. Is she collecting souls or something?"

"First," I countered, "she is not my ex-girlfriend. Let me be clear on that. We had a little fling back in the day, which I still regret, so let's just say it was a spontaneous energy exchange. Harmless. My wife never found out, but she probably knows on some level.

"Now, when that weirdness happened out at Bell Rock, Kali, or Aura, or Alexis, was some kind of half-baked psychic who was chasing and photographing orbs and gets struck by lightning and winds up in the hospital basically untouched, which is pretty weird right there, and then becomes some kind of different person. And now she's a goddess with her own temple, promising miracles to the unwashed masses!"

"Thanks for the recap, bro', I know all that, especially the part about shagging the goddess, or the half-baked psychic, but what do you really think happened out there on Bell Rock? You were there, you saw the whole thing. Tell the Hacker everything you remember."

"I dunno, Hacker. It was pretty surreal. A wild thunder and lightning show, pouring rain, chaos, my wife disappears, Aura gets struck by a huge bolt, which I saw with me own eyes, the weird electrical smell in the air…then the medics come and then the cops and I pass out. Leela thinks that during the storm Aura was invaded or taken over by these orbs from another dimension, but, you know, she believes that stuff. I don't."

"But you saw these orbs, right? What in the friggin' hell is an orb? What's it look like? I read in some New Age rag that you can only see the things in photos, digital or whatever."

"Okay, okay. I saw—I *thought* I saw—these glowing little balls of light, flying and floating all around the place. About the size of a golf ball, maybe a baseball. Like I said, it was raining like hell and lightning strikes every few seconds, so I wasn't sure of anything. So this bolt hits Aura on the top of her head, and it looks like—*looks like*, dude—one of the freakin' orbs follows the bolt into her freakin' head!"

"Hey, Marty, you weren't on any serious drugs, right? Smokin' weed up there or maybe you had dropped some Ecstasy?"

"No way, my brother, not around either one of these psychics. They say it interferes with their connection to Spirit. Or the Great Spirit. I dunno. Anyway, Leela had disappeared, so I was kinda looking out for her, and after the bolt smacks Aura and she's on the ground, Leela shows up and she's dancing around in the rain—starkers. Friggin' naked."

"Wish I'd been there with my camcorder, dude," jibes my old friend. "That scene would have gotten millions of hits on YouTube."

"Take me home, Hacker," I said, tired of the questioning. "I gotta meditate on all this. There is something very strange going on here. Leela is off to god-knows-where on some secret gig for the warmonger U.S. gummint. Some tacky broad I balled a lifetime ago is suddenly a freakin' sex guru selling miracles after an orb enters her skull. I don't get the big picture yet."

"Don't forget the hot sex scene with you and Aura in her hospital bed," chided Hacker. "After the weirdness on Bell Rock. You told me it was like sex on acid, remember?"

"Yeah, yeah," I sighed. "How could I forget? It was more like being sucked into a throbbing vortex—on acid. Maybe I was really shagging an orb in a woman's body."

"There is more to this than meets the eye," said Hacker, falling into his annoying Sherlock Holmes shtick, as he pulled a sharp left on Mountain Shadows Drive to take me to my remote hideaway. "The game's a-foot, Watson," he continued, irritatingly. I didn't miss the pun.

"No shit, Sherlock," I fired back. "The foot *is* the game for you, right? Meet me tomorrow morning at the Third Eye and we'll compare notes with our buddies. Let's see what the word is on the street. And what about Jill? How do you think she fits in?"

You'll recall that Jill and Hacker were once an item. It was very intense for a while. Then Jill wanted some space. Hacker was devastated.

He ignored my "what about Jill" question. We arrived at my house and parked in the driveway, as Hacker looked straight ahead, obviously in pain.

"Jill holds the key," I said, disregarding the awkward silence. I wasn't trying to hurt my friend with a painful reminder. I needed information. "She's been working with Leela. She knows things."

"Maybe," said Hacker sadly, as I carefully closed the Porsche passenger door. "And Jill also has the most beautiful feet in Sedona. Maybe in the whole Western hemisphere."

CHAPTER FIVE

Everything Is Bugged

The Third Eye was abuzz with activity when I walked in a few minutes after nine a.m. All of the twelve or so tables were filled with talking, laughing, excited people. Most seemed to be locals, with a few tourists hanging around the fringes. The new breakfast bar was in full operation, serving up all the pastries and muffins and sandwiches that a microwave and toaster oven could handle.

The young, dark-eyed, bleached blonde behind the counter had recently graduated from Red Rock High School, had ambitions to be a Sedona psychic, and had been coming on to me since she started working at the Third Eye a few weeks ago. She said her name was Destiny—yet another mono-named person, common in Sedona.

"Yo, Desty, whazzup?" I said as I approached the counter. "How 'bout a nice cuppa house coffee, black, for your Uncle Marty?"

"Marty," she sighed, her black tank top providing a revealing look at tight, ample teenage breasts, unencumbered by a bra. The words "Ask me about the vortex" were printed in red across the front of the garment.

She put her face close to mine and sent a faint breeze of sweet breath my way.

"Pisces, right?" she said, not blinking. "Aries rising?"

"Libra," I answered, "and I don't know my rising sign. I think my moon is in Uranus."

She giggled. "That's pronounced 'YER-a-nus,' not 'your anus,' silly."

"Whatever," I said. "Your anus, my anus. Can I just get a cup of java?"

She didn't back away, and now I noticed that her soft hand covered my hand. "Marty, I love your eyes. Are they blue or are they green? I can never tell for sure when I see you in here. Hey, listen, can I do your whole chart sometime? Just tell me when and where you were born and I'll do the rest. Call me here when you're ready and we'll get together, okay?"

"Destiny, how old are you?"

"Eighteen. Actually, I'll be eighteen in October. Scorpio. You know."

"Right. How about some coffee, and I'll call you when I'm ready." I didn't bite on her offer, although she was a lovely morsel—and my wife was out of town.

I took my steaming cup over to the round oak table where my friends and I usually gathered. Hacker was there already, giving me a strange look. Claude "Picasso" Imperioli was waving a colorful brochure, laughing and commenting on the various items contained on its pages. It was the same brochure that Hacker and I had been handed the day before at Kali's Tantric Temple.

"Hey, Marty, look at this—a menu of Tantric services they serve up at Goddess Kali's place!"

"This is your kinda action, dude," snickered Benny Bravo. "Matter o' fact, ah hears you and the Hackerman made the scene up there yesterday. How'd it go?"

"I hate it when you talk in that mixed-up street dialect, *señor*," I cracked. "Please be either a yid or a beaner. Or else a straight-shootin' citizen of the US of A." Benny's consciousness was somewhere between *La Bamba* and *Hava Nagila*. He was probably the only Mexican in Arizona who had had a Bar Mitzvah.

"Yo, *jefe*, but please share with us, your fan base and support team: Did you and *Señor* Hack get any action up there yesterday wit' dem *putas*?" Bravo was a short, intense, funny-looking brother, with a Jewish nose, a shaved head, and tattoos from elbows to shoulders. He was one hell of an investigative reporter, however, real smart and persistent, and was writing for several websites that specialized in exposés and scandal.

"Okay, okay," I said, my cover blown, "how did you wise guys know that we were there yesterday? We didn't tell anyone. We were on a mission."

"It's a small town, Marty," piped up Dan Strange. "News travels fast."

"Plus," said Picasso, "we all know a guy who was in the same audience for the video as you guys. He wondered if you signed up for anything."

"*He* did," said Benny. "This *cabrón* plunked down his three grand for the first level. The ladies call it 'The Cleansing.' Supposed to clean out all the do-do that's in your *cabeza*. So's they can fill it back up with their own bullshit, I guess. Turn your brain into a goddess burrito or somethin'."

Hacker laughed and shook his head. "Three grand. Unbelievable."

"Gimme a break," I muttered. "No wonder they can duplicate the Taj Mahal out there."

"But take a look at their brochure," insisted Picasso. Neither Hacker nor I had bothered to examine it yet; we should have.

"Check it out," said the long-winded Picasso. "'Astral Tantra. You will learn how to travel via your astral body and never leave your easy chair. Go any-where you want, even off-planet. Remote viewing also possible.'

"And this one: 'Techno Tantra. Music that affects your brain wave patterns and puts you in a higher state of consciousness. You will be able to read people's minds and channel ancient entities with this technique. Warning: Brain damage can occur with overexposure to this music.'"

"You'd have to be brain damaged to even go into this bullshit," muttered Hacker. "Tell us more, Picasso."

"I like this one: 'Past Lives Tantra. Recall and relive your past lives with our guaranteed Tantric exercises. With or without a partner. Results guaranteed.'"

Our table was stunned into silence as Picasso read on: "This one must be the ultimate: 'Cloud Tantra. The pathway to living in a permanent higher state of consciousness. Enlightenment can become your reality.

Learn how you can live forever with this unique form of Tantra.' Wow," said Picasso.

"Whew!" was all I could say. Hacker was muttering to himself. We all took a collective deep breath. Past Life Penelope, who had been silent up to now, spoke up, with fear in her eyes.

"This is all very dark, dear friends. I have an ominous feeling about Kali and her Tantric circus. She has some heavy karma to work out. I have seen her past lives. I fear for all of us and everyone in Sedona and—"

"It's okay, Pen, Hacker and I are on the case," I said reassuringly. "We have lifetimes of good karma on our side." Hacker nodded in agreement.

"Your lives are in danger," answered Penelope. "Be very careful...."

"Speaking of lives," I said, "has anyone heard anything more about those people who went over the cliff into Oak Creek Canyon? There's been nothing in our local paper, or the daily rag down in Phoenix, or on TV that I know about. Anybody...?"

"Yo, I called *mi amigos* at the Sedona PD and at the Sheriff's, and nobody's talking," said Benny. "They said the investigation is ongoing, and, you know, the usual bullshit. So I called my buds at the FBI and they said they were on the case but couldn't talk about it yet. Know what it smells like to me? Cover-up. Big time. International stuff. Very, very suspicious."

"Suspicious is right," I said. "Penny? Have you channeled any I.D. on those people who burned up in the fire?"

Before she could answer, my secure cell phone, the one in my pants pocket which is set to "vibrate," started doing its dance. I checked the display. It was Jill. Just the person I needed to see.

I stood up quickly. "Excuse me, guys, gotta pick this one up," and headed out the back door of the Third Eye.

I flipped open the handset. "Jill! Where are you?"

"Look up and to your left. I'm in the parking lot in my car. Come talk to me."

I found her silver Lexus and hopped into the passenger side. We had a big, juicy hug. I hadn't seen Jill for months. She looked great: tanned, toned, and excited.

She spoke first. "Marty, I've got to talk to you. Immediately. It's about Leela, it's about what's been going on, it's—" She stopped abruptly.

"Is Leela all right? Where is she? Have you heard from her? I've been sending her e-mails, but she hasn't answered."

"Marty, we've gotta meet someplace to talk. Everything is bugged. They're listening. Your table at the Third Eye is bugged. Your house, Hacker's house, bugged for sure. Your phones, your cars, bugged. Maybe my house too. Look, get in your car and meet me at our spot. You know, *the* spot. Don't say any more here, okay?"

"Got it. See you there."

I got out of her car and headed for my own wheels in the parking lot. My head was spinning. I certainly knew *the* spot. It was out in Boynton Canyon, a place known as Mystic Vista. It was where Jill once channeled a transmission from Leela from several thousand miles away.

Knowing my car could have been bugged gave me a creepy feeling. I turned on the car stereo as I headed to our rendezvous, punched in some numbers for the Stones' "Stray Cat Blues," and sang along as loudly as I could.

There were a lot of questions. Jill would have some answers. I hoped. I kept one eye on the rear view mirror to make sure I wasn't being followed as I swung the car onto Dry Creek Road and headed for the rendezvous spot.

CHAPTER SIX

Ecological Blackmail

Mystic Vista is located in the shadow of the awesome red rocks of Boynton Canyon, not far from the sprawling Enchanted Forest Resort and far enough (about four miles) from the amphetamine rush of traffic on main street Sedona. Not many people know of Mystic Vista. It is considered an energy vortex by the local cognoscenti; clueless tourists know it only as a lovely, quiet spot to take a short, easy hike. Sometimes a local Jeep tour company would bring their customers here for a quickie "secret trail" adventure, but not often, so the place was usually deserted.

There are only two parking spaces at the trailhead. I pulled my all-electric Honda Lightning into one of the spaces, turned off the silent engine, lowered the windows, and breathed in the amazingly fresh air. The smell of pine was overwhelming, intoxicating.

Two minutes later Jill pulled her hybrid Lexus into the other space. She got out and we nodded silently to each other, then proceeded up the dirt road, Jill in the lead. The first quarter mile or so is a deeply rutted track, so intimidating that only an experienced and fearless Jeep driver would dare to negotiate it. Then the road levels out and takes the intrepid hiker through a forest of juniper, manzanita, and piñon pine. Cactus thrives here as well—a community of cacti, welcoming the rare visitor with bright colors and otherworldly shapes.

Nearly a mile in, a little path takes you to a small atoll known as Mystic Vista. We had arrived. I had been busily studying the local flora as well as keeping an eye on Jill's shapely backside, which was encased in a pair of tight designer jeans.

They say Sedona has four major energy vortexes. Mystic Vista is the fifth vortex, the one they don't talk about, and maybe the most powerful of them all. The energy was palpable on Mystic Vista that day. Jill watched as I spun around and around, like a Sufi mystic, a whirling dervish soaking up the energy. She took me by the arm and led me to a spot on the atoll that overlooked a small valley below, and beyond that, the high desert forest dotted with juniper and cactus.

Gently, Jill guided me to sit on a section of crimson red slickrock under the sheltering arms of an ancient alligator juniper tree. We sat facing each other, legs folded neatly, as if we were about to meditate together. Jill held me with her mesmerizing hazel eyes, set in a heart-shaped face, long brown hair cascading around her shoulders. She wore a yellow t-shirt with the letters "OM" stenciled across the front. A floppy straw hat protected her delicate skin from the blazing sun.

It was near the end of summer, which in Sedona can stretch all the way to mid-November. The monsoon season was winding down, another dismal summer for precipitation, but there were hopeful, fluffy clouds floating in the blue sky with just a hint of rain contained in them. Jill looked funky and ancient and lived-in and high as a kite, all at the same time. She was beautiful and alive. She had things to tell me.

A word about Jill: She came to Sedona about five years ago to start a new life, as so many others do, and to get away from an abusive husband. The guy was a talented singer-songwriter, name of Jack Robbins, and Jill was the other half of a duet called Jack & Jill. Jack unfortunately got into hard drugs. Jill was into yoga, which wasn't compatible with Jack's drug habits or his violent rages, so she packed it up and moved to red rock country.

When she arrived in Sedona, I was riding a wave of financial success and notoriety with my website, Sedona Confidential. I needed some help, so I ran an ad in the local paper for an assistant, she answered it, and I hired her.

Jill and Hacker hooked up after a brief flirtation in my office. Jill later played a major role in a plot to take down no less than the entire nation of China. Out of that nightmarish business, Jill and Leela formed a psychic bond. In fact, on the very spot where Jill and I sat on that beautiful pre-autumn day, Jill had channeled a critical message from Leela which came all the way from Tibet.

"Jill, I have a lot of questions," I said firmly, looking this magical woman directly in the eyes. "Hard questions."

"First question," she said simply in her velvet voice, melting my hard edge immediately.

"Okay, why are we being bugged? Who is bugging us? What the hell is going on anyway?"

"The answers to those questions will emerge the more we talk, Marty. I'll just say now that Leela and I think the bugging is being done by the U.S. Government—by the State Department, the FBI, the NSA, the CIA. Yeah, our own government. You know that Leela and I work for the State Department, and we are on to some pretty serious stuff. So the big boys, the ones in the black suits, want to know what we are doing and who we are talking to."

"No doubt. So me and Hacker are on the quote-unquote watch list because of our, uh, our relationships with our wives and girlfriends."

"Well…yeah. Sorta. You got that about half-right," said Jill, mysteriously.

"Okay, the big questions," I said. "Where is Leela? Is she safe? Some people tried to kill us up in Oak Creek Canyon the other day. What was that about?" I could feel a deep trembling begin somewhere deep in my guts, just below the bottom of the rib cage.

I closed my eyes and took a deep breath. Jill waited patiently. "And Leela pulled off some incredible hocus-pocus to save our asses up there—some kind of psychic mind trick. She won't tell me anything about what she's involved in. It's all top secret. Jill, I…our…we…okay, our marriage is in the toilet. I don't even know this person anymore. And we've been together a long time." I was on the verge of sobbing uncontrollably.

Jill leaned forward and put her hands on my shoulders.

"Marty, Marty," she half-whispered, "I'm sorry it's come down this way." She paused a beat, tossed her long hair back with a jerk of her head. I caught myself on the razor's edge of tears, straightened up, and smiled grimly. Real men don't cry, I thought, cringing inwardly.

"Real men do cry, Marty. Real men do show their—"

"Jill, did you just…" Damn! She did read my mind! I temporarily forgot that this stunning woman was a gifted telepath.

"Listen carefully," said Jill, continuing on as if nothing had just happened. "Leela is fine. She is safe. She is in deep cover somewhere in Europe, probably London. You know about the State Department. Check. You kinda know she was at an environmental conference in Moscow and looked into some people's minds and saw what they were planning to do. Check. Then she called in Interpol and four bad guys got locked up somewhere, now awaiting trial. And then some people who are connected with the bad guys tried to force you and Leela off the road and down into Oak Creek Canyon."

"Yeah, they tried to bump us off. Literally. Off the friggin' cliff, two thousand feet straight down to a fiery death." I snickered inwardly at my little joke. "But who are these bad guys and what are they up to? Is this the Russian mafia or something?"

"Eco-terrorists. They are into eco-blackmail. And much worse. This is an international cabal, Marty, bigger than you can imagine." She paused and spread her arms wide, palms up. "You know our planet is facing an environmental catastrophe."

I couldn't help smirking. I had never really bought the concept of global warming. It had just seemed like a PR stunt to me, some kind of propaganda to make some rich guys richer. That was one of the issues between Leela and me. She was hardcore on climate change.

"Well, you know, Jill, after I closed down Sedona Confidential I became an environmentalist, sort of. Hacker designed my new website—you know, SedonaGoGreen.org—and we have big plans to take it national and start selling eco-friendly products for the green revolution."

Jill's eyes danced and she quickly covered her mouth with the back of a hand to stifle a laugh. The laugh trickled out anyway. "Marty, you dear, sweet, naïve boy. I know you're a clever guy, cuz I used to work for you! And you constantly surprised me with your smarts and your awareness. But this is serious. This is—"

"Jill," I interrupted, "I damn well know what's going on. I saw it on the History Channel last week. 'Last days of life on earth' or something like that. Too much carbon dioxide in the atmosphere. Climate change. Hotter every year. By 2050, the oceans will rise and everybody has to leave New York and London. Icebergs melt. Greenland disappears. So? We won't be here to see it. By 2050, sweetheart. Maybe later. Fifty years, a hundred years."

"How about in six months?" she said calmly. "Maybe a year at the most."

"Wha—"

"In the next six months," Jill explained, "we will see things happen on this planet that are totally beyond belief. I mean catastrophes. Big time. And not just natural disasters, which were already happening because of human greed and stupidity.

"No, Marty, it's much worse than that. Because there are people on this earth who want to make money on our environmental collapse, on human misery. These people are already making money—big money, billions—just on threats and blackmail alone."

"Well, just who is behind all this?" I asked, already feeling mentally exhausted from inputting too much information. "And I suppose my dear wife is right in the middle of this international intrigue, trying to save the world?"

"Listen, Marty," said Jill sternly, "it's because of Leela that a huge chemical complex in Germany, Düsseldorf, you know, near the Belgium border, wasn't blown up by a suicide bomber. If that had been carried out, it would have sent a cloud of chlorine gas for hundreds of miles downwind, and killed or sickened millions of people. Leela read this plot in the minds of these four fellows—saw it like a movie, she told me—and helped to get them locked away. As well as about twenty other people that were involved in the scheme."

"B-but why did they come after her in Sedona? How did they know that she was the one who fingered them?"

"Well, I didn't want to tell you just yet, but here goes anyway. I guess you're ready for this...."

I closed my eyes, waiting. I could feel my jaw clench and unclench.

"There is a mole in the State Department. Someone who ratted out Leela. Now, Leela thinks she knows who it is, a translator who was at the conference. A young woman. Apparently a double agent who works for the other side. Leela is pretty sure this person is psi too. She is the only one we know of who is able to mask her thoughts around Leela. An American. Name's Tanya."

"Jesus H. Christ," I sputtered. "You mean, Jill, that this snitch fingered Leela and sent a gang of hitmen to our little hometown of Sedona, Arizona, where the biggest crimes are drunk driving and domestic abuse? That this bitch nearly got us bumped off by professional killers?"

"That's right, Marty. That's just about right."

"That is fuckin' amazing, Jill. I feel like we should go over there right now and whup some ass and bring Leela home. But where is 'there'? And who really is behind all this eco-terrorism?"

"They call themselves Black Swan. The name comes from some book about unexpected events changing the course of history, or something like that. It's an international cabal, Marty. It's huge.

"It started in Russia with some billionaires who cashed in when the Soviet Union collapsed. The Americans got involved when Bush Two stole the election in year Two

Thousand. Most of its elite members are rich and powerful. There are two U.S. congressmen involved, plus high-powered lobbyists, and several bigwigs from American corporations and Wall Street. Plus bigshots from other countries whose names we are unfamiliar with so far."

"Wow," I said, feeling smaller and smaller.

"This is the intel straight from Leela, Marty. Top secret. The media hasn't touched it yet. It's all hush-hush. These people are very well connected, including control of the media. Plus they have an enforcement arm called The Brotherhood, which is a bunch of hired guns and strong-arm types mainly from Eastern Europe, places like Bulgaria, Serbia, Albania. That's who came after you and Leela in Oak Creek Canyon."

"So just what is their scam? What kind of 'eco-terrorists' are we dealing with?"

"Blackmail, mainly. They warn a government what they intend to do, then put a price on not doing it. The starting price is about one billion euros. Leela has picked up a lot of gossip and random thought forms during her travels in Europe, so much of this stuff is still unconfirmed.

"Supposedly these thugs have the technology to trigger all kinds of environmental disasters. Earthquakes. Floods. Droughts. Glacier melting. Gigantic oil spills. They have developed micro-nuclear devices that could set off everything from an avalanche on the Matterhorn to a nine-point mega-quake off the coast of California. Plus there is a suspicion that they are tampering with the Internet. Too soon to know, though."

"Jill, I really hope that this isn't just another wild-eyed conspiracy story ripped from the pages of supermarket tabloids," I said, with a little too much glib. I saw Jill squirm. But I had heard enough conspiracy theories over the years, especially related to global warming, to add this one to the cuckoo column.

Jill stiffened slightly, her eyes blazing. Obviously, she was getting exasperated with me. Then she sighed, let her shoulders drop. "Marty, this is no fiction. And it's no joke. Leela doesn't speculate. She is in the heads of a lot of people and this is the information she has picked up. So far. And it's pretty scary.

"Marty, I am truly frightened by what could happen to our planet," continued Jill, and now those expressive eyes conveyed her for-real fear. "These criminals, if they don't get what they want, they could accelerate the whole ecological disaster that we've been talking about for years. They could literally take us beyond the tipping point, to where the planet's defensive systems start to turn on us."

"Just what do they want, Jill? These guys seem to have money, power, political control....What more do they want?"

"There are rumors, Marty, rumors that Leela has picked up and stuff I have overheard in State Department meetings. Something about a space station...a moon colony...exploring the solar system...a drug that lets you live forever. This is where it starts getting really weird. That they need trillions of dollars and euros to carry out their wild schemes. All of this is pure rumor so far."

I took several deep breaths, exhaled mightily, and raised my arms to the sky. "Jill, I know this is what you've heard, 'cuz you don't bullshit. But, really…blackmail? Ecological blackmail? That's how they figure to finance this project? What are they, religious fanatics or something, trying to escape Armageddon by escaping to the moon?"

Jill didn't answer, just looked at me. So I stood up and stretched, reaching for the moon, which hadn't yet risen. Jill stood up too, and I held her hands and looked into her eyes. I could feel the Southwest sun on my neck and bare arms. I wanted to take a shower, or jump into a swimming pool. The information shared by Jill made me feel kinda creepy and contaminated. And my wife was apparently in the middle of all this. Location unknown.

"Jill, this sounds like real madness. I know you haven't told me everything. That's okay. But just tell me one thing…."

"Marty, I told you Leela's okay. Not to worry." She paused. "Too much."

"You said she was in deep cover somewhere. Where is she? What is she doing?"

"Marty, I hope you're ready for this. It's getting hot here. Let's take a little walk."

The sun blazed down on us. Jill took me by the hand and led me down the trail that would take us deeper into the mysteries of Mystic Vista. I felt like I was floating on a cushion of air. A Monarch butterfly landed on my shoulder, and stayed there. A raven called to me from somewhere deep in the forest.

CHAPTER SEVEN

Bonding on the Astral Plane

Jill and I walked for several minutes over a narrow, barely visible trail into an inner sanctum I didn't know existed. It was actually a small grove of juniper trees, with a pair of ancient alligator junipers standing like sentinels at the entrance to the grove.

The trees shielded us from the blazing sun. Wild grasses covered the hard, rocky earth. A family of agave cactus, representing several generations, stood guard on the perimeter of our little retreat. Jill invited me to sit on a red rock that looked like a rocking chair. She sat on the grass opposite me.

Again Jill fixed me with those soulful eyes. "Marty," she said, "please listen carefully. Leela has taken on a new identity. In fact, she has taken on several identities. She has changed her appearance drastically. You probably wouldn't recognize your own wife. Right now she is playing the role of a BBC television reporter. She has dark curly hair, wears brown contact lenses, has a great upper class accent, and has put on about twenty pounds."

I shook my head. "My Leela? Twenty pounds? And what is this doing for the cause of truth and justice, this being a BBC reporter?"

"It gives her entry into some pretty high places. Right now she is doing a series called 'Captains of International Industry.' She has already done on-camera interviews with three members of the Black Swan cabal. Most of these guys have huge egos and legit corporate fronts. You can actually see her work on cable TV. She's good! And the only people who know what she's up to are the top BBC execs and our State Department."

I sighed heavily and tried to picture Leela interviewing these deadly big shots. Why? Why?

"Why?" said Jill, as if she were in on the conversation going on in my head. I was slowly getting used to her telepathic talents. "Because she can look into the darkness of their minds. She has been trained to say certain keywords during the interviews that trigger thoughts and images in the minds of her subjects. Words like crisis, shortage, ocean….You know, the mind is just a micro-computer. Leela is activating these guys' left brains while she's flirting with their right brains."

"Flirting? Does she have to, you'll pardon the expression, fuck these guys to read their minds?"

"No, no, Marty, no sex. Just innocent flirtations. Just to get the story. Anyway, she throws out these keywords. It's all very scientific. Using this technique, she has already scanned the minds of these creeps and stopped a scheme to blow up a dam on the Yellow River in China, which would have disrupted the lives of millions of innocent people; she has stopped a really ugly plan to release kilos of anthrax on three trains of the Paris Metro; she—"

"Jill, Jill, Jill!" I interrupted. "Stop! Please stop! What in hell is Leela doing in the middle of this terrorist nonsense! Where is that freaking mole who exposed her in Moscow? It sounds like Leela is totally vulnerable and needs a friend, or a husband around, or something. Maybe I need to book a flight to Heathrow right away."

I started to get up, but Jill extended her hands, palms down, in a kind of calming gesture. "Marty, relax, please. Leela is fine as of right now. The mole is not in London. Her next assignment for the State Department is in Capetown, half a world away; Leela arranged that to keep Tanya at arm's length. Next Leela goes to Paris to cover a big conference for the BBC. So she's fine."

I breathed a big sigh of relief and felt my muscles gradually de-stress. "Okay, Jill, now please answer for me a couple of questions. First. How do you know all this stuff? I doubt if you and Leela are talking on the phone or sending e-mails. Leela hasn't answered any of my e-mails. It's almost like she doesn't know me anymore."

"Marty, do you have a secure e-mail account? Are you running your e-mails through a server that can't be hacked or messed with by some agents working for god knows who? No, I didn't think so."

Jill locked her hands behind her head and eyed me playfully. "Marty, your wife and I have become very close. Every day at the same time we...communicate. It's a telepathic transmission. Except now it's like a two-way conversation. We've gotten very good at it. It's like Instant Messaging, but totally secure.

"Leela and I made several trips to that transdimensional portal at the Indian ruins not long ago, sometimes going into it together. It was pretty intense. And it really expanded the range of our telepathic abilities. So you could say that we bonded on the astral plane."

I remembered that Jill first realized that she was a telepath back when Leela had been kidnapped by a bunch of crazies who dropped her off on top of a sacred mountain in Tibet. You remember, the guys playing with vortex energy who wanted to take out China.

Leela had sent a brief telepathic message to Jill in my Sedona office, letting us know that she was all right. Jill was shocked at the time that she could receive a telepathic transmission. A few days later Jill actually channeled Leela's voice and mannerisms, a phenomenon that occurred right here at Mystic Vista. But how, I wondered—

"You're wondering how I know what Leela looks like in her disguise, what setting she's in, if she's safe or not…right?"

"Right."

"Remote viewing, Marty. With remote viewing I can transport my consciousness to wherever Leela is at any given moment. It takes a lot of energy and I'm exhausted afterward, so I don't do it very often. Only when I feel I need to. And part of my job with the State Department is to report to my superiors what Leela is up to.

"And by the way, you do know I can read your mind, right? When I want to. I'm not snooping. I'm very discreet."

"So then you already know my next question," I said. "Is she sleeping with this Anderson dude from the State Department, the one she's always running off with on some assignment or other?"

"Marty, that one is off limits. I'm a telepath, not a gossip. I don't do remote viewing into Leela's bedroom. If I knew, I wouldn't tell. And if she is sleeping with Mr. Anderson, what does it matter, really?"

"Well, I—" She had me there. Leela and I didn't exactly have an "open" relationship, but there was an understanding that we maintain a certain level of marital fidelity. Or so I thought. Infidelity in the line of duty, well, that's one level. Shagging the nubile teenager from the local coffee house? The jury is still out on that one. My brief affair with Aura slash Goddess Kali? Too weird to think about now. So maybe a "don't ask don't tell" policy would best apply to our marriage contract.

"One more question, Jill." I looked up at the sky. Fluffy cumulus clouds had begun forming overhead, strange shapes like dragons and spaceships and bunnies with the heads of rats. Could blessed rain be coming soon? Our little alcove began to darken. I looked at Jill and began to mentally undress her. Remembering her telepathic talents, I quickly tried to cloud my mind and shifted my thoughts to eating ice cream, watching a professional basketball game, hiking up Thunder Mountain, recalling James Cagney in "White Heat."

"One more question, Marty. Go ahead. Something about a movie?"

"You and Hacker were an item for quite a while. I had never seen him so happy. Now it seems you have dumped him, and he's been depressed and angry ever since. Care to fill me in? It will go no further than right here."

She laughed. "Sure, guy, sure. Okay, Hacker already knows why I can't date him anymore. I love him, I suppose, and probably always will, but he's a player. He has to have a lot of girlfriends going at the same time. Oh, you know, the man is obsessed with my feet, but I don't mind that. In fact, I kinda like the attention. What I don't like is that there are a lot of strange diseases going around out there, and Mr. Hack refuses to use a condom. Plus I don't like being a member of his harem. Satisfied?"

Jill stood up. I stood up. I moved toward her, wanting a big hug to seal the deal and put a cap on our amazing conversation. But I had a problem: An erection for the ages, the mother of all boners. This woman was like an aphrodisiac to me. Her mere presence was a total turn-on. And, it didn't take a psychic to figure out what I had in mind. The setting was perfect for a little tryst.

Jill extended her arms, holding me back. "Forget it, Marty. You know it's not possible. Not now, anyway." Her voice grew soft and very kind, as if she knew I couldn't help it, that my erection was purely a force of nature, the end product of millions of years of evolution. Or perhaps it was just the vortex energy working on me.

The woman had compassion. She took me by the arm and led me gently back to the main trail, me stumbling and lurching, beyond embarrassment. "Come on, big guy, let's go back. It's getting late."

I don't remember the hike back to our cars at the trailhead. I do remember Jill taking me by the shoulders, looking into my eyes, her face inches away from mine, and saying, "It would be better if you didn't stay in your house for a while. There is still a possibility that there are hired killers from Black Swan hanging around Sedona. I'll keep my psychic senses open."

I nodded numbly. "And remember that our own government has planted bugs everywhere, so be careful what you say and who you say it to. I think you should lay low right now. Maybe you could stay in Hacker's cabin on the creek for a few weeks. He'll know if there are any bugs. I'll stay in touch and give you updates on Leela."

I looked Jill in the eyes and kissed her gently on the cheek. No words were needed. It was dusk. The smell of a distant forest fire wafted past my nostrils. The coyotes were already out, yipping and barking and yowling; I figured they were talking about an early dinner, raw bunny rabbit a la carte. I was hungry too. And for some reason, I felt as if I was just coming out of a trance.

CHAPTER EIGHT

Not Quite the Tipping Point

Three Months Later

Driving down the main drag through Uptown Sedona on a frosty winter morning, I noticed how light the traffic was. Uptown, the main tourist ghetto and economic engine for the area, was practically devoid of visitors. A light dusting of snow still accented the red rocks, fresh from last night's snowfall. This time of year is definitely not the height of tourist season, but still, the town felt deserted.

In a way, it was. The economic crunch had badly crippled Sedona's only industry, tourism. Many businesses were shuttered; whole office complexes were vacant. The housing crisis had hit Sedona big time, and many upscale homes had been foreclosed. Business in Uptown restaurants and shops and hotels was lousy too; workers fled to nearby towns to find jobs. Driving along the quiet, lonely highway, I had a strong feeling of entropy, as if the whole enterprise called Sedona was winding down.

Leela and I had first come to Red Rock Country in the mid-nineties, and had fallen in love with the place immediately. We moved in, got jobs, got a loan, bought a house. I worked as a waiter and a tour guide; Leela worked in Uptown tourist shops for paltry wages until she looked around and saw that a lot of people she knew were making big money as psychics. Since she had some pretty strong psychic abilities, she decided to become a professional, a working psychic reader.

I'll cop to something right now: I was a major scoffer when it came to the New Age, which used to permeate the Sedona atmosphere like a giant gas cloud. Millions came to Sedona, like pilgrims to Lourdes, for psychic readings, to have miracle healings, to discuss UFO sightings and abductions, and basically to rub shoulders with those of us who lived among the mysterious vortex energies of the red rocks.

I scoffed until my wife started making some big money as a practicing psychic, and finally became a believer when I realized I was living with a rare being possessed of powers that defied the laws of physics. Not only could Leela move objects with her mind and teleport herself from one location to another, she could see the future and read people's minds and transmit messages to other telepaths. She was also pretty good at remote viewing.

All this was a little hard to accept for me, basically a country boy from hardy and practical Midwestern stock, German and Swedish DNA on one side and English roots on the motherly side. I grew up in Omaha, back when the winters were so brutal you wanted to curl up and die. Now, of course, winter in Omaha is so warm that homeless people can actually sleep outside in December. Climate change, perhaps?

My father was an executive for an insurance company. He had a nasty, scary temper. He claimed he didn't have a drinking problem, but he downed two six-packs of Schlitz beer a day. He died of a heart attack at age fifty-five. My mother was a former high school beauty queen, vain and self-absorbed. She smoked like a chimney, had several nervous breakdowns, and died of lung cancer at sixty-two. I guess longevity is not on my side. What the hell.

I barreled through West Sedona, which also was shrouded in a cloud of gloom. "Going out of business sale" signs were everywhere. I had been staying, at Jill's suggestion, at Hacker's cozy little cabin up in Oak Creek Canyon. Hacker had scanned the whole place and declared it free of bugs—that is, hidden recording devices.

Over the past three months I had met with Jill every few days for updates on Leela's activities. We met at a different spot each time, usually on one of Sedona's many hiking trails. Although I still lusted after Jill—but only in my mind, which Jill of course was keenly aware of—she made sure our relationship stayed on the platonic level. Leela was doing fine, Jill said, safe and relatively secure, supposedly watched over by that Anderson dude of the State Department.

According to Jill: After her BBC gig, Leela had changed disguises several times, next passing as an overweight secretary to the British ambassador to Italy;

then as a glamorous, cleavage-baring cocktail waitress in a swank lounge frequented by the rich, famous, and politically connected in Lucerne, Switzerland; and finally as a personal trainer who accompanied her client, a powerful Israeli arms dealer, wherever her deadly business took her.

All of these transmutations brought Leela into contact with—or in the vicinity of—many leaders and various lieutenants of the Black Swan organization. Consequently she was able to glean vital information from their unsuspecting minds. This often came in the form of images, not words, thus bypassing gaps in her knowledge of languages. (Although she did speak fairly respectable French.) She then passed on the information to her handlers in the State Department. This stolen intel helped to thwart several deadly schemes in the cabal's agenda of environmental destruction. More than a hundred people were arrested by Interpol as the result of Leela's efforts in the past three months.

Except for my meetings with Jill, and a visit from Hacker about once a week, I had been relatively out of touch with the outside world. I didn't watch TV, except for old movies downloaded from the Web, nor did I visit my favorite news sites on the Internet; I didn't want to contaminate my mind. I spent my time reading Sherlock Holmes and James Bond books from Hacker's quirky library; meditating down by the creek, which was just fifty feet from the cabin's back door; doing a little writing on my book, "The Way of the Psychic;" and taking long walks in the forest. I thought about Leela often, but I didn't worry about her safety. Her adventures in Europe seemed like a TV soap opera—distant and surreal. Jill's updates helped my state of mind, and seeing her often helped the state of my heart. I was falling for this woman, big time.

One frigid evening Hacker and I sat huddled around the cheery fireplace in his cabin, sipping from crystal beakers filled with warm Courvoisier, having already sampled his new stash of gourmet weed from Humboldt County, California. It had been snowing for an hour, so Hacker decided to spend the night—on the convertible couch in the living room, since I had already claimed ownership of the luxurious king size bed.

Hacker leaned back in his rocking chair and gave me The Eye, that penetrating look of his that signals a "don't bullshit me" attitude. "How's Jill?" he asked. "I know you been seein' her for info on Leela, 'cuz you told me you were. But really, how is she?"

"She is a fine, fine lady, bro," I said. "Too bad you—"

"Never mind," said my friend. "I know all about the 'fine lady' and the 'too bad.' You wouldn't be, uh, getting' it on with her, would you?"

I could see by his body language, his slumped broad shoulders, that he didn't really want to know if I was. "No, man, I'm not. And if I was, I probably wouldn't tell you. Besides, that would be too close to home," I said.

Hacker looked out the window at the falling snow and quickly changed the subject. "Hey, Dude, you said you're not watching the news these days, but some really weird stuff is happening out in the world. I think you should know."

I nodded, vaguely interested. The world and its troubles seemed far away.

"You know there's this thing going on called global warming, right?" he said sarcastically. "Well, dig it: A huge piece of Greenland just fell into the ocean. The ocean got pissed off about this and now they're evacuating coastal towns like Dover in England and Le Havre in France because the ocean levels got raised about a foot or three."

"Uh huh," I muttered, slowly nodding off. Actually, my snotty, unconcerned attitude was mainly an act. Jill had sworn me to secrecy re the Black Swan organization and their eco-terrorism campaign. I couldn't even tell Hacker, my best male friend, what I knew about the eco-disasters caused by human mischief. Yet.

"And a huge earthquake in Upstate New York last week, and another big quake in Indonesia and a tsunami hit the South Pacific, and fires everywhere and all kinds of weird weather stuff. And food riots in Africa and people running out of water and—"

"Hacker, thanks for the intel, man, but this sounds like old news. Plus earthquakes and tsunamis are not caused by global warming. Look, I gotta go nighty-night now. You'll excuse me," I said, as I struggled to my feet and headed for the master bedroom.

"Check the TV news, Marty," my friend called after me. "I think you oughta know about these happenings. Something strange is in the air."

Something strange, indeed. Hacker should only know. Well, he will soon enough, I rationalized.

I closed the bedroom door with his words ringing in my ears. I had vivid, nightmarish dreams that night, mainly about Leela in scary, dangerous situations. In the morning Hacker was gone. He left a pipeful of his premium ganja with a note: "Start your day with Super-weed. Yes indeed!"

I pulled into the parking lot of the Third Eye Coffee House, shook my head to clear away the multitude of thoughts fighting for attention, and tried to focus on the present moment. I couldn't shake off the creepy feeling that something was very wrong—not only in Sedona, but wrong with the planet as well. It felt like the horizon was slightly off-kilter, that the long-predicted planetary shift had finally happened; that our whole civilization somehow had become unhinged.

I walked through the door of the Third Eye and was immediately swept up in the vibe of the place, which was frantic and fearful. The new, huge TV dominating one wall of the place was fairly throbbing with Breaking News, and the forty or so pairs of eyes in the coffee house were glued to the TV. "...millions of refugees on the move from one end of Africa to the other," intoned a solemn announcer voice. I watched transfixed as a montage of human misery played across the giant screen in HD.

Benny Bravo came rushing up to me, breathless. "Marty, Marty!" he said, grabbing my shoulders. "It's happened! It's finally happened, *vato*!"

"Get a grip, homeboy. What's happened?" As I pried his fingers off my torso, a shudder of icy dread crept up my spine. I had an idea what he was going to say.

"The tipping point, Marty. The freakin' tipping point. All hell is breaking loose like all over the planet. One disaster after the other. Just like they been predicting. Check it out, brother!"

The TV was tuned to CNN, and the assault on the senses was relentless. It looked like doomsday, with vid clips of fires, explosions, floods, oil spills, refugees, from all over the planet. Most of Southern California was on fire; millions had been evacuated. Half of Australia was on fire.

And equally scary, CNN showed a montage of banks around the U.S. closed and locked with thousands of account holders screaming outside for their money. Some computer hackers had messed with the banks' core networks, freezing accounts and even transferring large sums to secret Swiss accounts, so no public transactions were possible. Pharmacy computer networks had been hijacked, so nobody could get their prescriptions. Or food, because the big computers had been put out of commission and supermarkets couldn't function. Looters had taken over the business of food distribution.

I turned away and took Benny Bravo by the arm. "Benny, *mi hombre*, this ain't no tipping point. The tipping point means that us humans have fucked with the environment for too long and Mother Earth is tired of it and starts fucking us back. No, this is somethin'

else. Yo, homey, let us go outside and discuss this,"
I said, aware that our communal table might still be
bugged.

"Wait," he said. "I know about that shit. We talk
outside. First, go in the bathroom. Wash your hands,"
he said, with a strange, twisted smile on his Sephardic-
Mestizo face.

"Why? Are they dirty?" I looked down at my hands.
They looked normal. "I haven't done number one or
number two for awhile. Why should I wash my hands?"
I asked, that same feeling of dread surrounding me like
foul cigarette smoke.

"Just go," said Benny. "Turn on the faucet. Then I'll
meet you outside."

I went to the rest room behind the coffee bar, looked
in the mirror, noted that my eyes were wild, and turned
on the faucet. In an instant my worst fears were realized. What oozed from the faucet was an ugly, lumpy
brown substance; it looked like a cross between lique-
fied dogshit and raw sewage. The water, the water! I
muttered to myself.

I started to bolt from the restroom, but my iPhone
was vibrating crazily in my right pants pocket. I flipped
open the cover. It was an urgent text message from
Jill. "ND C U NOW. SO AAK. MP OK. A99. LOL. J."
This meant, in text talk code: "I need to see you now.
Significant other is alive and kicking. My place is okay.
Security high. Lots of love. Jill."

WTF—texting code for "what the fuck," but I mumbled it out loud. Must be about Leela. Where is she in

all this chaos? I dashed outside and hustled Benny to a quiet spot on the wooden deck of the Third Eye.

"Benny, I just got an urgent message from a very close friend. I gotta go, and soon. Give me a quick rundown of what's really going on."

"Okay, *jefe*, listen up. The word on the street, and the word from *los* blowhards on CNN, the freakin' experts, you know, they say that all this environment collapse is some sort of conspiracy. All these disasters happening at the same time, no? They saying that some big group behind it. The prez, she declared a national emergency. That means National Guard troops are fuggin' on the way, man! And the mayor of Sedona, he say why not have martial law here! City council bigwigs say yo, why not! It's gettin' hairy, Marty. Hairy and scary."

"Jesus freaking Christ," I said, feeling a shakiness in my legs, a burning in my gut. "And the water?" I asked, perhaps inappropriately, "What's with the goddamn water?"

"You remember that *grande* subdivision near Prescott everybody against?" asked Benny. "Ten thousand *casitas*, golf courses, shopping malls, the whole freakin' thing, got approved by the county last year? All them warnings about a shortage of water, and the fools didn't listen?"

"Yeah, yeah," I said impatiently, looking at my watch. "What about it?"

"So a lot of that stuff been built and now wells been dryin' up all over the place. The Verde River dried up last summer, you know. Poof! Our aquifer been hijacked. All them gloom and doom predictions? All come true. We're out of water, *vato*. Better get used to that brown sticky shit coming outta yo' faucet."

I clapped Benny on the shoulder, gave him a big hug, and looked into his deep, dark, troubled eyes. "Hang in there, Benny. I'm on the case. I gotta meet someone who can help us. Keep your cell phone close, and I'll meet with you later. Maybe for dinner."

I turned on my heel to leave, but Benny stopped me with a hand on my shoulder. "There's something I haven't told you yet, Marty," he said. "It's Kali. Out at her Tantra Temple. Some really weird *mierda* going down there right now. Lots and lots of people hangin' out there. Thousands of people. Don't get it, Marty."

I had a sudden inspiration. "You'll get it, Benny," I said slowly. "Because you're going out there. Undercover. You're still on my payroll. You'll be my man at Kali's temple."

His eyes brightened. I remembered that he still had my company's credit card. "Go," I said. "Enjoy. Keep me posted. Text me. Go right now, if you can."

Benny gave me a big, big hug and a huge grin. I watched him walk away, back toward the Third Eye. He would get "it," that was for sure.

CHAPTER NINE

Beyond Clairvoyance, Beyond Empathy

Jill had bought herself a beautiful little house on nearly an acre of land in West Sedona, with stunning red rock views, a rock and cactus garden for a front yard, the property dotted with stately juniper and cottonwood trees, all surrounded by a high security fence. There were security cameras all around the fence. Jill wasn't taking any chances.

She greeted me with a warm hug as she ushered me into her cozy living room, a wood fire blazing away in the fireplace. Jill wore a loose-fitting, well-worn red cardigan sweater and a pair of old cotton sweatpants that nevertheless accented that wonderful ass. Jill rarely wore makeup; she was one of those rare women who are more beautiful without cosmetic enhancement.

Jill's is a shoes-off house. She is a spiritual lady. Clumsily I pulled off the high-top hiking boots I often wear in the Sedona winter. Jill's feet, Hacker's obsession, were sheathed in a pair of brown wool socks, which probably helped her to negotiate the cold wood floors of her house. She sat me on her big old comfortable couch while she unwound herself into an upholstered rocking chair. I noted, to myself, that she had gradually been putting on weight the past few months. She was nearing voluptuous stature now. Or at least statuesque.

"It's true, Marty," she said softly, an admission that she had just read my most private thoughts. "I *have* put on a few pounds. For one thing, I've been pumping some iron. Also, I eat more when I'm nervous."

"Damn it, Jill, can't a man have any privacy anymore? Are my thoughts just open to public scrutiny?" I acted serious, but I wasn't, really; Jill probably knew that too.

"I'm sorry, Marty, just force of habit, I guess." She closed her eyes and breathed deeply. *I* was definitely nervous. Jill had summoned me with an urgent text message.

"Jill, please tell me what's going on. You said my SO, my Significant Other, was alive and kicking, but what else is going on? And by the way, I thought your house was bugged."

"It *was* bugged, Marty, but it's been debugged by a friend. Not Hacker, a new friend. I'll tell you more about him later."

My eyebrows must have lifted about a foot when she said "a new friend." I felt immediately jealous of whoever this guy was, but I shouldn't have. I'm a married man, I said to my inner horndog.

"Listen carefully, Marty, because I have much info to share with you. You're just gonna have to breathe through some of this. Leela is okay. Sort of. Some weird stuff happened, but she's okay. She was in Paris with her Israeli lesbian arms dealer—"

"What?" I said, in a state of shock. "Her *lesbian* arms dealer? I think you left out some details in your latest update on my wife's career path!"

I was sure Jill had looked into my mind and seen the fantasy images of a wild, naked, girl-on-girl orgy with Leela right in the middle of it.

"Oh…sorry, Marty, but I wasn't sure you were ready for that little tidbit. I guess you weren't." Jill chuckled briefly, then got very serious. "No, Leela has not become a lesbian," she hastened to add. "She was on duty, gathering intelligence, trying not to look sexy."

"Jill, could you start from the top? I seem to be missing some of the details of this sordid tale."

"You're right, Marty." Jill sighed. "Here goes. Leela was playing personal trainer, you recall, to one Rani Rifkin, a butch lesbian for real, and a real arms dealer who the State Department hired to make the rounds with Leela so she, your wife, could scan some minds and do her job. So they're in Paris at a gay bar on the Left Bank called Le Sexytime, guys and gals, a rough crowd, where a lot of dirty business was conducted."

"*Incroyable,*" I said in a crude French accent.

"So some of the ladies were hitting on Leela. Rani, who is more than a little drunk, wanders off to hang out with some of her buddies and leaves Leela alone at the bar. So now Leela, who is nursing a beer, is having a great time chatting with two French hotties who Leela knows are involved with Black Swan. By scanning their minds. She does speak a fair amount of French, you know."

Jill paused, closed her eyes, and took several deep breaths.

"And?" I said, leaning forward until I was about to fall on my face. "And? And? C'mon, Jill, don't play games with me," I demanded with growing impatience.

"And now Leela is in the hands of the Black Swan organization."

"Whaaaaaaatttttt?" I cried, incredulous. My heart started beating so hard and fast that it threatened to leap from my chest.

"I knew you'd say that," said Jill, almost smugly, sitting back in her rocking chair. "I left out a few parts of the story," she said apologetically. "Marty, this is hard on me too. Your wife and I are very, very close."

"Out with it, Jill. How did she get from the gay bar into the clutches of the Black Swan people?"

"Leela was so busy chatting with the two Frenchies that she didn't sense the energy field of a young woman who had slipped onto the barstool next to hers. It was Tanya, the American double agent who was working for Black Swan. Remember, Tanya is also psi. She apparently set up a psychic barrier so that Leela couldn't tune in to her. Leela has done the same thing to Tanya, but this time that little bitch turned the tables. She also dropped a tablet of some powerful drug into Leela's beer, so the next sip she took, well, Leela just passed out at the bar."

"Wait, I thought this Tanya bitch was supposed to be in Africa, South Africa, and safely out of Leela's hair. What happened?"

"Dunno, Marty. She must have gotten a tip from a European connection that Leela was in Paris. And then slipped away from her State Department post in South Africa without being noticed. Tanya is very powerful, you know, and supposedly can plant thoughts and ideas in people's heads."

"Damn. Please, Jill, continue with this horror movie."

"Okay, hang on tight. Apparently Tanya and a friend helped Leela from the bar while Rani was, uh, occupied in one of the private rooms, and took her off to a Black Swan hideout. That's the late-breaking news about Leela. The last I heard from your wife she is okay, she is in a holding cell somewhere in Switzerland, she is being fed and waiting to be taken to a surgical suite where they plan to implant a tiny computer chip deep in her cerebral cortex."

All I could do was laugh. I laughed until tears streamed down my cheeks. Then I laughed some more, until I cried. I sobbed, unashamedly, unable to stop. Finally:

"You're playing with me, right, Jill?" I said through tears. "This is a test to see how I'll react to really weird information. This is for your psychic study group or something, right?"

"Marty, it's all true." Jill handed me a box of tissues. "And you're wondering how I know all this, down to the tiniest detail, right? Almost as though I was there. Am I right?"

"Yes, of course you're right Jill. You know you're right. But please explain it to some poor slob who hasn't been to psychic school. Explain how you know the tiniest details of this disaster."

"A few months ago, Marty, you asked me the same thing, how I know what Leela is doing and where she is doing it. I told you at the time that it was remote viewing. That was the short, easy answer. It's actually more complex than that."

"I'm ready, Jillo, my mind is open and ready for anything. As you well know, since you can see right into the damned thing. Enlighten me, sweetheart!"

"Your wife and I are now transmitting not just thoughts and messages to each other, but Leela can now transmit pictures, almost like a hologram. Or better yet, like a movie. And in real time. I have learned to tune in to the higher cognitive centers of her brain so that I can experience exactly what she is experiencing."

"Clairvoyance."

"Beyond clairvoyance. That's just your basic ESP. What Leela and I are doing is more like clairsentience. Which means you can directly experience the thoughts or feelings of another person."

"You mean empathy?"

"This is way beyond empathy. Deepak Chopra described it as 'morphic resonance fields' that connect all living organisms. Even the Buddhists say advanced meditators are able to practice clairsentience."

"Spare me the lecture, Jill," I said impatiently. "In layman's terms, just what exactly is it that you and my wife are doing?"

"Basically, Marty, when the connection is open, whatever she is experiencing or thinking or feeling, I am too. It's like I am there. She is talking to someone, I am there. Being touched by someone, I am there. Passing out from the drug, I am there."

I just stared at Jill, but my mind was in overdrive. Then I remembered her telepathic abilities, and quickly cut off the thought process. Too late.

"To answer your question, Marty, it does work both ways. When Leela is tuned in to me, she experiences what I am experiencing."

"Then…" I ventured.

"What you're thinking is correct. It's true. But it can't happen now. Between you and me, that is. Not yet. Leela is locked up in a cell in Switzerland. They have put some kind of a force field around her cell. Communication between us is impossible. For now. So we have to wait until Leela gives the word. She has already told me she wants it to happen. Us—you and me, yes. But not yet. We have to wait."

She paused, looked down, studied her slender fingers. With what sounded like a tinge of regret, she said softly, "Waiting is delicious, Marty."

I was sweating profusely under my sweater, ready to implode. This woman was indeed my aphrodisiac. I started writhing, unable to sit still. My mind could barely contain the thought: Jill and me in a hot sex romp, with Leela experiencing it all as if she were there!

"Jill, I—"

She looked at me with an intensity, a longing, that I had never seen in her eyes before. "Marty, I want you so much. I always have. There, I said it. But Leela and I have a code—well, it's a code between women, something that men could never understand. It's a code of honor. Guys and gals are just built different. Leela and I are playing with such powerful forces, it's as if we have to really honor the gifts we've been given. Understand, you sweet man?"

She stood up and touched my forehead with a cool hand, then covered my third eye with two delicate fingers. Immediately I relaxed and felt as if I was floating upward, then gradually sinking into a soft, soft cushion of air.

Jill walked into her kitchen, leaving me in a state of bliss. "I'm going to put on a pot of tea," she said. "Then we'll wrap ourselves up in blankets and go outside and drink our tea and talk some more.

"I need to tell you about my new friend," said Jill over her shoulder from the kitchen. "Once you meet him, your life will never be the same," she said provocatively.

Life changes had been coming at me so fast lately that I felt swept up in a whirlwind. Outside of Jill's little compound, the planet itself was changing. "Life is change; how it differs from the rocks." I remembered the line from a Jefferson Airplane song, circa 1968. The red rocks...?

CHAPTER TEN

Eye of the Hurricane

I was wondering, to myself, just how serious the situation really was, as Jill and I sipped our tea from big warm mugs, sitting across from each other at a wooden table near the edge of her Zen garden. The water in the little ponds had frozen over, and icicles hung from the miniature wooden bridges. Off in the distance was an awesome backdrop: the panorama of red rocks etched in amazing shapes by Mother Nature across many eons: chimneys, coffee pots, lizard heads, ship's sails, penises, animals, comic strip characters. Mother Nature seemed fine, immutable; still, I wondered to myself if the world situation had gotten worse with Leela out of the picture.

"It couldn't get much worse," said Jill, following up on my thought forms conversationally. This was becoming the new paradigm of our communication.

"It was out of control before Leela got snatched. Now the Black Swan people are getting even more aggressive. They just issued a demand this morning to all the wealthy governments of the Western world: the U.S., Canada, France, Switzerland, Germany, Holland, and so on, plus China, of course, and India. They are demanding trillions of euros and dollars in blackmail money. The State Department sent me the message this morning. I'll make you a hard copy if you'll keep it to yourself."

"Why? Why keep it to myself? The whole world should know about this! Why isn't the media all over the story?"

"For a very simple reason. Secrecy. Only the top honchos of the governments know about Black Swan. They have decided to keep a lid on the story. For now. So the masses don't panic in the streets, mainly. The only reason I'm on the government's secure e-mail list is because of Leela. Your wife, dear friend, is a key player in the strategic operation to take down Black Swan and maybe even save the planet."

"A cover-up," I said. "It's a freakin' government cover-up. The public should know about this. And a whole regiment of special ops goons should be sent in to rescue Leela. Right now, without any more diddling around!" I said, nearly losing it, my voice rising steadily.

"No, Marty," said Jill calmly, "this is when sensible people don't panic and rational people take action. The situation is very delicate, extremely sensitive. The Black Swan agents say they've got everything in place to trigger massive disasters unless their demands are met. Mini-nuclear weapons ready to be deployed. Bombs wired to chemical plants. We know their threats are real because of Leela's work."

Jill took a deep breath and continued: "Little brush-fire wars have already broken out all over the place between tribes and between countries and between religious groups over food and water. Black Swan has influenced and inflamed these situations and made them worse. They have managed to destabilize several shaky governments with bribes and political sabotage.

"Now, North Korea is ready to fire missiles into South Korea. Pakistan and India have got their fingers on their nuclear triggers. Israel and Iran have got their nukes pointed at each other, ready to fire at the slightest provocation. All Black Swan has to do is anonymously drop a little nuke into somebody's turf to ignite a nuclear holocaust. And on, and on, and on." She paused and looked deeply into me. "How do I know all this? Remember, I also work for the State Department. They keep me updated on all this stuff."

I felt exasperated. "Jill, honey, the whole world is about to blow up, my wife and your best friend is about to have her brains defiled by madmen, and our little red rock town is about to have martial law. And you sit there calmly sipping tea!"

"Marty, look at me as the eye of the hurricane, the quiet place in the center of the storm. Why? Because I know things. Leela, you know, she has great powers now. Greater than you can imagine. She is also a precog. She can see into the future. She can see all the possibilities.

"That's why Leela is so valuable to Black Swan. Plus they know she has been sabotaging some of their stunts and that she has sent a lot of their people to jail. They want her working for them, spreading disinformation. They think if they implant a chip in the cognitive centers of Leela's brain, they can control her behavior and turn her into a double agent."

I let out a low whistle. "Whew. This is almost too much for me, Jill. Isn't it possible for you to communicate with Leela now, to send her some support or maybe work out some kind of a plan?"

"No, Marty. I wish I could. Leela's psychic senses are blocked right now. I told you that they've created some kind of force field, an energy field, around her cell. So we can't communicate in any way."

I wasn't giving up. "Then why doesn't she just teleport the hell out of there? We know she can teleport, 'cuz she did that big jump from Mount Kailash in Tibet to India, right?"

"Because, Marty," Jill said patiently, "Leela was hooked into some serious vortex energy for that jump, remember? A lot of wattage, plus all the processing power from the hack on Google's server farm. Now all she has is her own resources, which are awesome, but she needs our help."

"Our help?" I said incredulously. "How can we help her? We probably can't even get a plane out of here, or Phoenix, or anywhere!"

"Relax, Marty. I've got a plan. You will be happy to learn that you are part of that plan. Plus the State Department is real eager to get Leela back; she is a very important 'asset' for them. So have a little trust in ol' Jill, okay?"

"Okay, Jill, but..." My state of bliss from the golden moments with Jill was fading fast. Anxiety started to gnaw at the edges of my consciousness.

"Hey, Marty, I want you to meet someone. Remember that new friend I told you about? Here he comes now."

I looked up. A small, slightly bent figure, wearing a shabby coat and a black wool cap pulled over his ears, came through the back gate. He shuffled over to our table and sat himself down in a straight-back wooden chair. His eyes jumped out at me; they were coal-black and shiny, with a tiny golden glow in the center.

"Marty, this is Harry. Harry the handyman. He is also a gardener. He's been working around my property for the past three months."

I shook his hand. "Glad to meet you, Harry," I lied. His hand was cold and vaguely damp, his handshake limp and tentative. Dude gave me the creeps, instantly. He had a nose too big for the face, huge jug ears, a very long neck, and a chin that protruded out a little too far. It looked like a face that had been hastily thrown together.

"Looks like he's been doing a fine job here," I said to Jill, sarcastically. "I love your Zen garden, too. So… How did you find him? An ad in the paper? A referral? Where did he come from, anyway?"

Jill laughed nervously. "Marty, I hope you are ready for this. He came from the orbs."

The freakin' orbs. Just the spoken word triggered all kinds of crazy memories and unwelcome cross-references in my fevered mind. "Right, Jill. I suppose he squeezed himself into one of those orbs and was cruising Bell Rock during a thunderstorm. Next you're gonna tell me he entered Aura through her head, did his dirty business, and exited through one of her, uh, lower orifices. Right?"

"Marty, I realize you are the only eyewitness to the incident on Bell Rock. You saw lightning strike Aura, followed by an orb disappearing into her body. I know that's true; I saw the police report."

"Right. So? How does this dumpy dude fit into the picture?"

"Listen carefully, Marty. Harry is from some faraway star system; maybe a quantum dimension—a long, long way from Earth. He is a shapeshifter. And yes, you could call him an extraterrestrial, an ET. He has come to the Earth on a very important mission."

"An ET, eh? Where's the mothership?" I scoffed.

"Harry, please explain to my friend why you are here and how you got here. My friend is a bit of a skeptic."

Harry the Handyman—unusual name for an ET—looked me straight in the eye. His voice was gravelly and forced, right on the edge of computer-generated.

"Mr. Powers, sir. I came to Sedona with a partner via inter-dimensional travel, using the orbs as vehicles. Our assignment was to save you Earthlings from committing global suicide."

"A worthy objective, sir," I sneered, "but what does that have to do with lightning striking some bimbo in the noggin followed by an orb worming its way into—"

"Please, Mr. Powers, let me finish," said the Handyman, his voice whiny and irritating. "My partner was in a hurry and arrived here out of phase. That is, out of sync with me and our waveform frequency. He got here first, a few milliseconds before I arrived, and merged with your Aura Adelstein. That was a serious mistake. I arrived too late to intervene. Now we are seeing the consequences of his error. That is all I can tell you right now."

I turned to Jill. "This is such a mountain of bullshit, sweetheart. Who is this joker and what does he want from us? How does he know so much about the Bell Rock thing? Please look into this dude's skull and tell me what's going on."

"Marty, I tried to scan Harry's mind when he first arrived, but there was nothing there—emptiness. Leela had told me before she left for Europe that I would meet such a person as Harry and that he would play a very important role in our future. She has a strong ESP sense, you know—I told you that your wife is a precog. Sometimes she can see what will happen in the future."

"So what about the *now*?" I protested. "Why is Mr. Handyman hanging out here and what does he intend to do…to save us all from global suicide? And why does he look like he lives in a cardboard box?"

"Uh…" said Jill.

"And I've got more questions," I railed. "Maybe your Harry has got some answers. What caused that kinda monsoon rainstorm in April, three months early? Thunder and lightning and…"

"Oh, poor Marty," said Jill, mocking me. "Questions and more questions. Well, Harry looks like he does because he visited Uptown Sedona after the Bell Rock thing, looking for a body template. What you see is a composite of several tourists."

"Oh. Tourists. That figures. Look, Jill, I still can't get my head around the idea that this guy is an ET with some kind of super powers, or that he came from another dimension. Got any real proof of this dude's alien street cred?"

"Take my word for it, Marty, Harry is a real alien. And he's here on some very important business."

"He looks like a real alien, all right—an illegal alien. He better be careful walking around. He could be asked for his papers and wind up in the pokey. You should tell him he's in Arizona, not on Mars."

Harry stepped forward and took my hands in his. I tried to get away, but his steel grip held me tight. His eyes were filled with stars. I felt suddenly relaxed. My mind drifted into space, beyond the Earth, out through the planets, gliding freely and laughing at gravity; floating among the moons of Saturn, wandering boldly into the Uranus energy field, past the cold, dead rock fields of Pluto, and—whoosh!—out of the gravitational pull of our solar system.

How tempting to linger forever in the cosmic free-fall, to let go and just go with the flow….Into the clouds of Magellan, into the dark matter of space, hurtling toward the black hole at the center of the Milky Way….

And then I freaked. My old mind kicked in; fear had me by the throat.

I shook my head violently and returned instantly to Earth. To Sedona. To Jill's Zen garden.

"Whoa! Whoa! Whoa!" I sputtered, pulling my hands away. "Jill, who is this dude? What's he doing to me?"

"Marty, darling, this 'dude' is for real. He is here to help us. Please believe me. Now, pull yourself together. Time is short. We've got a job to do—a really, really important job."

"I don't know, Jill, I…" I was waffling, out of fear, I suppose, and confusion, and lack of control over the situation. An alien had just taken me on a trip beyond the stars. I really didn't know what the—

"I know you're confused, Marty, and you're not sure what is going on," said the lovely Jill, reading me accurately, as usual. Her energy was strong, no-nonsense.

"Go home and pack a suitcase. You and I have got a reservation on a military jet leaving Luke Air Force Base in Phoenix in two days, less than forty-eight hours from now. We'll take a chopper from the Sedona airport to Luke around noon. Bring your passport and some warm clothes. It's cold in Europe right now. And please bring that black leather jacket that Leela likes so much."

"W-w-w-wh—" I sputtered. "L-l-l-Leela?"

"You and I have a date with Leela, somewhere in Switzerland. First we make a short stop in Cyprus for a briefing at our embassy in Nicosia. We also gotta get you a Top Secret security clearance there. Then we head to somewhere in Switzerland, which will be our base of operations, then we find Leela. She's wearing a GPS device."

"She's *wearing* a GPS device?" I said. "Won't those Black Swan creeps find it and destroy it or something?"

"Nobody will ever find it. Hopefully. It was implanted under her skin by State Department people in Europe a few months ago. Just below her tailbone at the base of the spine. Even to an X-ray or MRI it will show up as tissue. Leela's GPS emits a strong signal that can be tracked from many miles away. Don't worry. We'll find her."

"And when we find her—"

"Just relax into the situation, Marty," said Jill reassuringly. "It will all work out. Trust me. I can see the future, too. Sort of. Just keep breathing. And start packing."

I closed my eyes, took several very deep breaths, then opened my eyes. We were still in Jill's Zen garden. Jill was there, as was Harry, the ET. I wasn't dreaming.

CHAPTER ELEVEN

Into the Lion's Mouth

Time was truly short. Before I left for Europe, I wanted to meet with Hacker and get us both caught up on all the gossip and news of the day. Hacker could be trusted with any information, any deep sharing of feelings, any crazy wild dangerous thought forms lurking about one's left brain, any confession of any deed or scheme done or undone.

With one exception: The Black Swan business. I was sworn to secrecy. Maybe he knew about it already. Hacker had many sources of insider info.

We met for dinner at Sushi Town. It was too cold to sit on the outside patio, so we slammed into a big roomy booth inside. The place was empty except for us, plus one bored waitress of unknown ethnic descent, probably from Taiwan or Singapore; and one cook dancing in his open kitchen with headphones on.

Hacker did a quick scan of the booth and the whole place with his Microsoft Bug Cleaner. The place was clean, so we could talk openly. I noted that the economic crisis, combined with the disasters happening planet-wide, had created a climate of fear and anxiety in our little town. Bad for business, I said. We were lucky this place was still open, I said.

"Plus don't forget martial law," added Hacker. "The city council is meeting in emergency session tomorrow to decide if they're going to impose it or not. If they do, it means police checkpoints, curfews, a lot more paranoia, and more restrictions on our freedom."

I leaned in close to Hacker. "Okay, dude, you are in touch with the happenings, you know what's going on. Time to share with your old friend Marty Powers."

Hacker sat up straight and squared his broad shoulders. "I will do that, good buddy, I will tell you what I know. But I also expect you to share what you know. For example, I know you were up at Jill's house today. I know about the trip to Europe. I know about the weird little fellow up there who is from somewhere west of the dark side of the moon."

Oh-oh. "How the hell do you know all that?" I asked, nearly falling out of the booth. "Are you psychic too? Jesus Christ. I must be the only one who—"

"Don't forget who you are dealing with, my man. Remember that annoying moth that was flying around Jill's living room when you first got there? My latest creation. Audio plus video. Great picture, perfect sound. No psychic could pick that up."

"Jesus," I muttered.

"Outside," said Hacker matter-of-factly. "Remember the squawking little red bird up in the tall pine tree? An Arizona cardinal? My masterpiece, so far. A living creature, equipped with a wire, sending a signal up to fifty miles. Again, perfect audio and video. Remotely controlled by me."

"Shhhheeeeeessshhhh," I exhaled. I shuddered inside. Nothing was private anymore. Privacy once was sacred; now the very concept was old school, outdated, ancient history.

"These are strange times, my friend," Hacker said, in a voice deeper than usual. "Things have changed. None of the old rules apply anymore."

I went silent, staring at the wall, embarrassed, wondering if my lust for Hacker's ex-lover showed up on his surveillance recordings. Wondering if my body language, my eyes, my attention to her, were a dead giveaway. Did I say anything suggestive? Wait a minute! Didn't Jill say she'd always *wanted* me? Weren't our tongues basically hanging out with unrequited lust for each other? Didn't Hacker know—

"Wake up, Marty, here comes the waitress. Do you know what you want to eat?"

I sighed, hoping my thought forms weren't showing. So much for openness. I managed to order my favorite meal at Sushi Town, pad thai with tofu. Extra peanut sauce. Easy on the chilies.

"You folks got good water?" I asked the waitress, who was actually quite attractive, young, Asian, short skirt above knees, probably had her own stories to tell. Why had she come to Sedona? What were her plans for the future? What future?

"Bottled water in storage," she answered with twinkling eyes. "Not much left. Cost three dollars glass. You want? Oak Creek beer only two dollar."

Hacker ordered chicken teriyaki and we both ordered a glass of local Oak Creek beer. I breathed deeply a few times to clear my head and wipe away any emotional flotsam. My friend gazed at me, knowingly.

"As you say, Hacker, these are strange times. All bets are off. Now, what's the big story? Late-breaking news, dude. Give it to me. I know you're tuned in. Know you got your sources. I've been out of the news loop lately."

"Okay, Marty, here are the headlines. Our environmental crisis was coming to a head of its own accord, the droughts, the warming, the glaciers melting, the sea levels rising, the fires, the whole shot. Volcanoes erupting. Earthquakes. Running out of water. You know. Then a few months ago some new people suddenly made the scene—Black Swan Galactic. They decided to exploit the situation and make it even worse. They blackmailed governments for huge amounts of money so they could do their thing, which is this cockamamie scheme to launch a satellite and live forever, or explore the solar system, or something."

"Uh, Hacker, my man, you must know from your intrusion, uh, your surveillance of my meeting with Jill that we discussed the Black Swan business. So tell me something I don't know about these creeps."

Hacker exhaled long and deeply, took a short time-out to munch on his dinner. "Okay, Marty, you asked for it. This is what I found out on HNN, the Hacker News Network. Black Swan Galactic Limited is registered and incorporated in Geneva. They have offices all over the place: in Moscow, in London, Paris, Rome, Tokyo, New

York, Mexico City, you name it. They started out a few years ago as a group of wealthy investors who made a lot of money in the international markets and especially in currency trading, and gave huge donations to environmental causes. But that was just a front."

"A front for what?"

"For their real business, which is to fuck up the planet, scare the bejeezus out of the politicians, blackmail their ass, take the money and run. To outer space. They got some crazy space travel agenda. Marty, do you know what 'Black Swan' means?"

"No, not really," I said. I remembered that Jill had some intel on the Black Swan thing, but she was vague on it. "Is there such a thing as a black swan?" I asked my friend. "I thought all swans were white."

"That's just the point. Black swan is all about the unpredictable. The unexpected. You can assume that all swans are white, but if you just see one black swan, it disproves the whole friggin' thing."

I shook my head. "What the fuck are you talking about, Hacker? What do swans have to do with an environmental crisis?"

"Okay, my man, here's the intel I got from my hacker network. A few years ago a former Wall Street hotshot named Nassim Nicholas Taleb wrote a book called *The Black Swan*. According to this book, life is totally unpredictable. Just about anything really significant that happens—historically, personally, whatever—is a black swan event. Something really game-changing. Usually catastrophes. Nine Eleven, for example. The atom bomb we dropped on Hiroshima. The stock market crash of 1929. Political assassinations in the Sixties.

"In short, a black swan event is an unexpected event that has a major impact on the world. In other words, shit happens. Life can never be the same again."

Hacker stopped and took several deep breaths. "So this book is their bible. These freakin' billionaires and power-mad bigshots who think they can do whatever they want and fuck the rest of the world. They think they can *create* black swan events, and, by the way, live forever. They're all taking some weird drug called EMC-2. They think it jacks up their cells and gives them eternal life. This stuff has weird and unpredictable side effects, like boosting testosterone levels. You know what that means: unchecked male aggression. One of the core problems on this planet for thousands of years.

"So. Black Swan Galactic Limited. That's who they are. They are very interested in your psychically gifted wife. And they have got her pretty ass under lock and key right now, according to my surveillance data. So if you, my friend, and my ex-girlfriend, Jill, are headed for Europe to try to find Leela, you are headed right into the lion's mouth."

"Lion, schmion," I sneered. "It's something we've got to do. And there are also rumblings about the Internet being fucked up. Any connection with Black Swan? Know anything about it?"

Hacker paused for a beat or two, looked around, and whispered conspiratorially, "This is strictly on the Q.T., Marty, okay? It's a very delicate situation. Just about all business, public and private, is run on the Internet today: power grids, dams, banking, communications, stock markets, airport traffic control, you name it. And the Internet is definitely fucked up. Somebody, or a group of somebodies, is doing a major hack on the Web. A bunch of malicious attacks that have already created chaos all over the world, okay? Try to go to your favorite websites and you'll end up somewhere you didn't intend to go. I tried to bring up my bank's website the other day and wound up at a porno site.

"So, my hacker buddies and me are trying to track down the source of this big-time sabotage. We suspect Black Swan Beta, the company's software branch located somewhere in Switzerland. We can't prove it. They are very clever, my friend. We want to keep it very quiet so we can slip in and launch a counterattack. It may take a week or two. But in the meantime, power grids all over Europe have been shut down. Airports are closed. Traffic lights don't work. It is a very, very ugly situation."

"This is real spooky stuff, dude, real spooky," I said. "Armageddon time. Pretty soon there'll be mobs rioting in the streets. Born-agains will be running around screaming for the Rapture. Hope your guys can move on this soon, Hacker."

"You know, Marty, these Black Swan people may seem like crackpots, but they are damned serious. They've got money, influence, weapons, connections in high places, high-tech and computer savvy. And with all the other enviro disasters going on in the world, they've kinda got us all cornered like trapped rats. Unless the politicians come up with some big dough. I don't know if there's enough money in the world to pay off these assholes."

I shoveled a huge portion of pad thai noodles into my mouth with expert chopstick moves, then nodded to Hacker to continue. He cleared his throat, looked skyward.

"Black Swan wants the dough to build rockets to take them to Mars or some virgin planet so they can start a human colony and explore the stars. I hear rumblings that they are secretly building a space station as a starting point.

"Plus there is some connection to a fundamentalist religion. I hear they have started their own religion based on eternal life."

Hacker paused, closed his eyes, took a deep breath. "These people are vicious killers, man. Already tens of thousands of people have died because of their shenanigans. Millions of refugees are wandering around the planet without food or water or a place to sleep thanks to Black Swan's war on humanity. And they're just getting started."

"So how much money do they need, for chrissake?"

"Lots. They have laid out exactly how much money they want from each country. For the rich countries, it's trillions. Even poor countries in Africa have to cough up money or oil or some other resource. It's global blackmail, Marty. Nothing like this has ever happened in human history. We could all be headed for the trash heap unless something happens to turn this around."

"Hacker, dear friend, for some strange reason I feel almost optimistic. In a few hours I'll be flying to Europe with Jill to find Leela and get closer to the Black Swan organization. I have a strong feeling that these two ladies are the key to our survival. And this strange dude Harry the Handyman, whatever his story is. And our old friend Kali, who fits into the big picture somehow. I've got a meeting with Benny Bravo tomorrow to find out what's going on out at the Tantra Temple."

"Marty, I wish you luck. More than luck. Good karma. And may the angels protect you, and surround you with love. May the deities protect you. May the—"

We both cracked up. At least we still knew how to laugh, even in the face of...what, a series of staged black swan events? Unexpected, unpleasant surprises that would change the course of human history?

"I'll get the check, Hacker," I said, chortling and signaling to our waitress. "The angels can wait. I've got *white* swans on my side: two beautiful psychic ladies."

I stood up and gave my dear friend a big hug, holding my cheek against his. He is a big man, possessed of powerful energy. I felt as if he was transmitting his energy to me. I hoped we would both live to see each other again. As he said earlier, things have changed.

Indeed.

CHAPTER TWELVE

Wired

Benny Bravo was fairly quivering with excitement when I sat down with him the next morning in his trim little West Sedona house. For a guy who never married and lived alone, his home was neat and tidy, decorated in used Ikea, funky but functional, wood floors plus expensive Persian rugs, framed posters of dead rock stars. His views out of huge picture windows encompassed the entire Thunder Mountain range.

"Yo, *jefe*," he began, as soon as I had flopped down on his well-worn tan couch. "How about a cuppa java? Maybe some hot tea or good water? Or how about a couple tokes of the new ganja just arrived in town?"

I said no to all of the above, but did silently note the faint aroma of marijuana smoke that seemed to linger in every corner of his abode.

"Marty, you're not gonna believe this. I'm in love. I am really in love this time."

"One day at the Tantra Temple and you're already in love? That Goddess Kali sure works fast. Who is it, one of her Dakinis?"

Benny proceeded to tell me in wild, amped-up prose about his day at the Temple. For starters, he was taken in hand by the Dakini named Satori, who had made some moves on him months ago at the Third Eye. Satori was both his guide and his consort. She gave him the tour, showed him all the various rooms in the main temple building, signed him up for several programs—charged on my credit card—and introduced him to Kali.

"You wouldn't believe what she looks like now, boss. A real *gordita.*" He giggled. Benny was one of the few humans who knew about my trysts with Kali before she was a goddess.

"She must weigh about two-twenty. She looks kinda like the Buddha, heh heh. So Satori takes me into this room, like a chamber, you know? With golden curtains and soft light, everything kinda glowing, a really delicious smell in the room, like vanilla crossed with musk. And there's Kali herself, sitting on this golden throne, wearing a golden robe. And I swear there was this aura around her, a white and golden aura. Now you know, boss, I don't believe in that New Age ca-ca—"

"But an aura is an aura, bro," I reassured him. "If you experienced an aura, that is what was there, for you. Go on, Benny."

"So Kali just looks me in the eyes for a long time, like she knew me really really well, then she sat back and said to Satori, just two words." Benny closed his eyes and fell silent.

"Well, what were the words? C'mon, homey, don't mess with my mind!" I said impatiently.

He sighed, and smiled, as if cherishing a memory. "*Transport him.* That's it, boss. Kali said 'transport him' and the next thing I remember is Satori shoving me into this big room where about thirty people were floating in the freakin' air. The place smelled like oxygen or something. Satori said this was the Levitation Chamber, and all I had to do was run a few steps and jump and I could levitate too. So I did it. Sheeeeeeit!"

My rational mind wanted to poke holes in his story, tell him he was hypnotized or dreaming. But something in me believed everything he was telling me. Obviously, Kali had attained incredible power.

"Go on, Benny," I urged. "Tell me more."

"Okay, *vato*. So I floated around in this room with all these other people, and it was a real blast. Everybody is giggling and laughing and we're bumping into each other and some people are hugging and one couple was dry humping while floating around! It was like there was no gravity. It was amazing."

"And then...."

"Then after about half an hour Satori came in and waved for me to come down. So I just floated right down to the floor, like it was a natural thing, you know? She showed me around some of the other rooms, the session rooms. She took me around the campus. It was amazing. About a thousand people live there. They have dorms, they have big kitchens, they have their own food, their own farms, *jefe*, they have their own water supply from Oak Creek, they have—"

"Wait a minute," I said. "A thousand people live there?"

"I told ya, Marty, it was amazing. The parking lots were full. You had to take like a shuttle to get from the parking lot to the main temple. Satori told me there were about three thousand people out there at any given time, which includes two thou visitors, doing all the stuff they offer. Or just visiting, checking it out. A lot of these people were there to get healed. You know, healed? Like Jesus did? Sick people, cripples, cancer, AIDS, bad hearts, the whole shot. And Kali does these healings."

I didn't know what to say. I simply sighed.

"And they freakin' get healed!" Benny said. "That's what Satori told me. She let me look into a big room where Kali was, about two hundred people sitting in folding chairs, some of them in wheelchairs, and Kali waving her hand over the people and speaking in tongues or some weird language."

"Jesus Christ," I muttered.

Benny looked at me funny. "No, *like* Jesus Christ. Healing the sick. Satori told me that Kali could even raise the dead. If she wanted to. But that it would mess with the cosmic slipstream, or something like that."

"Go on, Benny," I said, feeling kind of sick in my stomach. I knew there was something really wrong, something dangerous and threatening about all of this.

"So we had a great time, Satori and me, swimming together in the big outdoor pool, everybody naked, and what a bod on this chick, hey? She's about eighteen or nineteen and sweet as halavah. She showed me how Kali could be in more than one place at the same time."

"Huh?"

"You know, be in one place, doing her thing, and being in another place at the same time, doing her thing."

"Holograms?"

"Nope. The real deal. Blew me away. Satori showed me. Kali was in the healing room, and she was also in a Tantra session. And she was also in the big channeling room across the hall, about fifty or so people in there, and she was channeling some old dude, talking in this weird voice, like a ghost."

"Go on, Benny."

"Well…okay, so after lunch Satori took me to one of the private rooms, and—"

"And…."

"And she gave me one hell of a great massage, man, then took off her clothes, lit some candles, some incense, turned down the lights, and showed me some, uh, ah, some tricks. I mean, she did some shit with *mi huevos*…"

Benny's voice trailed off and he turned his head away. "You mean, she turned you on to Tantra," I said. "She showed you the Tantric sex ritual."

"Tantra, schmantra, Marty! This *chica schtupped* the shit outta me, homey! I have been with a lot of women in my time, you know that, but this was from outer space! I almost didn't come back! I don't know where the hell I went, but it was righteous out there, it was—"

"I got it, Benny, I got it. Been there, done that."

Benny went on to describe more of his experiences at Kali's Tantric Temple, and after awhile I started to feel a weird kind of overload. Most of what he told me defied logic and the laws of physics. "Are you sure that wasn't some sort of illusion, Benny?" I asked at one point. "Mass hypnosis, or maybe a series of holos?"

"No, Marty, there was no tricks. Yo, Satori gave me a video clip of some of the stuff I did and saw out there. It's all here on this little memory chip. Wanna see it?"

"Homey, I can't take much more, tell ya the truth. Plus I gotta get on a plane in a few hours and try to find my wife. Make a copy of that chip and I'll watch it later, okay?"

"Done, boss." He dropped the chip in a tiny copying device, and a duplicate popped out seconds later.

"Tell me something, Benny." I leaned in closer to him. "You know, there's a lotta stuff going on out there in the world, like the whole place is falling apart. All kinds of disasters, everywhere. You know that, Benny, you told me about some of the shit goin' down. People are freakin' out all over the planet, homey. Don't these people out at the Tantric Temple know about all this? And aren't they kinda, you know, concerned?"

Benny stood up suddenly. "Marty, I saved the best for last, okay? Satori told me if I got home and there was anything *yo no comprende*, or any question I couldn't answer, to do a little thingy and Kali herself would show up to help me out. So I think we need Goddess Kali here, you know, to answer your question."

"Whaaaaat?" I said, my jaw dropping about a foot, ready to believe just about anything.

"She said to stand up tall and put both hands on my crown chakra—you know, the top of my *cabeza*—and face toward the southwest. Think positive thoughts. And Kali would come to me." Benny proceeded to do just that, putting both hands on his crown chakra.

What happened next was almost too much. Goddess Kali materialized. Right in Benny Bravo's living room. Looking just as he had described: Overweight, Buddha-like, swathed in golden robes and bathed in a golden light. She seemed very real. She stood there and looked right at me.

"Marty," she said, in an ethereal voice. "Marty, don't worry about the world. Kali will take care of everything. Kali has the power now. Kali protects you. Come to Kali now." Kali, or whatever passed itself off as Kali, held out its arms to me.

I couldn't help myself. As if in a trance, I stood up and moved toward the image, arms outstretched, ready to embrace my former lover. I passed right through Kali's image and out the other side. I turned around and the image had disappeared.

"A hologram, Benny! A fucking hologram! They must have planted a wire on you, homey, and transmitted the holo when you gave the signal from your *cabeza*. Friggin' hell! Probably our whole conversation was monitored and recorded. Benny, you are a walking wiretap!"

I gave Benny a big hug and whispered in his ear, "Meet with Hacker *muy pronto*. Tell him what happened.

All of it. Show him the vid clip from the temple. But first let him debug you. Got it? When you're clean, let's keep in touch via v-mail. Send me streaming vid, if possible. Use the encryption code. You okay, homey?"

I held Benny Bravo by the shoulders at arm's length. Tears were running down his cheeks. He looked like a wounded child.

"I— I thought I was in love, Marty. It really felt like love. It still does, kinda, but, but, but—"

I put a finger up to my lips to silence him. "Love, lust, they all seem like the same thing sometimes," I said philosophically, pulling on my winter coat. "Gotta go, brother. See ya around. Take care."

I was out the door and in my car in thirty seconds. I was in a big hurry: I didn't want any more data about me or my plans to get transmitted back to Kali. I looked back and saw Benny at his door, waving at me. I waved back and took off down the road, fast. Benny was hot, he was wired. Everything seemed bugged; the whole world suddenly felt unsafe. Adding to the creepiness was that holographic image of Kali, which refused to leave my mind.

As I headed up Oak Creek Canyon toward Hacker's cabin, I thought about Leela, held prisoner, somewhere. My guts churned. And I ached for Jill. Tomorrow we would be together on a military transport plane headed for Europe. Into the unknown.

A flock of fantasy black swans flew across the screen of my imagination. I blinked my eyes to drive them away as I powered my Honda Lightning into the wild curves of Oak Creek Canyon.

PART II

In Search of Leela

"Mr. Powers, you have a key role to play in this drama. You will pass yourself off not only as an expert on computer software and Internet function, but also as a shaman with supernatural powers."

—U.S. Secretary of State

CHAPTER THIRTEEN

Trust Is Enough

This was a first: Flying across America in a sleek C-20 Gulfstream III aircraft at 600 mph with a beautiful psychic by my side as the fate of the planet hung in the balance. We had taken off at dawn from the runways of Luke Air Force Base, home of the 56th Fighter Wing, forty-five hundred acres of hair-trigger military readiness located in the suburbs of Phoenix, Arizona.

The C-20 is a twin-engine, turbofan aircraft whose mission is to shuttle high-ranking government and Defense Department officials. It is the Rolls Royce of military transports, and is, in fact, powered by two Rolls engines. Our plane featured pure luxury throughout, with wooden interiors and cabinets, roomy, comfortable seats, two bathrooms, one with shower and tub.

In the rear was a small bedroom with a queen-size bed, surround stereo system, and large-screen TV with a collection of the latest movies. And, of course, a high-speed Internet connection. There were fourteen seats and a crew of three, two pilots and a foxy stewardess in Air Force uniform, Staff Sergeant Annabelle Hunter.

As we flew over the ragged checkerboard squares of the "united" states, my eyes glazed over and I visualized Jill and I having hot sex on the queen-size. My hand drifted to her thigh. She let it rest there for a few seconds, then politely removed it, snapping me back to reality. I had forgotten that I was with a psychic.

"Don't go there," she whispered in my ear. "I am *not* having sex with you on this plane, Marty. Don't rush me. Behave yourself. We are on a military mission, remember?"

Our mission, right. The U.S. State Department had arranged our trip on this fancy VIP flying machine after Jill convinced her boss of the gravity of Leela's predicament. Our mission was to find Leela, appraise said predicament, and rescue her if possible. That was it. If Jill and I thought we couldn't pull it off by ourselves, we were to call in an elite American special ops unit ready and waiting somewhere in Europe. In other words, Plan B would be a covert operation to rescue my wife, featuring a gang of sharpshooters with a take-no-prisoners attitude.

The whole idea made my blood run cold. Yet, I have to admit, it also was tremendously exciting.

Oh yes, we also each carried our own PDA's—Personal Digital Assistants. I had the latest version of Mojo Corporation's Amigo, which had about a gazillion gigs of memory and could do just about anything, including downloading and projecting holos. But Jill carried the ultimate PDA: the brand-new Psi-Fi handset, which could do anything any other PDA on the market could do, and more. And—get ready for this—the Psi-Fi had the ability to translate Jill's thoughts into text onto the handset's huge LCD!

Crude translations, yes, Spelling errors, yes. Grammar, sometimes awkward. But it actually worked, it freakin' worked! We beta-tested it during our flight.

"Jill," I said softly, when we were well underway, "I'm really curious about what Benny Bravo saw at Kali's temple. Want to play the chip that Benny made for me?"

She whispered in my ear, "Don't talk. Just think it. Leave the rest to me. Check out the screen of my Psi-Fi. You know we are being monitored, right? There is a vid camera in the light above your seat and there is an audio bug in the window shade button on my side. Pretty cool setup."

I suspected as much, I thought. *Guess our government doesn't trust us yet. I'll run the chip on my Amigo. Let's put on the wireless headphones and I'll hold the screen away from the vid cam.*

Carefully, Jill showed me the LCD on her Psi-Fi. Words, her thoughts, were actually materializing! *Gotcha! Loud + clr. Run da chip, deer.*

It was quite a show at Kali's Tantric Temple. All of the craziness described by Benny was right there on the data chip: Kali on her golden throne, the levitating, the various rooms and chambers, the "private" Tantra sessions, Benny's wild Tantra session with Satori, nude swimming, Kali in more than one place at a time (not too convincing), the gorgeous temple grounds and dormitories.

Whadda think about that, Jill? Instantly her thoughts appeared as words on the Psi-Fi LCD: *Imprsive & ominas. May-be sum iz fake but obvsly th womn haz great pwr.*

I turned off the Amigo and we removed our head-phones. "I'm tired of this game," I whispered in Jill's ear. "Why don't we continue this conversation in the bedroom? We'll crank up the stereo. I've got some nice romantic tunes on my Amigo. We can talk in there. With impunity."

"You're a hopeless case, Marty," whispered Jill. "Let's just go silent and meditate for awhile. We can talk more openly when we make our refuel stop."

Jill was right: I was a hopeless case. Probably a sex addict. Mental note: Get into one of those twelve-step programs for the terminally horny when things get back to normal. If ever.

Meanwhile, we were on our way to Andrews Air Force Base in Maryland, the home base of our Gulfstream. We were scheduled to refuel there and have about a half hour break to stretch our legs and breathe some real air. Our destination was the American embassy in Nicosia, Cyprus, a distance of seven thousand, two hundred eight miles from Phoenix. The C-20 has a range of forty-one hundred nautical miles. Total trip time, not counting refueling stop: twelve hours.

Andrews is a huge military installation just ten miles from the Pentagon, and even today a cloud of suspicion hangs over the base after the 9/11 terrorist attacks. Many conspiracy theorists say the two squadrons of fighter jets at Andrews assigned the job of protecting the skies over Washington D.C. failed to do their job. Not a single Andrews fighter was ordered to take off to protect the city despite a one hour advance warning of a terrorist attack in progress.

On this day, the 9/11 attacks seemed like ancient history. Jill had turned her head away from me and appeared to fall asleep. I meditated for awhile, or at least tried to help my mind go silent and give me a break, but it was a beehive of thoughts, fantasies, memories, analyses, and on and on and on. Soon it led to a light, troubled sleep.

I was awakened with a hand softly shaking my shoulder and a female voice whispering, "Mr. Powers, Mr. Powers. Please, Mr. Powers." I awoke to the not-unpleasant face and presence of Sergeant Annabelle Hunter. She was holding a tiny data chip in her right hand. "Urgent message for Miss Appleton from the State Department. It came over the secure server in the cockpit. The pilot put the message on the chip for her. He has a Top Secret clearance; I don't. Would you give the message to Miss Appleton?"

I nodded a sleepy "yes." Sgt. Hunter left quickly. Jill was not in her seat. I figured she must have gone to the bedroom to sleep. Oh well, later for her. I felt that I needed to look at the message immediately, so I popped the chip into my Amigo. I didn't worry about the bugs monitoring our every move. I didn't have a Top Secret security clearance, or *any* security clearance, but I didn't worry about that either.

URGENT. TOP SECRET, flashed across the screen. ATTENTION JILL APPLETON. EYES ONLY. Came the message in smaller type: "Leela Powers has been located via GPS by Agent Anderson using helicopter overflights. Location: Davos, Switzerland: Black Swan Beta headquarters. Your assignment: Infiltrate their operation. Rescue agent Powers if possible. Your cover: software designers from USA. We are preparing background profiles for Web + corporate creds. Advise you begin studying Internet protocols. Details @ Cyprus. Gambit foolproof."

Incredible! Where was Jill? I left the chip in the Amigo and dashed to the back of the plane and the bedroom. Not there. She had to be in one of the bathrooms. One had been designated as my bathroom; it was fairly drab and ordinary, with just a toilet and a sink. The other was Jill's. It had a large tub and a shower. I was so excited I ripped open the door without knocking.

"Jill! I've got some good news and some bad news! I just saw—"

"Eeeeeeek!" screamed Jill, a stage scream. She didn't attempt to cover her semi-nudity, which was masked with a tapestry of bubbles. "What's with you, Marty?" she scolded. "Can't a girl have any privacy? What's up?"

I told her the good news about Leela and she shrieked again, this time with joy. I told her about our assignment. Suddenly she stood up in the bathtub. It was the first time I had seen Jill's nakedness, partially concealed as it was with the bubbles. Her body was awesome; I gasped in spite of myself.

"Throw me that towel, would you Marty?" she said, seemingly unconcerned about the effect she was having on me. "And then give me a minute or two to get dressed. I wanna see that message. We're supposed to be software designers? Sheeeeeeeeee!"

Our landing at Andrews was smooth and uneventful. We were met by a small welcoming committee of military types, and allowed to walk around the grounds while our plane was refueled. There was a winter chill in the air and patches of snow around the little park we stumbled upon. "Can we talk here?" I asked. "Jesus, Jill, I'm not used to being so paranoid."

"Let's just go for a walk and talk in low voices, Marty. And stop thinking about giving my booty a big squeeze, okay?"

"Damn, Jill, you are one hell of a sexy bitch. Too bad you know everything I'm thinking. That kind of spoils the male-female dichotomy, you know? Unfair advantage to the female of the species. And now that I know what you really look like...."

"Marty...." Jill was wearing a strange smile when I looked over at her.

"Okay, Jill, here's what I'm thinking about. You probably already know, but I'll say it anyway. First, this is amazing news that they have found Leela. That's the good news. But why does this Anderson guy have to have his nose in everything? And also, how the hell are you and I going to become software experts in such a short time? That was the bad news, by the way."

"Marty, no need to be worried about Mr. Anderson. Jealousy doesn't become you. He has been Leela's control guy for quite awhile, and he works for the same people we do. That's all he does. So get over it.

"Then…we will learn enough about software design to bluff our way past these boobs at Black Swan Beta. We will have a crash course. I have a few memory tricks up my sleeve. Also, I have a sneaking suspicion that these people are behind the Internet attacks. Maybe that will be part of our assignment: rescue the Internet. I think we could pull it off with Leela's help."

"Okay, okay, Jill, I respect your confidence. I have my doubts about the whole caper, but I'm with you all the way. Now, one more question, please. Why are we going to Cyprus, which is way the hell out of the way, instead of checking in at the American embassy in Rome? Much closer to Switzerland, where they're holding Leela. Or Florence, or Nice, or Geneva, or some other fun city. I found out that Cyprus is about fifteen hundred miles from Zurich or any cool place in Europe."

"Marty, there are things you don't know about yet. Most of Europe is a mess. There are food riots in Rome; in fact, all over Europe. Tent cities everywhere. The computer saboteurs have shut down the power grids all over Germany and France. In Paris, they are rioting in the streets. Little wars are breaking out. It's a bad scene everywhere in Europe, and getting worse. Only in Switzerland is everything running smoothly, which happens to be where the main Black Swan operations are located."

I looked around. No one in sight. A few drab military buildings off in the distance, the drone of aircraft, birdcalls, the bare trees, elm and oak and some kind of pine. So peaceful.

"Jill, I said, "I get the picture. But really, how can I help rescue Leela? I don't have your psychic abilities. All I've got is my good looks and charm and a little experience creating websites."

"No time to tell you the whole story, dear one. There are some surprises in store for all of us. We land in Cyprus, which is a safe place and still relatively civilized, and get a briefing from the State Department honchos there.

"Marty, I got a message from the State Department while you were in the shower. In Cyprus, after our briefing, a high-speed chopper will take us to somewhere near Davos. We set up a base camp and meet with our support people. Then we drop in on the Black Swan Beta headquarters and—"

"Oh, right. Just walk right in and tell these armed-to-the-teeth cyber-terrorists we want to see a friend. Who we understand is being held prisoner in their dungeon by means of an electromagnetic force field."

"Not exactly. We have our cover, which is the computer software thing. Black Swan will want to meet us for our expertise. Once we are inside, we will figure out what to do."

"That's fine for you. How about me?"

"I promised you there would be some surprises when we got to Cyprus. You worry too much, Marty. Just trust."

"Trust and....Too bad I don't believe in prayer. I'm not sure if just trust is enough, Jill."

We had been walking shoulder to shoulder toward the terminal. Jill stopped suddenly, planted her beautiful self in front of me, took me by the shoulders, and gave me the warmest, lovingest hug I have had in quite some time. She looked me straight in the eyes.

"Trust is enough, Marty," she whispered. "Now let's get on that plane and fly off into the wild blue yonder."

Jill stepped away from the hug, gave me a big smile, and extended her warm hand to mine. That's how we walked, briskly, hand in hand, back to our waiting C-20. My heart was beating wildly. My mind was empty.

CHAPTER FOURTEEN

Darkness Prevails

The flight to Cyprus was uneventful. Dinner was served somewhere over the British Isles—vegetarian, at Jill's request—while our pilots navigated us through choppy skies. Jill and I kept our spoken conversations to a minimum while aloft. I managed to fall asleep on the queen size bed, alone, after popping two or three Melatonins and putting some sleepy music on the wrap-around stereo.

I dreamed of Leela in some kind of great danger, locked in a room guarded by a vicious, snarling dog which lunged at me as I tried to enter the room. Several men with lizard heads and human bodies came at me, but I escaped by waking myself up. In a cold sweat. A real nightmare. I stretched, thought about a threesome with Leela and Jill, and drifted back to sleep with a smile on my face.

Hours later. "Marty. Wake up. Time to get up and prepare for landing." It was Jill, calling from the doorway, a dark silhouette in the harsh gray backlight of the aircraft.

"C'mon in, Jill," I called sleepily. "We just have time for—"

"Don't be crude, dear boy," she said, shimmying and smiling her way into the tiny bedroom. Jill looked almost translucent. She was wearing a white blouse and tight jeans, her hair tied back in a ponytail, no makeup as usual, gorgeous and unattainable. For the moment. She sat on the edge of the rumpled bed, put her hand on my forehead.

"You've been having some bad dreams, huh, Marty?"

"Oh, just my wife being abused by lizard-men and attack dogs, that's all. And then the falling from the sky dream, and something about you, far away beyond the mountains, disappearing in the mist...."

"Just your mind processing some useless information, that's all, dear one. Dreams aren't real, you know." She looked at me with such kindness that I felt tears forming behind my eyes.

"What've you been doing while I was dreaming?" I managed to ask.

"Plenty. I watched the vid again from Kali's temple that Benny Bravo gave you. Verrrrry interesting. Kali is a force to be reckoned with. She has incredible powers and seems to be just getting stronger."

"Yeah, I agree. Stronger, and weirder. Hey, is this room bugged?"

"No. I did a scan earlier. It's clean. We can talk."

"Well, nobody's perfect, Jill. Not even you. I know a bug you missed. Maybe even two."

"You mean that moth at my house? I know Hacker's work. I wanted him to tune in on that scene. And that noisy bird outside? Yeah. No problem."

"Migawd, Jill, you are one hell of a—" I reached out to encircle her waist with a long arm. But she was off the bed and at the doorway before I could connect.

"Marty, we land in Cyprus in less than an hour. You've just got time to take a shower and get yourself together. Come join me and I'll show you the decoded message I got from the State Department. We've got a great adventure ahead of us. Hurry up."

A cold shower was just what I needed. It felt like things were heating up, and that I needed to be ready. Ready for what...? I had no idea.

Cruising across Western Europe in the middle of the night was eerie: darkness prevailed, everywhere. What happened to the great cities? Swinging London; Paris, city of lights; eternal Rome; vibrant Athens. Someone, or something, had turned out the lights.

I turned to Jill in the next seat. "That is one of the problems you and I are facing," she said, scanning my mind. "The hackers have done a thorough job of disrupting the electrical grids in most European cities. You see the results. Only it's worse than just the lights. Anything electrical is being messed with. And it's intermittent, so nobody knows when the juice will be turned off. Or back on."

I shook my head in disbelief. This was the cold reality of Black Swan's ruthless sabotage of the world's infrastructure.

"It gets worse. Take a look at this decoded version of the message I just got from Cyprus." She showed me the screen on her Psi-Fi.

SITUATION URGENT. BLACKMAIL DEMANDS GROW. WANT NASA FACILITIES. NUCLEAR THREAT SOUTH ASIA. HURRY.

Jill quickly deleted the message and closed the device. She put her index finger to her lips, silencing all but my busy mind. Nuclear threat? "Look down," Jill said. "Dawn is breaking over the Med."

I looked. It was an awesome sight, the first glimpse of a fiery daybreak over the Mediterranean Sea, reflecting the color palette of red, orange, and deep purple. A miniscule piece of land poked out of the mighty ocean. Is that Cyprus? It looked like a tiny piece of meat about to be devoured by a giant mouth.

"Cyprus is surrounded by all these countries hostile to each other," Jill said. "Egypt, Syria, Jordan, Lebanon, Israel, Turkey, Greece. And yet it has survived all the turmoil."

Not to be outdone, I chipped in with my own tidbit of information. "Okay, how about this: For hundreds of years the Greeks and Turks fought humongous wars over this little island, really Islam versus Christianity, what else is new. Now the Turks occupy the northern part of the island, and the Greeks the southern part, which is most of the land. They are separated by the Green Line, which the United Nations has to enforce. They still don't speak to each other."

"Almost right, Marty. But I've got an update. While little wars are breaking out all over the planet, people fighting for food and water and territory, the Greeks and Turks on Cyprus are finally getting along. Not only that, they are partying together. And sharing resources. Cyprus used to depend on oil imports for ninety percent of their energy. Now oil is hard to come by, so nearly everything runs on batteries and solar power.

Sgt. Hunter, in her crisp Air Force duds, walked slowly down the aisle as the plane gradually nosed downward. "Please fasten your safety belts," she purred. "We'll be landing at Nicosia International Airport in fifteen minutes."

"Nicosia International?" I asked Jill. "I thought it straddled the neutral zone and was closed down in 1974. And that it was being used by the U.S. military as a playground for military-type toys. You know, boys and their toys."

"It's been reopened, Marty, secretly, as a high-tech military superbase. That's where we're landing. No customs or check-in for us. We are being met there by some spooks from the CIA, who will whisk us to the Cyprus Hilton, where we check into our rooms, and then we have meetings at the American Embassy in the morning."

All I could think of was our "rooms" at the Hilton. "Did you say 'rooms,' Jill? Why don't we share a room and save the taxpayers some money?

"Get real, Marty. This is a very serious thing we are about to get into. I need my rest, so do you. In the morning we have a meeting with the Secretary to get briefed and to get our orders."

"The secretary? Why don't we just meet with the ambassador and skip his secretary? Aren't we important enough?"

"The Secretary of State, you idiot. Herself. My boss. Your new boss. She is meeting us at the American Embassy. We have some very important business to discuss with her. And she has a big surprise for you."

"Oh? A surprise? What kind of surprise?" I tried to close my mind to Jill and visualize the Secretary. She's probably middle-aged, attractive, big tits, tall, good legs, divorced...Maybe she's heard about me and wants to....

"Marty, you are impossible. That line of thinking is almost sacrilegious right now. What is your problem? Are you a sex addict or something? I can't wait until you get your—"

Jill stopped in mid-sentence. Not like her. She usually spoke in well-considered sentences. "Until I get my what, Jill?"

"—until you get your Top Secret security clearance," she said hurriedly. "The Secretary is going to ask you to volunteer for something that you never thought possible. Something that could affect the outcome of our mission."

My mind went berserk. "What, Jill, what could it possibly be? Do you know? Don't play with me."

My hand covered Jill's as I glared at her anxiously. She pulled her hand away. We were both exhausted from the long flight, but she was also a little pissed off at me. Maybe more than a little. Well, sometimes I just can't help the way I think and act. Sometimes, truth be told, I get a little tired of myself.

Suddenly the landing wheels extended noisily, our plane hit the bumpy runway, and we slowly cruised to a stop. I opened my eyes. It was dawn at the airport, five a.m., Nicosia time.

What now? I looked at Jill. Her eyes were closed, her mouth a grim line.

Suddenly I felt very, very alone. The world was closing in on me. The roar in my ears was the C-20 engines revving up before shutting down.

Then, silence.

CHAPTER FIFTEEN

Because They Seek the Stars

At eleven a.m. the next day, after a short journey by Mercedes stretch limo from the Hilton, Jill and I were ushered into the spartan offices of the U.S. Secretary of State. Nicosia, population around three hundred thousand, has been the capital of Cyprus since the 12th Century. We didn't see much of it from the blackened windows of our limo. It appeared to be a pleasant, thriving, Mediterranean-style city, full of life and tall, modern buildings, busy thoroughfares, colorful markets, happy people. But sightseeing was not on our agenda.

Jill and I were silent for most of the ride. The vibe was neutral. I had slept deeply in my own room at the Hilton, and Jill informed me she had slept deeply in her room. It wasn't enough snooze time, but what the hell. Yesterday was history. I reached out my hand for hers in the limo; her warm hand gave mine a squeeze and held on tightly.

"Madame Secretary, this is Marty Powers and Jill Appleton," said our guide.

Madame Secretary sat on a plain brown couch, long legs discreetly crossed. She wore a long dark skirt and white blouse, no jewelry. She was about fifty-five and had the look of a long-time civil servant: serious, no-nonsense, emotionally closed. Still, with kind brown eyes and a strong, jutting chin, she was basically attractive, underneath the signs of strain, and looked like she hadn't slept peacefully for weeks.

"Folks, I'll be brief," she began. "We don't have a lot of time. The situation, as you know, has reached a planetary critical mass. Our world is threatened not only by man-made ecological disasters, but by a type of enemy which we have never faced before. Possibly you already know some of what I'm going to tell you, but please bear with me."

I took a deep breath. I looked over at Jill, elegantly funky as usual in a floppy black sweater and tight jeans, the picture of composure. I knew her mind was working on several levels.

"We know that the people behind the whole operation—the Internet sabotage, the power outages, the attacks on infrastructure, the disruption of communications systems, the human-caused volcanoes and earthquakes and massive forest fires, the blackmail, the whole thing—is the work of a front organization called Black Swan Galactic. Black Swan is actually a whole web of companies, all connected by a common goal, which I'll talk about in a minute.

"They also have an enforcement arm called The Bratva, Russian for 'The Brotherhood.' Mr. Powers, they are the ones who tried to murder you and your wife in Arizona recently. They are ruthless killers, mainly from Russia and its former satellites."

I wanted to ask about Leela, was she all right, did anybody know anything more about her, but Jill, scanning my mind, put a strong hand on my arm and quieted my demons.

"What we know so far is that Black Swan has divided up the planet into twenty sectors. And that there are about two hundred district managers who run the company's various operations, including hiring engineers, scientists and thugs to carry out their missions, which have resulted in the deaths of at least a million people, maybe more. Black Swan has thousands of operatives around the world. Some are 'temps,' hired for only one operation. Many of these temps have been 'disappeared' after their participation.

"There are maybe six people at the top of their organization, including a shadowy figure named Wolfgang, who seems to be the head of the enterprise. We think he's a naturalized American citizen, born in Hungary. We don't know his whereabouts. About two thirds of the two hundred managers are men. This is their elite group. They all belong to a cult called 'Eternal Flame' which sprang from the notion that it is possible to live forever."

The Secretary paused, rearranged her long legs, shuffled her notes. I looked around the drab little office. The pale yellow walls were bare, save for two framed photographs. One was a portrait of the Secretary, not too flattering. The other was a photo of the Secretary with the President of the United States—the two most powerful women in the world.

"All of these people, the elite group of two hundred, anyway, have one thing in common," the Secretary continued, "a drug called EMC-2. They take it daily. It is a synthetic compound that comes from a secret laboratory somewhere in Switzerland. It supposedly rewinds the clock on cellular aging, allowing one to live forever. We have samples back in the States which we are studying; we haven't yet figured out all of its components. But we do know one dangerous side effect: a testosterone overload. The individuals who take this drug seem to display all of the negative male characteristics, including aggression and belligerence—and that includes the women."

Again the Secretary paused. She took a sip of coffee and looked for a long time first at me, then at Jill. She knew well of Jill's psychic abilities, so she must have factored that into her presentation.

"I know you must be wondering," she said, "why these people are doing all this. Why they have become the most dangerous criminals in human history. Why they have robbed trillions of dollars and euros from bank accounts, why they are holding the world hostage, why they are blackmailing the planet's great nations, why they have helped bring the world to the very brink."

"Why?" I blurted, remembering Hacker's intel about Black Swan's crazy space travel plans, but still wanting to hear the official explanation. "Why are they doing this?"

"Because they seek the stars. They want more than eternal life. They want to explore the planets. They want to explore the solar system. They want to develop technology that will allow them to time travel, to go beyond the Milky Way, to go where, as that famous sci-fi series says, to go where no man has gone before. And in their testosterone-fueled minds, they think— they *know*—they can achieve this.

"According to our intelligence reports, many of which came from your wife, Mr. Powers, they feel that the politicians and governments of the world have wasted so much money, manpower, and technology on fighting wars in the last hundred or so years that space exploration has been neglected. In fact, they feel it has been ignored. All of the NATO countries plus other major players on the world scene got an e-mail to that effect from the Black Swan people a few months ago. Now they want to take over our rocket launching facilities or they say they will trigger a nuclear war.

"You see what we are up against. The Eternal Flame-slash-Black Swan members are willing to do anything to achieve their goals. Their first goal is to set up a space station that will be at least ten times bigger than the International Space Station now orbiting the earth. The hardware is being assembled somewhere in Europe. This space station will be a closed-loop eco system, able to feed and support the two hundred Black Swan pioneers who will form the gene pool and eventually carry the group into outer space.

"They want to launch their shuttles and eventually their spaceships from somewhere in the U.S. They need launch facilities already in place, such as our

Cape Canaveral in Florida or Edwards Air Force Base in California. That's what they demanded. But both of those launch sites have been deactivated since this crisis started. So we are offering our White Sands Missile Range in New Mexico. It's still up and running. Theoretically, we could launch ICBMs from there, if our national security was threatened by an enemy from the Middle East, for example."

"Hmmm, White Sands," I mused out loud. "The site of the first atomic bomb test. Now, *there* was a black swan event. How ironic."

"What's that?" said the Secretary, eyebrows slowly elevating.

"A black swan event. You know, an event that changes history, like Hiroshima or 9/11 or….That's where Black Swan Galactic got their name."

The Secretary didn't respond to this information, only sighed deeply and stood up, walked to her desk, and picked up a folder marked TOP SECRET. My head was spinning. I wondered what I was doing there, why I wasn't back in Sedona, in my own home, kicking back in my big easy chair, a brewski in hand, a fire in the fireplace, and a good Clint Eastwood action movie on the TV.

"In this folder you will find all the background information you will need to carry out your mission," said the Secretary, handing me the thick file.

"Mission?" I asked innocently.

"Mr. Powers, you and Ms. Appleton are about to launch Operation Algorithm. It may be one of the most dangerous covert missions ever attempted by Americans. Should I continue?"

"Yes, yes," I blurted, feeling my armpits suddenly emitting a pungent liquid. This was it—the Big One.

"You and Ms. Appleton will infiltrate the headquarters of the Black Swan Beta operation—their software branch—in Davos, Switzerland. We have located your wife there, Mr. Powers, via her GPS transmitter. This was accomplished on a hunch by our agent Richard Anderson, who crisscrossed a huge area of Switzerland for days in a helicopter and finally caught her signal. This was an extremely high-risk operation on his part, considering the security around all Black Swan facilities.

"So: Your first priority is to rescue Leela Powers and return her to safety. It could be extremely difficult, but our government is confident that you will figure out a way to accomplish this. Mrs. Powers is an extremely valuable asset. We have also been informed, by Ms. Appleton, I believe, that the Black Swan people planned to turn her into a double agent and use her skill set for their evil purposes. This simply cannot be allowed to happen."

"Uh, c-certainly n-not," I stammered.

"We have someone on the inside, a mole, if you will, a spy who works for us, who—

"Wait a minute!" I interrupted. "Your Mr. Anderson just discovered that she was in the Black Swan building. If you have a spy inside their building, why didn't she tell you days ago, weeks ago, that Leela was a prisoner there? What kind of—"

"Take it easy, Marty," said Jill, sensing that I was losing it. She covered my hand with her soft hand, which instantly neutralized my growing anger.

"Our spy, Mr. Powers, was unaware of your wife's presence in the building. That information was withheld from her and other employees in the company's headquarters. Now our mole has located exactly where in the building your wife is being held prisoner."

"Oh," I said, gradually calming down. "That's good news."

"Our mole has already set up an appointment for you and Ms. Appleton with the head of Black Swan Beta. In other words, the leader of the software firm that has corrupted the Internet worldwide is anxiously awaiting your arrival."

"And do we simply have afternoon tea and crumpets?" I asked sarcastically. "Why would this dude—ah, this gentleman—even want to see us?" I felt a new wave of anger tightening my skull. Suddenly, this whole business seemed like a futile exercise.

"Marty," whispered Jill. "Let her explain. The best is yet to come."

"Our inside connection at the computer firm has assured their leaders that Ms. Appleton possesses an algorithm that they need. Something that will tighten their grip on the Internet, and the glue that holds it together, the World Wide Web. And that she can help Black Swan create an impenetrable firewall so that no one will be able to fix the Internet. This would give Black Swan tremendous power and leverage.

"This, then, will be your second priority: to cripple their hold on the Internet and try to destroy whatever they are doing to accomplish their 'hack', or whatever it's called. Your first priority, of course, is to rescue Mrs. Powers. So you see, it is a good thing, a lucky coincidence, that Black Swan agents decided to hold Leela in the computer building.

"Now we can kill two birds...uh, I mean we can accomplish two important things with one ingenious plan. Our mole will be of tremendous help on your mission. And Jill's algorithm is a major piece of our plan."

"Now wait a minute," I said, anger level rising again, dangerously. "This is all about a mathematical formula? Then I'm just tagging along to carry Jill's laptop?"

"Mr. Powers," said the Secretary, in a condescending tone, "you have a key role to play in this drama. You will pass yourself off not only as an expert on computer software and Internet function, but also as a shaman with supernatural powers. The head of Black Swan Beta, Mr. Klaus Lieberman, is very interested in such phenomena and also in various hallucinogens. You will demonstrate your psychic abilities, such as telepathy and ESP, and you will move objects with your mind, and—"

"Wh-whaaa—" I interrupted. "Hold it right there. Telepathy? ESP? I can't do any of those things. How can I fake—"

The Secretary held up her hand and stopped me in my tracks. "Jill," she said softly, gently, "is he ready?"

I looked at Jill. She was nodding vigorously. I thought I saw a mischievous gleam in her eye.

"Mr. Powers, I suggest you take a deep breath. That's right, relax. Let your shoulders drop. Now then. We would like to implant a microchip in your brain. It will be a relatively painless outpatient procedure. The chip will activate the pineal gland, which will give you greatly enhanced psychic abilities. For a period of about two hundred hours. After that the chip will dissolve and you will return to your normal state.

"We need you to possess these special abilities so that your mission can be carried out successfully. Also, we will give you a Top Secret clearance. A temporary one. You will be an employee of the U.S. State Department. Quite an honor, sir."

There was a gap of perhaps five to ten seconds where I was unable to speak. Suddenly, something snapped in me. I felt very reckless, almost intoxicated. As if from a distance, I could see my personality splitting into millions of pieces. I rode with the energy; it had a life of its own.

"Why, shore, Madame Secretary," I drawled, adopting a fake Texas accent. "Y'all jes go raht ahead an drill a hole in mah haid. Ah shore don't mind a teeny weeny bit. Y'all jes drop a little ol' chip down in there. Shore thing."

Jill reached over and pinched my right triceps, hard. "I think he means yes," Jill said, turning to the Secretary of State. "He's probably in a state of shock. Mr. Powers is just a little bit, ah, delicate right now, sensitive, due to the dangerous and unknown status of his wife."

"Ah, yes," said the Secretary, standing up, signaling that the meeting was over. "Very good. My assistant will explain the details of your mission, then escort you and Mr. Powers to our laboratory in the basement, where Doctor LeBoeuf will carry out the chip implantation procedure. Thank you both very much. Your plane departs today at nineteen hundred hours and will deliver you to the Switzerland drop-off point. Good day."

I managed to get to my feet, stagger the short distance to the Secretary of State to shake her hand—I didn't feel a hug was appropriate—and lurch to the door with Jill holding me up. My stomach gurgled. I was hungry, but I had an appointment with a brain surgeon. Lunch would have to wait.

CHAPTER SIXTEEN

The Light in the Head

The doctor's basement lab was very white, anti-septic, and claustrophobic. The doc sat me in a big leather chair that reminded me of an electric chair, or perhaps the kind of chair they use for ECT, you know, Electroconvulsive Therapy. There were wrist and ankle restraints—a precaution, I was told, against the patient moving even a millimeter during this delicate procedure. Jill stood close by, holding my hand and murmuring soft reassurances to quell my fears and misgivings.

"This will make you psychic, Marty, so we can work together and get this mission accomplished. It will increase your brain processing power by a factor of at least one million. You'll be a super-genius! And it will be a blast to mind-link with you, even if it's just for a short time. You'll also be able to mind-link with Leela, once we get her out of her little pickle."

The good doctor, a stocky American with a red face framed by a bushy gray beard, hovered over me with a hypodermic needle in his hand, a serious-faced nurse by his side. "Ready, Mr. Powers? Good. We're going to put you to sleep for just about thirty minutes so we can get the job done swiftly and efficiently. This hypo-dermic contains a general anesthetic and a new type of amnesia agent. You won't remember a thing. And you won't feel any pain. We've added just a touch of morphine to insure that. Okay?"

"Okay," I managed. "And where is the drill?"

I was referring to the instrument that would drill a tiny hole in my skull so that a tiny wire could be inserted into the opening—a wire which carried an entire nano-sized tool kit, including a video cam, a searchlight, a gripper, and the payload: a nano-chip which would turn an ordinary schmoe into a super brain capable of...what?

"The so-called drill, Mr. Powers, is actually a high-intensity laser beam which will cut through flesh and bone without even drawing a drop of blood. It is the most efficient surgical tool ever invented by human science. The microscopic wound it creates will heal in minutes thanks to a solution called adhesivan. You have nothing to worry about. Right, Ms. Appleton?"

"That's right, doctor," said Jill reassuringly. I closed my eyes and surrendered to the whole idea. And to Jill, who was my guide for this strange trip. Om om om, nothing to worry about, surrender to the...and that's all I remember.

An hour earlier Jill and I had been briefed on the procedure and its possible results by an assistant secretary of state named, appropriately, John Danger. He was from New Orleans and spoke with a soft drawl. He had a sort of owlish look, with big horn-rimmed glasses and a military brush haircut. He explained that the procedure I was about to undergo had been done successfully, but never used "in the field." Mr. Danger said the purpose of the nano-chip implant was to turn on, to activate, the pineal gland, which, he explained, was sometimes known as the Third Eye.

"Now, Mr. Powers, I am not some kind of giddy New Ager who believes all this superstitious stuff about the mystical powers of the pineal gland. I know that by activating it with the chip implant you will have psychic abilities for several hours. But I don't want to bore you with—"

"Mr. Danger," I broke in, "we are from Sedona. We eat and drink this mystical stuff. We live it every day. So please: don't hold back. Tell us everything you have heard about the powers of the pineal. And call me Marty."

"Got it. Marty. Okay, well, the pineal is a tiny little gland about the size of a pea, and it lives in a dark cave just behind and above the pituitary gland, with which it has a relationship. You know, a symbiotic relationship." Mr. Danger seemed to blush for a moment.

I looked at Jill and thought, This is gonna be good. She grinned at me and touched a finger to her lips to shush my mind.

"It is located in the center of the brain directly behind the eyes. Some people say it is a dormant organ which can be awakened to enable telepathic communication. Many famous philosophers, including Descartes, who was also a scientist, have called the pineal the 'Seat of the Soul' and our source for inner vision. Should I go on, folks?"

"If you stop now, Mr. Danger, I will put a spell on you," said Jill, grinning wickedly and rubbing her hands together.

"Okay, okay. You probably know that the pineal gland produces melatonin, a brain chemical which promotes peaceful sleep. We don't care about that. This gland is activated by light. That is why the nano-chip that we will implant in your brain, just outside the cave where this little gland lives, is fitted with a kind of mini-floodlight.

"When this floodlight is activated by you, using pure thought, the gland becomes the so-called 'light in your head,' and your telepathic and psychic powers will be greatly enhanced. We don't yet know how much power you will have. We hope you will give us a full report when your mission is completed."

"Phew," I exhaled, a long, low whistle. "And won't I have psychic powers anyway without turning on the light? How do I activate my 'normal' telepathic abilities?"

"You won't have to activate anything, Marty. You will be capable of telepathic communication immediately after the chip is implanted and you wake up from the anesthetic. The chip will send signals to the pineal gland to activate it. You can greatly enhance your psychic powers, when necessary, by simply focusing your mind on the chip. But I must warn you of something. There could be a serious side effect."

"Oh?" I said, my breathing suddenly becoming erratic. Damn! This whole psychic adventure sounded so great. Now, a side effect? Jill nodded, reading my thoughts.

"You. Could. Go. Mad." He said the words one at a time, with great drama.

"Oh? Oh? Please explain, Mr. Danger. Leave nothing out."

John Danger cleared his throat and took a deep breath. "Marty, the pineal gland secretes trace amounts of the drug Dimethyltryptamine, otherwise known as DMT. The substance was compounded in pill form and taken as a psychedelic drug starting in the late Sixties. Its effects were compared to those of LSD, but more intense."

"DMT! The fifteen minute super-trip! I always wanted to try it, but it was never around. I know people who tripped on it. They said you had to be an advanced tripper or you might never come back."

"Exactly. And we here at the embassy are concerned that you might accidentally trigger a sudden DMT experience while carrying out your dangerous mission. Let me quote from an American website: 'DMT experiences can include profound time-dilation, time travel, journeys to paranormal realms, and encounters with spiritual beings or other mystical slash trans-dimensional modalities.' If this should happen to you, Marty, well, you have been warned...."

"Are you kidding me? I would love to hang out with some spiritual beings from other dimensions! And by the way, what exactly are the details of our mission? Nobody has explained that yet. To me, anyway. And Jill...?" She shook her head, smiling.

"Basically, Marty, you and Ms. Appleton will be flown into Switzerland. You will use the on-board mini-chopper to exit the aircraft and land at a heliport, then make contact with our friends in Switzerland, keep your appointment at Black Swan Beta headquarters, sabotage their device that is being used to manipulate the Internet and other computer networks, rescue your wife, and escape." Mr. Danger winked at Jill and smiled flirtatiously.

"Is that all?" I said, grinning. "And me half if not completely mad, stoned on a powerful psychedelic, hearing voices in my head, and reading Jill's wicked thoughts. I thought this was going to be difficult. Do you have any more details?"

"Well, uh, yes, Marty. Actually, it's all contained in the Top Secret folder that the Secretary handed to you. I suggest you and Jill read it carefully, memorize the contents, shred or burn everything in the folder, and report to the airport at eighteen hundred hours for your flight briefing. It's only noon now. Plenty of time. Now I must lead you to the surgical suite for your chip implant."

"One more question, Mr. Danger," I said, suddenly growing more than a little paranoid. "How do I know the chip isn't—"

Jill quickly cut in, having picked up my question from the quagmire of my nagging mind. "It's definitely not a spy chip, Marty," she said softly. "It's not one of those radio frequency I.D. chips the government wanted to implant in everybody during the Bush years. Not to worry."

John Danger looked startled. He didn't know about Jill. "Ms. Appleton," he said, with a quiver in his voice. "Are you a natural telepath? Or did you have a chip implant too?"

"As natural as they come, Mr. Danger," she said cheerfully. "Well, actually I had a little help from a trans-dimensional portal back in Sedona, and some training from a friend of mine named Leela. You've heard of her, I'm sure."

"You bet I have. Well, let's get Marty over to the lab. The good doctor awaits."

The operation must have been successful because I survived it, and felt wonderful when it was over. I remembered nothing of the procedure. I felt a little woozy for a few minutes, then my head cleared, and everything was different. At first it felt like I had two sets of eyes, like double vision, and I had to concentrate to bring the two images together. There was a low babble in my head, like a crowd of people murmuring. I looked at the doctor and brought him into focus.

Thank God it worked, he was thinking. *You never know with this crazy shit. This man looks wonderful. What have I done, what have I done?* His thoughts came in bursts, like raspy whispers, with little clouds surrounding each word. I felt his feelings, and shuddered. He was worried.

"You have done a wonderful thing, doc," I said, and he looked at me with alarm. *I hope he can't read what I'm thinking, or I'll be ruined. Ruined! He'll know all about me and Lance, and that horrible boy from the French embassy....*

"Don't worry about anything," I said softly, as I reached out and embraced his bulky body in a big bear hug. I looked deeply into his dark eyes and kissed him on the forehead. "Thank you for what you have done. You have done all of humanity a favor."

I turned on my heel, draped my arm around Jill's waist, and we marched together out of the American Embassy, onto the street, and into our waiting stretch limo. My first exposure to the thoughts of people we passed was startling at first, like walking through the babble of a madhouse, or being in the middle of a mob, everyone mumbling to themselves. This would take some getting used to.

In minutes we were back at the Hilton, in Jill's room, studying the details of our mission, munching on raw vegetables and humus. I was able to read, absorb, and memorize the contents of the folder, all fifty-six pages of it, in an hour.

At one point I looked up at Jill—she was sitting on the bed, me at the desk—and she was looking up at me, her eyes filled with love and compassion. I felt joined with her like never before. Her mind seemed empty of random thought, but loaded with feelings that seemed to generate a kind of heat in the room, or perhaps only

in my mind. My new nano-chip was working beautifully. It might take a little time to adjust to the expansion of consciousness. All of life seemed larger.

Everything was illuminated, now.

CHAPTER SEVENTEEN

Hanging Out with the Monkey Mind

We streaked through the night sky over Europe at forty thousand feet, Jill and I and our pilot, Captain Jake Fisher. A sky bright with stars, nearly devoid of clouds. And devoid of other aircraft. It seemed as if we were the only airplane aloft that night; most European airports had closed down because of widespread computer "irregularities."

Our little Gulfstream G600, although a civilian craft, could zip along at more than seven hundred miles an hour (Mach 0.94), which meant we could cover the distance from Nicosia to somewhere in Switzerland, about fifteen hundred miles, in little more than two hours. Any aircraft hitting Mach 1 (or 761 mph, the speed of sound) would probably create a noisy sonic boom; we didn't want to wake up anyone on the ground or call attention to ourselves.

The G600 is equipped to carry eight passengers in American-style capitalist comfort: leather seats, giant screen 3-D TV, broadband, you name it. We had flown a military-owned Gulfstream from Phoenix to Cyprus, but this craft was sleeker and faster. For our journey, half of the eight seats had been ripped out so that a special cargo bay could be installed. The cargo bay held a

163

piece of equipment vital to the success of our mission: the Bell Spyder helicopter—a tiny aluminum chopper that runs on batteries, barely seats two humans, and is designed to be dropped out of an airplane and immediately become airborne.

Jill had assured me back at the Hilton that she could pilot the Spyder, although she had never flown anything in her life and never had a lesson. She told me she had read the manual for the Spyder and was confident that together we could figure the thing out. I believed her. Our destination: somewhere in the Swiss Alps.

You are probably wondering what happened between Jill and I back at the Hilton. After the nano-chip was implanted in my skull, I found telepathic communication with Jill to be easy and natural, an extension of our already deep connection, with a new layer of intimacy. I didn't go too deep at first, as I was still exploring the possibilities and the boundaries of my new abilities. There was no doubt that my mind's processing power had been greatly expanded.

Jill and I found that we had a few hours left to rest after digesting our Top Secret file, and before we had to report to the military airport at Nicosia. She crawled under the covers of her king size bed and invited me to take a nap with her. It was an offer I couldn't refuse. Hold me, she whispered, and pressed her warm body to mine. We kissed, deeply. Clothes came off.

We made love, yes: sex in hyperspace. Cosmic lovemaking. Actually, it was more of an out-of-body experience than anything else. I knew her great body, visually, at least, having seen it back on the flight to Cyprus. But to touch her womanly flesh, to melt, flow, taste, penetrate, become one with, turned into a hallucinogenic experience. I saw her DNA signature; I saluted her ancestors; I lived and shared her past lives in a split second of holographic awareness. It was an awakening, an opening of the thousand-petaled lotus.

Marty.

Yes, Jill. Back on the Gulfstream. We were holding hands. I woke up from the daydream of our shared journey to the farthest star. Had it really happened?

It happened, darling, and it was glorious. It was worth waiting for. I am still tingling! Jill had just "flashed" me, which meant she had sent me a telepathic communication. That's what psi people called it.

Soon Jill dropped the flashtalk and reverted to voice mode. It was easier to communicate that way on matters that were less intimate or private. "Now, Marty, please listen. The Secretary back in Nicosia gave me a vid chip to plug into our player. It has all the details of our mission. And it's got some great clips of the Black Swan headquarters which our mole managed to send out of there to a transceiver in Switzerland. Put on these headphones and let's start gathering some data."

"Yes, sir, er, ma'm," I said, and resisted the impulse to plant a big wet kiss on her juicy lips. Grow up, Marty, I mumbled inside my head. My annoying horn-dog character, the alter ego that had haunted me for years, seemed to have dissolved with the chip implant. Still, ancient echoes remained. Jill glanced at me and looked away. I tried to tune in to what she was thinking, but there was nothing on her mind's thought-screen except an empty space and a few random notes from Beethoven's Third Symphony, the Eroica.

Reading someone's thoughts is not like reading text. Thoughts rise endlessly like bubbles from the conscious and subconscious mind, pop into life as waveforms and become neurons, or brain nerve cells, dancing across trillions of synaptic junctions propelled by chemicals called neurotransmitters, looking for receptive cells in order to form coherent thoughts. No wonder humans are crazy.

I have heard that the average human brain produces at least 50,000 thoughts a day. Most of these thoughts are just nonsense—endless loops of worry, regret, fear; revenge fantasies; memories, nightmarish or otherwise; pictorial sexual fantasies; re-creations of scenes from the past, with embellishments; projections of what will happen in the future; rehearsals of what to say to a wife or husband, to a boss, to a cop, to a bully. To add to this neurotic cesspool, endless repetition rules the human mindscape.

In other words, the average human mind is a mess. Buddhists talk about the "monkey mind," an out-of-control thought generator. What to do? The average mind lives everywhere but in the present moment.

My work now is to "watch" the thoughts that enter my head, according to Jill, my teacher. She said this is the basis of meditation. Watch the ongoing parade of thoughts from a distance, she said, and the thoughts will simply dissolve. Okay, that's meditation. So far, so good.

Using my newly-acquired supermind, my job was to focus on the thought forms of others that related to our mission. This wouldn't be easy. Which thoughts are coming from the outside into my head, and which thoughts are mine? Thoughts have no voice; they are more like a whisper. Also, Jill said that if someone is running a pictorial fantasy about something or other, a common activity of the monkey mind, I could actually tune in and see the pictures, which appear like a fuzzy movie or You Tube video.

The trick I had to learn was how to screen out unwanted thought forms. Otherwise, the cacophony could drive a novice telepath insane in seconds.

Jill is very clear; her thought forms have little or no baggage attached. There is no inner censor standing over her mind's shoulder, no residue of guilt and regret and ancient trauma lurking in her unconscious mind waiting to contaminate her thoughts. The woman seems to have no ego.

Unfortunately, I do. Whenever my thought forms come up tainted or tricky or "unclean," she will bust my balls immediately. Telepathically, that is.

"Marty, please pay attention to the video, hey?" Jill impolitely interrupted my daydream state. "We need to know the layout of this place before we barge in there." The video was intriguing and revealing. Black Swan Beta designed custom software programs for big corporations worldwide. Its client list was impressive. The firm had branch offices in San Francisco, New York, London, Paris, and Tokyo. Big time.

The head of the computer operation was a gentleman named Klaus Lieberman. His bio came as a readout on our airplane's giant TV screen:

Klaus Lieberman, born in Cologne, Germany, age 52. Parents moved to USA, settled in Bay Area, No. California. College: UCal Berkeley, Master's degree computer science. Subject worked for various Silicon Valley firms as programmer, software designer, systems analyst. Wrote first security detection program in UNIX for military, banks, Wall Street brokerage houses and oil companies. Dropped out of corporate computer business in 2001 and began taking powerful psychedelic drugs. Had brief notoriety as hacker-prankster. Became disciple of so-called Indian guru/shaman Shree Rama Shivanandadas, a native of Newark, New Jersey. At the guru's ashram in New York City, met and became friends with Wolfgang von Neumann aka Wolfgang Maximus. At von Neumann's urging, joined cult org Eternal Flame, became involved in immortality movement. Subsequently had business association with von Neumann. (More intel on von Neumann forthcoming.) Resurfaced in Davos, Switzerland, in 2007, formed Black Swan Beta, software firm which grossed over $500 million worldwide last year. Subject never married, no children, linked with half dozen gay male European celebrities.

"Jill, this dude is heavy duty. Plus this is great footage of the Black Swan layout. But I got one question:

Where's Leela?" I spoke out loud, because there was no need for secrecy. And it felt better. We had scanned the plane for bugs; it was clean.

"Leela is definitely in that building," said Jill reassuringly. "Mr. Anderson verified her location by code matching. Our mole knows exactly where she is being held because of Leela's GPS signal. Leela is still being restrained with a powerful electromagnetic field. I hope we can break through it when we get in there."

"Yeah, me too. So let me get this straight. We have been invited to Black Swan Beta h.q. because of our reputations in the computing field? Better explain, sweetheart. I built a website once, but I can barely talk zeroes and ones, much less write code or discuss Internet protocols and stuff like that. And Black Swan has pulled off some of the major hacks of our time. What do they need us for?"

"Marty, do a recall on that Top Secret folder. Our friends at the State Department have paved the way for us. Supposedly I am a mathematical genius from MIT who wrote an algorithm that will solve all of Black Swan Beta's problems. You know they are having trouble maintaining their attacks on the Internet worldwide, right? They can do short-term attacks, and cause a lot of trouble for infrastructures and power grids and so forth. But they can't sustain the attacks because their victims do short-time patches and fixes. There could also be a problem with Black Swan's attack software shutting down and crashing. So I am supposed to have the answer to those problems."

"Wow."

"My cover story says I am the author of several books, I have a website, I have won numerous awards in the scientific and computer fields, I have tenure at MIT. My name is all over the Web. The State Department has taken care of all that. I have solid credentials. Black Swan needs me."

"Great. But if the Internet is disrupted all over the planet, how can Black Swan access all your online info?"

"Somehow Black Swan Beta's Internet access is still up and running!" said Jill with a grin. "All of my fake info will be available to them."

"Great," I said. "But what about me?"

As the word "me" left my mouth, our fierce little Gulfstream hit some turbulence and seemed to drop about a thousand feet in a millisecond. My stomach did a flip-flop. Jill looked a little pale.

"Sorry, folks," said our pilot over the P.A., "just some weather up here for a few minutes. We'll drop to thirty thousand feet for now and begin our d and d, descent and deceleration. The drop-off point is about a half hour away. Better get your flight suits ready."

The drop-off point. That meant Jill and I would be getting into our tiny Bell Spyder helicopter for the final descent to our designated helipad in St. Moritz, a tiny resort town in the Swiss Alps for wealthy skiers and snow bums. St. Moritz is about seventy kliks from Davos, a journey to be negotiated in a rental car. In St. Moritz we would meet our contacts from the State Department, and be given last-minute instructions—

plus luggage, clothes, paperwork, fake passports, and whatever else we needed to carry out our very dangerous mission.

The video continued, revealing that the Black Swan people were running their software enterprise with a business-as-usual attitude. Very few people outside of the firm knew of their worldwide computer sabotage campaign, whose victims included private corporate and government networks as well as the very core of the Internet. It seemed that our whole computer culture was under attack by Black Swan Beta's twisted geniuses.

We learned that the software business was headquartered in a historic, chalet-style office building in downtown Davos. Most of their legitimate business was conducted on the two surface floors of the building. Their dirtiest business was conducted in the two basement floors beneath.

The vid chip footage was amazing. On the first basement level were hundreds of servers in high-ceilinged, frigid rooms; skilled hackers were hunched over keyboards and monitors in myriad cubicles, triggering worldwide chaos, blackouts, dam breaks, bank failures, system breakdowns, airport closures, train collisions, everything imaginable where computers were vital parts of the human endeavor in the Twenty-first Century.

The second basement level was a mystery, and what went on there was a closely-guarded secret. This level was off limits to most employees, including the State Department mole, one Greta Eisen. She was a Swiss-born American citizen who was a hotshot programmer and superbrain, supposedly a member in good standing of Eternal Flame, eating the immortality drug EMC-2 every day. Except she wasn't; she faked it.

Black Swan Beta's malicious mischief was reported to the State Department by Ms. Eisen. She shot the incredibly revealing video using her mobile phone. For about a month Ms. Eisen worked in the special basement unit, first level. Every evening when she got home from work, she sent a deeply encrypted message to the State Department in Cyprus—audio, video, photos, and text—on the current state of affairs at Black Swan Beta.

Greta eventually was sent back upstairs because her supervisor didn't trust her. She never managed to get to the second basement level; that required a special elevator key and a nine-digit code. But by staying alert and keeping her ears open, she did manage to gather two critical pieces of information. One, that Leela was being held in a locked room in the second basement unit, unable to use her psychic powers or communicate with the outside world because of the electromagnetic field that had been in place for weeks and basically neutralized her.

And two: Greta learned that the real secret weapon of the Black Swan Beta organization also was located in the second sub-basement. The people at the U.S. State Department called it the Secret Internet, which was just a fancy term for cluelessness. They really had no idea what it was that powered Black Swan's attacks. "It" had awesome, unheard-of processing power; "it" could override and defeat any patch or fix that ordinary humans could effect to counteract the damage done by Black Swan's programmers and hackers.

Temporarily. It had one shortcoming: It kept crashing. The program might run successfully for hours, then crash for no good reason. It was a bitch to reboot. That was why Jill's algorithm, a supposed patch for the problem, was so important to Black Swan Beta.

There were some in the CIA's inner circle, and even some analysts at State, who thought the "Secret Internet" device was sentient, was possibly AI, Artificial Intelligence. Reasonable, intelligent people in the government believed that the big breakthrough—a machine that could outthink people—had finally been accomplished. And that the breakthrough was being used by madmen to get what they wanted and totally fuck over the rest of the human race.

"Time to go!" came the cheery voice of Captain Fisher over the intercom. The video was over. Jill and I had already slipped on our thermal, full body flight suits. We squeezed into the tiny helicopter. It looked like a bubble with a single propeller on top. Was this a toy or a flight-worthy craft that would deliver us to our destination?

"It'll be fine, Marty," said Jill. "Remember, I read the manual. I know I can run this thing."

"Great," I said tentatively. The Bell Spyder weighs less than two thousand pounds, has a top air speed of one hundred thirty knots, can stay airborne for at least three hours, and runs on the new super-batteries.

I closed the Plexiglas bubble and fastened it securely. *Seat belts, Jill,* I flashed. I could feel the Gulfstream descending and decelerating.

"Opening the cargo bay in ten seconds," said our pilot. "You two only have to descend about eight thousand feet. Don't forget to press and hold down the starter button for at least five seconds. Be sure to wait until you have left this aircraft before you do that, okay?" Good luck!"

Whooooosh. The bottom seemed to fall out of the Gulfstream and our Spyder was falling fast through the night sky. It was very, very dark. "Hey, Jill, how about that starter thingy?"

"Where is it?" she said, a bit panicky.

"I thought you said you read the manual!"

"I did, I did, but I can't—Marty, turn on the lights, huh?"

We were falling, faster and faster. There were no interior lights, only exterior. I was very calm about it all. Earlier, back on the plane, I had had a vision of the near future: Our Spyder would have a crisis coming in, would appear to be falling out of the sky, but we would have a smooth landing on a surface very slick and cold. I trusted my intuition to find the starter button. It was just under the control panel. I held it down for five seconds. The rotor began to turn and whir and we were on our way.

"Thanks, Marty," said Jill with a big grin. "Sure glad they drilled that hole in your head back in Nicosia!"

"No problem, Jill. Hey, where do they keep the heater switch? It's freezing in here."

"Heater? There is no heater. This is supposed to be a short trip. And we're running on power cells anyway. Hey, watch this!"

Jill was in full control of the tiny chopper now, pulling and pushing on handles and levers and gears, making the craft rear up and down, like a bucking bronco, laying it on its side, having one hell of a time.

"I didn't know you were such a hot-rodder, baby!" I teased. "What else can you do? Let's see if you can really haul ass in this hopped-up taco wagon. Floor it, you cool kitten!"

"Dig this, Daddy-O," she shouted, jamming some lever down to the floor. Our Spyder hovered briefly, then went into a sudden sharp nosedive.

"Wheeeee!" said Jill, laughing hysterically. I had never seen her like this, so I sat back and enjoyed it for a few seconds. Then:

"Hey, Marty, I can't get this thing back up in normal position," she said, pulling frantically at the stick. "Got any good ideas?"

We were heading nose down at a pretty good clip when the rotor suddenly died and all I could hear was the sound of wind whipping around our little bubble. Jill looked over at me with fear in her eyes, another first. We were about a thousand feet from the ground, which appeared to be a huge, jagged iceberg.

I put my hand over hers on the stick. "Relax, sweetheart," I said, totally confident that I knew what to do.

With closed eyes, I put two fingers over my third eye and focused on leveling the chopper. It worked. Then with pure mind energy I started up the rotor. The Spyder slowly glided downward. Jill missed the descent because her eyes were tightly closed.

I put my hand on her shoulder. She turned to look at me, a helpless female look. I had never seen that before either. So many firsts. "Marty, how did you pull that one off? That nano-chip must be a lot more powerful than we thought."

"Jill, could you manage to land our chopper now? We're almost touching down. Look, we were supposed to trigger some radio signal to alert our contacts that we're coming in to the helipad at our hotel. Do you know where that button is? No?" She was shaking her head, embarrassed, slack-jawed.

My earlier vision of a safe landing came back to me. "Hey, there's a nice frozen lake just below us," I said. "Let's land here. The hotel isn't too far away. Oh, and I've found the radio signal button, see?"

Silently, Jill pulled gears and levers and made a perfect landing on a frozen lake. She turned off the engine and the rotor slowly came to a halt. She sat back in her seat, trembling and breathing heavily. I put my arm around her shoulders, brought her closer to me. My lips felt numb from the cold. It was definitely below zero outside.

"Kiss me," I commanded. Jill melted into me, her warm lips exploring mine. We had a few minutes to kill before our friends showed up. It was late, and it was cold. Making out with this beautiful psychic in a helicopter on a frozen lake in the Swiss Alps seemed like a perfect way to pass the time.

CHAPTER EIGHTEEN

The Internet's Invisible Underbelly

The Palace Hotel is the top of the line at the top of the world, the grande dame of hotels in the ritzy resort village of St. Moritz.

Our contacts had rescued us from our tiny chopper on the frozen lake, whisked us to the elegant Palace, helped us check in, supplied us with luggage, clothes, an iPad, everything we needed. Joe and Kate Jeffers, our angels, a young married couple from Durango, Colorado: their cover, ski instructors for the Palace; their real employer, the U.S. State Department.

They ushered us to our suite and smiled a lot and wished us luck and handed us a sealed Top Secret folder with updates on our assignments. They didn't know that both Jill and I were telepaths. I scanned them, just for laughs. Joe was running a wild fantasy about he and Jill naked together in an outdoor hot tub, surrounded by snow; his wife was visualizing me in jockey shorts, all muscles and washboard abs and ripped, sculpted pecs. Quite a fantasy, that.

They left with hugs and continental-style air kisses. Jill and I immediately thawed out in front of one of our two wood-burning fireplaces. Our suite had a separate bedroom, a huge tub with Jacuzzi, and a view of the lake and snow-covered mountains. The tab, to be picked up by the State Dept., was two grand U.S. a day. We had our own butler, Wilhelm, a sweet little Swiss gentleman from Zurich; he wasn't in on the game.

Jill scanned the rooms for bugs: no recording devices, aud or vid. We had a little supper sent up by room service. Jill wasn't interested. She warmed her innards in the Jacuzzi, took a quick hot shower, and jumped into our king-size bed. Exhausted, she fell asleep as soon as I kissed her eyes, nose, and lips and tucked her in with the big down comforter.

My chip implant was working overtime. I had been warned by the docs back in Cyprus. Because the pineal gland regulates sleep as well as other bodily functions, they said, and because my pineal had been slightly "reprogrammed," I might find it difficult to sleep. The docs were right.

I meditated in front of the roaring fire that Wilhelm had fixed for us, looking inward at this mind that so recently had been expanded. I felt like I had attained warp speed in brain processing power and added several dozen points to my IQ. I kind of understood who I was and what this existence was all about. And the thoughts, the endless thoughts: It was easy to watch the thoughts passing by, like watching the river flow— silent, unattached, non-judgmental. As the Buddha said, just watch.

Yeah, and this whole thing was crazy, absolutely friggin' crazy. It seemed as if there were two Martys: the Marty of the past, the neurotic, sarcastic, always edgy

Marty, a wiseass horndog who somehow had managed to live an incredible life. And the *now* Marty: calm, confident, mature, super-intelligent, telepathic, telekinetic. Who knew what other powers I had been granted, albeit temporarily? How could I ever go back to the old, pre-chip-implant Marty?

I pulled out my Amigo, which had been turned off for a few days so I could focus on the business at hand. There were urgent messages from Benny Bravo, sent via the new, highly secret message delivery network called REBEL. This program had been written by Hacker and some of his cyber-pirate buddies when it became obvious that persons unknown were sabotaging the Internet and e-mail was no longer viable. Data was transmitted with absolute security via de-activated NASA satellites that the genius programmers had managed to hack.

I brought up the REBEL app on my Amigo, spoke the access code and password, let the photo cell take a snapshot of my retina, and passed through the virtual security gates. There were Benny's three messages, beautifully encrypted—a final, fail-safe security measure. In times of crisis, you can't be too careful.

I spoke another password and the decoding program kicked in. Benny's videos were a little shaky, and a little out of focus. Which didn't matter, really; my assistant was just learning to use the Amigo I had given him back in Sedona.

First message: Goddess Kali had gone completely over the top since I left Sedona a few days ago. Now she was healing terminally ill people, just by touch.

Word had gotten out and the ensuing traffic jam had clogged all the roads into Sedona. Her next project, she announced, would be to bring people back from the dead—carefully selected historical figures who would help solve our planet's present problems. She would install their consciousness in bodies of living volunteers. Holy cadaver, Batman. Zombie time.

Second message: Martial law had been declared in Sedona. There was a curfew after sunset. Police were having trouble controlling the crowds coming to be healed by Kali. Meanwhile, city water coming into homes and businesses was sporadic, and toilets were overflowing everywhere. A terrible stench pervaded the town.

Many residents had started to move to a tent city growing up near the wastewater treatment facility, five miles south of town. Treated wastewater was there, potable water, millions of gallons of backlog, safe to drink. Somebody had brought a bunch of chickens to provide food, so they called the place Chickentown. Jesus H. Kee-rist.

Benny had attached a video clip of Sedona's empty streets, police checkpoints, a parade of cars, bicycles, and pedestrians heading out of town on the main drag for Chickentown.

Third message: Benny got a call from Hacker, who asked for a meeting. My two buds managed to dodge the cops and the curfew and got together at our old secure meeting place, Mystic Vista. Hacker said he was involved in a project so important and so secret that it would affect the entire planet. He couldn't discuss it, but he wanted to know my whereabouts and what I was doing. Benny asked if it was okay to give out my Amigo access info to Hacker.

I wrote back to Benny that Hacker was a welcome guest in my Amigo anytime. Benny said Hacker had told him to send me a three-letter message: DNS. Suddenly I got it.

For weeks, computer criminals had been messing with the Internet's Domain Name System, or DNS, the unglamorous, invisible underbelly of the Internet. DNS has great power: It could be called directory assistance for the Internet. It also routes every piece of Internet traffic in the known Universe. Hacker had told me back in Sedona that he suspected attacks on the DNS system were behind the Internet sabotage. Now, my expanded mind and super-intelligence were able to put all the pieces together.

DNS had been the subject of malicious attacks by hackers for years, but the keepers of the WWW gates always managed to patch it up. Without a fully functioning DNS, the Internet would be chaos. That was what had happened. Now, e-mail messages were being rerouted to the wrong addresses; websites and search engines were either inaccessible or fakes, full of ads or porno photos; bank accounts were raided, and huge amounts of money transferred to secret accounts.

The whole global Internet system, which most of the world's population had come to depend on, was hopelessly scrambled and virtually impotent. The watchdogs of the Internet, scattered around the world and possessing incredibly powerful tools, were unable to keep up with the attacks. Every patch was met with a new style of hack. Also, malicious viruses had been distributed by the saboteurs to millions of computers around the world, further snarling the system.

The primary suspect in this plot to take down the Internet was Black Swan Beta.

I closed my eyes, put a finger over my third eye, and tried to look into the future. All I got was a blank screen, then a snowstorm on a blank screen, then a high-pitched, screeching noise which forced my eyes open and gave me a headache.

I was restless, not even close to sleepy. I decided to visit Jill's dreams, and allowed my consciousness to drift into the bedroom. Dreams are weird at best, and rarely make sense—fragments of mind dust, a synaptic free-for-all, the brain simply letting go and allowing data to dance like the notes in a Bach cantata. Jill was dreaming of Leela, alone in a cage, naked, like a trapped animal, desperately grasping the bars, a look of despair on her face.

Suddenly I felt like a voyeur and ducked back into my own head. Visiting the dreams of a telepath is risky. She might be doing lucid dreaming. She might be dreaming of a future you don't want to know about.

I thought about Leela and my lust for Jill and the consummation of our hot flirtation just a couple of days ago. Did our tryst have Leela's stamp of approval? It must have. Jill had said back in Sedona that she had "wanted" me for a long time, but the code of honor between women, especially powerful psi women, precluded any kind of a coital experience between Jill and I. At that time! That was then! Also, guilt didn't seem to be in my repertoire of emotions anymore. Strange.

Wide awake. I picked up the Top Secret envelope, broke the seal, pulled out the sheath of papers. Contained therein were further details of our mission.

Jill and I were to pose as Simone and Roger Hightower, an American couple with special skills. Jill/Simone was a noted computer scientist who had never met a computer problem she couldn't fix. Her whole history—college, post-grad, articles, books, websites, blogs— had already been created by the CIA. A Google search on her name would bring millions of hits—when the Internet was functioning normally. In reality, all she knew about computers was how to send e-mail.

Her scam: She would connect telepathically with Greta Eisen, our mole at Black Swan; Greta would think or visualize the steps necessary to help Jill seek out and sabotage whatever was disrupting the Internet. This sounded like a ridiculously reckless plan to me, but Jill lived in an unwavering state of trust, so what the hell. In her bag Jill would be carrying several data storage units, in order to download incriminating information from the Black Swan Beta servers. She would also be carrying a data chip loaded with the most malicious computer virus ever created, courtesy of the State Department's computer scientists.

My cover story: I am known as The Raven, a "psyche-delic shaman" who has lived among Native Americans and whose skills in healing, ESP, and inter-dimensional travel are widely recognized. I am also an expert on psychoactive drugs, and have ingested most of them: LSD, psilocybin mushrooms, peyote, salvia divinorum, Ecstasy, DMT. The State Department knows well of Klaus Lieberman's great interest in drugs. My life is very secret and no official documentation exists on Roger Hightower. My job is to keep Klaus distracted while Jill works on the Black Swan problems.

The fire was starting to die. I shuddered. It was four a.m. There was a single sheet of paper left in the large Top Secret envelope. It was headed "Wolfgang von Neumann aka Wolfgang Maximus." There was one short paragraph on the purported founder and head of Black Swan Galactic:

Wolfgang von Neumann (Maximus), born in Budapest, Hungary 1960 of German and Hungarian parents. Natu-ralized US citizen. Education: Stanford University, MA, computer science. Worked for Silicon Valley firms as pro-grammer, software designer. As freelance, created "Blujay," sophisticated spyware which he sold to U.S. government for 250 mil. Blujay used by National Security Agency (NSA) for surveillance, wiretaps, database management, e-mail hacks after 9/11. Became wealthy investor, started Eternal Flame and immortality movement, founded Black Swan Galactic, set up Klaus Lieberman in software business called Black

Swan Beta. Twice divorced, no children. Supposedly char-
ismatic man who inspires confidence and even worship.
Probably addicted to immortality drug EMC-2. Known to
be ruthless in business and personal relationships, although
ostensibly charming and likable. A mystery man never seen
in public. Former therapist diagnosed him as psychotic with
murderous tendencies.

So that was the man behind the whole operation: a
charming, violent psycho who had the wherewithal and
the smarts to create a worldwide organization bent on
destruction of Planet Earth. And who planned to use
his ill-gotten monetary gains to finance a mission to the
stars!

Jill and I, two vulnerable, small-town psychics, were
assigned to take down one of this egomaniac's prime
business operations—the firm that seemed to have a
stranglehold on the world's most valuable resource,
the Internet. And while we were in their headquarters
building we were to rescue my beloved Leela, who was
also, by the way, a very important State Department
"asset." How could we ever pull this off? It seemed like
Mission Impossible. And yet, we had to make it work.

I needed to sleep, needed darkness. I put a finger
over my third eye, hoping to trigger a deluge of melatonin, the brain's natural sleep chemical. In minutes
I started yawning and my muscles seemed to relax all
at the same time. I ripped off my clothes, hurried
into bed, put my blindfold in place—melatonin needs

darkness to really trigger its effects—and snuggled up next to Jill.

She was naked. She moaned softly as I wrapped myself around her. I slept, a deep, dreamless sleep. Blackness.

CHAPTER NINETEEN

In the Belly of the Beast

"So you have taken zuh trips on DMT, Herr Hightower? May I please call you Herr Raven? Thank you. So, what iss it like?"

"I have indeed, sir. It is very profound, almost too intense for the human mind to accept without going mad. Fortunately, it is a very short trip."

I was sitting with Klaus Lieberman, CEO of Black Swan Beta, the computer arm of Black Swan Galactic. Klaus was the chief mastermind behind the malicious computer mischief that was helping to bring down the planet's financial and communications systems. We were in the outdoor patio of Beta's headquarters in Davos, enclosed by a transparent bubble of some unknown material, immune to the below zero temperature outside. The view of nearby snow-capped mountains was stunning.

"Details, Herr Raven, details, please."

"Klaus, even veteran trippers such as Leary and Terence McKenna say the experience defies verbal or visual description. How about this: time travel, visits to paranormal realms, encounters with spiritual beings, meetings with trans-dimensional entities.... Whenever I took it, I felt like the Ruler of the Universe—"

"Like God?"

"Beyond God. The god behind the god. Like I knew everything and had experienced everything past present and future and could do anything, be anything I wanted."

His eyes were very wide. Klaus admitted he had never taken DMT. In truth, neither had I. Everything I told him came from Wikipedia.

"Can you read my mind, Herr Raven? If so, you must tell me. We have done considerable research on you and your genius wife, Simone. Our research shows you have some extraordinary abilities. Please demonstrate, now."

His tone was demanding, with Germanic overtones. Although Lieberman spent most of his life in the USA, he was basically German; his first language was German. He had a very Arian profile, high cheekbones, piercing blue eyes, fit and pumped up, a little over six feet, just about eye level with me, and an intimidating kind of energy. I knew he was gay, but he was very butch, very aggressive, like a street punk from Berlin or a queer Moscow gangbanger who had learned his moves in the gulag.

He had been taking large doses of the mysterious drug EMC-2, which not only kept cells alive forever, or so it was claimed, but it also flooded the body with massive doses of testosterone. That might explain the man's macho energy. Allegedly, the drug also boosted brain processing power exponentially. The jury is still out on that one.

"Herr Lieberman, Klaus, that ESP stuff is just bullshit. No human can read another human's mind; that is a myth promoted by TV and tabloid writers. During psychedelic journeys I have undertaken after ingesting certain, uh, plants and chemical substances, I have demonstrated some amazing abilities which were recorded on video. Perhaps that is where you heard of my so-called ESP abilities. I cannot see into the future. I can, however, move objects with my mind. Watch."

I don't know what possessed me in that moment, but I knew I could do something I had never done before if I just focused my mind. So, using my amped-up super-brain, I lifted the man's half-full porcelain teacup into the air, slowly, hovering it a full meter from our table. I tilted the cup so its golden contents spilled out onto the tiled floor. Then I let the teacup fall onto the floor, shattering into hundreds of pieces.

Lieberman simply gaped at me. His mouth moved, but no words came out. Finally, he stuttered, "How—how did you do that, Herr Raven?"

I stared at him, then let my mind drift over to Jill's world. I found that I could easily allow my consciousness to function on two levels: one, sitting with the German, carrying on a conversation; and two, experiencing the world through Jill's eyes, mind, and body.

Jill and I had arisen early that morning, enjoyed a leisurely breakfast on our patio with the heat lamps on full force, showered together, dressed, and left our room with nothing incriminating left behind. We took our iPad and mobile devices with us as we piled into our rented Porsche 911.

It was an exhilarating drive through the countryside on a narrow, winding, sometimes icy road, but the Porsche hugged the pavement and gobbled up the kilometers like a hungry panther. Jill was silent but tense as I tried to impress her with my driving skills. When she finally spoke, it was with authority. Just the energy in her voice could shrivel a man's scrotum.

"Marty, please slow down!" I did, of course. I looked around. On our left was a vertical wall of snow and ice. On the right, a vertical drop of several thousand feet into the valley below. There was no guardrail on the road. I geared the Porsche down to second and glanced over at Jill.

"Marty, I'm worried. Are we walking into a trap? It all seems too easy, us being invited into the belly of the beast. Can you take a peek into the future for me? Does that chip of yours give you that kind of power?"

"First of all, Jill, our handlers back in the U.S. have done a fantastic job of preparing the way for us. Our cover is secure. Second, the Special Ops people are standing by, ready to bail us out with some serious force if we get into trouble at Black Swan HQ. All I have to do is press this little button here on my turquoise bracelet and the Army warriors will come storming in." I showed her the nearly invisible button. "They're camped out in some five-star hotel nearby." Jill smiled sardonically.

"And thirdly, last night after you fell asleep I tried to take a little peek over the horizon, but all I got was a blank screen and some static. I guess there were too many variables and too many possible outcomes, and my chip just kinda shorted out. You know how the future is, Jill….You never know what's gonna happen."

"Granted."

"But I did visit your dreams to see if there were any clues there and—"

"You did what? You voyeur, you!" Jill said with mock seriousness. "What did you see? I hope you didn't catch any of that wild business with you and me doing it all over the rings of Saturn!"

"No, all I saw was just Leela naked and in a cage. That was enough to freak me out. So I went back to studying our game plan." I told her about the intel on Wolfgang Maximus that was in our Top Secret packet.

Jill let out a big sigh, sank back in the luxurious Porsche upholstery, and went silent. We passed through tiny villages with names like Schmitten, Monstein, Glans (my favorite), and Frauenkirch before cruising into Davos. The trip from St. Moritz is only about thirty-three kliks, and we did it in less than half an hour.

Davos is primarily a ski resort, your typical overpriced alpine village, elevation eight thousand, five hundred feet, permanent population about eleven thousand. In the wintertime the temps range from around zero Fahrenheit during the day to unthinkably cold at night. Davos used to be famous as a refuge both for the super-rich and tuberculosis victims, back in the early 1900s, and also as the setting for Thomas Mann's most famous (and most bizarre) novel *The Magic Mountain*.

More recently, Davos was best known as the home of the World Economic Forum, which every January brought together the planet's most powerful bigwigs—financial wizards, corporate CEOs, presidents and prime ministers—to discuss how to get more money and more power. Until the crash of '08-'09. At the 2009 forum, these mavens were clueless as to what to do about the pending worldwide economic collapse. This year, the forum was cancelled, of course, what with airports closed, spotty electricity, transportation and communications systems disrupted, riots in the streets, and so forth.

I guided the Porsche onto the town's main commercial street, the Promenade, which contained the major hotels, eateries, and coffee houses. Most of the buildings were painted white. I opened the window for a better look, and immediately we were hit by a rush of frigid air.

The car's GPS spoke in a flirtatious female voice, German accent and all, "Schiaweg Strasse Sixty-three, please turn right," which led us to a little side street where we found the headquarters building for Black Swan Beta. On the outside it looked like a fancy chalet from the early 20th Century, perhaps ripped from the pages of Thomas Mann's novel. The Black Swan sign was set on a huge piece of metal on the building's second story.

Jill and I hurried across the windy, frozen parking lot, hand in hand. I could feel her heartbeat speeding up; probably mine was too. We rang the doorbell at the huge wrought iron door, held still for the security camera, and gave our fake names when requested: "Simone and Roger Hightower." We carried fake passports in case they were asked for; they weren't.

Inside, the building was a surprise: all stainless steel and right angles and high ceilings and wild colorful murals done in Jackson Pollack style. Spacious enclosed cubicles with transparent walls housed dozens of employees hunched over keyboards. The whole place had a buzz, a sort of high-tech energy feel to it. I had experienced this feeling before at successful software firms in California's Silicon Valley. I did a quick scan of the place and discovered that bugs were everywhere, including video cameras mounted on walls and rafters every few meters. We expected that.

We met Herr Lieberman, who was charming and gracious and even kissed Jill's/Simone's hand. He explained briefly the problems his programmers were experiencing with their new artificial intelligence application, and quickly turned Jill over to Greta Eisen. Klaus and his programmers thought Greta would be the perfect person for the job because she spoke flawless English, and language was vital in finding and fixing the glitches. Our luck was holding.

Greta took Jill on a tour of the building. I was able to follow them through Jill's cognitive pipeline, the psychic link that enabled me to see, feel, and experience everything in her reality. Greta knew that Jill was a telepath, and that her job was to mentally feed Jill the data that would allow her to appear to fix—but, in reality, sabotage —the Black Swan supercomputer and world-wide networks. Greta, a petite, pleasant woman with short dark hair and sparkling brown eyes, wasn't aware that I had a chip implant and possessed some psi abilities in my own right.

As I sipped tea with Klaus and made small talk about the various planetary crises and the ski and toboggan conditions around Davos, the two ladies took an elevator to the level below the main floor. This was the first basement level, familiar because of Greta's excellent photography.

"This is where the programmers do the serious work using our AI application," said Greta, sweeping her arm across a vast, bizarro room which contained about two dozen walled-in offices with neither windows nor visible humans. Banks of humming servers lined the perimeter of the room. There was a constant whirring, buzzing sound, absent human voices. The sight and feel of it, through Jill's POV, gave me a chill.

"Most of the staff here are working twelve-hour shifts to stop the hackers around the world who keep trying to sabotage our servers and our AI application. That's why you're here, Miss Hightower, to give us a permanent patch and an impenetrable firewall. To help us carry out our mission and put a stop to this futile resistance once and for all." Greta looked and sounded angry; an excellent acting job.

"Miss Eisen," Jill was saying, knowing full well that their conversation was being monitored by the ubiquitous bugs, "I saw another button on the elevator for a level beneath this one. Is that where the—"

"Yes," said Greta quickly, "that is where the AI application is located." Greta formed a mental picture of concrete walls enclosing an area about fifteen by twenty feet. Meaningless; what was inside those walls? She also visualized Leela in her nearby cell, a sad and lonely picture. Leela was curled up in the fetal position on a thin mattress, wearing an orange jumpsuit, convict-style.

Had Greta really seen these things on the second basement level? Or was it just her fantasy of what might be there? One of the problems with mind scans, for me, anyway, is that I can't tell fantasy from reality. The mind can project a perfectly formed image or mini-movie of a scene or an event, and it can be pure fantasy. Maybe an experienced psi like Leela or Jill could tell the difference.

The image of the imprisoned Leela in Greta's mind lasted only three or four seconds, but that was enough for me. Whether it was real or imagined didn't matter. I felt sick inside, desperate to spring her from captivity.

Klaus Lieberman continued to stare at me after my floating teacup trick. His eyes, both curious and angry, demanded an answer. "How…"

"Elementary, my dear Lieberman," I said. "As you may know, I have spent great amounts of time in Mexico and Central America and Peru and Brazil studying with Indian shamans. I have studied medicinal plants with native healers. I have ingested huge quantities of ayahuasca in the desert and seen God. I have…"

I rambled on and on, watching the man closely, while plagiarizing whole sections of Carlos Castaneda's books about the mythical Don Juan and the narrator's search for truth in Mexico, his psychedelic adventures with the Yaqui Indians. Klaus watched me talk, riveted. Meanwhile, I shifted my awareness to Jill, who was in a tiny enclosed office with Greta by her side, both hunched over the interface keyboard that linked them with the company's huge server farm and AI app. Greta called it The Matrix.

How's it going, Jill? We don't have a lot of time, you know. I can only keep this rube entertained for a few more minutes.

Relax, Marty. I am inside the master computer and Greta is beautiful, feeding me all the data and keystrokes I need. There is definitely something very curious going on here. I suspect that we're not dealing with artificial intelligence but sentient *intelligence. Some kind of superbrain that is making this whole thing work. The attacks on the Internet, the infrastructure sabotage, the bank—*

Jill, can't you just drop the virus into that thing, whatever it is, put it out of its misery, so we can rescue Leela and get the fuck out of here? C'mon!

"Herr Raven! Herr Raven!" The somewhat whiny voice of Klaus Lieberman brought me back to reality number one. "Your story sounds vaguely familiar. It reminds me of a book I read once when I lived in Berkeley and hung out with hippies. But tell me: How did you learn to move objects with your mind? Presuming that you didn't hypnotize me, of course."

"Well, Herr Lieberman, it is a trick I learned from the Indians of Bolivia while under the influence of peyote. One scorching October day...."

I felt Jill knocking at the door of my consciousness. I tuned into her immediately, while on the other level I rambled on to Klaus Lieberman.

Marty, Marty, Marty! I have found something incredible! I'm looking at all these hacks to the main operating system, from servers all over the world, and I keep seeing a familiar digital signature. I think it's Hacker! Right, our friend Hacker of Sedona! I think he's the one who has been coordinating the sabotage of the Black Swan cyberterror campaign!

What? My friend—our friend—Hacker? Is behind all the sabotage of Black Swan Beta's nasty business? Impossible. No, probable. Any other evidence?

One more thing. This...symbol...keeps showing up on his hacks. Almost like graffiti. Hacker is trying to tell us something. It looks like that Christian symbol for a fish, you know, Jesus, loaves and fishes and all that, but this fish looks more like a whale or a shark. No. Wait a minute: It's a freakin' dolphin, Marty! I get it! Their AI app really is sentient intelligence...a dolphin!

Okay, Jill, it sounds crazy, but then again it sounds right. See if you can get Greta to take you to the bottom level. Maybe that's where it lives. Anything is possible right now. But please stand by, 'cuz I have a feeling our host is getting wise to our scam.

"…So that is how I learned to practice telekinesis, Herr Klaus. How to move objects with my mind. Just a little parlor trick, that's all."

"Computer!" ordered Klaus. A holographic image of a huge computer screen materialized out of nowhere. "Source of my guest's story, *bitte*." In about a nanosecond, a readout appeared. "Carlos Castaneda. Teachings of Don Juan. Separate Reality. Yaqui Way. Ixtlan."

I was temporarily stunned. I did a quick scan of Herr Klaus's speeding mind: He was emanating fear, suspicion, and paranoia, like steam from an overheated engine. This was dangerous.

Trying to mellow him out, I said calmly, "Herr Lieberman, allow me to explain. I have had many experiences similar to the narrator in the Don Juan books. Same territory, same drugs. Naturally there would be some overlap."

Klaus was adjusting some tiny object in his ear, as if listening to something over earbuds. I froze. Scanned his mind. He knew.

Jill. I think Klaus knows our scam. Be prepared for anything. Maybe you should drop that virus on our fishy friend now before we run out of time.

"Herr Raven," said Klaus Lieberman in an odd, flat voice. "We are onto you. We know who you are and why you are here. You are Martin Powers, a rabble-rousing journalist, and your so-called wife is Jill Appleton, a telepath from Sedona who works for the American State Department. The woman being held in our subterranean prison is your real wife, the dangerous psychic Leela Powers."

He didn't have to say any more. I read the whole thing in his mind. It was like scanning a report of the most recent past, the previous hour or two, with mental video and jerky, urgent thoughtforms. Fortunately, his thoughts were in English.

Black Swan Beta's supercomputer had analyzed DNA samples we left behind on the doorknob as we entered the building, on various objects we had handled, and on various hands we had shaken. The firm's global computer network, working at lightning speed, had matched our DNA with our photos and our profiles out of billions of possibilities in a huge worldwide database. I had feared this very thing would happen. He had us. Or did he?

Klaus reached into his jacket pocket, pulled out a small, deadly-looking pistol, and pointed it at my head. "Please do not move, Herr Raven—or should I say Herr Powers— or I shall be obliged to blow your fucking brains out."

Jill, are you with me? Do something, will ya'?

Are you joking, Marty? There are six thugs in here with guns and tasers and some kind of high-tech weapons, all pointed at me. Greta has been handcuffed and hustled out of here. I'm not sure I have too many options. These guys are killers. I think they're from that Russian Brotherhood that tried to take out you and Leela back in Sedona. Their minds are cursing in some kind of angry Baltic languages.

Stand by, sweetheart, I flashed back to Jill. *I've got a plan.*

Bearing down hard with my new supermind, I managed to slowly slowly move Herr Lieberman's gun-wielding hand until the pistol muzzle was stuck in his ear. His eyes were wide with terror and rage.

"Now maybe we can see what your brains look like, you sick motherfucker," I snarled, totally ready to engage the trigger.

"I wouldn't try that, Herr Powers," snarled Lieberman. "Two floors down—remember, your wife? She is in our cellar. In a cell. At my signal, my assistants have disabled the energy field that has kept her safely in our keep, and have now entered her cell. They will not hesitate to kill her if I give another signal or if I am suddenly terminated. Of course you are aware that this room is monitored with video cams."

I sat back, took several deep breaths, scanned the man's mind and knew that he meant what he said. I was aware of a cloud of insanity around his consciousness. The scope of his mania astounded me.

Jill. We are in deep shit here. Got any ideas?

Keep breathing, Marty. I'm thinking. I'm thinking.

CHAPTER TWENTY

The Om Protocol

"So. You two are probably wondering why we call our organization Black Swan, isn't it?"

Jill and I sat in the enclosed outdoor patio with the madman Klaus Lieberman and watched dark clouds float slowly across the sun through the transparent roof. A chill entered the space and hung in the air like dense fog. Klaus had put his pistol away, but there was nothing we could do. Yet. I always had the option of calling in the Special Ops people with the push of a button on my bracelet, but that could have endangered Leela's life.

Menacing thugs had ushered Jill into the patio at gunpoint. Greta's whereabouts were unknown. Leela was being watched by gunmen somewhere in a subbasement. Her neighbor was possibly a dolphin held prisoner within concrete walls. Hold on a minute. If the electronic force field holding Leela captive had been disabled, maybe, just maybe....

"Perhaps I should tell you a little about us, eh? Or perhaps Frau Appleton will simply read my mind and then tell you what she reads. Eh? Eh?" The German's thin lips twisted into a sadistic smile which quickly morphed into a sneer.

Jill and I sat silently, watching him, both of us busily scanning the cesspool of thoughts, memories, fantasies, and real-time information that swirled about in his mind. Jill flashed to me that she was going to dive deeper into memory storage areas to gather more intel.

"The book *The Black Swan*, eh? Perhaps you have read it. About the impact of the highly improbable. A rare event, totally unexpected. The unpredictable. For example, the assassination of your President Kennedy. Your country's nuclear bombs dropped on the innocent people of Japan. The 9/11 attacks...quite a black swan event, hmmm? Something happens with great impact that changes the world forever, hmmm? Or as an American friend of mine says, shit happens. Isn't it?"

"What does the *Black Swan* book have to do with your firm's malicious attacks on the Internet, which has totally fucked up our planet?" I asked with undisguised hostility.

"Because, Herr Raven, we are using the Internet— perhaps the greatest tool ever devised by man—as our ticket to the stars! Unpredictable, eh? Totally unexpected, eh? We will change the world! The world will never be the same!" He smirked at us and looked skyward.

Don't mess with him, Marty, I've opened some memory folders in his cerebral cortex. See what you can pick up in his real-time ruminating. Then we'll compare notes.

It was very weird, probing around in this man's mind while Jill was in there too. There was nothing tangible, nothing to see, not much to really grok, except the scrambled images and memories of our host's very busy mind; but I could *feel* Jill there too.

Marty, get this. It's info from this dude's short-term memory. The dolphin is the source of Black Swan's Internet attacks and the superbrain behind their processing power. It is a conscious and aware being capable of incredible cognitive function. And it is constantly drugged! The clicks and whistles and groans and squeals that dolphins put out, this one is sending out binary code. Wow.

I took a deep breath while looking Herr Nutjob right in the eye. *Amazing, Jill. A dolphin? Far friggin' out. Now get this. Klaus is thinking about a rocket somewhere in the desert of...wait a minute...somewhere in southern New Mexico, must be the White Sands facility, a rocket on a launching pad...a rocket that is headed for an orbiting platform in the...wait a sec...a space station that is already launched and orbiting the earth! Could this just be a fantasy, or just wishful thinking? I can't be sure.*

All of this communication was happening at the speed of thought, faster than the speed of light. Meanwhile, Klaus droned on.

"You two have probably heard of the Eternal Flame, eh? The organization that guarantees its members eternal life? Good. You of course want to live forever, isn't it, Herr Raven? As an expert on certain plant and chemical compounds, perhaps you should know about a chemical called EMC-2, eh? I take it every day, Herr Raven. I plan to live forever! Are you interested?"

It took a major effort to shift my focus from exploring this madman's mind to actually conversing with him in real time. "Of course I am interested, Herr Lieberman. What exactly is in this drug? And who produces it?"

"Ah ha!" he said, enjoying a small triumph. "Perhaps Miss Appleton can tell you. Are you reading my mind now, Miss Appleton? Are you? What am I thinking? Answer Mr. Powers' questions, otherwise I may have to kill you."

"You give me too much credit, Herr Klaus," said Jill smoothly. "I give psychic readings to clients in Sedona, Arizona, USA, at the Crystal Grotto, and to a few of my private clients by telephone. I cannot read your mind, or anybody's mind. If I could, I certainly wouldn't be interested in reading yours," she said, turning angry. "Why are you holding us here? We are tourists, on a skiing vacation, who have accepted your invitation to help your firm solve a software problem."

Easy, Jill, this dude is already on the edge....

"Ha ha ha!" he laughed, throwing his head back in an exaggerated gesture of hilarity. "You work for the American State Department. You are a spy. You know our prisoner, Leela Powers. You are traveling with Ms. Powers' husband, Herr Raven. We have a complete dossier on you. We have big plans for you and your companions."

Keep him talking, Marty. I have more exploring to do. See if you can find out what he's got in mind for us for the next hour or two.

"So, Herr Lieberman," I said, "tell me more about your Eternal Flame and this drug you are taking. You know of my interest in advanced pharmacology."

"Ha! So. Everyone wants more of the precious life, eh? This special drug that I and my brothers and sisters take every day, EMC-2, it is composed of many enzymes and even a bacteria extracted from the DNA of extinct wooly mammoths and Siberian rhinos! Prehistoric Viagra! Get my point? Not only will we live forever, but the men among us will 'keep it up' forever! Ha ha ha ha ha!"

Marty. Tune in to me, please. It was Jill. Just in time; this whack-job was getting on my nerves. Jill, undisturbed, sitting next to me, was deep in the man's head. *Lieberman's databases show that they are using the dolphin's processing power and their hijack of the Internet to transfer huge amounts of money from banks and individual accounts into secret Swiss bank accounts. They have stolen billions of dollars and euros, maybe trillions. They are funneling most of that money into building their rockets and orbiting space station. This software operation with all of its branches is only a small part of an international conspiracy. Stay tuned, Marty. The plot thickens.*

"...and each of us is made of cells that have been around since the dawn of life on this Earth, Herr Raven! Imagine that! We come from a cell lineage that has continued unbroken since life began! Now, listen, please. Why do our cells normally age and die? Why are they programmed to age so quickly and send us to an early grave? Eh? Eh? Do you know why? Of course you don't."

The people involved in this scam, Marty, you wouldn't believe. I can send you their images. Political bigshots and bankers and scientists and celebrities and.... Well, they all think they can live forever. They don't care about what happens to planet Earth and its people. They just want to get away from it, away from our problems. And they are causing many of our problems. They want to set up a moon base and launch space flights through our solar system and beyond. All of this info is stored in this joker's subconscious mind. And it just confirms what the Secretary told us back in Cyprus. The scope of this thing is unbelievable.

"...So it's all about the cellular clock that limits the lifespan of our cells, Herr Raven. The DNA sequences at the end of each chromosome which get shorter and shorter and finally give you a 'fatal error' message. *Verstehen*, Herr Raven? The germ-line cells that reproduce forever? Do you get me? *Ach.* You are hopeless. Stupid American. You will never understand."

Looking frustrated and resigned, he sank back into his overstuffed lounge chair. He looked at his watch and closed his eyes, falling into a silent reverie. I looked into his mind and what I saw shocked me. It was an image of a woman whose picture I had seen before, a woman who represented a potential disaster. Klaus was thinking about her imminent arrival.

Hey, Jill, check out what's happening in our friend's real-time ruminations. I know that woman from somewhere.

That is Tanya, Jill flashed, *the bitch who used to work for our State Department, then got flipped and went to work for Black Swan and was responsible for Leela getting exposed and captured. Klaus is thinking about her arrival here in Davos, which will be in less than an hour. She is flying in via helicopter from Zurich, and if she gets anywhere near this building, she will know there is a heavy psi presence here, namely you and me. Plus Leela. I know one thing for sure: this woman is very dangerous. She has tremendous powers.*

Which means, I flashed back to Jill, *that we had better get some escape plan going in the next few milliseconds or we are all going to be in deep doo-doo. Got any fresh ideas?*

Hey, guys, what's going on?

Jill, who's that? I must reiterate something here: Thought transmissions have no voice. When telepaths communicate with each other, it happens on another level and in another realm: Call it the brainwave realm, the cognitive domain. There is no sound. There are ripples in the cerebral cortex; a kind of *knowing* occurs. And it happens at the speed of thought.

Jill: *Leela! Leela! Marty, it's Leela! She's back with us!*

Leela: *Marty? You're tuned in! How? When?*

Sweetheart, it's a long, long story. Are you okay? What's happening down there?

Leela: *When Klaus and his boys turned off the electromagnetic energy field, I got my mojo back. It took awhile, but these six goons guarding me are all in a theta state, ready for delta. Hypnotized and immobilized. Take a look.*

I looked through Leela's eyes. It was amazing. Six burly thugs armed to the teeth were seemingly frozen in place, their eyes glazed and staring into space.

Jill: *Leela, we gotta get you out of there! Can you do a jump?*

No, I'm too weak. Jill, Marty, have a look around this place and see what we're up against. I'm accessing the central monitor panels for all the cams around the building. Have a quick look, guys.

I looked through Leela's eyes. The ubiquitous surveillance cameras showed all of the employees in the building, save for the six goons and Klaus, in battle-ready positions, everyone, including the female secretaries, armed with pistols. Most of these people were computer nerds and geeks, but dangerous nevertheless. A monitor of the first floor showed tiny Greta, stuffed into a corner, handcuffed and helpless.

What about our dolphin friend, Leela? I asked.

I had to hypnotize and disable the poor creature. She's not sending out binary code anymore. The dolphin has been drugged for months, floating around in a little salt water pond, programmed, and exploited. These creeps picked an innocent member of the most advanced species on the planet to do their dirty work. Despicable.

"What are you thinking about, Herr Raven?" came the raspy, lizard voice of Klaus Lieberman. "How to escape, isn't it? See, I just read your mind. Maybe you can show me another one of your parlor tricks, eh? While we wait for a friend of mine. Perhaps you know her. She will help us decide what to do with you and how to chart the future of our enterprise."

I scanned his real-time mind. A sharp, clear picture of Tanya emerged out of the mist. She was beautiful, with sinister eyes. Klaus visualized Tanya as a leather-clad dominatrix, bursting through the front door and attacking my two favorite ladies, smacking them with her fists then flattening them with yellow beams from her eyes.

Hey, Jill, Leela, this fruitcake is running some fantasy about Tanya as an evil Superwoman, messing you two guys up. Is this anything to be concerned about? Help me out here, I'm new at this.

Jill: *I caught a little of that fantasy. Nothing to be concerned about. Tanya is definitely on her way here. She could cause big trouble, so we have to be prepared. Right now we've gotta move fast. I set a software bomb in their computer network that will go off when someone hits the RETURN key. Marty, you could handle that, you've got a good touch on moving things around remotely. When that "bomb" goes off, it will bring down their entire global network. I got the code from Hacker.*

Hacker! Isn't he still in Sedona? Did he get a chip implant too? This was Leela, being mischievous. How did she know about my chip? Oh yeah, she scanned my "long, long story" less than five minutes ago. Leela sees all, knows all. *Listen up, folks, I have an idea. We have to put the rest of the crew here out of commission. We have to shut this operation down, post haste. Marty, you can trigger Jill's software "bomb" and call in the troops with your little magic button. Next we'll have to deal with my old friend Tanya. And then slip out of here. Jill?*

Here's how we do it: the Schumann Resonances. Right, Leela?

The what? I said. *This is no time for piano concertos by 19ᵗʰ Century German composers, ladies.*

211

The frequency of the earth's magnetic field, silly. (It was Leela, of course, my smarty-pants wife, staying in character even in the psi domain.) *Dig: A continuous wave of sound that puts the brain into higher or lower states. Lower, like sleep. That's what I used downstairs to render those big bozos helpless. All we have to do is tune in to that brainwave frequency. It's around 7.8 Hertz. Hey Marty, listen to Jill and I and join in. It won't take long to disable these people. I'll turn on the P.A. system for the whole building. There are hidden microphones everywhere.*

Whereupon the two ladies launched into a sweet, high-pitched sound that was like nothing I'd ever heard before. Klaus looked up, startled, jerkily tried to get to his feet, then crumpled to the floor and lay still. The girls wanted me to join in? I am a baritone, not a mezzo soprano.

Come on, Marty, we need you to make this work on everybody in the building. Just sing "om" in the lower registers of your lovely baritone voice. Then watch the video monitors through my eyes as everybody in this whole place goes into a delta state. Okay?

I sighed. Damn that Leela and her big ideas. Singing in public was never my thing; too shy, I guess. I closed my eyes and let go. The ladies started up their song again in perfect sync with me.

"Om. Om. Ommmmmmmmmmmm." Deep breath. "Ommmmmmmmmmm."

Our song, delivered in some weird kind of cosmic harmony that felt like it could throw the Earth off its axis, seemed to bounce off every surface and consume the whole building in a vibrating wall of sound. There were mics and vidcams everywhere, which helped to amplify our symphony. Through Leela's eyes, I watched Black Swan employees on three floors slowly crumple to the floor, sound asleep, probably in a deep hypnotic state.

This was serious medicine, this Shumann business. In fact, I was feeling a strange, unfamiliar tingle behind my third eye, perhaps in the pineal gland area. Oh oh, I thought, maybe this resonance thing is triggering some kind of reaction around my chip implant and an unwanted, untimely DMT trip is imminent. If so, well....

Jill: *Everyone's asleep, guys. Including Greta. We'll get her in a minute or two. Time for the next chapter. Marty, please remotely press that RETURN key at the main computer interface and trigger the software bomb. Know where that room is? Just follow my energy signature.*

I did, without thinking. Just did it. The experience was something like astral travel or an out-of-body experience. I followed Jill's energy trail; suddenly, there I was; there was the keyboard. I experienced my body in two places at the same time: weird. I pressed the RETURN key, using PK, psychokinesis, and lights started flashing and alarms went off all over the building.

You did it, Marty, congratulations! It was Leela. *Now would you press that button on your bracelet and call in the Special Ops guys? Your short-term memory says they'll be here in ten to fifteen minutes to clean up this mess. So let's be gone when they get here.*

"Marty, all the lights are blinking off. Part of the alarm system, I guess. The emergency generators are kicking in." It was Jill, speaking out loud, which was a relief. She was standing next to me on the patio and holding my hand tightly.

"Think you can disable all but two or three of the generators? Remotely? Sure you can. Keep one going in the computer interface office. That's so our software bomb will take out their worldwide network before they can patch it from another location. And one on the lower level so the dolphin can survive. And another one that controls the lights so we can see what's going on here. Okay?"

"What about the freakin' elevator, Jill? We've gotta get down to the lower level to get Leela out of there. We'll need some juice for the elevator."

"No we won't. We're gonna do a jump, Marty. But first, would you please take care of the generators? Oh, and don't forget to press that button and call in the troops."

Don't ask me how it all happened. All I know is it went down fast, very fast. I disabled all but three generators in seconds by following the electrical fields to their source. Then: My first-ever jump was painless and easy, passing through time and space and solid matter while tightly holding Jill's hand, scooping up Leela and taking another jump back to the first floor. Down in the sub-basement, Leela and I didn't even have time for a hug, but we made up for it on the main floor.

In fact, the three of us had a hug in the atrium that could have fried the circuits of the remaining generators. Engulfed in the loving energy of these two sexpots, I grew a boner so invasive that it had to be calmed down with psychokinesis. Greta stood a few feet away, trying to look disinterested. Jill had freed her minutes earlier.

"Let's get serious, guys," said Leela, stepping out of the hot energy, looking almost glamorous in her orange prisoner jumpsuit, despite also looking thin, pale, and malnourished. "In about ninety seconds, my old friend Tanya is going to show up. She is very powerful and very crazy and probably has already sensed what's going on here. So get ready."

"Let's hit her with some heavy psychic energy," suggested Jill. "Marty, as soon as Tanya steps into the security threshold, we will create an electromagnetic energy field around her. But wait until you see her physical presence."

Around these two very advanced psychics, you don't ask why or how. You don't think about it. You simply do. Somehow, the right thing always seemed to happen.

The massive front door of Black Swan Beta headquarters swung open and there was Tanya herself, a shocked look on her face. She was tall and thin, with high cheekbones and those penetrating eyes. She wore a wool cap and a white parka. We hit her with everything we had. She simply stood there, arms at her sides, her head lolling from side to side, her eyes wide and unfocused. Our energy field around her was firm and holding.

Leela waited about half a minute and then said to Jill and I, "Hey, guys, let's drop the field for just a few seconds while I take care of some overdue business, okay?" We let go, and Tanya staggered around, as if lost or drunk. Then my wife stepped up to the woman and did something amazing. And totally out of character.

"You rotten, traitorous bitch," Leela snarled. She wound up like a fastball pitcher, and delivered a fist directly to the other woman's jaw. Tanya staggered backyard and fell to the frozen ground at the entrance to the building. She struggled to get up, finally falling, face first, into a dirty snowdrift near the entrance. Leela stood over her, reached down, and pressed a point near her jugular vein.

"Forget the energy field, folks," said Leela. "This bitch will be in a semi-coma for about twenty-four hours. Gives the Special Ops boys a chance to get her immobilized, drugged, and harmless. Otherwise she would be in their heads, making them do weird stuff to each other."

"Let's go," said Jill, grabbing Greta by the arm. "Our car is right over there. Let's get out of here before all hell breaks loose."

"An alarm has been set off in a nearby building," said Leela. "I think some of those Brotherhood goons are on their way. Marty, how good are you at driving on icy mountain roads?"

"You know me, baby," I said. "Remember those motorcycle trips in Oak Creek Canyon?" We piled into the Porsche and I fired up the powerful engine. Leela sat in front with me while Jill and Greta scrunched into the tiny back seat. We roared off and skidded onto the Promenade, then headed out of town. I looked in the rear view mirror and saw two vehicles about a hundred yards behind: a black SUV and an equally black Hummer. I felt their threatening energy crawl up my spine.

"The Brotherhood?" I asked of anyone who might have a clue.

"Yep," said Leela, calmly.

"Step on it, Marty," said Jill, with equal equanimity. "Be ready for anything. Maybe even a Black Swan event. You know, shit happens?"

"I know, Jill, I know," I said shakily. I floored it; the Porsche responded like a lover who was ready for a long night of hot sex.

CHAPTER TWENTY-ONE

What's the Anti-Matter?

My two psychic consorts seemed unshaken as I whipped around icy corners and downshifted like a crazed monkey. Greta, however, seemed to be frozen in a state of panic, her eyes wide, her arms encircling herself. She is a physically small person, pretty face but perpetually furrowed forehead. Basically, she was scared shitless; I didn't blame her. The two black vehicles following closely behind us skidded dangerously around the switchbacks. Fortunately, the Porsche hugged the road like a jealous lover.

"Marty, can you coax a little more muscle out of this baby?" asked Leela. "Those monster cars are staying with us and the goons are just about to break out the guns. Whoops! There they go!"

I heard several shots and instinctively ducked. "Jill, is your force field holding? Marty and Greta, Jill has put up one of her famous force fields just behind our car and the bullets will just seem to die and fall to the ground. Okay, sister?"

"The force field is holding, yeah, but Marty's driving is making me nauseous," Jill giggled. "I'm doing my best, guys."

Five tense minutes went by, bullets flying and dying. Leela finally broke the silence: "They've given up on the gun-and-bullet thing, folks, and I think they're gonna break out their new EMP weapons, you know, electro-magnetic pulse? Like what happens when a nuke goes off. But these gadgets don't involve nukes. They basically shut down anything electronic or mechanical. Like our car engine."

"Like when those creeps tried to take out China?" I asked. "Using the power of the vortexes to generate an EMP? Yeah, I remember, sweetheart. You mean these Black Swan people have crammed all that power into some kind of handgun?"

"You got it, Marty. So in about ten seconds we're gonna get hit with some very strong radio pulses that will look like bolts of lightning. Jill, our lives are in your hands!"

"Are we gonna die?" croaked Greta, scrunched down in her seat.

"No, not yet," said Leela, just as the lightning bolts started hurtling our way, a truly frightening sight in my rear-view mirrors. "You okay, Jill? Is your force field holding? You look a little pale."

"I'm st-starting to l-lose it, Leela," said Jill, uncharacteristically shaken. Her facial muscles were straining, her teeth showing. "Can I get a little h-help?"

As she spoke, the car shuddered; I could see the blue bolts of lightning whipping toward us, then falling away as they struck Jill's invisible (but vulnerable) force field.

One bolt seemed to penetrate her shield and strike the back of the Porsche.

The engine died. I stomped feverishly on the gas pedal, but got no response. The car was hurtling around a sharp curve on a patch of black ice. I dared not use the brakes; they were power brakes and probably useless anyway. I slammed the gearshift into third and then second. We lurched around the curve.

From the back seat, Greta was wailing, keening, as if we were already toast. "I am calling in all of the angels, deities, and ascended masters for this one," she moaned. "God is great. *Allah Akbar.* Praise the Lord. Hari Krishna. *Shalom Aleichem. Mungu U mwema. Mazeltov.* Amen! That should do it!" She sat up triumphantly, shook her shoulders, and observed the unfolding drama.

"I've got your back, Jill!" yelled Leela. "And your front! Hang in there, kiddo!"

With peripheral vision, I could see Leela kneeling in the front passenger seat, head thrown back, arms outstretched, fingers aimed at the menacing car right behind us, like some kind of Wiccan high priestess casting a spell.

"Jump start this beast, Marty!" said Leela. "The force field is holding! Jump start it, please!"

I did as she asked, popping the clutch and stomping on the accelerator. The Porsche sprang into action, the engine fired up and our powerful little speedster again charged down the winding, hazardous road at breakneck speed.

"It is definitely holding, Leela," said Jill. "Thanks for the help. Maybe you can take a break now and… whoops, there's something new coming at us! Watch out!"

Leela hadn't changed her position. Arms outstretched and fingers spread, she now appeared to be holding something back. "They've upped the stakes!" she announced with some alarm in her voice.

In the rear view mirror I could see red streaks zooming toward our car. "Leela!" I shouted. "What the hell are those?"

"I think those are missiles, my beloveds," she said. "Mini-missiles with nuclear tips. Holy shit. They're trying to nuke us right out of existence. What do you read, Jill?"

"I don't think so, Leela," argued Jill, her voice quavering as she held up her end of the protective magnetic field. "If they were nukes they would not only put us out of business, but cook their butts too. And when those missiles hit the ground they would probably detonate. I don't get the feeling these bozos are suicidal types."

Leela groaned from the strain of holding up her end of our protective shield, her energy obviously starting to ebb. "What is it then?" she said. "Let's find out soon, cuz I'm getting tired. And I'm sensing there is something up ahead on this road that could change the course of history."

"Okay, here's what I get," said Jill. "Somehow they are sending atoms of anti-matter at us. That's right, anti-matter. If a single atom penetrates our field and hits the car, we would be vaporized. No evidence, no record of us, nothing."

"Anti-matter?" groaned Leela. "Doesn't it cost, like, trillions of dollars to produce a single gram of the stuff?"

"I dunno," said Jill. "I know these Black Swan creeps have practically the whole planet's money in their Swiss bank accounts, so they can do just about anything they want. But my scans say that they are sending anti-matter atoms our way. And that we will be less than dust if one penetrates our shield."

Leela: "Okay, listen, everybody, breaking news. Here is what I see clearly now." What she meant by "see" was that her psychic sense was at play. My wife's psi powers were greater than they had ever been before, many times greater. Scanning her real-time thought forms, I knew that something seriously life-threatening lay just ahead. I couldn't see what it was, though. Danger in front, danger behind. How could we survive? I took a deep breath, consciously breathing in and out as deeply as possible.

"Less than half a mile up the road, around several curves, there is some kind of obstruction," said Leela. "Some huge object is blocking the road. I can see some letters, some name, on the side of it. There is no way we get can around it. Unless we do something, we will have to stop the car and those hoods will have a clear shot at us." She paused for several seconds and time seemed to expand, a kind of crystalline field of energy filled the car, a great stillness descended. We were on the cusp of something: a Black Swan event, or....?

"Marty, do you remember that motorcycle ride we took into Oak Creek Canyon last summer in Sedona? When those hoods tried to run your Harley off the road and into the canyon? Remember?"

"I remember, sweetheart. Just at the right moment, my Harley lifted off the ground and the guys chasing us went straight over the side of the canyon. I always kinda knew that you had saved our butts by lifting the bike off the ground before we went over the side. Yeah, I remember."

"Okay, listen Marty, because this one is up to you. I can't do it. All my energy has to go into helping Jill keep this magnetic field going. You're gonna have to do what I did —that means lifting the freakin' car off the ground, over the obstruction, and onto the road on the other side of it. With PK. With mind power."

"Uh, Leela, I can't even start to imagine how—" I protested, feeling like some kind of wimp.

Leela was kind, as usual. But firm. "All you have to do is focus real hard, set your intention, and know that you can do it. Got it? Okay, Marty? I know you got it in you to make this happen, sweetheart. Ready? Cuz time is short, real short. A few seconds, and..."

I rounded a sharp curve, and there it was: A huge semi, an 18-wheeler, was stretched across the road. The tractor section, where the driver sits, had broken through the guardrail and was hanging over the edge at a crazy angle. The narrow road was totally blocked. Again time seemed to slow down, and I clearly saw the letters on the side of the huge trailer section: BLACK

SWAN GALACTIC ENTERPRISES. Under these were words in smaller letters: Danger: combustible.

No time to think about it. I focused, focused hard, visualized our car moving through the air, and basically *willed* our Porsche up and over the hopelessly marooned semi. It seemed to happen in slow motion. Leisurely, I took in the view of the snow-covered mountains, the valley below, the clouds, a hawk circling lazily in the sky. With pure thought, I brought our Porsche down easily on the icy road, a few feet beyond the semi. I hit the gas pedal hard, and squirreled us around a tight hairpin curve.

The explosion came a few seconds later—at first a whoosh, then an all-encompassing, violent shockwave of energy that rocked our little car and threatened to hurl it over the side of the cliff. The explosion seemed nuclear in scale. The sound was ear-shattering. I saw a huge fireball rising from what must have been terrible wreckage.

"Faster, Marty, let's put some distance between us and that mess," urged Jill. "There could be several explosions, especially if that stuff they fired at us was anti-matter. We don't know what that truck was carrying, but I suspect it was some kind of rocket fuel. It's probably very unstable. Please hurry."

I put the pedal to the metal and the Porsche shot ahead. Multiple explosions were happening behind us. Then, silence. The ladies and I fell into our own quiet space. A minute later, a new sound emerged. It started as a low rumble, gradually growing in volume and intensity. I looked in the rear-view mirror.

"Avalanche!" I cried. "The whole friggin' mountain is coming down behind us!"

Huge chunks of ice, snow, and rock were raining on the road that we had passed just a minute ago. The roar was deafening. It sounded and felt like an earthquake. The mountain, an ancient rock glacier, was disintegrating and falling into the valley below.

"Hurry, Marty, hurry!" said Jill. She seemed to be enjoying the thrill ride. "Hey, Leela, I guess I was right about the mini-nukes, eh? I hate to say I told you so, but...."

Leela was also bouncing in her seat with excitement. Only Greta, hunkered down in the back seat and looking nervously behind us, was, again, scared witless.

"You were right, Jill, spot on," laughed Leela. "I guess I don't know a nuke from a noogie. It must have been anti-matter. By the way, Marty, you did a great job back there, lifting our car up and over that truck. I knew you could do it."

"Thanks, Leela. It was nothing." The two psi ladies giggled; I laughed, and checked my trousers to make sure I hadn't soiled myself. I checked the GPS display and saw that we were only a few kliks from St. Moritz. Fearless, I ran the speedo up to 130 kpm on a smooth straightaway. The mood in the Porsche had definitely lightened. We were still alive.

"You know, ladies, I'll be expecting some sort of *reward* when we get back to the states. I still haven't experienced that thing that Jill told me about that you two had going —uh, I call it Remote Screwing."

I glanced into the back seat and saw that Greta was blushing. "Oh, you mean the Unified Psychic Energy Field of Universal Love," piped up Jill. "The remote coupling experience."

"Yeah, something like that. I'm ready to try it."

"Count me in too," said Greta, surprising everyone, including herself. She cleared her throat, blushed again. "Marty is my hero. I would do anything for you, Marty. You saved our lives." She put a hand on my shoulder.

Jill gave Greta a sidelong glance that had jealousy written all over it. "Sorry, girl, but remote coupling is only for people with enhanced psi abilities. Maybe when this crisis is over...."

Leela came alive. "Marty, just how long is your chip supposed to last? I hope it holds until we get back to Sedona!"

"They told me two hundred hours, sweetheart. So far, so good. I wish it could go on forever. Maybe... maybe I'll get lucky and my chip won't dissolve."

"I hope so. I love you even more with psi abilities. It's like having a born-again husband!"

Just ahead, a road sign: St. Moritz 10 km. Did we dare check back into the hotel? Would the Brotherhood goons be waiting for us? Could we even fly safely back to Cyprus and catch a plane to the US? Lots of questions, and no answers. Wait....

"I have a couple of answers, Marty," said Jill. She had been listening in to my thoughts. She had also been fiddling with her handset, the wonderful Psi-Fi device, which delivers data at lightning speed: audio, video, 3-D holo, and text. She had apparently been in contact with the Special Ops team back in Davos as well as with our contacts at the Palace Hotel.

"Here's what I just learned," said Jill. "We have probably destroyed their whole Internet sabotage operation, or at least seriously crippled it. Lots of people were arrested by the Special Ops guys. Including the bitch Tanya. And our friend Klaus. Operation Algorithm was a huge success. We got Leela back. We saved a dolphin. And I told our friends in St. Moritz that we'll be there soon. They've got security people all over the place. Our hotel rooms are waiting and the Jacuzzis are heated up. Any more questions?" She wore a huge grin.

"Yeah, " I said. "When is dinner? All this excitement really works up a man's appetite!"

CHAPTER TWENTY-TWO

The Man in the Blue Parka

Icicles hung like silver daggers from the roof of our patio, accenting the luminous winter postcard scenery outside our cozy suite at the Palace Hotel in St. Moritz. A light snow was falling. I shook my head to clear the cobwebs and to make sure I wasn't dreaming all this.

Yesterday....Ah, it had been quite a homecoming, returning to the relative security of the stately Palace. We were greeted by our friends from the State Department, Joe and Kate Jeffers, the young couple from Colorado who had rescued Jill and I from the frozen Lake St. Moritz just, what, twenty-four hours earlier? Forty-eight hours? Time seemed telescoped and meaningless in light of what we had just been through.

I was physically and mentally exhausted; it took a lot of energy to lift our Porsche, using psi power, over the semi truck and then driving us to safety over the icy road. I was hoping for an invigorating massage from my two psi lovers.

We had a debriefing session with Joe and Kate in our suite, and they delivered the news that our little group was to be picked up in St. Moritz by a special high-speed military helicopter and delivered to the American Embassy in Cyprus, where we would be given new orders before departing by military aircraft for the USA.

"But be warned," said Joe, with a sidelong glance at Kate, "that things have changed in only the last two days. The world is a more dangerous place than ever. Plus the Brotherhood boys are going to be looking for you. We've got security all over the hotel—even the head waiters and the concierge are working for us—but watch your backs anyway. The chopper will pick you up at thirteen hundred hours tomorrow. Please stay in the hotel until we call for you."

They were a beautiful couple, late twenties, rosy-cheeked and healthy looking, rugged American outdoor types who had somehow gotten themselves involved in this very dangerous scenario. I saw some dark energy around the two of them, saw something sinister in their future that gave me a chill. I looked over at Leela and Jill; both nodded almost imperceptibly in agreement.

"And you two please be very careful too, okay?" I said, looking deeply into their eyes. A vision had come to me. "Watch out for a guy in a blue parka and ski boots who will be a threat to all of us. He is carrying a gun and he will be looking for us. He is very dangerous." Now Jill and Leela nodded vigorously in agreement.

"What are you guys, psychic or something?" laughed Kate. "Oh yeah, I almost forgot: Leela here is a world-famous psychic. And husband Marty too, I s'pose?" I nodded modestly. "Well, don't worry; Joe and I are armed and we have a nose for trouble."

The two psychic ladies and I shared a two-room suite, while Greta had her own room. We all felt that would be the wisest arrangement. At first, it was a little awkward for me to share a space with my two lovers, although jealousy had never been a factor in our unusual relationship. How could it? Hanging out with telepaths, and being one yourself (if only temporarily), nothing is hidden—thoughts, feelings, fantasies, emotions, memories. One is basically naked.

And physically naked too, at least in our suite. Both ladies pranced around shamelessly nude. Leela was terribly thin after her weeks as a captive. She had lost at least twenty pounds, which brought her down to around one hundred. The Black Swan m'fuggers had fed her slop, and she had had virtually no exercise. Yet she still looked delicious, perfectly proportioned, with radiant skin and fine long hair.

Jill, by comparison, looked well-fed and filled out. She was a buxom lass anyway, with a big caboose and finely shaped legs. The two of them gossiped and tittered and laughed, occasionally giving each other high-fives. I was all but ignored, except when they paraded in front of me in the fine new clothes provided by Joe and Kate.

I had been watching the news on the giant screen TV in our living room. The big story was about a terrible explosion on the highway leading into St. Moritz. A large truck and two cars were apparently involved, but no bodies were found, only a few pieces of metal and plastic. The explosion had caused a terrible land-slide, and the road would be closed for several weeks while huge chunks of granite were removed by bulldoz-ers. No cause for the explosion was apparent, but Swiss police were on the case.

Dinner was at Le Bistro, the Palace's trendy French restaurant, with prices to match the hotel's upscale ambience. Our rooms alone cost more than four thou-sand US a day. Fortunately, the State Department was picking up our entire tab. The ladies, including Greta, wore high heels and low-cut, sexy dresses to dinner.

The restaurant was located right next to the hotel's elegant disco, the King's Club, the town's major hot spot, which attracted the rich and famous who were vis-iting St. Moritz. Through a transparent red wall, we could watch the beautiful people writhing to the music.

"Isn't that Madonna over there?" cried Greta.

"Sure looks like her—and moves like her," I said. "And isn't that Johnny Depp dancing with Beyonce? Where's his wife, I wonder. And her husband, you know, Jay-Z."

"Oh, let's go there!" said Jill.

"How about after dinner?" said Leela. "I haven't had a decent meal in weeks. Hope they got some tasty veggie food here."

Leela and Jill scanned the area around our table for bugs, found no recording devices, and we all breathed easy. I scanned the room for video cams; it was clean.

In a low voice, Leela described her experiences as a prisoner of the Black Swan organization. It was a shocking, frightening story. They had planned to turn her into a double agent for Black Swan by implanting a device in her brain that would rearrange a few million of her neurons, turning her into a virtual slave of the organization. Fortunately, Jill and I had shown up just in time to snatch her away from the crazies.

They had taken a DNA sample from her body in the hopes of creating a genetic line of psychics who could be trained and conditioned to work for Black Swan Galactic. When early tests on the DNA sample failed, they had taken some of her eggs to create clones of Leela in a Petri dish. We gasped at this revelation.

"It wasn't too bad," said Leela softly. "I just surrendered to it. A lady came in while I was asleep, rolled me over, did the job with equipment that seemed sterile, and it was all over in a minute or two. Maybe they'll name the clones after me: Leela Two, Leela Three, Leela..."

She laughed, breaking the tension, and we all laughed with her. The best part of the story was her connection with the dolphin, and the data she got from the poor creature.

"She called herself Piscea. She was a very beautiful being."

"The dolphin had a name?" said Greta.

"She had a name, she had a life once, she had a whole story. I only had a short time to communicate with her, but it happened telepathically and very fast. You know, dolphins are the most highly evolved creatures on this

planet. Their intelligence and their capacity for learning are way ahead of humans.

"Anyway, she had lived at Sea World for a few years
and was very happy there. She had a mate and she loved
performing for people. A year ago she was kidnapped
by Black Swan agents and flown to Davos, where she
was drugged, programmed, and hooked into their
computer system. She was connected to their servers,
became a kind of dolphin cyborg, and with her vast
brain power she could do computations faster than
any known computer network. So Piscea was exploited
to the max by these lowlifes. Unwillingly, she was the
super-processor that caused all the trouble with the
Internet."

"Shhhhh!" whispered Jill. "Here comes our food.
To be continued."

After the dessert dishes were cleared away, Leela
dropped a bombshell. "I was able to download some
of the data from Piscea's databases. You know, she had
an incredible memory capacity, at least seven petabytes.
Compare that to the human memory capacity of just
over three petabytes."

"How much is that?" I asked, not ashamed to display
my high-tech ignorance. Greta jumped in.

"It's like poetry," she said. "Kilobyte, megabyte, gigabyte, terabyte, petabyte, exabyte. A megabyte is about
a thousand kilobytes. A gigabyte is about a thousand
megabytes. And so on and so forth."

"Huh?" I said. "I think I got it. Sorta."

"Someone once said that five exabytes would be equal to all the words ever spoken by mankind," continued Greta. "That's a lot of memory."

"No wonder the human mind is stuffed with so much useless garbage," mused Jill. "Lot of room in there for junk. I wonder if humans can drag and drop useless material into their Trash bin."

"I don't know about that," said Greta, feeling good that she was finally in her element. "But the computational capacity of the dolphin's brain is three times faster than that of the human brain, and twice as fast as any computer known to man. Or woman."

"Listen," whispered Leela. "Listen to what I got out of my download. The names of the top players in Black Swan Galactic. All taking that EMC-2 drug, all members of the Eternal Flame cult, and all major players on the world stage. Listen to these names: Snitzer. Breedlove. Wilfong. Shestak. Nerdski. Von Trump. Harry Wong. Patel. Turkulu. Glinka, Chekhov. The list goes on and on. Heads of corporations. U.S. congressmen. Prime ministers. The World Bank. It is truly unbelievable."

"How much data were you able to download, Leela?" asked Greta.

"Probably about a terabyte. That's it. It's all in my own deep memory, which I can access pretty easily, anytime I want. Still, there's a lot left in that dolphin's databases. I downloaded an index that lists files for all of their plans, all of their personnel around the world, the whole shoddy criminal enterprise. Plus their schematics for the space station and their rockets. I'd love to have another mind meld with that dolphin some day."

Greta leaned in close and whispered, "I have a surprise for all of you. I was saving it for the plane trip to Cyprus, but there's no time like the present." She paused for effect and looked around the table at each of us. "While I was working at Black Swan Beta, I managed to download most of what was in the dolphin's memory storage. I didn't realize at the time that the processor was sentient! Anyway, it's all on these little flash drives."

She rummaged in her purse and pulled out a device that looked like a fat thumb with a USB plug at the end of it. "These just came out a few months ago. Each one holds about a hundred terabytes. I've got forty of these, not counting this one. This one's blank."

"Jesus H. Kee-rist!" exclaimed Leela, a little too loudly, drawing the attention of a number of uppity, white-haired patrons at nearby tables. "I mean, Greta, where are these things now? That's our whole case against these people!"

"Well, uh, I, uh...." stammered Greta, red-faced. "They're upstairs, in my suitcase, you know, in my, my, uh, room."

Jill was exasperated. "Omigod. Greta, I don't know how you could...Now listen to me. Let's all stay calm, people. I'm sure no one could get into our rooms. We've got security everywhere. But Greta. Did you back up all of this priceless data, by any chance?"

"Of course I did," she said, obviously annoyed that anyone could doubt her intelligence or computer savvy. She reached into her purse and brought out a silver rectangular object about the size of a credit card. "It's all backed up on this. All of it."

"That's a hard drive?" I asked. "How much memory?"

"Almost five petas. More than enough to handle the Black Swan files."

Leela, Jill, and I all breathed a collective sigh of relief. "Oh, Greta, I could kiss you!" said Leela, and reached over to put her arms around our diminutive friend.

Suddenly, a sound like firecrackers filled the air. Gunshots? Women screamed. A cacophony of shouting and confused voices drifted into Le Bistro. It was coming from the disco in the next room. We all looked at the transparent red wall separating the two rooms, looked into the King's Club, and saw a scene of utter chaos and terror.

On the small stage where the DJ had been working the crowd with sweaty techno and trance music, a man was waving a pistol in the air and shooting at the ceiling. He had his arm around the neck of a young woman. We could vaguely make out what he was shouting. The music had abruptly stopped. A long-haired young man, apparently the DJ, lay still on the floor in a pool of blood.

"It sounds like he's saying, 'Bring me Leela Powers or I will...' and I can't hear the rest," I said. "He seems to have a strong Russian accent."

We all pushed away from the table and stood up. "Let's go!" said Leela.

"Waiter!" I shouted. "Charge this to our room! Add a thirty percent tip!"

We ran out of Le Bistro with Leela leading the way, barged into the King's Club past the startled guardian of the door, and planted ourselves near the back of the club. About three hundred patrons stood motionless, like statues. On the stage was the man I had seen earlier in the vision—blue parka, ski boots—and he was waving his pistol around and screaming into the DJ's microphone.

"Bring me Leela Powers now or this woman dies! Now! Now!" He punctuated this with three more shots into the crowd. One man in front fell to the floor. Blue Parka was holding Kate Jeffers securely with his arm around her neck. Occasionally he pointed his gun at her head. Then he fired two more shots into the crowd. A young woman in a white gown screamed and fell to the floor.

"Marty, Marty," said Leela, grasping my arm, "we've got to move on this guy now. We gotta get his gun. Let's see if we can lift it right out of his hand. I'll help you. Go now. Go."

No time to think about it. I focused on the gun, visualized it leaving the guy's hand and moving through the air. Leela stood next to me; we were joined at the hip; I could feel her energy working in sync with mine. Focus, focus, focus. Bear down. It was working. The gun left the man's hand and moved slowly through the air over the crowd. The gun came right into my hands. I looked at it with disgust and threw it into the shadows behind us.

On the stage, Blue Parka seemed to be in shock. He released Kate. She quickly kicked him in the crotch, and as the man bent over to protect his jewels, she nailed him in the jaw with an elbow. He crumpled to the floor. Six uniformed security cops were on him in a flash. It was over.

"Let's get out of here," said Leela, starting to gather her posse.

"Wait just a second," I said. I noticed a dude standing next to me who looked vaguely familiar. I felt like I needed to connect with him.

"That was quite a trick, pal," said the guy, an American. He was an actor. I recognized his voice, his eyes. Right. Johnny Depp. "How'd you do that, anyway?"

"Magic," I said. He grinned. "Hey," I said, "I really liked you in...let's see. *Fear and Loathing in Las Vegas.*" It was the only movie of his I could think of in the moment. It was released in 1998.

"That film where I channeled Hunter Thompson? Right. I've made a few since then. Whadda ya want, my autograph?" he said, still grinning.

"No," I said. "I would like you to look at my screenplay."

"Sure. I've got a production company, you know. People are still making movies, crisis or no crisis. What's the name of your movie?"

"*I Married a Psychic.* It's kind of a sci-fi fantasy."

"Bring it on, man," he said, and handed me a card. "Send the script to my e-mail address. And come to visit me anytime. You know, I've got a place in the South of France, near St. Tropez. Pretty safe there, so far. You and your friends are always welcome."

Leela and Jill stepped up, each one grabbing me by an arm, and hauled me away. "Hey, guys, that's Johnny Depp!" I protested. "He invited us—"

"And I'm Martha Stewart," said Jill. "Let's go to our rooms, dudes. I'm exhausted."

When we got to our suite, the door was open. Joe Jeffers was inside, as well as four uniformed security guys. Across the hall, Greta's door was also open and security people were buzzing around inside. "Come on in, folks," said Joe. "Looks like the party's over. Sit down and I'll tell you a little story."

"The guy in the blue parka, I'd guess," said Jill. "But how—"

"Here's how," said Joe. "He was prowling the halls and somehow slipped past all the security cams on this floor. He knew the numbers of your rooms. While the maid was turning down your bed and placing the Swiss chocolates, you know, he slipped into the big suite, snuck up on the maid, and knocked her out with a blow to the head. Then when he tried to pick up your laptop, the one we had loaned you...."

"I know, I know," I said. "The alarm on the laptop went off. If you don't say the code word, anybody touching it will set off the alarm."

"Right. So he apparently took the master room keys off the maid, went into Greta's room, and was rummaging through her suitcase when the security team came into the room. The guy pulled a gun and ran off down the hall and down the stairs with the security boys in hot pursuit."

"Quite a story," said Leela, her eyes wide. "Now let me guess: Mr. Blue Parka runs into the lobby, sees Kate, grabs her and holds her at gunpoint and then drags her through the disco and onto the stage. That's where we came in."

"How did you—" began Joe, then said, "Oh, right, I forgot who the psychics are around here! Well, sorry about the little security slip-up, folks, but as you know, shit happens. By the way, Mr. Blue Parka was thoroughly searched and didn't have any of your stuff on him. We'll I.D. him right away. I'm sure he's with The Brotherhood, part of Black Swan. Sleep tight. I'll see you guys tomorrow."

We all sat around the fireplace in our suite for a good twenty minutes, just breathing with eyes closed and letting the events of the evening wash away.

"I feel violated," sighed Greta. "The thought of that creep rummaging around in my stuff....I hope he didn't mess with any of the flash drives. But anyway, I've got the hard drive backup."

"You can sleep on our couch if you would feel safer," offered Leela. "It converts into a big bed."

"No thanks," said our new friend. She looked haggard and exhausted, and her makeup was smeared. "I'll be fine. I need to take a nice hot bath."

Leela, Jill and I needed a nice hot bath too. The three of us squeezed into our Jacuzzi tub and let the powerful jets soothe our aching muscles. Afterward, we crawled naked into our king size bed with the big down comforter. The two ladies sandwiched me, delightfully. I spooned Leela and Jill spooned me. Sex was not on anybody's agenda.

I slept deeply by consciously triggering a big dose of natural melatonin from the pineal gland. My implant was still working beautifully. I wondered how long I could keep my psychic gifts. The docs said two hundred hours. Maybe, maybe....

CHAPTER TWENTY-THREE

Hostile Forces

The Black Hawk 90-A Panther Cruiser is quite a helicopter. Not only can it carry up to eight passengers in cozy comfort, but it is loaded with electronic gear and enough firepower to take out nearly any airborne attacker. It has a top speed of 250 mph and a range of about sixteen hundred miles, just enough to take us from St. Moritz to the Nicosia airport in about six hours.

Why the State Department in Cyprus had decided to assign us to a top-of-the-line, heavily armored military chopper instead of an airplane would become blatantly obvious in a few hours. Just for security purposes, our chopper was accompanied by a loaded Apache gunship. This awesome machine is really a flying tank, a helicopter designed to survive heavy attack and inflict serious damage. Some experts say it is the most lethal helicopter ever created. Knowing all this, I felt both secure and scared shitless.

Helicopters are by nature noisy creatures, so our little group of four spent most of the trip in silence. I had noise-proof headphones and some heavy Stones on my Amigo, so the non-stop roar of the chopper's mighty engines didn't bother me. Leela and Jill huddled over our laptop, studying the files on the Black Swan organization that Greta had so cleverly downloaded. Greta was also studying those files on some hand-held device she had borrowed from Kate Jeffers.

I had other priorities: opening several messages that had accumulated on my Amigo over the past forty-eight hours. All came via REBEL in deep encryption mode. There were three from Benny Bravo, and one—surprise!—from my dear friend Hacker. Hacker's had to be opened first, of course.

I ran my unscrambling program. Hacker never bothered much with punctuation. He figured you had to have at least a little sense to understand him anyway.

"Dear Dude hope you are well Internet up & running again…you and Jill musta picked up on my code… good work! BS (his own code for Black Swan) had servers in fifteen cities - bit of a challenge but I think my Bird Flu Virus shut em all down…no more DNS problems now… so what's with the fish? and did BS have AI to fug with the web? explanation please

"also Jill sent me coupla fotos of her pretty feet via private wireless network I set up when we were still interfacing…as thank you for me sending the code via her psi-fi gadget and wireless network? what a gal! wish she'd take me back dot dot dot Sedona? oh nothing serious just martial law has seriously kicked in… streets blocked razor wire concrete walls…cops everywhere army units in flagstaff… only way to get around is auto rickshaws new in town just like india…drivers illegal aliens barely speak english take any currency like pesos and rupees bicycles OK too… very 3rd world here Also strange shenanigans Kali's place benny b tell you more... most people who stayed in town moving to tent cities... me still home got three teens living here (female o course none jailbait) water on only sometimes no electric... stay safe write soon hacker

I closed my eyes and let it sink in. My beloved Sedona. Martial law? Razor wire? Tent cities? I tuned in to the Stones music pounding through the headphones: "What's confusing you/Is just the nature of my game," belted Mick Jagger in his tribute to Lucifer. Whoever *he* is. I felt an urgent need to get back to Sedona to help sort things out, to make some sense out of the gathering madness—a madness that seemed to have infected the entire planet.

We had been in the air for maybe an hour or so when I looked earthward from the big windows and saw, what, Mount Etna in Italy? Maybe we would see that damned thing erupt? There had been several volcano eruptions lately, almost an epidemic of eruptions. Pele in Hawaii. Mount Rainier in Washington, Mount Hood in Oregon. Yellowstone's volcano had finally blown its top, sending thousands of homeless campers running for cover. Worse, the ash blotted out the sun over three states.

I tapped into my short-term memory: Recent volcanic eruptions in Greece; Japan; the Philippines; Guatemala; New Guinea; Mexico; Iceland. All over the planet. Had the Black Swan organization figured out a way to trigger volcanoes? Earthquakes? Tsunamis? Or was it just the natural progression of Mother Nature's current rampage?

Greta had fallen asleep with her handset still on and running data from the pilfered Black Swan files. I turned it off, put it in a safe place, and covered her with a blanket. It was getting cold in our chopper. My two fellow telepaths were still poring over the Black Swan files and chatting away. Earlier we had all three scanned the copter for bugs; it was clean.

I turned back to my trusty Amigo and brought up Benny Bravo's messages. He reported that things were getting weirder across the board. Goddess Kali had actually succeeded in bringing some dead people back to life. Her insane scheme to plant the consciousness of famous people in the resurrected bodies had failed, however.

Still, she had managed to create a race of zombies. Zombie temps. They were a great source of entertainment, while they lasted. The resurrected bodies lasted only two or three days, started to stink, and then died again. Ghoulish.

Still, the suckers poured into her temple to be healed or reborn or...whatever. Many came for the zombie entertainment. The only way to get into Sedona, and to Kali's temple, was through Cottonwood via the divided four-lane State Route 89A. The roadway was often clogged with cars, the drivers honking and shouting at each other. Traffic came to a complete stop for an hour at a time. Cars would run out of gas and be pushed to the shoulder. Many frustrated motorists simply abandoned their cars in the middle of the highway and walked miles to Kali's temple, Benny reported.

Benny was still staying in his house. He got water deliveries from a black market source, a brother who filled up huge containers from the spring up in Oak Creek Canyon, and made deliveries in a fake pizza van. Benny had a large supply of powerful battery cells which he had "collected" over the past few months. The batteries supplied his household electrical needs, and also powered his tiny motor scooter, which gave him wheels for tooling around town.

So far so good. Message Two was a little more dire. Several days had passed. "Yo, Boss," he began. This message was in audio, and he had returned to his annoying reggae-punk patois. It meant he was nervous. "Things dey get a li'l weirder here since message one. Now, I deduce dat de Mexican gangbangers has taken over de fancy subdivisions, you know, de ones with gates and code numbers and all. So we got the Mystic Hills gang, we got the Casa Contenta gang, we got the Foothills South gang, you know. But I dunno what dey be doin' here cuz dere's nobody buyin' drugs, there ain't much cash around anyways. So methinks dey just be squattin' in dese fancy digs and killin' each other for turf just out of habit."

Benny said Kali's temple seemed to be winding down. "The Dakini chicks has left and I hears dey be offering Tantra sessions out at Chickentown. For food and cigarettes, you dig?" He was referring, of course, to the major tent city out by the wastewater treatment plant. "I goes out to de temple yesterday on me scooter just to snoop around and it look to be a dying scene.

Some tourist from Kansas, he be all about leavin', he tell me only Kali and a few die-hard followers still hangin' out. I no try to get inside. Who know what happen to me skinny ass in dere."

I took a deep breath, then another, then brought up Message Three from Benny. Still in audio. "Late-breaking news, Boss. Kali has split. Word on de street. Destination unknown. On me way out to de temple yesterday, me squirrel down main drag and note dat odor of de town from mass toilet unflush now over de top! No water, remember? Hold yo' nose, brudder! And also dis: High school now big tent city, football field gots hundreds o' folks, cooking fires everywhere, people catch rabbits for dinner, I hear. We get water through tap sometimes, usually brown sludge, sometimes jus' copper color, okay for shower-shave but no drinkee. Also no flushee. No prob, I got me pizza service for drinking stuff."

I turned my ahead away from the Amigo and looked out the window. We had been aloft for a little over three hours. It had been a smooth and uneventful trip so far. Through the clouds I could see a large land mass below. I figured we were just about over Greece, probably Athens. There was our escort, the Apache, about three hundred meters to the right of our craft.

I saw the flash just a meter or so from our chopper, then the explosion. "We're under attack!" screamed a male voice from the cockpit. The source of the voice, the co-pilot, suddenly appeared in the passenger section. "We are under attack!" he repeated, more calmly.

"Be sure your seat belts are fastened and get ready for some rough weather!"

"Who is it? Who's attacking?" I asked without thinking, because I already knew from scanning the man's mind that he had no idea. *Gotta be Black Swan*, Jill flashed to me. *State Department said big Black Swan presence in Greece. Hang on tight.*

"Just stay in your seats," said the co-pilot, and disappeared back into his little alcove, slamming shut the heavy metal doors.

Another flash, plainly visible, another explosion. Then another. "The Apache! They got the Apache!" yelled Greta. A missile had indeed struck our companion helicopter, but it's armor held; then the beast fired back at the source of the firepower, followed by a huge explosion on the ground and a fireball that leaped into the sky.

"Bingo!" said Leela excitedly. "Got 'em!"

"We're not out of danger yet," said Jill, calm and unflappable. "There's no guarantee our armor could survive that kind of attack. Plus the State Department told me that Black Swan could have surface-to-air missile installations from Sicily to Cyprus."

The co-pilot appeared again in the doorway and had "bad news" written all over his face. He was tall, lean and angular, slightly hunched over in the cramped space. He didn't need to speak, because Leela, Jill, and I already knew what he had to say. Greta obviously didn't. We let him deliver the news.

"Folks, it's decision time. We're about five hundred miles from the Nicosia airport. Under ordinary conditions, it would take just a little over two hours to get there. Now, we got a problem. We just got a transmission on the secure channel that civil war broke out on Cyprus this morning.

"It's all about water. The Greeks control what little is available, and they cut off the Turks' water supply. So the Turks attacked the Greeks. Then Turkey, the country, started firing missiles at the Greeks on Cyprus. Now the whole island of Cyprus is on fire, chaos, fighting, just a hellhole. All of Embassy Row in Nicosia has been wiped out. Thank God our people in the American Embassy evacuated before the bombing started."

"The American Embassy...gone? How am I supposed to get my new orders?" asked Greta, somewhat inappropriately. "Oh....I get it. Sorry. Well, what are we going to do, Mr. Co-Pilot?"

"That's what I'm here to talk about, ma'm," said the soldier with strained politeness. "We can take our chances and fly you into Nicosia International, which is right in the neutral zone between the Greeks and the Turks and hasn't been touched by the fighting. There are still some good aircraft there we can all escape in. We hope. Unless the place gets bombed out before we get there. Then we're stuck."

"Where else could we land?" I asked, already knowing the answer. "Doesn't America have any friends left in the Middle East?"

"First, forget Turkey," said the co-pilot. "There is an American airbase there, but the Turks on Turkey have gone completely insane. Then...Well, forget Syria.

Lebanon. Jordan. Iraq? Iran? Ha ha! Okay, Israel. Airbase in Jerusalem. At least they still love us there. Only trouble is, Jerusalem is two hundred miles beyond our chopper's maximum range. Chances are good that we would run out of fuel and have to ditch in the Mediterranean."

"Hmmmmmm," I murmured. "And we noticed that some people on the ground are using us for target practice."

"That's another thing," said the co-pilot. "Hostile forces have launched an attack against our resources in the area. Our intelligence says it is the Black Swan organization, and that they may have weapons emplacements along the corridor we need to negotiate in order to land on Cyprus. Also, we may come under attack from other hostile forces on Cyprus. Intelligence says they are firing on any aircraft that attempts a landing on the island."

"In other words," said Jill, "it appears that we are fucked."

The co-pilot stiffened. "I wouldn't use that word exactly, ma'm. I would say that we are in imminent danger of being neutralized. Or better yet, obliterated." He turned on his heels, said over his shoulder, "Please discuss your options and let us know what you decide to do. Our orders are to honor your decision to the best of our ability." He looked out the window.

"Holy shit!" he cried, suddenly dropping all military demeanor. "INCOMING!"

He quickly disappeared into the cockpit. We all saw the missile fast approaching our chopper. The pilot executed an evasive maneuver and the thing missed us by about three meters. It exploded just above us, creating a concussion that shook the chopper like it was a limp doll.

I glanced over at Leela and Jill. A look of understanding passed between us. When the chopper stopped trembling, I knocked on the cockpit door. "Yo, pilots! We have reached a decision!" The door opened slowly and a shaken co-pilot stood staring at me. "Full speed ahead, matey," I said. "On to Cyprus, to that airport in the neutral zone. Take evasive action. We will do our part to keep us safe."

He shook his head and retreated back into the cockpit. I sat behind my psychic ladies and we began our secret operation: Together, we would create and maintain a force field around our chopper until we got to the Nicosia airport. It would take a whole lot of effort. Silence would need to be maintained. We would need to pool all of our psi mojo to pull this one off. We looked at each other, and joined hands.

"All kinds of heavy firepower is gonna be coming our way, ladies," I said softly. "That means bombs, rockets, heat-seeking missiles...Is this force field gonna work?" Leela and Jill nodded vigorously. I glanced over at Greta. She was busily biting her nails. "Anyone believe in the power of prayer?" I asked. The two psychics shook their heads; Greta nodded vigorously.

"Then hold on tight and everything gonna be all right," I said confidently, squeezing the hands of Leela and Jill and giving Greta a wink and a knowing smile. "I want to go home. I miss Sedona."

PART III

Dateline: Beyond the Stars

The Transition

"My friends," said the alien, "your planet is at a crossroads. I am here to help facilitate your transition to the next phase."

—Harry the Handyman

CHAPTER TWENTY-FOUR

Like a Virgin

Laughter rippled through the restaurant as I described our frightening helicopter journey from Switzerland to Cyprus, then the aftermath at Nicosia International Airport, then the shaky flight back to the USA.

"And I was singing the Star Spangled Banner to keep our morale up!" I said. '…and the rockets red glare, the bombs bursting in air…' That's all I could remember of the friggin' song. But that was the scene in the helicopter: bombs and rockets bouncing off our force field and falling back to earth. Our force field held. We survived."

"Obviously," said Hacker smugly.

"*No mierda!*" said Benny Bravo. "Whad'ja do then, Boss?"

"Do you guys remember South Vietnam? The last helicopter out of the place before the war was officially over? Americans scrambling to get on that chopper and get the heck out of there? That was how it felt for us." It was Greta, speaking up from behind a tall glass of Oak Creek Amber that nearly hid her from view.

Hacker looked affectionately at the newest member of our little posse, the diminutive Greta, who had flown to America with us because her job as a mole at Black Swan Beta was over and no new orders from the State Department were forthcoming and she had nowhere else to go.

"Listen up!" said Leela, cutting through the maze of cross-talk at our table. We were the only people in the Navajo Room of the luxury Enchanted Forest Hotel. "Thanks to my beloved husband, Marty, here"—she paused to give my reddening cheek a pinch— "we were able to bluster our way onto the last plane at the Nicosia airport, which was a decrepit Russian Condor military transport, which already had sixty nuns from the Russian Orthodox Church in Nicosia on board."

Everybody roared. "The plane was already overweight because they had hundreds of cases of vodka and half a ton of caviar in the cargo hold," said Jill. "They were on their way to someplace in Canada, Nova Scotia, I think, but Marty convinced the pilots to drop us off at Andrews Air Force Base. We also felt we should take the two American helicopter pilots who had flown us into Nicosia with the bombs bursting in air. The Russkies agreed to give them a ride if Leela and Greta and I would give them an erotic massage when we landed. The Russkies, that is."

More laughter. "And…and…and…?" said Hacker.

"Well," I said, picking up the thread, "when we landed at Andrews, practically nobody was minding the store. The place seemed to be deserted. So we found a nice hospitality room for foreign VIPs. We ushered the Russian flight crew in there, and about six of the youngest nuns. Then Leela hypnotized all of 'em, ordered everybody to strip down, and the erotic massages just kinda happened on their own. We split when the moans and groans got too loud."

"And now you are here," observed Hacker. "How? Did you three psychics teleport from Andrews to Sedona and take Greta along for the ride?"

Oops. Unknowingly, Hacker had given away my secret psychic identity. Everyone at the table knew it except Benny. I tapped into his *cabeza* to see if the remark had registered. He was thinking in English, fortunately. When Hacker dropped his giveaway line, Benny thought, "What the fu—", then his thoughts went skittering off to something about women's legs and breasts. I would tell him later, at a better time, I decided.

"No, we didn't teleport back to Sedona," I told the group. I explained that we had hitched a ride from Andrews on some ancient U.S. military transport plane, which lacked such amenities as flush toilets and padded seats, but which delivered us directly to the Sedona airport after the ladies promised to give the pilot a psychic reading and a chakra energy clearing upon arrival.

The Enchanted Forest (which we nicknamed the EF), once the plushest resort in Sedona, had become both our hideout and our headquarters. We had the whole place practically to ourselves, save for a skeleton crew of cooks and waiters, room cleaners, masseuses, one concierge and one assistant manager. The staff all lived on the property. A few wealthy guests were also there, including two movie star couples, a former NFL quarterback, a rapper, and four CEOs of big corporations. The rich and famous were apparently fearful of leaving the secluded resort and going back into the chaos that the American landscape had become.

My little group was welcome at the EF, first because of Hacker's specialized hacking skills, and second because Benny Bravo used to work for the gas company. The computer genius hacked a nearby electrical power pole and delivered a constant flow of juice into the EF's little grid; Benny managed to tap into a working gas pipe, directing enough gas to the resort to supply its needs. The EF had its own wells, so water was not an issue.

Leela, Jill, and I moved into a two-bedroom casita on the edge of the property, alternating sleeping arrangements so that all three of us were satisfied. It was absolutely wild. Hacker had fallen in love with Greta—actually, the incurable foot fetishist had fallen in love with her tiny feet—and they had moved into a luxury suite together. "Most beautiful feet I have ever tasted…er… ever seen," my old friend told me, "and that includes Jill's tasty tootsies!"

Hacker and Greta: this was a true odd couple. John Hack, the kinky, dope-smoking ladies' man, and Greta, the naïve nerd who had been with only one other man in her forty years, her ex-husband. But both were computer geniuses, and they spent hours huddled over a laptop in their suite, presumably swapping algorithms and hacking secrets. I would wager that they also discussed Hacker's deadly Bird Flu Virus, whose launch code he had transmitted to Jill at Black Swan Beta HQ—and which helped to take down that firm's Internet sabotage scheme.

Benny Bravo had his own suite, but he insisted on also spending time at his Sedona home, threading his way through the roadblocks and military checkpoints on his tiny electric scooter. One evening I sat him down and told him the whole story of my newly-acquired psi abilities, including some of the incredible adventures that had just happened in Europe.

Benny was very cool about it; he shrugged and said, "In Español we would call you a *psíquico*, a psychic, or *un lector de la mente*, a reader of the mind. *No problemo, vato.*" He laughed heartily. "I'm safe. Most of my sexy thoughts are in Spanish!"

Our casita arrangements went like this: Leela and Jill each had their own bedroom, and I was like a roving ambassador, spending a night or two with Leela, and a night or two with Jill. It didn't seem to matter to the ladies which one I was with, as they had the remote coupling mode turned to ON. Whatever Leela was experiencing with me was fully shared by Jill, and vice versa.

The first time with Leela since the rescue at Black Swan Beta in Davos was a true memory-maker. It was almost like being with a virgin. At first Leela was trembling, scared, her legs locked together. She was still thin and bony; she seemed like a young teenager. I took my time, my mouth brushing her full lips, her erect nipples, her concave belly, her soft bush. After what seemed like hours of foreplay, I rolled on top of her. Her chest was heaving and she was thrusting her pelvis toward my rigid maleness.

"Please…please…please, Marty, now now now now now!" Leela begged. When I finally penetrated her, in the next room Jill let out a scream that must have frightened away every coyote within a mile of the resort. "Ohhhh!" Jill howled. "Ohhh, Marty, yes yes yes yes! Harder! Harder!"

This was new to me. This was so new, and so astounding, that I almost lost my precious erection. Fortunately, I didn't. Suddenly, I thought, I have to satisfy two demanding women, two for the price of one, double your pleasure double your fun, two screamers, two women who I loved deeply, and… Suddenly I realized that I had to get out of my head, and fast. I focused on the physical phenomenon that was underway, the joining—three psi people, through our loins—of body, mind, and spirit.

Leela moaned, jerked violently, and exploded under me with a shudder and a primal sound that I had never heard from her. In the next room, Jill also exploded. "Omigod!" she screamed. "Omigod! Ahhhhhg! Ahh-hhhggggg!" And then I exploded, a kaleidoscope of lights going off in my brain, a synaptic firestorm, a gusher of white liquid heat passing through me into Leela, wave upon wave of volcanic eruptions, Leela's body slowly and finally coming to a full stop.

I rolled off her, exhausted. Silence. After five or ten or twenty minutes, a voice from the next room: "Hey, that was pretty good, guys! Was it good for you too?"

Jill appeared in the doorway, naked, backlit by moon-light, her body a sensuous silhouette. "Mind if I join you?"

Without waiting for an answer, Jill sprang into Lee-la's bedroom like a cat on the hunt, wedging herself between Leela and I. She faced me, her full breasts pushed against my chest, her legs tangled with mine. "Let's do that again," she murmured in my ear. Leela, picking up on the verbal as well as non-verbal cues, snuggled up against Jill, her hands cupping those big breasts and kneading the hard nipples.

The heat was rising. This time around I entered Jill, we lying face to face, belly to belly, while Leela held on to Jill from the back and absorbed the energy. This was a delicious arrangement, pure Tantra, almost no movement, silence save for deep breathing, a Zen ballet of heightened consciousness. The energy contin-ued to build, we three breathing as one, until finally we reached a kind of inner explosion. Together. This peak seemed to last forever.

I can say this about the female orgasm: It is awe-some. We poor males are orgasmically challenged. I appreciate the male's rocket-into-outer-space effect, the fireworks, the explosion, the release. But it is essen-tially genital-centric. The female orgasm is a full body event, a shuddering, tingling, wave upon wave upon delicious wave. It goes on and on and on. Multiple orgasms. Whew!

But don't get me wrong. I'm not complaining, and I'm not jealous of woman's orgasm. Actually, I am one lucky sonofabitch. I was able to experience the coveted multiple orgasm sandwiched between two lusty women, to feel every sensation, to travel to that sacred zone of pure female energy.

During our stay at the EF, I climbed to these climactic heights many times, thanks to remote coupling—which wasn't so remote when we three shared a bed. But how long, I wondered, would my psi gifts last? I had already gone well beyond the two hundred hours the docs in Cyprus had promised me. The pineal gland chip implant should have dissolved by now. And yet, my psi powers seemed to be getting stronger. The remote coupling switch was turned on!

What happened? I loved my new state of being. How could I ever go back to being plain ol' Marty? I drifted off sandwiched between my lovers and dreamed of blue skies and flamingos and tall pine trees and naked people dancing like faeries through the woods. But from somewhere in a remote corner of the dreamscape, an alarm bell was sounding. Sirens, explosions, screams, the rise and fall of frightened voices. Awareness of dream state. Suddenly the sounds stopped. Duly noted. Lucid dreaming, take one.

CHAPTER TWENTY-FIVE

We've Gone Too Far

A Day Earlier

Hacker knew right away that there was something different about me. We were sitting on the deck of his West Sedona home, taking in the red rock views. It was ten a.m., and below us, the little jewel of a city was amazingly quiet. Anybody with any sense had already left town.

Leela, Jill, Greta and I had just arrived in town the day before, and after piling into an auto-rickshaw at the airport, we made our way to our house, Leela's and mine, up in the hills near Sugarloaf Rock, an isolated and quiet part of town. Exhausted, we spent a quiet night. Jill and Greta each had their own rooms.

"What's up, Marty?" inquired Hacker, peering deeply into my eyes. "Something's happened to you, hasn't it. Something new. Something...awesome. You feel like, like, damn, I dunno, like more than you were before. Explain, dawg."

I told him everything: the chip implant I got in Cyprus, the Davos adventure, the Leela rescue, the dolphin, our escape, the huge explosion and rockslide on the road back to St. Moritz. Patiently I tried to describe my new psi abilities, what it was like to read people's thoughts, the tricks I could do like move objects with my mind, the enhanced memory, and the ability to communicate with other telepaths.

Hacker wasn't impressed. "So you're probably reading my thoughts right now, right? You know what I'm thinking about, what my schemes are, what ladies I want to get it on with, feet feet feet fuckin' feet! You know my deepest, darkest secrets, dude! That just sucks! How can I ever hang out with you again? How can I get the edge on you with my superior brainpower?! You know what I'm gonna say before I say it!"

"Look, Hacker, I've got better things to do than read your mind. It's just not that interesting. Plus I only use my new abilities in the line of duty—you know, serving our country, rescuing fair maidens, saving the world from arch-villains." I told him about the supposed time limitation on my chip implant, that it could dissolve at any time and I would be right back to plain ol' ordinary Marty.

Hacker seemed to soften. He sat back in his easy chair and released a mighty outbreath. "Sounds like a mixed blessing to me, Marty," he said quietly. "If that chip melted right when you're in the middle of some crazy trick, like teleporting to Las Vegas or jumping over the Grand Canyon, you might get trapped between dimensions. We'd have to hire a, what, an exorcist to get you out of there."

"Hacker, old friend, we have some serious work ahead of us. We could use another trusted psychic on our team. How about you getting a chip implanted in *your* thick skull? It's painless, and the rewards are many." I was half-serious, half-kidding. Actually, more serious than not.

"Ha! Are you putting me on? I don't wanna be like some kind of zombie, like a walking seed pod with higher consciousness linking up with other seed pods. Know what I mean? Remember that great film from the Fifties, that *Invasion of the Body Snatchers?*"

"I don't know what the effin' hell you are talking about, brother, but I know it's time we got serious. Forget the chip implant. Now, could you please fill me in on what's been going on in this troubled world?"

My friend sighed, closed his eyes, was silent for a minute or two. "Where should I start? Okay, after Jill dropped my Bird Flu Virus into the Black Swan hardware, me and some hacker buddies from Silicon Valley fixed the Internet, so it's up and running again. We put up some new electronic barbed wire around the DNS, you know, the Domain Name System that Black Swan Beta attacked and completely fucked up and used to extract big bucks from innocent people's bank accounts. And totally screwed up the way business is conducted on this planet right now.

"You remember that message I had Benny send you? Just the letters DNS? I was trying to tell you that that was the heart of the Internet's problems. Didja get it?"

"Yeah, bro', I got it, and I got it. I ain't exactly a retard, y'know. You and I had already talked about your suspicions regarding DNS attacks months ago. So

I passed the info on to Jill and she used it to start the counterattack on Beta's attack programs."

"Well, just checking, Marty. I know you're a hip dude and all that. Anyway, we patched up the damage and tried to make sure it can't happen again." He paused, took a deep breath. "Unless it does happen again. And it could. But don't tell anyone that."

"Hmmmm, okay, I promise. What else, Hacker? How bad is the world situation? My little group has been out of touch for a few weeks."

"Oh. Right. The Web was down, so you couldn't get the news. Well, it's pretty bad, Marty. The infrastructures in most countries have just collapsed, you know, electricity and water and fuel oil supplies are just sporadic. Most of the airports of the world are closed so people can't fly anywhere. The trains are still running in most places, at least for now. Unless they run on electricity."

"Sounds pretty bad, man. What else?"

"Well, people can't drive their cars like they used to either because oil production and delivery has broken down everywhere. Gas is around ten to twenty bucks a gallon. In the good ol' USA there is looting going on everywhere. People are desperate. Some cities are just finished. Caput. Detroit. Oakland. Philly. Little Rock. Baltimore. There is no government left in those places. Anarchy. Tent cities springing up everywhere."

"What about D.C.?" I asked.

"A real mess. An Army battalion is surrounding the White House as we speak. Angry mobs trying to break through, thousands of people. The president has declared a national state of emergency and is sending troops and National Guard into every big city to restore order. Good luck, I say."

"Wow. Amazing. And what about the rest of the world? What's been going on?"

"More bad news, bro. Little wars are breaking out everywhere because people are totally freaked out so they turn against their neighbors. Religious wars, too: Muslims versus Hindus, Christians versus everybody else. Millions of refugees on the move, starvation, genocide, even cannibalism, I hear. People eating their babies. It's a bad scene, Marty, scary as hell. Lots of people waiting for J.C. to come back, lots of folks praying for the end of it all, a lot of suicides and just a black cloud coming down on the whole damn thing."

"Look, Hacker, I—"

"You know me, Marty, I may be a sarcastic asshole and a skeptic about New Age-type shit and miracles and auras and angels and psychic readings, etcetera, etcetera, and especially a skeptic about a higher power and God and all that, but I have always believed in people. And technology. And the future. I always thought the people of Earth could have a good life, that someday we could all get together and share the goodies, and everybody get along. Now...I don't think so. I think it's too late. We've gone too far. Hate has won. I think we are all doomed."

I looked at Hacker, stared at him for a long time. His eyes were filled with tears. I had never seen that before. I looked into him. His mind and his heart were enveloped in a great, overwhelming fog of sadness. It was almost more than I could bear.

"Hacker," I said gently. "Hacker, old friend. You remember last winter we had dinner at Sushi Town and we were talking about Black Swan Galactic and what the name 'Black Swan' was all about? And the weir-does who were triggering these environmental disasters and taking strange drugs and blackmailing all the governments? And you said, I remember your exact words, you said, 'Nothing like this has ever happened in human history. We could all be headed for the trash heap unless something happens to turn this around.'"

"Yeah, yeah, I remember that dinner. I was worried about the future. I got a bunch of intel from the hacker network about these creeps and I was totally freaked out. And I remember that good beer was cheaper than water that night at Sushi Town. And I remember the great legs and cute toes on our waitress, who was from Singapore or something. And we talked about you and Jill and—"

"Right. Right. We talked about your surveillance of my meeting with Jill, and blah blah blah. We talked about the whacko sci-fi fantasies of the Black Swan Galactic leadership, their quest for the stars, etcetera, etcetera. Yesterday's news. Here's some late-breaking, my brother.

"Their space station is nearly complete and they are preparing for a manned rocket launch in the very near future. They blackmailed the mighty U.S. Government into letting them use the White Sands Missile Range in the New Mexico desert for their launch site. This is the next step in their plan to conquer the stars, dude!"

"Wha-a-a-a-t?" said Hacker, his eyes darkening with anger. "So that's what it's really all about, eh? All this global disruption, this hijacking of the planet's operating systems, millions of innocent people dying, just so a few crazies can escape this mess we're in and beat the Grim Reaper and fly to the moon? Have you got any documentation on all this, good buddy?"

"Yeah. Me and the girls brought back petabytes of data that we downloaded from the Black Swan matrix in Davos. We've got their organizational chart, who the bigwigs are. You won't believe some of that. We've got their business plan. We've got their training videos for building a space station. We've got little animated movies on what life will be like on their space station. We've got CGI versions of their vision for exploring the galaxy. Amazing stuff, Hacker."

"How do I get my hands on this data, Marty?" His eyes were suddenly on fire; the dark clouds were gone.

"First, I want you to meet our new friend, Greta Eisner. She was the State Department's mole at Black Swan Beta. She helped Jill upload your killer virus to take out the Black Swan matrix. She's the one who risked her life to download all these petabytes of data onto flash drives which she smuggled out of the building, don't ask me how. We brought her back to Sedona with us. You'll meet her maybe later today. She is a real sweetheart, real smart, and a computer nerd."

"Does she have pretty feet?" asked the Hacker, suddenly innocent and boyish.

"I, uh, didn't really notice," I said. "Probably, I dunno. She is a small lady, kinda pretty, wears glasses, shy, perky, sorta naïve."

"Hmmmmm," said Hacker, deep in thought and fantasy, and I couldn't resist: I looked into his mind and saw an image of a face—Hacker's, looking skyward—with a big smile on it and a petite foot planted squarely on the face. Hacker suddenly snapped to attention. "Hey! Are you rummaging around in my mind? I think I felt something in there."

"Why, Hacker, I wouldn't think of violating your mental privacy. If you want to fantasize about feet, I... oops!"

"I knew it!" he cried. "Damn you, Marty!" And then he exploded into a fit of hilarious laughter. Soon I joined him. It was a joyous relief, after the tense talk about the world situation. Then Hacker got very serious.

"Marty," he began, "we can't come back here anymore. To my house, I mean. At least for now. It's too dangerous."

"What do you mean?" I asked, although I already knew from a quick mind scan. The three teenage girls who had been staying in his house had fled the day before; destination: Chickentown. There had been telephone threats by men with Slavic accents, graffiti spray-painted on his wooden fence, loads of feces, human and otherwise, dumped into his front yard. Drive-by shootings had become a daily occurrence, but only his fence had been hit with sprays of bullets. Hacker had electrified his wooden fence and studded it with alarms and videocams, but that didn't stop the thugs who were harassing him.

"You just read me, right?" said Hacker. "I think I felt you inside my skull."

"Yeah, I got it, brother, I got the pictures. What do you intend to do?"

"These guys mean business. I think my life is in danger if I stay here. They know I'm connected with you and Leela and Jill. I've got a plan. I'll give you the details later."

"The Brotherhood," I said simply. "A gang of goons from Eastern Europe and the old Soviet Union. The enforcement arm of Black Swan Galactic. They're the ones who tried to bump us off in Switzerland, and they're the ones who tried to run us off the road in Oak Creek Canyon last summer. They are a vicious bunch of killers. If they are the ones who have been harassing you, it would be best to evacuate the premises, my man. Immediately."

"I hate to give up my humble abode, Marty, but you're right. Let me pack up a few things, including an ounce of primo weed and my favorite bowl, and we'll get the hell out of here. Plus the toilets haven't worked for two weeks and the smell is starting to get to me. That's one of the main reasons the teenies left—they had to do their business outside. They didn't appreciate that. I told them to pretend they were camping out. Okay, Marty, I—"

A tremendous explosion interrupted Hacker mid-sentence. It seemed to come from just outside the front door. The house shook; framed photographs and paintings of women's feet fell off the walls. Smoke and an acrid chemical smell filled the house.

"What was that?!" I shouted. "Hacker, I think we have just been bombed." I ran to a window and saw that his sturdy redwood fence had been decimated, probably by a pipe bomb. What remained of the fence was on fire. "Get your stuff together, my brother, and let us flee this scene! Or maybe you should put out this fire first!"

Hacker dashed through the front door carrying a miniature fire extinguisher, spraying the fire dead and stomping angrily on the still-burning embers that littered the front yard. "Damn! Shit! Fuck! *Mierda*! Friggin' sumbitches!"

It was a wonderful catharsis for my friend. It seemed to calm him down and to help him focus on the job at hand, which was to get the hell out of there. Ten minutes later we were on his sleek Harley Volt 100 series motorcycle, the first all-electric bike to be available to consumers. The saddle bags were packed with clothes, a laptop, and his potent stash of top-grade marijuana.

I scanned his thoughts during the wild ride through West Sedona, avoiding the checkpoints and the cops, on the way to my house to wrap things up there. Ol' Hacker had something up his sleeve, all right. He had made arrangements with the Enchanted Forest Resort for us to stay there. It was all arranged. We needed a headquarters and a hideout. He didn't seem surprised that I had read his thoughts and deduced his plans. It saved a lot of needless chit-chat, he said.

And for all of us—Leela, Jill, Greta, Hacker, myself—it was to be a new beginning, another leap into the void. I tried to peek into the future, but all I got was chaos, upheaval, non-stop noise, the shrill cry of birds on a mass migration. And darkness.

But one image came through very clear: a confrontation with Goddess Kali, now an all-powerful entity with madness in her eyes. In my vision she had a new name: Big Mama Lakshmi. This made no sense at the time.

It would soon enough.

CHAPTER TWENTY-SIX

The Road to Chickentown

We spent a joyous week at the Enchanted Forest resort, soaking up much-needed R&R for our exhausted bodies and stressed-out minds. The spa was our favorite hangout. We ate like royalty. We hiked on nearby trails. We made love. We meditated. And we made love often, the two psi ladies and I. My chip implant seemed to enhance every sensation, every feeling, every moment.

We even put together our own little rock band, using instruments that had been left behind by a group that had stayed at the EF, a Christian heavy metal outfit called Loaves & Fishes. When the musicians and their roadies heard the end of the world might be approaching, they left immediately with only the clothes on their backs, leaving their instruments behind.

The Seventh Chakra, we called ourselves. Hacker on lead guitar, Benny Bravo on bass, me on keyboard, Leela on drums, and Jill on flute and vocals. At first Greta declined to join us, falling back on her claim of terminal shyness. In time she joined Jill on vocals, and turned out to have an amazing knack for singing harmony. We created several original songs spontaneously, chords, melody, lyrics, just by tuning in to the creative

Source. Of course the synchronous mindscape of the three psychics helped to make it all happen.

Meanwhile, we were all anxiously awaiting a message from the State Department. What next? With the Internet back up and running, Leela took a chance and sent an encrypted message to the Secretary. Her whereabouts were unknown, we were told; we knew she and her people at the embassy in Nicosia had escaped before civil war enveloped Cyprus. Within an hour we got an encrypted message back from the Secretary's deputy.

Our orders were clear: First, turn over all computer files that we had liberated from Black Swan Beta headquarters. This was to be accomplished thusly: a military helicopter would land on a grassy area of the Enchanted Forest property, a colonel in uniform would rappel down to the ground, spot Leela by sight, and give personal information about her that was known only to the State Department. This would be like a password; nobody was taking any chances of subterfuge. Leela would then turn over the hard drive containing precious petabytes of information. (Secretly, we would keep a copy.)

Second: Our little group was to locate a person of interest named Wolfgang Maximus, the purported head of Black Swan Galactic. He was last known to be in New Mexico, somewhere near Santa Fe and Los Alamos. We were to take him into custody, if possible. This was a tall order, as he was rumored to be protected by several layers of security.

Third: We were to locate a white female who had joined Maximus and Black Swan to further their dark and dirty agenda. This person's assignment was to trigger eco-disasters, sabotage the global economy, and essentially screw up all of the fragile systems and procedures that once kept the planet Earth glued together. She allegedly had the supernatural ability to make things happen. She formerly lived in Sedona and was known then as Goddess Kali. Now she was known by another name, Big Mama Lakshmi. Our assignment: If possible, terminate Big Mama Lakshmi, with extreme prejudice. *If possible.*

"BINGO!" shouted Leela, reading our orders to Jill and I from the decoded transmission. "Big Mama Lakshmi, is it? My old girlfriend, Aura Adelstein? She's hit the big time now! It wasn't enough to be a goddess and have her own Tantra temple, now she has to hook up with the biggest villains on the world stage!"

"The orb that invaded her body out on Bell Rock must have something to do with this," I said. "Aura, Kali, Lakshmi—whoever she is now—must have learned how to manipulate that entity and use its power to fuck things up!"

"Right on," said Jill. "How are we supposed to 'terminate' this person, anyway? I have heard she has enormous power now—probably due to that freakin' misplaced orb, as Marty said—and that she can do things like affect the weather and cause earthquakes and volcanoes and hurricanes and floods and get inside people's heads and make them go insane. And be in two or

three places at the same time. Not to mention bringing people back from the dead and other weird stuff
too gross to talk about. How could we even get close to
her? Sorry, Leela, this gig freaks me out. Plus 'termi-
nating' people was not in our job description."

Leela nodded. "I understand where you're coming from, girlfriend, I really do. Possibly you and I and
Marty could pool our psi power and set up a force field
around the Big Mama, but she could probably flick us
away like mosquitoes. And she would know that we
were approaching and create some horrible event to
keep us away, like a forest fire or a tornado. Plus our
lives would be in danger. No, kids, we need something
else for this assignment."

"Like a whole elite battalion of marines, with futuristic weapons and air cover?" I said sarcastically. My
recent vision of an opponent named Big Mama Lakshmi made sense, now.

"No," said Jill, "just one little man with shabby
clothes and mismatched facial features and an empty
mind, remember? He's got some inside info on
Big Mama. You met him at my house not that long
ago."

"Harry the Handyman," I said with a sigh. "The
dude who held my hand and took me into outer space."

"Right," said Leela. "That's our guy. We need him
with us on this gig. I've got his Psi-Fi handset code somewhere in my memory banks—oh, thanks, Jill." Obviously a quick transmission had just flashed between the
two telepaths, a reminder that there were no secrets in

our little triad. "I'll give Mr. Handyman a holler and find out when he can join us."

Leela ducked into her bedroom, leaving Jill and I in Jill's room. I looked at her, sprawled across the big bed, wearing a skimpy halter top and short shorts. I looked into her mind and to my surprise caught an image of Jill and I writhing about, naked, on her bed. A projection of the future, perhaps?

I looked her straight in the eye and sent a message: *Tonight, Jill. Tonight is our night. Just you and me.*

She nodded, and a wicked smile played around her lips. That was definitely a yes.

Leela flowed back into Jill's room and said just one word: "Chickentown." She paused a beat, then: "Harry said to go to that tent city outside of town as soon as possible and find Kali's Dakinis. Bring 'em back here. They're wearing amulets that might be the key to taking down Kali, or Big Mama Lakshmi, whatever. He said he would join us when we came back here. And he said to pack our bags and get ready for a road trip."

"A road trip to New Mexico, no doubt," I said, dubiously. "For a showdown with a very powerful, very dangerous, and probably psychotic woman, and the head of the organization that has been trashing our planet. Brilliant."

"Don't worry your pretty little head, Marty," said my beloved wife. "Harry will be coming with us to New Mexico. He may hold the key to this whole operation. In fact, I have a strong feeling that he holds the key to the future of the human race, no less."

The next morning we all piled into a big van that we had appropriated from the resort. Stuffed in the back were our borrowed instruments. We had spent much of the previous day rehearsing, actually just jamming together and learning each others' moves and grooves, trying out some rock and roll riffs, Jill and Leela creating songs spontaneously, amazingly, a virtuoso display of psi togetherness. Speaking of which....

I spent the night in Jill's boudoir, and we went at each other like cats in heat. It happened on some animal level, with yowls and howls, clawing and scratching, in full animal modality. In the next bedroom, although Leela's door was closed, we could hear her own animal sounds as she joined us in the Remote Coupling adventure.

By the time Jill and I slowed down—she on her fourth or fifth, or ninth or tenth thunderous orgasm—and moved into deep kissing and heavy breathing, Leela had broken the connection and seemingly fallen asleep. Jill soon followed Leela into the arms of Morpheus. A curious expression, that. In Greek mythology, Morpheus is the god of dreams and the son of Hypnos, the god of sleep.

Even with the help of Greek gods, I couldn't fall asleep right away. That damned pineal gland of mine was refusing to release even a small amount of the sleep-inducing chemical melatonin, due to my chip implant still shining its ever-lovin' light on that tiny gland. So I used the sleepless time to reflect on the day's events. Specifically, the successful transfer of one hard drive containing pirated petabytes of data from the Black Swan organization into the hands of one Air Force Col. Parker. I allowed the painful scene to replay on my memory screen:

The helicopter made a noisy appearance mid-afternoon, hovering over the grass carpet of the Enchanted Forest resort. A rope ladder emerged, and the colonel climbed down it onto the perfect green lawn. Leela was waiting for him, hard drive in hand. I watched and listened in through Leela's eyes and ears.

The colonel uttered very few phrases: "Birthmark on right scapula resembling state of Florida." "Uh huh," said Leela. "Tattoo of ankh on right inner thigh." "Um huh, yeah," said Leela, and handed over the hard drive to the colonel. He saluted, did an about face, and climbed up the rope ladder into the still-hovering chopper. From the doorway he waved and shouted over the rotor noise, "Have a nice day!"

I remembered floating in the spa's indoor swimming pool when I observed this little scene. At first I was furious, then simply jealous. How could anybody in the military, or the State Department, know such intimate facts about my wife's geography?

Wait a minute! That freakin' Mr. Anderson again. The "hero" who located my fair beauty in Davos. Oh, shit, I can't stand the thought of him seeing Leela naked, of him touching her beautiful skin, seeing her secret places, kissing her all over, sticking his… NO-O-O-O-O-O! A silent scream filled my brain.

Lying in bed, shivering, I quickly deleted the memory. I spooned the naked and softly purring Jill. The light in my head went out. Hello, Morpheus. Good night, cruel world.

We decided to take the back roads to Chickentown because of all the military checkpoints along the main highway. The alternate route is a Forest Service road, which is paved for about a mile and then suddenly becomes a pothole-ridden gravel road littered with huge rocks and other obstacles. Hacker was at the wheel, me in the passenger seat next to him. Everyone in the van was silent for the first fifteen minutes of the journey. When more than half of your crew is psychic, there really isn't much to say.

"Hey, look to the right, guys," Hacker said, breaking the silence. "The entrance to Palatki, those Indian ruins where we went into the portal. Wish we had time to stop and go through that thing again. Maybe I could get my psychic chops on too and join the rest of you."

"What's a portal?" asked Greta innocently from the back seat.

"It's kind of a doorway," said Leela. "A doorway into other dimensions. It takes you deep inside your being and gives you insights and information that aren't available in the so-called real world. The four of us experienced it couple of years ago. It was fun!"

"Oh, wow!" said Greta, sounding like a high school girl who'd just discovered kissing. "Could we stop there for just a few minutes? I'd love to try it."

"No time right now, Greta," said Jill. "Maybe another time. You know, I heard that there are people squatting over there. About a hundred people living among the ruins. No running water, and they're growing their own food. Also hunting rabbits. Eating anything that doesn't eat them first. Saving up rainwater. Survival...just like the Sinagua Indians who lived here six hundred years ago. *Sin. Agua.* Without. Water. Get it?"

"Got it, Jill, thank you very much!" said Hacker a tad sarcastically. He hadn't shown much emotion lately around losing his ex-girlfriend, but I detected some strong feelings in him regarding this issue. I scanned his mind and immediately tapped into sadness, guilt, and remorse, seasoned with plenty of anger. He didn't seem to understand that Jill couldn't tolerate his playboy ways, and he couldn't square that with the reality of the hot threesome that Jill and Leela and I seemed to be enjoying immensely.

Hacker also was carrying around no small amount of anger toward me. It slipped out occasionally. Still, he loved me. I was his brother beyond blood.

"Hey, Marty, I been wondering," said my friend. "When is that freakin' chip in your skull gonna dissolve so we can be equals again?"

"I dunno, man," I said. "The docs said it would be good for two hundred hours, just so we could pull off the operation in Davos. Now it's way way past that. Many days past that. And the power just seems to be getting stronger. I'm beginning to wonder...."

"I've got a theory, folks." It was Leela, leaning forward and putting a warm, tingling hand over my crown chakra. "Remember the Schumann Resonances, that singing we did in Davos at Black Swan Beta that put everybody to sleep? We tapped into that brainwave frequency, remember?"

"I remember," I said. "I was ommmming like my life depended on it. And I guess it did."

"We were singing at the frequency of the Earth's magnetic field," explained Leela to everyone in the van. "See, the Earth is a receiver of cosmic energy. It radiates this information outward as long-wave signals which we humans then receive via our spines and our craniums. Like an antenna, hmmm? So our antenna captures this information and sends it to the pineal gland, which transmits it to the pituitary gland, which is the master control center of the brain. Does that make sense? That's all I remember. I saw it in Wikipedia."

"And so...." I commented, dryly.

"And so the brainwaves we generated with our singing back at Black Swan Beta passed through Marty's pineal gland, where his implant is located, and amplified its effects. So maybe he'll retain his psychic abilities forever. Or occasionally he'll need a booster, and we'll sing to him again. If Marty joins us on baritone, we'll do three-part harmony. Ommmmmmm."

Everyone in the van joined in the om. Three times. Then we all breathed deeply together. And fell into silence again.

Half an hour later, Hacker was bouncing up and down in the driver's seat, yelling excitedly. "Hey, you guys, check it out! The highway is just up ahead! We're almost to Chickentown!"

The last few minutes of the ride had been horrific, the tortured shock absorbers of the van stretched past their breaking point. We could see the occasional vehicle moving along the divided road up ahead. We could also see what appeared to be a military checkpoint where the gravel road met the concrete highway.

And then we saw something else: a gate made of barbed wire stretched across our crummy road. There was no way to go around it. Everyone in our van moaned. Hacker cursed. Jill swore like a sailor. Leela shook her head in disbelief. Benny Bravo, who had been uncharacteristically silent during the trip, swore in Spanish.

"Let's ram it," I said, "just ram right through the frickin' thing and shoot across the highway."

"Yo, homies, let us crash the barricade like my bloods crash the wall down at the border!" said Benny, waving his fist in the air. "I can see a bunch of tents across the highway. *Vamonos, hombres*! We didn't come all this way for nothin'!"

Hacker agreed with us, and gunned the van's tired engine. "Let's do it!"

"Wait! Wait!" said Leela. "I've got another idea. We can't risk running into that checkpoint. There's a small army of trigger-happy soldiers just around the corner. Plus the barbed wire would rip our van to shreds."

"I can see it all happening, too," said Jill, who was a pretty fair clairvoyant. "It will be very ugly. Let's try something else."

"Hey, Marty," said Leela. "Remember what you did on that road from Davos to St. Moritz? That little psi trick where you lifted our car with mind power and saved our lives? How about you do that again and land us right in the heart of Chickentown?"

I turned around to face Leela, horrified by her idea. "Oh, sweetheart, I don't think I could do—"

"Yes you can," urged Jill. "Come on, we'll help you. Right, Leela? We pitch in and lift this meat wagon up and over the barbed wire and across the road and into the Chickentown parking lot. Okay? There's no time to think it over. Hacker and Greta, Benny, maybe you guys could close your eyes and visualize us already in Chickentown. Ready, Marty? On three: one, two, three, and—"

I concentrated, I focused, I gritted my teeth and madly massaged my third eye. I clenched my fists and screwed my eyes up tight. Nothing. Nothing at all. The van didn't move. I looked up and saw a small contingent of soldiers approaching. The others in our van saw them too; I heard a collective sharp intake of breath. The soldiers, wearing camouflage uniforms, pointed their huge combat machine guns at the van as they moved ominously toward us.

"Now, Marty, now!" encouraged Leela.

"Git 'er done, dude, get 'er done!" ordered Hacker.

"Go, man, go!" encouraged Benny Bravo.

"Please, Marty?" said Greta in a small voice.

Suddenly the van floated into the air; higher and higher, twenty feet, thirty feet, fifty feet. The soldiers on the ground broke formation and looked frantically for the van. To them, it had disappeared. Seventy feet, eighty, one hundred feet, still rising.

"How do you stop this thing?" I shouted. "Where's the brakes?!"

"I don't know!" shouted Leela.

"I have no idea!" shouted Jill.

Hacker instinctively slammed on the vehicle's real brakes, but that of course had no effect on our trajectory. My psi powers were in control. Actually, out of control.

When we looked down we could see the huge dimensions of the tent city, a beehive of activity, thousands of people. There was a stage where a band was playing. Nobody on the ground noticed our flying van. Higher and higher, farther and farther from the highway we drifted, away from Chickentown.

"Marty!" screamed Jill. "Do something! We are headed for Jerome!"

CHAPTER TWENTY-SEVEN

City of the Future?

Violating the law of gravity by flying over the Verde Valley in an aging Chevy van was not my idea of a good time. Still, it was a necessary maneuver; we all knew that. We knew there were risks. What we didn't know was how to control the beast. I focused my mind and found that I could control the vector, the direction of the van, as well as the altitude; but I had no control over the speed. The ride was getting bumpier by the second. The Mingus Mountains loomed just a few hundred feet away.

"Leela! Jill! See if you can slow this buggy down, okay? Concentrate!"

They did something, and it worked. The van slowed down and went into glide mode. I caused the van to swoop in low over Jerome, a tiny former mining town built into the side of a hill. Jerome was once a thriving center of sin and excess; now it is primarily a tourist magnet.

"Land this thing, Marty!" shouted Hacker, holding onto the steering wheel for dear life. "I can *drive* to Chickentown from here, dammit!"

"No way, Jose," I snorted. "We've come this far, and I'm gonna drop this baby right into the parking lot. Chickentown, here we come!"

Over everyone's protests, I guided the van expertly back to our destination, and in less than fifteen minutes we were hovering over the parking lot. The vehicle was almost noiseless, and no one on the ground seemed to notice. The parking lot was vast. I dropped the van right between a rusted Dodge pickup and a 1965 yellow Cadillac convertible. No one in the van said a word, but I heard a lot of sighing and heavy breathing. The engine was still running. Hacker turned it off, swearing to himself.

Chickentown is located about five miles from the western city limits of Sedona on the site of the city's wastewater treatment plant. For years we sent our human waste and ground up garbage and unwanted fluids and general detritus a-rushing to the treatment plant, where, through some alchemical miracle, it was transformed into drinkable water.

That worked well for years, until the water in Sedona wasn't flowing regularly anymore and the city defaulted on its bond payments for the plant and the whole place was closed down. Sedona's raw sewage, having nowhere to go, backed up into the sources from whence it came. Meanwhile, the plant had gazillions of gallons of treated water in storage, primarily in holding ponds that looked like clear blue lakes and in humongous storage tanks that looked like giant toilet bowls. This perfectly good water had for years been sprayed uselessly over three hundred acres of nearby open fields, creating a lush riparian habitat for creatures large and small.

A tent city sprang up in this location as the economy collapsed and desperation grew like a cancer.

The first settlers of the new city discovered and appropriated the pipes that would make the treated water available for drinking and other human needs. The ponds supported colonies of fish. The largest pond was available for swimming and boating and also served as a reservoir for drinking water.

All manner of fruits and vegetables thrived in the lush soil of the new city. One resident brought in a flock of chickens, which multiplied into the hundreds and supplied fresh meat and eggs and gave the tent city its name. In short, Chickentown was a huge success, a triumph of human ingenuity and engineering. It could have been, should have been, a kind of model for the City of the Future, a loving, sharing, supportive commune, a place of peace and happiness, a community of equals.

And it was. For about six months. Then human nature kicked in.

When our little group arrived at Chickentown, the place was a model of anarchy, greed, fear, and violence. Arguments and physical fighting were commonplace. Most occupants had gone tribal and divided themselves into various ethnic, religious and cultural groups. There were the atheists and anarchists and born-agains and Catholics and Jews and Mexicans and Protestants and New Agers and hippies and junkies and homosexuals.

Every group had its own little enclave. Most of the fights were over food and water. Money didn't exist. You bartered and traded and worked in the fields for your food and did your best to survive. Motorcycle gangs rampaged through the place, stealing whatever they could and selling protection and cheap drugs. Mexican gang-bangers strutted and postured along the narrow lanes and alleys, but were not taken seriously.

This was the scene our little group walked—or rather, flew—into. The population was about three thousand when we arrived. In spite of the atmosphere of danger and potential violence, the place had a feeling of celebration and what-the-hell spirit. Colorful tents were everywhere, as well as booths offering food, cheap clothing, prescription drugs, booze, speed, and marijuana. Massage parlors were everywhere, as well as closed tents offering exotic sexual delights and degradations.

It was like a giant circus: loud, rowdy, exploding with energy. There was no sign of police or authority figures. The leaders of Chickentown, both Sedonans—a former politician and a former Jeep tour operator—decided that the best way to mellow out the rowdy, restless populace was with daily rock concerts.

Our job was to entertain the masses with some kick-ass, danceable music. Jill had arranged our gig. We were one of the opening acts for the featured group of the afternoon, a sinister-looking bunch of heavy metal thugs called Foreskin.

Because we arrived a little late for the gig, there was no time for a sound check. We had already put on our costumes by the van: long hair wigs for everyone, dark glasses, ratty, hole-filled jeans, and Grateful Dead t-shirts. Greta dressed herself in Janis Joplin hippie drag.

The rickety wooden stage was about twenty feet wide, fifteen feet deep, and ten feet above the excited, murmuring crowd. Huge stacks of speakers and amplifiers bookended the playing area. Leela's borrowed drum kit glistened in the sun. We plugged in and dashed backstage for a quick briefing by Leela. Backstage was a tiny room where we huddled together in a tight circle in the dingy space with our arms around each other.

"Okay, guys," whispered Leela, "you know the drill, right? We do the rock and roll for about twenty minutes and get the mob dancing, then we do that techno stuff. The techno is basically bass and drums so it's me and Benny and the rest of you improvise the melody. Our job is to lure those Dakini girls up to the stage so we can nab 'em and take 'em with us. Jill will hit some notes on the flute that will bring the chicks to us without fail."

"Right," said Jill. "Harry the Handyman taught me this sequence of tones that will resonate with the crystals in the amulets the girls always wear. Kali gave the amulets to the Dakinis, and they can't be taken off. No one else will hear the tones. Except maybe you, Marty, you might be affected because of your implant."

"For chrissake, Jill," I protested, "what if your freakin' tones launch some kind of psychedelic trip while I'm up there cookin' on my keyboard? You know, the DMT thing they warned me about."

"Lucky you," said Hacker. "Just go with the flow. Give me a signal and I'll go all Jimi Hendrix on you with my guitar."

"And I'll go all Keith Moon on you, my brother," said Benny. "Wait, who was Jimi's bass player?"

Outside the tiny room, a roar punctuated by shouts and clapping was emerging from the audience like an ominous black cloud of sound. The crowd was getting ugly.

We hopped onto the stage, moved toward our instruments, and looked out at the mob. There were thousands of people screaming and shouting and waving fists in the air. "Let's go bitches! Let's go bitches!" they chanted.

I turned on my keyboard. I had the sound controls for our group at my fingertips. Cranking up the amps all the way to ten, I hit a power chord in B flat and we were off and running with Chuck Berry's "Johnny B. Goode." The crowd went berserk, screaming and dancing and slamming into each other. We played cover versions of faves by the Stones, early Beatles, the Doors. We jammed on old rockabilly riffs and killed with Jerry Lee Lewis tunes. Benny introduced his just-composed new rap song, "Show Me Ya' Paperz," which he called "a tribute to the State of Arizona." Greta took center stage, grabbed a cordless microphone, and did a dead-on impression of Janis Joplin singing "Piece of My Heart."

I looked up and saw that the thing was getting out of hand. The audience had turned into a giant mosh pit. Both guys and gals were ripping off their shirts and throwing them toward the stage. Many people writhed together on the ground. The sweet smell of marijuana filled the air. Two punks on chopped Harleys tried to bully their way through the crowd, knocking down several people in their path. The crowd quickly turned on the bikers, throwing them to the ground.

It was a monumental, apocalyptic sight. This is how the world will end, I thought. What I didn't see through all of our musical numbers was any of the three Dakinis. Neither had anyone else in our group, I learned with a quick mind scan. Leela had told us earlier that the Dakinis had fled to Chickentown after Goddess Kali split without warning. Now, she said, the girls intensely disliked each other and never hung out together.

We stopped playing suddenly on a signal from Leela. The mob froze in place. Leela gave us another hand signal and launched into a hypnotic drum beat, wilder than any drum machine.

The average human heart pumps at around seventy-five beats per minute. Leela was kicking it at, what, a hundred beats a minute? One-fifty? One-eighty? That's it. Leela cooking on the drums at three beats per second, enough to potentially throw the unwary citizen into cardiac arrest. Benny Bravo kicked in on the fret-less bass, thunk, thunk-a-thunk, thunka-thunk thunka-thunk thunka-thunk. Our audience suddenly shaped it up, everyone standing and moving to the beat, no more mosh pit, no more pushing and shoving. Hacker came in on lead guitar, high and sweet and supernatural, channeling Jeff Beck and Carlos Santana at their trip-piest. I played chords and riffs I didn't know existed.

Jill raised the flute to her lips and begin to wail. Greta gripped her mic and started screaming, a high, pure sound that made my scalp tingle. Jill's sound sud-denly disappeared, and I knew what was happening. Those mystery tones, off the scale, off the charts, were calling the Dakinis. In a space inside my skull the tones were bouncing and echoing and vibrating. I was fine with that.

I looked into the crowd and saw three figures making their way to the stage. They looked like hippie chicks of the Twentieth Century, peasant skirts and tank tops and beads—and, most important, those mysterious but vital amulets around their necks. One approached from the center, one from the right, and one from the left. They came to the foot of the stage, looking up at us with glazed eyes. They had called themselves Karma, Satori, and Chakra while employed at Kali's Tantric Temple. There, they had driven men mad with their addictive sexuality. Now, occupations unknown. Now, names didn't matter. They were obviously in a trance.

Jill gave a hand signal to the three and they clam-bered onto the stage, shakily making their way toward

Leela. There they stood, heads bowed, surrendered to the Psi Queen herself: my beloved wife. With another hand signal, Leela told us that we would end this so-called song in four bars. Jill and Greta, in close vocal harmony, trying to stay with Leela's syncopated techno beat, thanked the crowd for their enthusiasm.

"Thank you for having us/Now we gotta get on our bus/Fly away to a distant land/Be kind to each other/ Understand?" sang our two songbirds. We stopped playing music. The crowd looked mesmerized. No one moved, no one uttered a sound. It was eerie. We unplugged our instruments, surrounded the three Dakinis, hustled them quickly off the stage and into the tiny room behind the performance area.

Harry the Handyman had told Leela to get the crystals contained within the amulets in order to render the Dakinis helpless. "Let's get those crystals now, in case these three sexpots try to run away," said Leela. She pushed the girls together, grabbed Karma's amulet and telepathically invited Jill and I to hold the amulets of the other two. *Push the amulets together so they're touching,* Leela flashed. We did. The three Dakinis went limp and had to be held by up the rest of our team. A strange buzzing sound emitted from the amulets. A golden beam of light suddenly radiated from the amulets, and a small round crystal dropped into our hands from each.

"That's it!" said Leela excitedly. "Hold onto your crystals, guys, and we'll see what Harry has in mind. I have a strong feeling these amulets and the three

Dakinis together are the key to taking down Kali. Help me get these zombies into the van and let's get out of here!"

We put our instruments back into the van, stuffed the limp Dakinis into the cargo area, and took off. To save time and trouble, Leela, Jill, and I lifted the van skyward and floated it just above the deeply rutted road as we made our way back to the Enchanted Forest resort. Hacker occupied the driver's seat, but I was doing the steering with my mind. Jill and Leela supplied the power.

There was no time to waste. A mysterious being we knew only as Harry the Handyman would be waiting for us. Benny Bravo, apparently over his crush on the Dakini once called Satori, ignored her presence in the van and logged onto the Internet with his own Amigo. He told us with alarm that the environmental crisis had reached critical mass, worldwide. Our home planet, our Mother Earth, was beginning to turn, violently, against its human inhabitants. Leela connected with a State Department source and learned that Kali already was creating all kinds of mischief from Black Swan headquarters in New Mexico.

I squeezed the crystal in my palm. It was hot and pulsing. A showdown with Goddess Kali, a woman whose erotic heat I had once known a lifetime or two ago, was looming. I knew it wouldn't be pretty.

CHAPTER TWENTY-EIGHT

The Human Virus

The bus was waiting for us when we got back to the Enchanted Forest. The being known only as Harry the Handyman was there, polishing the huge vehicle with a rag. The bus was awesome, overwhelming; it seemed to glow and vibrate in the late afternoon sun.

Harry waved. "Hi, folks! Say hello to your new home! Come have a look. But don't take too long. You need to pack up a few things and get ready for our trip to New Mexico."

Harry seemed so jovial. He looked exactly as I remembered him from our meeting at Jill's house in Sedona: a little bent over, shabby clothes, an odd-ball out of his element, almost like a character from a Grimm Brothers fairy tale. When he took my hands in his, I remembered, I felt like I was hurtling through outer space.

Hacker took an instant dislike to Harry; that was obvious, from the sneer on Hacker's face to the ugliness of his judgmental thought forms. I looked at Leela and Jill, and they gave slight nods of agreement. For openers, my bro' didn't believe in anything remotely New Age, which included space aliens and UFO visitations. (We had all dropped hints about Harry's alien roots.)

Also, Hacker didn't like the looks of this greasy little character, and was outspoken about it.

"Who is this dude anyway, guys? Lemme get this straight: You want me to get on this vehicle with some character from Skid Row, drive all the way to Nowheresville New Mexico, and confront some madwoman and the head of Black Swan? You gotta be joking. The Hacker is outta here, folks."

He turned to leave, but Greta grabbed his sleeve and hung on tight. "Hacker, please! I'm going to be on the bus, and look, I put on my special Manolo Blahnik toe-candy sandals, just for you!" Greta obviously knew of her new boyfriend's weakness, and, at Jill's suggestion, wore her very special shoes in case her BFF balked.

Hacker looked down—way down, he is about six-three—at Greta's dainty feet. He had seen them before, but not like this. Greta had pushed an old fetish button. Hacker gasped, staggered, wavered.

"Mr. Hacker," said Harry, unexpectedly. He caught Hacker's eyes and held him for a long time, a full half minute. Hacker looked stunned at first, then he relaxed and his arms hung loosely at his sides. Suddenly he brightened. Harry had flipped him, but good.

"Okay, folks, I guess you need me on this trip! My computer expertise, my good looks, and my new friend Greta obviously has some big plans for me!"

That was the signal for everyone to run back to our rooms, quickly pack a suitcase, and hustle back to the bus. The three lethargic Dakinis were hustled into the front compartment of the bus by Benny Bravo.

Benny elected to stay behind to keep an eye on the fast-changing planetary crisis, and to keep us updated with encrypted Amigo communications.

We left the resort about five in the afternoon and headed up Oak Creek Canyon toward Highway 40 in Flagstaff. Destination: somewhere near Santa Fe. I figured the Dakinis had been ordered by Harry to drive the bus. I didn't stop to think that they were in a serious trance, limp, nodding off, and in no condition to do much of anything. Apparently, neither did anyone else in our vehicle. Nevertheless....

The bus was gorgeous, inside and out. The outside was painted a pale blue, overlaid with surreal versions of Sedona's famous red rocks: The Thunder Mountain-Coffee Pot Rock-Chimney Rock range on one side, and Bell Rock-Cathedral Rock on the other. On the back was a detailed and psychedelic portrayal of the Milky Way Galaxy.

The bus itself was about sixty or seventy feet long, a late-model super-beast produced by Mercedes-Benz. Inside, pure luxury. Black leather seats and mahogany built-ins throughout. A front section included luxurious driver's and co-pilot's seats, then three rows of two seats each, all black leather. This is where Benny, on Harry's instructions, installed the three still-dazed Dakinis. The front part was separated from the back of the bus by a half inch-thick wooden wall.

Next came a living room slash conference room, outfitted with black leather couches, a round oak table, a huge flatscreen TV monitor, wrap-around stereo speakers, and laptop computers everywhere. Beyond this room was a full kitchen with granite countertops, built-in everything, and the ubiquitous flatscreen TV. Next were two small bedrooms with queen-size beds and mahogany cabinets—and of course a TV monitor and wrap-around stereo. Two bathrooms followed, one with a shower and one with a real bathtub.

Finally, at the back of the bus, a tiny recording studio filled with digital synthesizers and sampling keyboards, a setup so advanced it made me salivate. Harry had told us that the bus formerly belonged to a famous English rock group. He winked, as if he was keeping a secret. We didn't ask him for details about the group or how he got the bus to the resort. Did he simply drive the bus down the heavily-patrolled streets of Sedona, through checkpoints and roadblocks, nervous cops and military and National Guard troops everywhere? Probably not.

Harry invited us into the conference room and we sprawled indulgently on the black leather couches: Leela and Jill, me in between them; Hacker and Greta, holding hands and seemingly attached at the hip. Harry the Handyman sat by himself in the full lotus position with closed eyes: a meditator, I thought, or perhaps a would-be guru. Who was this guy? *Be silent and listen,* Jill flashed. *All shall be revealed.*

He opened his eyes and looked for a few seconds at each of us with what I interpreted as compassion. I tried to scan his mind, but there was nothing there—no thoughts moving, no images, no memories.

"My friends," he said softly. "Your planet is at a cross-roads. I am here to help facilitate your transition to the next phase. Allow me to explain."

I looked at Hacker. He was still not happy. I scanned him: he was full of distrust, anxiety, anger. Harry's spell had completely worn off. Hacker didn't accept the concept of ETs; he didn't feel secure around psi people; and he was depressed about the dire state of the planet. A toxic combination.

I scanned Greta: She was filled with both fear and excitement. This was her first meeting with Harry, and his presence seemed to trigger her insecurities about the future. This seemed to be her usual state: excitement, fear. She had shared and survived a series of hazardous exploits with three psi daredevils, yet her Christian conditioning and childhood fears kept popping up.

"Just who the fuck are you, sir?" said Hacker, his voice trembling. "It's time you told us who you are and what you are doing here and what exactly you mean by 'the next phase.'"

"You are correct, Mr. Hack," said Harry. "I do owe you all an explanation. My telepathic friends here"—he indicated Leela and Jill and I with a sweep of his hand—"have a bit of an edge because they have tried to look into my mind. You see, I have no mind, not in the human sense."

"Then what the fu—" exclaimed Hacker, his face reddening. "Keep talking, dude," he said menacingly.

"Harry" seemed unfazed. "I am not a humanoid," he said calmly. "I travel inter-dimensionally. I traveled to your planet as an orb. I am—" long pause, deep breaths all around— "I am what you might call a shape-shifter. A metamorph; a therianthrope; a change-ling. I can change shapes at will. I am basically a very advanced microprocessor contained in a ball of energy. I am here on a very important mission, important not just for the residents of Planet Earth, but for the residents of this quadrant of your galaxy."

"Why?" shrieked Greta. I could feel her phasing into freakout mode. "What have we done to bring you here?"

"Let me explain, please," pleaded the alien. "It is obvious that the people of Planet Earth have some serious psychological problems. First, your race, the human race, is very suicidal. You want to self-destruct. This is due to your religions, your priests, your concept of sin, your politicians. Perhaps even a defect in your collective DNA. But your basic defect is a two-sided coin. You also have a deep-seated need to kill each other. And you have an innate need to destroy this beautiful green planet. The people of Planet Earth—how can I say this delicately—are very, very sick."

Hacker was outraged. "Who are you to judge us, you friggin' alien creep!"

"Please listen carefully, Mr. Hack, all of you. I will put it simply. Planet Earth is on the verge of a global suicide. You are killing your planet, and you are killing each other. That is your business. But your tendency for self-destruction—what that means to the rest of your solar system and to this portion of the galaxy, that is my business."

"What do you mean, Harry?" I interjected. I too was in the dark. I had been quiet up to this point, but I couldn't stay silent any longer. "What exactly are you talking about?"

"First, Mr. Powers, my name is not Harry. Not Harry the Handyman or any such nonsense. I do not have a name in the human sense. I have a number, similar to the IP numbers you humans use on your primitive networks. The Internet Protocol numbers, every computer in your network has one. My number is twenty-four dot one twenty-three dot two eight dot eighty five dot, well, you get the idea. If you need to call me a name, call me...call me Nebula. Yes. Nebula Jones. That's a good, solid name."

"Nebula," I said. "Has a nice ring to it. Meaning a cloud of gas and dust in outer space, eh? Maybe a distant galaxy. Nebula, nebulous...."

"Good, Mr. Powers, you get the idea. Now. Our computer models show that—"

"*What* computer models, Mr. Nebula Jones?" said Hacker, his voice rising. "Who runs the computer models that you are talking about?"

"Good question, Mr. Hack. I will get to that eventually. Your galaxy, which you call the Milky Way, has a governing council which is headquartered near the galactic core. These entities monitor the progress of all your occupied planets. Your planet, Terra, which you call Earth, has been red-flagged for the last twenty of your centuries. You have been watched, not because of your warlike ways—again, that is your business—but because of your potential impact on the well-being of the entire galaxy."

"Wait a minute," said Leela, speaking up for the first time. "You mean this Planet Earth, this little backwater planet at the far edge of the Milky Way, is a threat to the entire galaxy? How could that be? We haven't even started to explore other planets in our star system. We've spent all of our money on weapons and wars."

"Precisely. And that is a big part of the problem. Our computer models indicate that by the Earth year 2018—much sooner than expected—a global nuclear conflict on your planet will trigger a violent shock wave of energy which in turn will trigger a massive explosion of the Earth's core. The Earth will blow into millions of pieces and become space junk. "

"So what!" sputtered Hacker. "Why should you and your effin' governing council care a rat's ass if we blow ourselves up or not? As you said, it is none of your effin' business!"

"Oh, but it is, in a very important way," said the alien, brushing the question, and Hacker's explosive temper, aside. "When Earth goes nova, which is a virtual certainty, it will leave a large hole in space. This hole will affect the orbits of all nearby bodies in space, because the gravitational pull of Earth will be gone. The orbit of the fourth planet in your system will go askew, and the Earth's moon, with nothing to orbit around, will go crashing into the fourth planet."

"Wait just a damn minute, Mister Spaceman," snarled Hacker. "I doubt if—"

"One minute please, sir. Allow me to finish. The fourth planet and its moons will go careening into space. This in turn will trigger other orbital anomalies in your solar system, eventually affecting every planet and every moon. Our models show that in less than one thousand Earth years every planet and every moon in your system will have crashed into your yellow star, your sun."

"Fine," said Jill, obviously agitated by this news. "Fine. Then our sun can have a picnic and eat the entire solar system. Again, so what? Will the Universe really care?"

"Perhaps. Perhaps not the entire Universe, but at least your closest galaxy and certainly every star system in this quadrant of the Milky Way. You see, your star, the sun, is a fiery nuclear furnace. As it consumes every piece of matter in your star system, it too will go careening off into space and possibly collide with nearby stars such as Sirius, Betelgeuse, Rigel....

"This could trigger a chain reaction that will affect all of the stars and planets in this quadrant. And possibly the entire Milky Way galaxy. Furthermore, these anomalies could hasten the Milky Way's collision with its nearest neighbor galaxy, Andromeda. This collision is predicted to happen in three billion years. That is as it should be. But when Earth goes nova, it could cause the collision to happen in less than a million years. A disaster on a cosmic scale. All caused by your insignificant planet's rush to commit suicide."

Greta, who had been carefully holding in her feelings, exploded with near hysteria. "But— but— but— it's not our fault! We didn't cause all the wars! Not everyone wants to commit suicide or— or— cause the planets to crash into each other," she sobbed.

"Look at it this way," said Nebula calmly. "Earth itself is a diseased organism. It is infected with a deadly virus that is slowly eating away at the planet's ability to sustain itself. I call this disease the Human Virus. If this condition is not corrected, the planet will be destroyed. Actually, the Earth itself will self-destruct and trigger the series of cosmic disasters I described earlier. This is unacceptable."

Hacker stood up, enraged. "And what exactly do you plan to do to stop the disease, sir? Kill us all? Wipe the planet clean of humans? Destroy this civilization that has taken thousands of years to evolve?" He started moving slowly toward the alien, his huge hands balled into fists.

Nebula also stood up. As we all watched, transfixed, he began to change shape. His Harry the Handyman garb seemed to melt away as the hunched over, shabby persona was replaced by a tall, stunning, broad-shouldered, golden male with long hair, rippling muscles, killer abs, and…naked.

Migawd, look at that schlong, thought Jill. *Who's he supposed to be? John Holmes, the late porno star?*

No, no, flashed Leela, *he looks more like some legendary god, maybe Mahavira, one of the deities of that obscure Indian religion, Jainism. Mahavira supposedly never bothered to wear clothes and only took food once a year. He was on the scene twenty-five hundred years ago, around Buddha's time. Hey, Jill, that is a pretty good-sized organ, yah.*

Pretty good role model for a dimension-hopping ET, eh? flashed Jill. *I guess he needed a more macho presence to deal with Hacker's rages.*

Nebula's new persona, topped off with a strong, ruggedly handsome face, sculpted cheekbones, aggressive chin, piercing golden eyes, and full, pouting lips, was pretty overwhelming. Also, his voice had changed, from a slightly quavery, nerdy voice to a rich, booming baritone. "Please sit down, Mr. Hack," he said. "I will explain everything.

"Leela, you are correct: I have morphed into a character out of your religious mythology, a god from thousands of years ago. Our computer models indicate that this identity will enable us to perform more successfully than we could as Harry the Handyman. I said please sit down, Mr. Hack."

He picked up several sheets of paper from a folder on the oak table. "Now. We do not intend to kill anyone. You humans can do that on your own. No, we have another plan worked out, based on our computer models."

Hacker collapsed into a black leather couch, intimidated and subdued. "Those freakin' computer models again," he muttered sullenly. "Please do tell us, master, what do those sacred computer models tell you? And could you put on some pants or something?"

Nebula ignored him. "What I hold in my hand is the solution to all of our problems. I intend to present this paper to a worldwide audience via television, radio, streaming holo, Internet, global wireless, mobile phone, texting, every form of communication possible on your planet. I would like all of you to hear it first, in case you have any suggestions. Because you five seem to have more intelligence than the typical retarded human."

"Well, what the fuck is it, pal?" sneered Hacker.

Nebula waved the papers at Hacker. "I call this my manifesto. Maybe you clever people can come up with a more colorful name."

"I've got it!" I piped up. "How about...The Alien Manifesto!"

CHAPTER TWENTY-NINE

The Ultimate Solution

Our bus was zipping along at a high speed—a *very* high speed—as I glanced out the big picture windows in our cozy little compartment. We were on Interstate 40 about two hours out of Flagstaff, barreling toward the New Mexico border. In normal times there would be huge semi-trucks clogging the highway, delivering their precious cargo to American cities. But these were not normal times. The semis were nowhere to be seen. Only the occasional passenger car or pickup truck which we left in our dust.

"Those Dakinis must be experienced drivers," I said to our little group. "Whoever is at the wheel is really kickin' ass."

"No one is at the wheel, Mr. Powers," said Nebula Jones in his new baritone voice.

"Then who the fug is drivin' this fuggin' bus?" demanded Hacker. His vocabulary was becoming ever more creative as his anger level escalated.

"I am. I am driving the bus, Mr. Hack. By remote control." The alien paused for effect. "The three young women in the front compartment are still in a trance state. Look at the TV monitor to my right."

313

The monitor switched on. It was an eerie picture. The three Dakinis were slumped over in their seats, chins on chests, nodding out. The driver's seat was empty. The steering wheel moved slightly, on its own, to adjust to road conditions. Our bus hurtled onward at a now-frightening speed.

A cloud of silence pervaded the cramped space now occupied by five humans and a…what? The powers of the entity we now knew as Nebula Jones seemed unlimited and untouched by our laws of physics.

"My friends," began the alien, reassuringly. He stood tall, towering above us. His huge organ was out of sight, below table level. He looked around the oak table at us.

"My friends," he repeated. "I ask you to clear your minds and hear what I have to say. Time is very short."

I tried to scan the alien again. There was no mind there to scan, just some white space and a faint crackle of static.

Forget it, Marty, flashed Leela, *this guy doesn't have a mind, only a link to a supercomputer that is orbiting the Earth right now. I think I've cracked their code. It makes our binary code look like a kiddie game. Jill, Marty, this dude's got some pretty heavy stuff to tell us. But—"*

"Thank you, Mrs. Powers," interrupted the alien, who had been monitoring Leela's transmission. Leela looked embarrassed. Jill rolled her eyes. I squirmed at this invasion of our privacy.

"You are good, very good. Very clever. But please let me explain the situation. There are many levels of data emanating from our satellite that only I can access and evaluate. When the time comes, I will incorporate that data into my Manifesto, which I intend to present to the citizens of your planet, as I mentioned earlier."

Nebula Jones sat down in his leather chair and folded his hands together. My mind, for unknown reasons, went to a mental picture of his big, muscular bum merging with the rich leather. Jill picked up this thought and nudged me with her elbow, hard.

"You are by now aware," said Nebula Jones, "that we are traveling to the nearby state of New Mexico for a confrontation with the being you have known as Goddess Kali and who now calls herself Big Mama Lakshmi, named, presumably, after a prominent goddess in the Hindu firmament. She apparently added the 'Big Mama' name to trigger an emotional response in other humans, probably fear. This entity possesses frightening powers and has been using these powers to trigger cataclysmic events on Planet Earth." The alien paused and took a deep breath.

"Big Mama," he continued, "can affect the weather. She causes earthquakes and volcanoes, hurricanes, floods. Just by using the powers of her mind. Advanced telekinesis. And it's our fault. It's our fault that she has such powers."

"WHOA!" roared Hacker. He had been silent for several minutes. Now he was in full voice, eloquent and unambiguous. "Wait just a minute, Mr. Alien. You just said 'it's *our* fault,' meaning that you and your buddies did something very stupid and created this monster.

Out of a woman who we all knew as Aura Adelstein. A former New Age sex queen and half-assed Sedona psychic who my good friend Marty here was hosing at one time and…whoops!"

Embarrassed, and more red-faced than ever, Hacker knew he had given away one of my deepest, darkest secrets. At least I thought it was a secret.

Hacker clapped a hand to the side of his skull and banged it several times. "Oh, Leela, Marty, I'm so sorry, I gave it away, I didn't mean to—"

"It's all right, Hacker, I've known all along," said my wife in a soothing voice. "You can't fool a psychic, you know." I felt Leela's warm hand covering mine. I scanned her mind and found a montage of memories of her former friend Aura. She recalled my weak lies and cover-ups of our sordid affair. She remembered how Aura had changed radically after one memorable stormy night. She gave my hand a warm squeeze.

"Watch," said Nebula Jones. "Then you will understand what has happened to your former friend Aura."

A hologram formed over the oak table. The images were about three feet high. The holo depicted that memorable night on Bell Rock, which began with a tremendous, unseasonable electrical storm, featuring torrents of rain plus a dramatic lightning and thunder show. Leela was not yet in the scene; when the incident in question actually occurred, she had disappeared behind some huge rocks. I watched an image of myself and Aura, standing out in the open, both drenched and wild-eyed, as bolts of lightning flashed around us and strange multi-colored orbs filled the air.

A lightning bolt struck the skull of Aura and clearly traveled through her body, followed by a brightly-colored orb, sending her writhing to the ground. Leela appeared from behind a rock. At this point the hologram froze.

"Look here," said the alien, pointing to the lightning bolt which glowed brightly inside Aura's body, which now appeared as a dark silhouette. The glowing orb was just behind the lightning bolt, clearly visible.

"This is the reason for our current dilemma. The bolt of electricity is actually the transport mechanism for the orb, which was implanted in the body of Ms. Adelstein. The orb contained the essence of my colleague. As I told Mr. Powers during an earlier meeting, I came to Sedona with a partner via inter-dimensional travel. My partner is a fussy sort, and it arrived on Bell Rock early, a few milliseconds before I arrived. It— he— and I triggered the unseasonable electrical storm and deluge of orbs. This is a common method of transubstantiation where we come from."

"Trans— what? Get to the point, asshole," snarled Hacker. "What is all this about?"

"Quite simply, my associate made a serious mistake. He was supposed to merge with another human. The other female on Bell Rock that stormy night. The orb was meant for Leela Powers."

The hologram flickered out.

My jaw dropped. I looked over at Jill and Leela and saw their eyes widen. Hacker looked like he was having a stroke.

"What do you mean MEANT for Leela?!" demanded Hacker, pounding on the table with a closed fist. "And who is this 'partner' you keep talking about?"

"My colleague, another trans-dimensional consciousness. We were sent to Earth to fix a problem: humans. Our assignment was to penetrate a high-vibrational, advanced human, a low-ego or no-ego person, to merge with the consciousness and physical manifestation of that human, to enhance its psychic and physical abilities, and to use the human to bring about a dramatic shift in the consciousness of your entire planet.

"We searched our databases for the most advanced humans on your planet, and found three: One, an autistic genius, a Siberian dwarf, had been locked away in a mental institution for twenty years; the second, an Indian guru from Benares, lived his life in the Ganges River and refused to come out. The third was Leela Powers. She was our best choice to save your planet.

"Our plan was that with her enhanced psychic abilities and spiritual enlightenment, she would start a movement that would change and uplift the consciousness of your species. A movement that would spread love and understanding and awareness. A movement that would neutralize the prevalent human need to destroy and self-destruct. Call it Plan A. Goddess Leela.

"We thought it was a great plan. Unfortunately...."

The alien paused, looked down at his folded hands.

"What do you mean, 'unfortunately'?" I raged. "What went wrong with your crazy scheme? Why was my wife passed over for an oversexed, overweight, half-baked psychic?"

"My associate—let's call it Cosmo, ah, Cosmo Kincaid—is that a good name? Cosmo became confused in the intensity of the thunderstorm and entered the, uh, the physical manifestation of your Aura Adelstein, merged with her brain and body, became one with her, and enhanced her being with its limitless powers.

"Unfortunately, because of Miss Adelstein's enormous ego and unstable mental state, our entire project has been sabotaged. As she became the self-anointed Goddess Kali, this woman became aware of her abilities and used them to build a spiritual and paranormal empire, even going so far as to bring the dead back to life.

"Now," he continued, choosing his words carefully, "you see the ultimate result of the human ego gone berserk, totally out of control. Big Mama Lakshmi is now a threat not only to your planet, to your solar system, and to its quadrant of the galaxy, but to a large swath of the Universe."

"So why doesn't this Cosmo character just escape from Big Mama and leave with all of those powers," asked Hacker. "Why doesn't the dude just slip out through her rectum or some other orifice and give us all a break?"

I couldn't help laughing at the mental picture this created. I scanned Leela and Jill and they shared the same mental picture: a roly-poly orb with a tiny head peering out of a giant rectum framed by huge, tree-trunk thighs. Both of my fellow psychics wore huge smiles.

"Why?" asked the alien, exasperated. "Why? Because Big Mama Lakshmi has learned how to control Cosmo. She has broken him into small pieces and has him stored in several places within her rather large physical structure. She has learned how to access his enormous power and use it willfully while essentially keeping him a prisoner. He cannot escape. I am no longer able to communicate with Cosmo because of his confinement."

Leela, who had been watching, with a bemused smile, this little scene play out, finally decided to speak. "I am certainly flattered by your choice of me as the goddess who could save the planet, Mr. Jones. Too bad it didn't work out. But it looks like we've got a real problem on our hands now. Hopefully, you and Cosmo have a Plan B."

"The real problem we have now involves time, Mrs. Powers," said Nebula Jones. "We are running out of it. Before Cosmo's, uh, miscalculation created Goddess Kali and then Big Mama, Planet Earth already was in trouble because of environmental damage. We had several years to work on that problem. Then Black Swan came on the scene and shortened the timeline by several years. Now Big Mama has reduced our window to a matter of weeks, if that."

"Then what do you propose to do, Mr. Jones? It looks like a hopeless situation," said Greta sadly. She had been sitting nervously next to Hacker, twisting and pulling on her short hair. She had been sullen and silent during this whole discussion.

"There are several things we can do—*must* do—and all carry huge risks," said Nebula Jones. "First, we must take down this Big Mama entity. That is of paramount importance. And then we must go after the Black Swan Galactic organization, which has already created havoc around your planet and still poses a threat to the future of humanity. We suspect that right now, Big Mama is meeting with Wolfgang Maximus, the chief executive of Black Swan, at the organization's ranch in New Mexico."

"Whew!" I exclaimed. "That's quite a challenge you've got there, Mr. Spaceman. Now that you and your boyfriend have totally fucked things up for us earthlings, what do you plan to do about it?"

"We are all in this together, Mr. Powers. You and your friends are here because you all have skills which can be used to deal with the present crisis. And because you can help prepare the citizens of your planet for the ultimate solution, which is contained in my manifesto, here." He again picked up a sheath of papers and laid them down on the oak table.

"Say what?" said Hacker, incredulously. "What exactly do you mean by 'ultimate solution'? And how do we fit into your crazy, effin' plans?"

"Please try to relax, Mr. Hack. You seem to be on the verge of a breakdown, and we need your strength and wisdom in the hours ahead. Number one: Let us focus on neutralizing the Big Mama entity."

"How?" asked Jill. "Sneak up on her? A surprise attack? She can probably sense us coming from miles away. And she could probably do some terrible mischief to stop us in our tracks."

"This is true," said the alien. "She does have frightening psychic energy at her fingertips. But we have one weapon, actually three, that can neutralize her. That would be the three females in front of our bus who you call the Dakinis. Remember, they were once disciples of Big Mama when she was known as Kali. Each Dakini wears an amulet given to them by Kali, supposedly to give them abilities such as telekinesis and ESP. The amulets did that, as long as the Dakinis were within psychic range of Kali, but the amulets also allowed the goddess to monitor and control them."

"So?" I said sarcastically. "How does that apply to our present situation?"

"First, the amulets now are virtually useless, for the Dakinis. But...they can be used *against* Goddess Kali! Do you remember the amulets? Gold and silver with strange markings and the legendary Eye of Horus? Take a look."

A hologram formed on the oak table displaying an enlarged version of the amulets. Sure enough, strange markings and that penetrating eye. A caption beneath the image: "Ancient symbol of strength and wisdom... spiritual guidance, insight, protection from evil."

Nebula Jones turned off the image and continued. "I studied the markings. They are an ancient code for stopping evil forces. These amulets are probably thousands of years old."

"As my friend Marty said, 'So…?'" said Hacker, with sarcasm equaling mine. "Let's skip the superstitious bullshit and get down to the source code here. What is the point of all this?"

"Patience, please, Mr. Hack," said Nebula Jones. "These amulets, when held closely together by the Dakinis, touching actually, *have the power to neutralize Big Mama.* Do you understand? The crystals that our three psychics removed from the amulets are a key part of the process. This process is extremely powerful. Each of you, Leela, Jill, and Marty, must hold a crystal securely in your hand."

The alien sighed, looked into the faces of our psi trio, and seemed close to showing emotion for the first time, as he presented his case. "As our three psychics and I direct the energy of the amulets and the crystals toward Big Mama, we will be sending a stream of anti-matter into her body. This anti-matter will release my associate, Cosmo Kincaid, from the grip of Big Mama, and hopefully reassemble his atoms back into his orb structure."

"Holy shit!" said Leela, uncharacteristically.

"That's the theory, anyway," shrugged Nebula Jones.

"But how can we ever get those three bitches together to pull this off?" I asked. "They hate each other. They attack each other at every opportunity, physically and verbally. They can't even stand to be in the same space together for more than a few seconds. I don't know why they haven't ripped each other to pieces already."

"They have been in a trance for hours, sir. As long as you keep those crystals in your possession, you can control them—turn them into passive slaves, if necessary. When we engage in Operation Shiva Baby, they will be in a deep hypnotic state and will obey my commands."

"Operation Shiva... Baby...?" I said.

"Yes. And for further protection against whatever weaponry Big Mama throws at us, we will all chant the mantra *Om Namah Shivaya* as we approach her. This chant will create a force field which is designed to repel any weapon up to a twenty-kiloton nuclear bomb."

"Howzat....?!" said Hacker. "You want us to chant some Hindu gibberish and create a force field? Do I look like a whack job? You ain't gonna get me to chant some—"

"Hacker, please, listen to the, uh, man," begged Greta. She had removed her thick horn-rimmed glasses, which gave her a distinctly bookish look, and without them she was actually quite beautiful.

"Mr. Jones," Greta continued, "what happens when Mr. Cosmo Kincaid is removed from the person of Big Mama Lakshmi? Will she lose her powers? Will she go back to being just a regular person?"

"Our computer models say that she will no longer be a threat. She may suddenly became no more than an overweight ex-psychic with an uncertain future."

We humans fell into silence again, eyes closed, absorbing and processing all that the alien had told us.

Hacker was the first to pipe up with one of his irreverent questions.

"Your computer models have been wrong before, buster," he began. "But tell us, dear alien, about your *ultimate solution*. You sidestepped my question when I asked you earlier. It sounds a little *Hitlerian*, don't you think, folks?" We all nodded in agreement.

Nebula Jones again picked up his sheaf of papers. "This is the address I plan to deliver to the people of earth. This will answer all your questions. I would appreciate your feedback." He cleared his throat.

"People of Planet Earth," he began tentatively, looking around the table. "You have nearly destroyed your beautiful home. You cannot stop killing each other. Your environment is in ruins. Now your actions threaten the entire galaxy and beyond. The Planetary Council has decided that steps must be taken to stop your reckless march toward planetary self-destruction. Therefore—"

"Whoa, whoa, whoa!" interrupted the Hacker. "Is this a joke? You must have stolen this from some cornball sci-fi movie from the Fifties. Get serious, dude."

"This is no joke, Mr. Hack. Please listen carefully." Now the alien looked ominously around the faces at the oak table. "Therefore, in approximately thirty days, Planet Earth will be dropped into a small, sentient black hole. Our computer models indicate that—"

"WHAT?!"

"How can you—"

"What the fu—"

"And then—"

"WAIT A MINUTE!!!"

Leela was the last to shout in protest. Of the black hole idea, that is. She was into that supercharged energy space that could bring any man—alien or human—to his knees.

"Let's say you could physically drop our planet into a—what?—*sentient* black hole? Do you know what a black hole does, Mr. Jones? Just what is your fucking *ultimate solution?*" My wife was unusually livid.

The alien jerked and seemed to be knocked backward about half a foot. "Mrs. Powers. All of you. Listen carefully. The sentient black hole, which we have carefully programmed with computer power you cannot even imagine, will take Terra, your planet, back in time and give humanity another chance. We did this once before on a planet in the Andromeda system. It worked perfectly."

"Just how far back in time are you talking about?" asked Jill. "Hundreds of years? Thousands? Do we have to rebuild the pyramids? Or go back to our caves and reinvent the wheel and start over?"

"Nothing that extreme, my friends," said the alien soothingly. "Only back a generation or two. Has anyone here heard of a person named Tiffany Tattlebaum?"

CHAPTER THIRTY

Linchpin of the Cosmic Plan

"TIFFANY TATTLEBAUM?!!?" we all shouted in unison, causing Nebula Jones to cover his ears with his ginormous hands. "What does she have to do with anything?" I shrieked. "She nearly brought down our government. Why is she even in your wild scheme to save the Universe?"

"My friends," said the alien calmly, "every civilization in every galaxy is at the effect of certain events that change or create history. A fly can land on someone's nose, and...poof! There goes the solar system. You could say that humanoid life is but a tapestry of accidents, coincidences, synchronicities, random acts, cosmic events. Chance. Luck. Fate. Serendipity. Call it what you will."

What the fuck is he talking about? I transmitted to my fellow psychics at the table. *Where is he going with this cosmic babble?* I didn't care if the alien was eavesdropping.

I think he's going to make a case for how Miss Tattlebaum's talents changed the course of history, transmitted Jill. *I'd better jump in here and keep this dude on message.*

"Mr. Jones? Hear me out, please," said Jill in her no-nonsense voice. "Let's say Tiffany Tattlebaum's affair with President Clinton changed the course of history. Clinton is impeached, the presidency is tainted, Al Gore loses by a hair, and the Bush-Cheney regime swaggers in. Now, Gore would have been the environmental president and global warming would have been his number one issue. Instead, the other guy wins, our country is attacked, we start unnecessary wars, America becomes a fascist state, the world economy collapses, we've got an ecological catastrophe on our hands.

"Then take all of these events to the illogical extreme, which would describe what is happening right now on our planet. America's downfall triggers a worldwide crisis. Chaos and panic ensue. And so on and so forth. You plan to send us into the past to make it all go away. So please enlighten us, sir: If Miss Tattlebaum triggered this whole series of events, what does your sentient black hole intend to do about the fact that she exists in the present? And that her whole life's history has created a path through time, influencing people and events?"

"Good questions, Miss Appleton. The entry on the world stage of the Bush-Cheney regime did indeed disrupt the psychic equilibrium of your planet. I am not a political scientist, nor do I care about the details of individual lives. But Miss Tattlebaum is what we call the pivot point. Her actions indeed changed the course of history. She is not to be blamed for subsequent events, because blame is irrelevant and childish. No. What we must do is slightly change the course of *her* life. We have studied her past, and fed the information into our supercomputers. Now—"

"And your computers can tell your black hole exactly how to change the path of her life, with all of its random events and the people she meets and her first boyfriend and the twists and turns of her life?" asked Hacker. "How is that possible? I'd like to meet the dude who wrote the code for this program."

"Very simple, actually, Mr. Hack. Tiffany Tattlebaum grew up in a wealthy family, attended Beverly Hills High School around Earth year 1990, and met her first boyfriend there. Then she went on to exclusive private schools and worked her way into a key job at your White House at the age of twenty-one. That's when the pivotal events started unfolding.

"We will send the Earth back in time to approximately 1990. In the new, custom-designed past, Miss Tattlebaum will take a class in Eastern religions, meet a handsome young man who will teach her yoga and meditation, and she will decide to become a Buddhist nun. After high school, she will move to a monastery in Nepal, over her parents' objections, live a quiet life of service, and never meet Mr. Clinton. The rest, as they say, is history."

"That is the craziest shit I've ever heard," said Hacker, shaking his head. "You can't mess with the past like that. Damn!"

"We are not 'messing with the past,' Mr. Hack. We are simply making a small, necessary adjustment in the time-space continuum. Our assignment is to save this quadrant of your galaxy from chaos and destruction due to the irrational behavioral patterns of the residents of Planet Earth."

"Fascists," muttered Hacker. "I told you guys that this dude is a Nazi."

"You see, by re-creating the past," said the alien, ignoring Hacker's insult, "we are creating a new future for the people of Terra—a future that will be less about war and more about honoring the ecosystems of your planet. A future where the planet's resources are shared by all and greed is disdained. A future where—"

"A beautiful vision, Mr. Jones," interrupted Leela, "but a little idealistic. Are you saying that just by shifting the karma of one sexy woman that everyone on the planet will be affected?"

"That's right, Ms. Powers. There is a Cosmic Plan, you know. Miss Tattlebaum is the linchpin of the Cosmic Plan. Our computer models are very clear on this."

Jill jumped in, excitedly waving her arms. "Okay, Mr. Alien, what about our memories? Our memories are stored in our brain cells, you know, and in our blood and our bones. You and your friend are messing with some powerful forces. Are you sure you know what you're doing?"

"Indeed we do," said the alien. "You see, when your planet is dropped into our sentient black hole, all memories from the time of the—let's just call it the Singularity— from that moment back to the moment in the past when time starts over again, all memories will be deleted by the black hole's sophisticated software. That includes every person's cellular memories in both body and mind."

Hacker was still seething. "Black holes in space eat whole stars, dudes. What goes in never comes out. Is this what Mr. Jones has in mind for us? Or is his whole rap just a bunch of bullshit? Some whacko fantasy? And what the fuck is a *sentient* black hole? Think about it, folks."

No one had an answer, and silence descended again on the oak table. I scanned some minds quickly. Everyone, including me, was not eager to lose twenty or twenty-five years of our lives and have to do it all over again. It seemed like being reborn into a new body after death and having to learn all of life's hard lessons one more time.

"Bathroom break!" shouted Leela, standing up and stretching. "Come on, girls," she said, signaling to Jill and Greta. They followed, both fingering their hair. Hacker got groggily to his feet and staggered to the men's, not looking at me. I stayed to have a few minutes of peace and quiet. Nebula Jones sat silent and unmoving, eyes closed.

I stared out the bus window, watching the miles fly by, the dull, brown scenery no more than a blur. Briefly I held a picture of Tiffany Tattlebaum in my mind. In many ways she reminded me of Aura Adelstein: big girl, big boobs, great insinuating eyes, radiating sexual energy, loves oral sex, giving and receiving; Tiffany and Aura merged into one naked, hungry she-beast, coming for me, closer, closer....

"Hey, Marty, that's a pretty wild thought form you're projecting!" It was Jill, catching me off guard, as she and the other two ladies swept into the cramped compartment. I must have blushed bright red; my cheeks burned beyond my control.

Aren't you violating the psi code of ethics, Jill? I flashed. I was serious. *I thought such things were just between us psychics.*

I caught your fantasy too, Marty, flashed Leela, *in the ladies room. It was like a bright, flashing hologram. It was pretty wild. I guess Jill couldn't control herself, right Jill?*

Jill nodded solemnly.

You owe me one, Jill, I flashed, grinning. *No, make that two: first, a good spanking, I give, you take. Then a good hour of oral—you give, I take. Okay?*

Pretty good fantasy, Marty. Okay, I'll think about it. An hour...?

Hacker didn't come back for about fifteen minutes. I knew he'd been smoking his primo weed in the john as soon as I saw the goofy grin plastered on his face. Then the smell of good ganja hovered around his clothes, radiating throughout our cabin. His mood was a lot lighter as he sat down next to Greta and draped an arm around her shoulders. This helped to lighten the mood of our whole group.

Our tour bus zipped along Highway 40, past Gallup and around Albuquerque and onto Interstate 25. Santa Fe was an hour up the road at normal speeds; we would do it in half that time. In fact, the trip from Sedona to

Santa Fe normally takes about eight hours. We were on schedule to do it in five.

Just outside of Santa Fe, a thought occurred to me.

"Mr. Nebula Jones, a question for you. Why are you helping us *now* to take down Big Mama Lakshmi—to *try*, anyway—and go after the head of Black Swan Galactic? This is a dangerous mission that we may not survive. Why not just let things take their natural course and then drop us into your friggin' black hole?"

"Because if things take their natural course, Mr. Powers, the Earth will implode much sooner than we had anticipated. *Much* sooner. That would be very unfortunate. So now our rendezvous with the black hole is in a little less than thirty days. The goal is to keep your planet in one piece until the rendezvous. The danger will be most acute in the next forty-eight hours."

"Please explain yourself, sir," said Leela. "I sense that there is something about this whole caper that you are not telling us."

"You are correct, Ms. Powers," said the alien, exhaling a breath, nearly a human sigh. He paused a beat. "My dear friends, are you aware of the location of Black Swan Galactic headquarters in America? Their ranch is located near the tiny city of Abiquiu, a ranch where the famous American artist Georgia O'Keefe lived for many years. If you were to look at a map of this state called New Mexico, you would see that the ranch is very near the city of Los Alamos, forty-five miles, to be exact. Do you know about Los Alamos? It is also known as

Atomic City. It is where the atom bomb was invented, and later the hydrogen bomb.

"The scientists who work there are still developing new weapons that will kill more people more efficiently. We know for a fact that there are still huge stockpiles of nuclear materials at Los Alamos, and other fissionable materials that are very very dangerous."

"So?" challenged Hacker, becoming hostile again. "So what? Is Big Mama going to nuke us all?"

"Not exactly, Mr. Hack. Please, try to relax. Now, I want all of you to prepare yourselves for the next piece of information." The silence in our compartment was deafening. A moment of truth—maybe THE moment of truth—had finally arrived. We collectively braced ourselves for it. I held my breath, closed my eyes.

"Black Swan Galactic, at its heart, is basically a religious organization. Fundamentalist Christian. Most of its members, and all of its leaders, believe in the Biblical prophecies in the Book of Revelation. The end of history, the last days, the end times. Apocalypse. They see the ecological disasters that have befallen Terra, not including the ones they themselves have caused, as the wrath of your God, fulfilling the prophecies in Revelation. They see *themselves* as the Second Coming; they don't consider themselves Jesus Christ, they are all *christs*, gods unto themselves, who have the gift of eternal life. Remember Eternal Flame? Their space station is their Heaven."

"Jesus H. Christ," I muttered.

"And to fulfill the prophecies—here comes the bad news—your Planet Earth must be destroyed. Incinerated. Fire and brimstone. And that is where your Big Mama Lakshmi comes in."

"What?" said Jill incredulously. "Big Mama destroys the world? I think you are exaggerating her abilities, Mr. Jones."

"Not really, Miss Appleton. Here is their plan. First, within the next twenty-four hours, Mr. Wolfgang Maximus will board a rocket ship with ninety-nine members of his organization and be transported to the Black Swan space station, which is in full operation and is now orbiting the Earth.

"In another twenty-four hours the second group of one hundred Eternal Flame members will board a second rocket and land on the space station. They need at least two hundred humans to create a viable gene pool to carry out their madcap scheme to live forever and explore the galaxy.

"This must not be allowed to happen. They must be stopped."

"But why bother to stop 'em?" asked Hacker. "Let the muthafuggas go! They took half the planet's money, so what? There's lots more where that came from. The Wall Street hotshots did that to the world in oh-nine, took our money and ran. And got away with it. Let these assholes play their little games in space—good riddance—and the rest of us will try to repair our planet."

"Here's why we can't do that, Mr. Hack," said Nebula Jones. "Once the second rocket ship has departed, the Armageddon prophecy must be fulfilled. That is where Big Mama comes in. The plan calls for her to trigger a series of earthquakes using her powers of telekinesis. The epicenter for these quakes will be near Los Alamos. The quakes in turn will set off several nuclear weapons now residing at the labs of Los Alamos."

"That is *more* of the craziest shit I've ever heard," mumbled Hacker. He closed his eyes and held his head in his big hands.

"Can she really do that?" piped up Greta, alarm and disbelief in her eyes.

"She can indeed do that," said Nebula Jones. "These high-yield nuclear bombs will reduce the entire Southwest of your America to rubble, and release a toxic cloud of radioactivity that will cover the entire western hemisphere of your planet within a few hours. This will in turn cause a global panic and trigger the worldwide nuclear war that will cause Planet Earth to go nova and...well, you know the rest. This is why it is up to us to stop Big Mama Lakshmi now before their plan can be carried out."

"Insanity," I said. "Fuckin' insanity. How do you know all this, Mr. Jones? Do you have spies? A team of psychic infiltrators? A mole inside Black Swan headquarters? How?"

"We have our ways, Mr. Powers. We have our ways of knowing what the key players in your little Earth psychodrama are thinking, plotting, and scheming.

Remember our orbiting satellite. That is all I can tell you. We know that Mr. Wolfgang Maximus is this very moment at the Black Swan ranch in Abiquiu, meeting with Big Mama and with his top advisors, planning the next steps in their plan to escape from this planet and then destroy it."

"And Big Mama. Does she plan to blow herself up in this nuclear holocaust, or...?" asked Leela. Obviously she still had some feeling for her former friend.

"She plans to ascend, literally, perhaps take another form, and ascend to the orbiting space station, where she would assume her position as head goddess," explained Nebula Jones. "Meanwhile, today, Wolfgang Maximus is scheduled to leave the ranch and board a high-speed helicopter which will take him to the Black Swan space-port, which is located about three hundred miles to the south near the White Sands missile range where, coincidentally, the first atom bombs were tested by your American military. Perhaps we can also stop Mr. Maximus and short-circuit the whole plan. Perhaps not."

Everyone issued a collective "whew!" This was too much information, even for the expanded consciousness of our psi trio.

"I have one more question, sir." It was Jill, her eyes wide. "What about this so-called Alien Manifesto you were talking about earlier? What do you really intend to do with it? Are you serious about broadcasting it to the entire population of the Earth?"

"Of course I'm serious, Miss Appleton. "The people of Earth need to know why their planet is in such a dire situation as well as the potential consequences of their actions. They also need to know what must be done to prevent a cosmic catastrophe. Thus, they will be told they are being dropped into a black hole, and that they will be sent back in time in order to have a second chance."

"That would be a big mistake, buster," said Hacker, belligerent once more. "If you tell the poor ignorant masses of this planet what is going to happen to them, they will totally freak out. The situation will be much worse than it is now. Millions of people will come looking for you with pitchforks and shotguns. There will be mass panic across the planet. I can see it now: Billions of people looking for a way off this planet before doomsday comes."

"What about that, Nebula Jones?" I asked. "How can the smart money avoid being sent back in time? What if some of us were orbiting the Earth in a satellite or something when the Singularity Day comes?"

"Good idea, Mr. Powers, but it won't work. You see, everything within the Earth's atmosphere, which extends about ten thousand kilometers from the planet's surface, will be, uh, recycled. There is one way out, however. There is one option that would transport certain individuals about one thousand years into the future."

"Please tell us how, O Alien," I said in a sing-song voice, laughing to myself. This was becoming more ridiculous by the minute.

"A handful of people on Terra, those possessed of highly advanced psychic ability, could travel a thousand years or so into the future by entering the wormhole that will be created when the black hole is activated. Two of you in this room, Leela and Jill, would have no problem in making this jump. You, Mr. Powers, are a borderline case, and there would be no guarantees. You might disintegrate during the procedure, or you might not."

"I'll take my chances," I said, going along with the joke. "But what will this planet be like a thousand years from now? Got any clues?"

"Life is a gamble, Mr. Powers. As the poet said, take your best shot. The black hole or the wormhole. Which will it be?"

I gulped, and went silent. The bus rolled on.

CHAPTER THIRTY-ONE

The Great Battle

The city of Abiquiu is no more than a tiny speck on the map, in the middle of New Mexico's nowhere lands, a landscape empty and forbidding, dry, endless plains framed by stark, naked mountains. A vast, sun-baked emptiness where the horizon never seems to end. Big sky country.

After zipping around the curves of Highway 84 in our sleek, driverless tour bus, we arrived unannounced at the Black Swan ranch. We were greeted by a gate that was almost a cliché in Western folklore, two tall wooden poles with a crossbar at the top, a sign hanging from the crossbar that announced BLACK SWAN GALACTIC RANCH with the abstract black swan logo and a sleek rocket ship blending into the background. No fence, physical or electronic, blocked our way.

"The ranch used to be owned by a church group," said Jill, who had done some research during the bus journey. "When the American economy collapsed, Black Swan took over the bank that held their mortgage, foreclosed the church group on some phony pretense, and moved in. One report I read says there are at least fifty Black Swan people living at the ranch, including their leader, Wolfgang Maximus."

"Good work, Jill," I said. "What else you got? I'd like to know what we're walking into here."

"Well, one blogger says they are all strung out on that eternal life drug, you know, that EMC-2. And all are members of the Eternal Flame. Mostly men, all jacked up on testosterone and aggression, all waiting their turn to be transported to their orbiting space station. These creeps bring in desperate young women from Santa Fe for recreation, feed 'em and give 'em a few dollars, then send 'em back on the daily bus that brings in the next batch of amateur hookers."

Our driverless bus came to a stop. "To be continued, citizens. Time to move out of here and look around." It was Nebula Jones, who had been moving about the bus restlessly. He had finally put on a pair of tan trousers and a white, long-sleeved shirt. He looked like a business executive on holiday.

We piled out of the tour bus and walked around on the hot, dusty earth. This was the first time the bus had stopped since we left Sedona. Nebula Jones opened the front door, woke up the three Dakinis from their long trance, and ushered them outside. They shook off their cobwebs and stumbled around in little circles, confused and angry, and immediately started complaining.

"Where the fuck are we?" screeched the Dakini formerly known as Karma. "How did we get here? You fuckers kidnapped us!"

"Hey, man, I really got to pee," said another of the girls to no one in particular, the one I recognized as the former Satori. "Where's the ladies room, you assholes?"

"Me too!" shrieked the third, the supersexy Chakra, who I had once taken a fancy to.

"Inside, inside!" insisted Nebula Jones. "Use the back door! Restrooms are right there!" Karma and Satori dashed inside the bus.

"Fuck it," said Chakra, who dashed behind the tour bus, raised her long skirt, dropped her drawers, squatted, and let go a long yellow stream that we watched with a mixture of horror and fascination. The stream kicked up the brown dust and created little pools that shimmered in the bright sunlight.

"Nice group of ladies you got there, Mr. Jones," said Hacker with a smirk. "Where'd you get these nasty bitches? Are these the brave warriors who will lead us into battle with their precious amulets? Good luck, everybody." He laughed, a hollow, mocking bark that gave me the creeps. I didn't bother to scan my friend, but I sensed that he had something dangerous lurking in the back of his cortex.

We stood around in a tight little group, surveying our situation, Chakra hovering on the outside of the circle. I looked up at the entry gate framing the entrance to the Black Swan ranch. Security cams, at least seven of them. A satellite dish. A holo scanner mounted on a nearby cell tower.

"We are being watched," I announced. "Big time."

"No shit, Sherlock," growled Hacker. "It doesn't take a mind reader to figure that out."

My friend was leaning against our bus, frowning, his arm around Greta's slender shoulders. He had barely spoken to me the entire trip. In fact, he had been seething for much of the journey, barely able to control his anger. My occasional scans of his cranium during the trip were scary, revealing a boiling cauldron of brain chemicals surging through his overheated synapses.

Actually, I couldn't blame him for being angry. For one thing, he was still very hurt and pissed off that Jill had dumped him over a year ago. Greta, his present girlfriend of convenience, may have been attractive in a nerdy sort of way, and wise in the ways of computers and high-tech, but she was no match for the vivacious, brilliant, sexually adventurous Jill. Hacker was also extremely jealous of my own relationship with Jill, and with our kinky psi threesome.

Lastly, he was nearly berserk with resentment that I—as well as Jill and Leela, plus our alien friend—could now read his most intimate thoughts, feelings, memories, fantasies, whatever was happening inside his head. Hacker was a very private person, loathe to show too much feeling or to share what was going on inside. He may have been a high-tech genius, but he was also very closed, an old-school male with chauvinistic attitudes toward women and competitive attitudes toward men. These qualities were irrelevant in the New World Order of Impending Doom.

"Listen, Marty, this place really creeps me out," said the Hacker. "How about if Greta and I stay here and handle recon. Think our alien friend will go for that?"

"Not hardly," I said. "We need both of you, good buddy, to help create the force field to take out Kali. We need you to chant with us."

"Me chant?" said Hacker incredulously. "Marty, read my lips. No, better yet, read my thoughts."

His thoughts said, and his moving lips expressed the same sentiment, FUCK YOU! AND FUCK THIS WHOLE—

His thoughts dissolved into dust as a ghostlike voice resonated over an unseen speaker system. It was wrap-around sound plus. The voice said:

"I am the great Mother Goddess of Creation. Surrender to the Goddess now. Fall to your knees in supplication. Surrender to the Goddess and you may be spared."

The disembodied voice repeated the words, again and again, in an unearthly echo. It was Big Mama's voice. We covered our ears. Nebula Jones suddenly emerged from the back of the tour bus, holding a Dakini by the nape of the neck with each hand. The two young ladies, both looking a little frazzled and ragged from the long bus journey, were snarling insults at each other.

The alien pushed them rudely through the front entrance of the bus. Chakra followed without being asked. All three assumed their seats and began bickering immediately. My own two ladies, Leela and Jill, looked at each other with mock horror.

"Let's go, everyone," shouted Nebula Jones to our little group. "Back on the bus. It's time for our rendezvous with Big Mama Lakshmi."

"At least do us all a favorite, dude," sneered Hacker, "and put these three hellcats back in a trance so we don't have to listen to them."

"Just as soon as we get underway. All I have to do is touch their third eye and they're gone," said the alien.

Jill flashed a message to Nebula Jones: *Do the Dakinis know the nature of this mission? Do they know why they're here?*

Nebula Jones: *The three of them hate Big Mama because she took away their powers back in Sedona and threw them back on humanity's scrapheap. Before Kali, they were a sex worker, a stripper, and an escort girl. Now they are just tramps living out their bad karma. They would love to take revenge on their former goddess. This is their chance. They know we are on the way to a showdown with her. They don't know yet that the amulets they wear have enormous power. Fortunately, they will be in a deep trance when we confront Big Mama.*

Leela and I intercepted this exchange, sent at the speed of thought. We smiled at each other and got on the tour bus. I squeezed her hand as we got in and helped her through the door with a solid pat on the ass.

Leela: *If we survive this thing, Marty, I've got a big surprise for you when we get back to Sedona. Remember that if things get rough out there.*

Jill, listening in: *Hmmmmm. Count me in, kids. All this danger makes me horny.*

Me: *The two of you are dangerous. I hope my psi powers don't go bye-bye. I'd be lost without 'em.*

Beyond the gate of the Black Swan ranch, our bus rambled along a bumpy gravel road that took us through the wild landscape of Northern New Mexico, awesome granite and sandstone rock formations providing a backdrop for the surreal terrain. About half a mile in, red rock formations cropped up out of nowhere.

"Funny how this place reminds me of Sedona," said Leela.

"Yeah, the red rocks plus there is some kind of powerful energy here," said Jill, awestruck.

Big Mama's disembodied voice went on in a continuous loop: "I am the great Mother Goddess of Creation. Surrender to the Goddess now...." Echoing off the rocks, the voice, a near-baritone that sounded like it was run through synthesizers, was ominous.

Our bus rolled on, driverless, deeper and deeper into Black Swan territory. It was creepy. My two psi lovers shared my feelings of vulnerability and dread as we rolled toward a showdown with...what?

The bus stopped, "Here we are!" announced Nebula Jones as he led us off the bus. "Don't forget our chant. We need it to create and maintain our force field."

"I can't chant some bullshit words without knowing what they mean," said Hacker. "What is this about, anyway, this chant?"

"It's not the words, sir, it's the vibration and the energy field created by the sounds of the words," patiently explained the alien. "These sounds are described in the ancient texts of India. This is the Shiva chant, Shiva, the creator and the destroyer! Please join us in this, Mr. Hack. If only one of us does not give it one hundred percent, our force field could collapse, allowing

Big Mama's weapons, whatever they are, to penetrate our shield. This could have disastrous consequences."

I did a quick scan of Hacker's mind, and what I read was alarming. He was thinking seriously of sabotaging our mission. His mind was full of doubt and scorn. He didn't believe we could pull this off.

Leela and Jill were into his mind too. *Duly noted,* they thought in unison. *It's Nebula Jones' party,* flashed Leela. *All we can do is watch how he handles it.*

"Let us practice our chant," said the alien. "All together now: *Om Namah Shivaya. Om Namah Shivaya. Om Namah Shivaya.*" He sounded it out, syllable by syllable. Slowly our little group got the rhythm and the pronunciation. We sounded pretty good. Even Hacker got into the flow.

We were outside the bus, standing behind a little knoll that the alien had selected as a sort of bunker. About a hundred yards in front of us was the main building of the Black Swan Ranch, a pueblo-style structure made of logs and bricks. And there she was, standing in the middle of the porch, arms folded, like a camp leader ready to greet the new arrivals: Big Mama Lakshmi.

"I can hold off her attacks for thirty or forty seconds," said Nebula Jones, "maybe a minute. Then we must have our force field in place."

She looked huge from a distance, at least three hundred pounds. She wore a golden robe, just as I had last seen her image in holo form at Benny Bravo's home in Sedona. Her puffy face displayed a frightening expression of power and destructive rage. Her arms were outstretched, fingers extended, pointing at our little enclave. The eerie soundtrack continued, "I am the great Mother Goddess of Creation. Surrender to the Goddess now...."

Nebula moved swiftly, arranging his little battalion on the hard, rocky soil as we prepared for the great battle: The three Dakinis in front, standing side by side with one hand on their amulets, their arms tightly linked at the elbow. In the next row, the psi trio, Leela, Jill, and I, standing shoulder to shoulder, each clutching a crystal from the Dakini amulets in our left hand. Nebula Jones had asked us to hold the crystals in order to stabilize the Dakinis, who were in a deep trance.

Behind us, the weak links, Hacker and Greta, holding hands. And behind everyone, the entity we called Nebula Jones had suddenly taken on a new shape: the Egyptian god Horus. In his new form he was huge, more than seven feet tall and rippling with muscles, naked to the waist and wearing black tights. His head was that of a bird of prey, a falcon, perhaps. I fought to suppress a wave of laughter when I first saw the alien's new incarnation. Jill whacked me with a hip and I regained control of myself.

Meanwhile, Nebula Jones, who didn't bother to explain his new persona, had already started the chant. "*Om Namah Shivaya. Om Namah Shivaya. Om Namah Shivaya.*" We all joined in, feebly and tentatively at first. I looked up at Big Mama on the porch of the ranch house; she seemed frozen in space as her extended fingers continued to point at us, looking like weapons. Maybe our alien friend really was holding her in place.

"Louder!" beseeched Nebula Jones. "Louder, please! And faster!" *Om Namah Shivaya.* Louder. Faster. We were all screaming it now, at the top of our lungs. Finally the force field began to form. I could feel it as a kind of crackling energy that smelled like burning plastic. It was invisible and transparent, but when I extended my arm it ran squarely into an immovable force, a kind of psychic wall.

"That's it, that's it!" yelled Nebula Jones. Suddenly the air was filled with pale blue bolts of electricity from Big Mama's direction. Each bolt hissed wildly as it came our way, then bounced harmlessly off our force field. It was working! "Keep chanting, people, keep chanting!" urged the alien.

We continued with renewed energy. "*Om Namah Shivaya. Om Namah Shivaya....*" Dancing in place, jumping up and down with the energy, celebrating our rejection of Big Mama's deadly weapons. And then I heard a foreign sound, like foreign words, inappropriate words, not in the rhythm and definitely not in the flow.

"*Shiva ram, Shiva om,* kiss my ass and let's go home." It was Hacker, my dear old friend, who was shouting out his own message, trying to sabotage our mission. His shouts nearly drowned out our chanting.

"Mr. Hack, what are you doing?" screamed the alien. "What on earth are you doing that for? You could weaken our force field! Please continue with our chant!"

Hacker ignored him and continued his own personal chant, even louder. "*Shiva ram, Shiva om*, kiss my ass and let's go home."

I heard a sharp cracking sound, like glass breaking or hard wood splintering. Suddenly our force field became visible, took on a rectangular shape and a pale, silvery greenish-blue color, shimmering; call it electric blue. There was a blinding flash, and something hit me hard in the middle of my forehead. My Third Eye. I crumpled to the ground, dizzy and disoriented.

"Marty, Marty, what happened?" cried Leela and Jill in unison. "Are you all right? Are you wounded, or...." Each of them grabbed me by the arm and helped me to my feet.

"Don't stop chanting! Don't stop chanting!" cried Nebula Jones, then he amped up the volume of his own chant. "If you stop, Big Mama's energy bolts will continue to penetrate our force field and kill you all! Keep chanting, everyone!"

Somehow I managed to continue the chant, but something was very wrong in my head. Something was missing. Oh shit. Oh no. My psychic powers were gone. The light had gone out.

"Don't worry about it, Mr. Powers!" said Nebula Jones/Horus. He knew what had happened, obviously by tuning into my panicky thought process. "I will fix you when we have taken out Big Mama! Meanwhile, everyone keep on chanting!" He grabbed Hacker by the shoulders, spun him around, and got into his face with that big falcon head.

"Mr. Hack, if you continue to sabotage this mission, I shall have to neutralize you. Do you understand? Now, turn around and continue chanting. Please!" Hacker meekly obeyed. You don't mess with the god Horus.

The chanting continued. The force field held. Nebula Jones made a sudden announcement: "The time has come, ladies and gentlemen. Time to confront Big Mama and strip her of her powers. Keep chanting. I will now move the Dakinis into position in front of our force field and ready them for the attack."

Which he did, quickly and efficiently, then shielded them with his huge physical form. Big Mama launched her energy bolts at this vulnerable little group, but the alien easily deflected them. "Now, ladies, now," he shouted to the Dakinis. "Put your amulets together, let them touch, and aim the lot at Big Mama. Put your heads close together. That's right. Don't be shy."

They were still in a trance, which was fortunate. If they had been awake, they would have been bickering and probably smacking each other. Instead, they meekly obeyed. I watched through the force field, which was again transparent and invisible, intact, holding. When the three amulets came into contact they seemed to lock together, as if magnetized. A soft golden light emitted from the Dakinis and began to spread outward.

"No!" shouted the besieged Big Mama Lakshmi. "No, no, no! Stop! Stop! Listen to me, Dakinis, listen to your goddess!"

Her deadly beams of energy had stopped. She raised her arms skyward. Suddenly a bright red beam of light shot out from the fused amulets, directly toward Big Mama's heart. She staggered backward. The red beam then swept over her body, from her head to her chest and to her ample belly. Nebula Jones must have been guiding it.

The chanting had stopped and our force field had dissolved, irrelevant. Our team watched the unfolding drama, breathless and speechless.

The red beam paused at Big Mama's loins, then swept down to her feet, and back over her entire body again. A very strange cry came from her lips, a moan, a keening, a sound of dying, a sound of total exhalation, of total exhaustion. She began to collapse, although collapse is not the right word. It looked like she was imploding, like her life force was draining away. She appeared to be *melting* as she slowly crumpled to the ground.

"The Wicked Witch of the West," murmured Greta.

But Big Mama Lakshmi didn't exactly melt. She lay on the porch floor on her side, twitching and jerking as if having a seizure. We moved in closer. She was foaming at the mouth. Her eyes were wide and wild. She continued to thrash and twitch like an android coming to a bad end. Then she lay still, on her back, her huge belly still heaving, her golden robe riding up her tree-trunk thighs, her eyes wide open.

Something was emerging from her bloated body: It looked like a small white cloud. "It's an orb," whispered Leela. "The orb is leaving her body. Her powers are gone. Finished."

"That's right," agreed Nebula Jones. "My colleague, Cosmo Kincaid, has finally escaped the prison of that woman's body. Now we can resume our program to save the galaxy. But first, observe." We watched transfixed as the orb gradually morphed into a white dove, spread its wings, and flew in circles above our little group. The Dove of Peace? Or were the aliens simply in bird mode, now, what with the falcon-like head adopted by Nebula Jones?

Greta suddenly shrieked, "Look, on the porch, behind Big Mama! I've seen that man before. In Switzerland!"

A tall, gaunt man in leather pants, vest, fancy boots, and cowboy hat, had been watching this spectacle from a doorway. My psi powers were gone, so I had no idea who it was. I suddenly felt helpless, ordinary, clueless.

"It's Wolfgang What's-His-Face, the head man of Black Swan Galactic," shouted Jill. "There's a chopper behind this building waiting to take him away. To the launch pad, you know, to their orbiting space station."

"Right," said Leela. "Big Mama was supposed to create a distraction so he could slip away unnoticed. Guess it didn't work out, eh?"

The man slipped through the door and disappeared into the house. The helicopter engines fired into life. "There he goes!" cried Jill. "I'm gonna stop that asshole!" And she jumped onto the porch, lithe and athletic as hell, and disappeared through the door into the ranch house.

"Jill! No!" cried Leela. "Stop! Don't go there! We'll get him later!"

"Don't bother," said Nebula Jones. "I already know what's going to happen. We have to let these events play out without interference."

"What do you mean?" demanded Leela, who could see what was happening inside the house through Jill's eyes. And feel what Jill was feeling as well. "Those horny bastards in there are holding her down and someone's coming with...oh, no, the chloroform! He's putting the chloroform rag over her...oh shit, she's out already. Marty! Marty, where the hell are you?"

Leela was freaking out, her body language unfamiliar and kinda scary. Her hands were twitching crazily as her bewildered mind tried to make sense out of what was happening. She seemed disoriented. I rushed to her side, but with my psi abilities shut down, the best I could do was hold her trembling body close to mine.

"They're carrying her out to the helicopter now, Marty," she whispered hoarsely in my ear. "Why would she do something as nutty as this?" She turned to Nebula Jones. "Mr. Jones! Nebula Jones! Please do something to stop this! You have the power to make things happen. Stop them, please," she pleaded.

"I can see what is happening, Ms. Powers. Your friend Jill is already on the helicopter, a prisoner. Let her go."

"*Let her go!*" cried Leela. "How can you just let her go? These people are crazy!"

The Black Swan helicopter was in the air and already headed south. To the waiting rocket and its launching pad. My heart sank.

CHAPTER THIRTY-TWO

Jill in Space

Soon we were in hot pursuit, heading south in a helicopter that had been commandeered by Nebula's colleague, Cosmo Kincaid, recent occupant of the body-mind of Big Mama Lakshmi and the source of her power. Nebula explained that the liberated Cosmo had flown to nearby Los Alamos in his white dove form, assumed the shape and attitude of an Army colonel, hypnotized a few security people, and "borrowed" a helicopter from the Air Force installation in Atomic City.

The chopper must have ranked among the fastest and most technically advanced on the planet. But the mood inside it was grim, to say the least, an emotional disaster. Leela couldn't stop crying; Hacker held his head in his hands, obviously wracked with guilt; Greta wavered between paranoid hysteria and paroxysms of laughter, her short-term memory completely wiped out. And I, feeling clueless and retarded without my psi powers and expanded consciousness, stared mutely into space.

Nebula Jones was calm and contained as he piloted the chopper over the brown New Mexico landscape at high speed. Cosmo Kincaid, now returned to his white dove persona, perched nonchalantly on

Nebula's right shoulder and seemed to be napping. Jill, the other member of our little team, was of course missing, having committed a totally un-Jill-like rash act by going after the head of Black Swan Galactic and getting herself captured, chloroformed, and spirited away in a Black Swan helicopter.

We had left Big Mama Lakshmi behind, still writhing, twitching, and foaming at the mouth, stripped of her awesome powers. We also left the three Dakinis at the ranch, still in a light trance, ordered by Nebula Jones to keep an eye on their former goddess in case she tried to escape. To insure that none of the fifty or so Black Swan personnel still at the ranch couldn't flee, the alien set up a force field around the perimeter of the property.

Leela had somehow managed, through wracking sobs, to send an encrypted message to the State Department regarding the situation at the ranch, and to suggest that they send a contingent of FBI agents to the scene to arrest everyone still on the property, including one overweight ex-goddess. Leela also managed to transmit the wireless ten-digit code that would allow the Feds to disable the force field and bust the bad guys.

As our chopper hurtled across the open sky, I finally summoned the energy to speak up. "What is going on here, Mr. Jones?" I demanded. Admittedly, it was a little weird talking to an alien with a falcon's head. "Why is everyone on this chopper, except you and your fucking bird, that is, an emotional basket case?" I was resting both hands on Leela's shoulders, trying to calm her down and get her centered. I had never seen her like this. She sat in the seat in front of me in the six-passenger helicopter, softly sobbing and mumbling something about Jill.

"It's basically simple, Mr. Powers. When your friend Hacker broke our chanting pattern and triggered a small rift in our defensive force field, some of Big Mama's energy bolts penetrated our shield. You knew that immediately because you were knocked to the ground and your psychic abilities were compromised; the light shining on your pineal gland was snuffed out by the blow to your head from an energy bolt.

"All of the humans behind the shield were affected, and all of you sustained a form of brain damage. The effect on Mrs. Powers and the others was more subtle, and took some time to manifest. I believe the damage occurred in their limbic system, that part of the brain usually associated with human control of emotion and behavior. Some of you are displaying the symptoms of damage to the limbic system, such as inappropriate crying or laughing, rage, fear, anxiety and depression. The damage to your own brain occurred in a different area, more toward the center of the organ."

"Just lucky, I guess," I said.

The alien was silent. The white dove spread and fluttered its wings, turned its head around to look me in the eye, then settled down.

"So can we be fixed? Or are we all stuck in this condition forever? After all, it was you who got us into this mess. Can you do something to help us?"

"As I said, Mr. Powers, it was your friend Hacker whose misbehavior caused your present condition. And, to be perfectly frank, it was the misbehavior of the people of Earth—all of you, collectively—which caused your planet to be in its unsustainable condition. Yes, I can probably fix you and your companions. Unfortunately, I cannot fix your troubled planet. The damage is irreversible. Now, please close your eyes and be silent."

In seconds I felt his large, cool hand on my forehead, then his powerful fingers massaging my Third Eye. I breathed deeply as the familiar feeling of expanded consciousness returned. Slowly, slowly, I was filled with pure energy and light. The babble of others' thought forms returned, like a whispering waterfall, and it was an untidy chaos: my poor wife, confused and distraught; Hacker, racked with self-condemnation; and Greta, a hysterical mess talking to herself in tongues.

Nebula Jones visited the others one by one, putting both his powerful hands on the crown chakra of each person for a minute or two after quieting them down. The chopper was apparently on automatic pilot; the white dove had taken up a position on a small shelf above the pilots' seats.

When he was finished, we all fell silent. There was nothing to discuss.

"I'm sorry I can't help your friend Jill remotely," said the alien minutes later. "I am sure the damage to her brain caused her to commit uncharacteristically rash acts. Perhaps I can help her when we reach our destination."

"And that would be..." probed Leela, tentatively. She had returned quickly to her "real" self, quick, sassy, and self-assured.

"The Black Swan spaceport at the White Sands Missile Range," said the alien. "America's largest military installation, thousands of square miles, desolate, mostly desert, most of its facilities now taken over by Black Swan operatives.

"The takeover was easy. Most of the US. military is now on the streets of your cities, trying to maintain order. Those military types who remained at White Sands were easily bribed or persuaded to leave by threat and intimidation. We are well on our way to the Black Swan launch site now."

We were at least an hour behind the chopper that had transported Wolfgang Maximus, his security detail, and a lass named Jill to their secret destination.

The Black Swan launch site was no secret to our two aliens. They used a powerful GPS device that homed in on the energy trail of the other chopper, and tracked it across the pale blue sky, across mile after mile of bleak desert landscape and endless fields of white gypsum sand dunes called the White Sands National Monument. At the southern end of this national park is the White Sands Missile Range, where the United States government has been secretly testing missiles, rockets, and laser weapons systems for decades.

"Look down," said Nebula Jones, "but look quickly because we don't want to be detected. I don't think

Mr. Maximus is expecting us, but I don't want their radar to pick us up."

We arrived at the launch site. What we saw, right in the middle of sand dunes, scrawny vegetation, and scorched brown earth, was a bunch of small wooden buildings arranged around a huge, spectacular launch pad. A mighty spacecraft array rested on the pad, apparently copies of the rockets and orbiting shuttles that the Americans had used for years to carry out their expensive but senseless missions.

Nebula Jones landed our helicopter several miles away in the middle of an endless sea of sand dunes, assuring us the dunes could prevent radar detection. But just to make sure, he set up a magnetic field around our chopper, basically making us invisible.

"Relax for a few moments, friends, and watch this," said Nebula Jones as we settled into the comfortable seats of the chopper. A huge, flat-screen video monitor unfurled in front of the pilots' section. We had a clear view of the launch pad and the lettering on the rocket being readied for blast-off: BLACK SWAN GALACTIC III.

"What happened to Galactic One and Two?" piped up Hacker, suddenly alive and kicking again.

"The organization has been conducting unmanned orbital test flights," said the alien. "This is the real thing. There are about a hundred Black Swan members on the spacecraft, mostly men but a few females. Several of them have been trained in space engineering and technology. The captain of the vessel is a former astronaut. Oh, and your friend Jill is also on board."

"Wh-a-a-at?" said Leela. "Of course she's on board, you idiot! She's in this situation because you allowed it to happen! Now maybe you can tell me why I can't establish a connection with her!"

Leela, I can see the situation through Jill's eyes, I flashed. *She is on that ship and unable to move. They must have her strapped in. But I can't scan her mind, not at all.*

I know, darling, flashed Leela, *I tried too. But we've got to get her off that space-thing. And soon. Otherwise she's going to be part of the breeding farm for a bunch of crazy drug-addled supermen living on a space station two or three hundred miles from Earth.*

"Synaptic derangement," said Nebula Jones calmly. He of course had been listening in to our private telepathic conversation. "Her mind is still in a deranged state from the energy bolts that leaked through our protective force field. Black Swan operatives are keeping her drugged. Her mind is very foggy right now. Please do not attempt to communicate with your friend. The Black Swan people have software on board that can read and interpret human thought forms."

"What do you expect us to do, Mr. Jones?" howled Leela, "just sit here while our friend gets shot off into space?"

"Please don't worry, Mrs. Powers," assured the alien. "I have a plan. Meanwhile, please watch the monitor. Our satellite cameras catch every detail, and will also follow the orbiter into deep space."

We watched. We were appalled. The launch pad was a beehive of activity. Men in white uniforms ran around frantically, checking the launch site for defects and preparing the rocket for liftoff. A voice sounded over the loudspeakers: "T minus two minutes...."

"What does that beast run on, anyway?" spat Hacker. "Liquid hydrogen? Oxygen? High risk of exploding. That is so early twenty-first century. How long before they are in orbit?"

"Please calm down, Mr. Hack, and I will try to explain. The twin solid rocket boosters that launch the craft, each producing more than twenty million horsepower, actually run on vortex energy. I see you are shaking your head. I am serious. Instead of the dangerous liquid hydrogen or liquid oxygen that was used for liftoff propulsion for decades, the Black Swan engineers have learned how to harness vortex energy using superfluid and an electric field to create incredible velocity. Voila! The vortex drive. Very advanced."

"That's just peachy," I said sarcastically. "And what takes our friends into orbit, Mr. Jones? I suppose they'll be using Warp Drive. Or maybe they'll find a wormhole and just land on their space station three hundred miles away in a nanosecond."

"After the rocket boosters have fallen away, the Galactic will reach orbit in about five minutes," said Nebula Jones, ignoring my snotty tone. "The three engines riding on the back of the shuttle, which supposedly will take it into space and into orbit at nearly eighteen thousand miles per hour, run on nuclear energy. Antimatter catalyzed nuclear pulse propulsion, to be exact. It is still in the experimental stage. It is based upon the injection of antimatter into a mass of nuclear fuel. The Black Swan people have already run several tests on this fuel. Only once was there an explosion."

"Oh, great," muttered Hacker. "Only one explosion."

"T minus thirty seconds," intoned the voice on the speakers at the launch site. The men in white uniforms withdrew to safe positions. A loud humming sound began to emit from the Galactic's huge nuclear-powered engines.

"Ten...nine...eight...seven...six...five..."

"Do something!" screamed Leela. "Get her out of there! You've got to rescue Jill! Now!"

"Too soon," said the alien, nearly whispering. I thought I saw a bead of sweat on his bird forehead. "Wait...wait...."

"...four...three...two...LIFTOFF!"

Leela held her head and groaned. I had an ominous feeling deep in my stomach. Greta was sobbing softly. Hacker produced weird grunting sounds. The two ETs were silent.

Galactic III broke free from its tower with a mighty roar and headed skyward, trailing a cloud of white water vapor. From the whirling vortex, no doubt. We humans all watched the monitor with rapt and fearful attention. For a few precious seconds we could see the spacecraft from our helicopter windows, blasting through the pale sky like a shooting star. Then it disappeared and the monitor was our only connection.

A minute passed. Two minutes.

"Watch the monitor. The rocket boosters are falling away now," said Nebula Jones softly. Was his voice at all sad? No, there was zero intonation. The boosters looked like huge metallic starships falling out of the sky. The cameras on the alien satellite gave us a clear picture of the craft's progress. Or was it all an illusion? A holographic projection of the alien's mind? Virtual reality?

Transfixed, we sat with our eyes glued to the monitor. Silence; there is no sound in space. Then it happened. A mighty explosion. The Galactic became a huge fireball, its parts flying into space in all directions. And then it all dissolved into a mushroom cloud. The picture on the monitor went black, with a few points of light—stars, apparently—piercing through the blackness. The silence of space was total.

"JILL! JILL! NO!" It was Leela, seeming to disintegrate, her hands covering her face, sobbing.

I too was wracked with sobs. I couldn't believe it. I refused to accept the death of our dear friend.

Hacker stood up and started walking down the center aisle of the helicopter, his fists clenched, a look on his face I had never seen before. Menacing. Beyond rage. "You— you evil sonofabitch," he spat at the alien. "You killed her. You killed her!" Literally snarling, he reached out and tried to grab Nebula Jones by the throat.

Suddenly the alien wasn't there, leaving Hacker grasping at air.

The white dove too had disappeared.

Silence.

CHAPTER THIRTY-THREE

The Manifesto Will Be Televised

Once again the interior of our helicopter sounded like an Iranian funeral. Two gifted psychics, two brilliant computer scientists—we all lost it completely over the presumed tragic death of our friend Jill, crying, caterwauling, and carrying on like a posse of tomcats on a three a.m. fence.

For about thirty seconds.

Then, about the same time as we heard a loud banging noise in the 'copter's tiny restroom, I...felt...something. Jill?

Leela, I think I feel Jill.

Me too, sweetheart. Could her spirit be with us already?

"Hi, guys, whassup? What's all the sniveling about? Turn off the waterworks already and give an old friend a hug, eh?"

We all screamed in unison: "JILL!!!"

"What the fu—" sputtered Hacker.

Jill danced gaily down the narrow aisle, stopping to give Hacker a kiss on the cheek, a high-five to Greta, and a huge group hug to her two psi buddies waiting at the end of the aisle. We kissed and patted and petted and hugged tightly and dry-humped until we were out of breath. Then we all four gathered around Jill, waiting for her survival story.

She looked great, all rosy-cheeked and bright-eyed, wearing a Spandex spacesuit that hugged every luscious curve on that tight hardbody. "Sorry for all the commotion when I landed in the, uh, loo," she said. "But I landed upside down right next to the commode. Good thing the lid was closed."

We cracked up. "Okay, Jill, take a few deep breaths and please tell us why your atoms are not scattered halfway around the galaxy," said Leela.

She grinned as she breathed, eyes closed. "Okay, here's the story. I'm on this spaceship, see, and strapped into a very uncomfortable chair, and we're going really really fast, and I wake up like out of a dream. Nothing makes sense. My head clears. I hear a voice in my head, 'Jump. Jump. Jump.' I go, Oh, yeah? Jump from where…to where?

"Then my psychic sense kicks in. It'd been missing for awhile. I remembered that you, Leela, my dear, once took a jump from the top of that sacred mountain in Tibet to the Ganges in India, riding on the wave of all that vortex energy. This thought process was happening in accelerated time, in fractions of nanoseconds, like it does on the psi level. I felt all kinds of powerful energies swirling around that spaceship, and I also knew that some kind of huge explosion was just around the corner. So I closed my eyes and jumped, riding an energy trail that just happened to be there, and that just happened to land me on my head in the lavatory of a fancy helicopter."

"Nebula Jones," said Leela. "The voice in your head."

"Dude's got a sense of humor after all," said Hacker.

"He must have sent a signal to the Galactic that fixed Jill's synaptic derangement," I contributed.

"My what?" said Jill.

"You were deranged, girlfriend," said Leela, gently. "We all were. Thanks to Big Mama's energy bolts. You never would have gone after Wolfgang if you hadn't been out of your friggin' mind. But the alien fixed our brains. Now, we've all got our marbles back. I hope."

"So how 'bout we get out of this friggin' hellhole?" said Jill. "Where's our pilot? Where are those cute bird-men, anyway?"

"The birds have flown the coop," I said. "Mr. Jones just up and disappeared when Hacker tried to commit mayhem on his person. He and his buddy must be around here somewhere. Remember, those orbs are not your ordinary shapeshifters."

"They're probably hiding out as cockroaches on the chopper," said Hacker. "That would be appropriate. Hey, anybody know how to fly this whirlybird? I've gotta get back to Sedona pretty quick. I've got an assignment from a certain alien to set him up for a worldwide all-media broadcast of a certain manifesto. Fucker's gonna go ahead with it against my advice."

"Assignment...?" I questioned. "After all that negative energy you threw at him on the bus, you took an assignment?"

"It's strange," said Hacker. "He must have planted that whole idea, the assignment, the details of it, when he put his hands on my skull and brought my brain back from Derangement City. Encouraged me to take on the job, too, with enthusiasm. Impressive! Hey, Greta, interested in writing some code with me?"

"You bet, handsome," she replied, snuggling up to the big guy. Greta had come a long way, personal growth-wise, on this craziest of adventures. She had been through hell, and come out a bigger and better person. "Take us home, Marty!"

So I was the chosen one. I climbed into the pilot seat, pushed a couple of buttons, pulled a lever or two, and we were airborne. Somehow I knew exactly what to do. And somehow I knew the chopper's computer responded to verbal commands. "Straight course to Sedona, Arizona," I said with authority. "Top speed. No stops. How's our fuel supply?"

"Please be more specific," said a ghostly voice through the helicopter speakers.

I looked at the fuel gauge. The pointer was in the middle. "Is the fuel tank half full or half empty?" I said mischievously, paraphrasing a famous Zen koan, trying to blow the computer's mind.

"Meditate on this," said the disembodied voice. "There is no fuel tank."

Marty, please cut the crap and get us out of here. I am hungry and horny as hell. The transmission was from Jill. Leela nodded in agreement, a crazy, crooked smile on her face, still beautiful after all we had been through, but showing some signs of wear and tear.

Jill, you are one oversexed little bitch, I flashed.

Marty, you know I am anything but little! Jill flashed back.

I pulled a mysterious lever all the way back and we were at top speed in ten seconds.

We covered the five hundred miles from the Black Swan rocket launch site to Sedona in just under two hours. I landed our chopper in a narrow parking lot at the Enchanted Forest Resort, near the suites we had staked out weeks earlier. Everything looked the same as when we set out on our tour bus with Nebula Jones. The personal belongings that we left on the bus, including the musical instruments, had to be forgotten. Our two alien friends hadn't shown up yet, but we knew they would at the proper time.

We all hustled into our rooms, cleaned up, and got to work. Time was very short; we had urgent jobs to do. Hacker and Greta needed to put together a mega hack that would enable Nebula Jones to deliver his Alien Manifesto simultaneously to every living human on the planet, in every human's native language. (There are more than six thousand spoken languages on Planet Earth.) This seemed to me to be an impossible task, even for our friends, who were brilliant computer scientists.

Leela and Jill huddled together in Jill's room to outline a report of our recent activities for the State Department. One item they debated was how much to reveal about our two alien slash orb colleagues, their plans for the planet, and how they had influenced the arrest and/or destruction of the Black Swan leadership. I knew what the ladies were discussing because I was tuned in to their psychic communication.

I also knew that State didn't consider me to be on their payroll anymore—I was a temp, with a pineal gland chip implant, a limited assignment, and an expiration date on my psi abilities—so I stayed out of the discussion. How would State know that my psychic powers had not only been extended indefinitely, but also expanded?

My job was to meet with Benny Bravo in the suite that Leela and I shared. He and I hadn't connected for awhile because I had been busy with an angry ex-goddess, spaceships, and, well, just busy. Benny had stayed behind to keep an eye on things. He updated me on what was going on in Sedona and the world situation in general.

The good news was that Sedona and all of Northern Arizona was beginning to return to normal. In Sedona, the cops and National Guard were no longer patrolling the streets; roadblocks had been removed; it was safe to move around again. Clean water was flowing through the taps, although serious rationing was in effect. The Western electrical grid had been liberated from the icy grip of Black Swan operatives, so the lights were on once more. Businesses were reopening, locals were moving back into their homes, and the Sedona economy seemed to be returning to some semblance of normal.

But the world situation looked grim. With the return of the Internet, plus TV, satellite connections, holo news feeds, and other media, Benny had been able to get a glimpse into the void.

"How bad is it, Benny?" I asked my friend.

"*Muy malo*, man. There are wars still breaking out all over. People fighting for food and water. Millions of refugees, people just walking around, with nuthin', man, I mean just the clothes on their backs. Huge refugee camps in every country, even in Europe. Greenland is melting. Africa is toast; cannibalism everywhere. Folks eating each other, man! People are in the streets, fighting with cops, firebombing the government buildings, all over Europe and Asia. North Korea launched two nukes, one for South Korea and one for Japan, but the rockets didn't work and the nukes landed back in North Korea. Sayonara, baby!"

"*Muy malo, mi amigo*," I replied in my limited Spanish, snatching the chilling images of worldwide carnage right out of his cerebral cortex. "Any word on the Black Swan group and what happened to 'em?"

"Oh, yeah, man, almost forgot. It's all over the news feeds. The whole leadership of Black Swan has been— ¿*cómo se dice...*¿— neutralized. The *cabeza* of the monster has been cut off. Seems that the top hundred Black Swans was on the way to their space station to set up some kind of new society when their spaceship exploded. Left nothing but a mushroom cloud. The other top fifty was busted out at a ranch in New Mexico, picked up by the FBI. And another fifty was busted at their launch site at White Sands, out in the friggin' desert. You know anything about this late-breaking, *señor?*"

"No, Benny, not a freakin' thing," I lied, winking. "*Nada*. Hey, we're all gonna meet in the fancy restaurant in a few minutes and compare notes. Come join us. Hacker and his new lady friend are gonna share some ideas with us. I think you met her before we left on the bus. Leela and Jill got some heavy shit to drop, too. I think they need our advice."

"I'm down wid dat, Daddy," said Benny. "Let us make our way to da famous Navajo Room."

Benny's consciousness was somewhere between *La Bamba* and *Hava Nagila*. He was probably the only Mexican in Arizona who had had a Bar Mitzvah. He liked to play the role of a barrio hipster, a faux gangbanger with a college degree; but he was whip-smart and my ace investigative reporter when I had the Sedona Confidential website.

Benny had been our link to the crumbling status of Planet Earth during the psi team's adventures outside of Sedona. Yet, he had only briefly rubbed shoulders with the ET called Nebula Jones, way back when that entity was known as Harry the Handyman. And he was totally in the dark regarding the alien's scheme to drop the Earth into a black hole to save the ass of, potentially, a whole galaxy. He would need to know about that piece, and soon.

The Navajo Room was indeed lovely, with its high vaulted ceilings and elegant furniture, Native American artworks everywhere, the place emanating a feeling of warmth and security. And we were all, of course, security conscious. Hacker and I both scanned the room for aud and vid bugs, and there were none. There were a few other guests at the far end of the restaurant; the tourists were starting to return to Sedona's most beautiful resort.

Our group was noisy, excited, enthusiastic. This was somewhat surprising, considering that in just a few days our home planet was going to be sent back in time—the most significant Black Swan Event in our history, to say the least. I suspected, as did Leela and Jill, that Nebula Jones had planted some positive attitudes in our minds, as well as Hacker's and Greta's, when he brought us back from our synaptic derangement.

But we also had plenty to celebrate: We had brought down the frightful monster most recently known as Big Mama Lakshmi; we had ripped the heart out of Black Swan Galactic and destroyed the organization which came close to destroying the world. Jill was safe and sound, rescued from certain death with the help of Nebula Jones. Our little group had been to the brink and back, returning to our beloved Sedona with barely a scratch.

Still...We all knew, except for Benny Bravo, that our two ETs intended to carry out their plans, regardless of the fact that the two biggest threats to our survival had been deleted. The world situation was more dire than ever. And our little group would play a major role in sending the world, our precious civilization, with all of its chaos and mayhem, its murderous and suicidal ways, into the past. For a second chance.

Hacker and Greta had been handed a nearly impossible assignment: Create a worldwide multimedia, multilingual network for Nebula Jones in less than two days. "So what did you guys come up with?" I asked our computer geniuses. "Did you solve the unsolvable?"

"You tell me, Mr. Mindreader!" snapped Hacker. "What are we thinking? Let us usher in a new paradigm in communication." He was testy, he was joking, and he was serious, all at the same time. I looked at Leela and Jill, and they nodded their OK. Benny simply rolled his eyes.

I went for it. "Okay, smarties, here goes." I scanned both their minds. Hacker the joker was trying to focus on women's bare feet and other female body parts, in a futile attempt to throw me off, but I went two layers deeper and got what I was looking for. Greta was more serious, and laid out their whole planned scenario in a nanosecond.

"Got it, Greta. Hacker, get real. Nebula Jones planned to broadcast his Manifesto worldwide in forty-eight hours. So for you, the heat was on. You and Greta tried everything in the Hacker's Handbook, but finally decided to drop your search for the perfect algorithm. You wanted to try something else. But what? And where? Time was not on your side."

"Right," said Greta. "Hacker said, 'If only we could hack into the alien satellite. It's got to have everything we need to pull this off. If only....' Then, for some unknown reason, I decided to take my shoes off. My feet were hot. And stinky. Hacker encouraged me to take 'em off. Naughty boy. In one shoe there was a small piece of rolled up paper I hadn't been aware of before. On this paper were several lines of code and number combinations that didn't make any sense."

Hacker broke in. "I had an intuitive feeling that Jones had planted the note in her shoe and that it had something to do with the satellite. You three are not the only intuitives around here, you know. I entered the code on a secret military website I hacked into a few months ago, sent the code into space via a military surveillance satellite, and sure enough—"

"Bingo!" I rudely interrupted. "The alien satellite's scanner grabbed your code and invited you into its central processor. Bingo again! A blinking cursor! You typed in the numbers from Greta's note and gained access to at least a section of the satellite's huge processing power, and—"

"Fucker," snarled Hacker, half under his breath. "So this satellite has, no kiddin', must be trillions of exobytes of memory. And unlimited processing power; it must get energy from the sun, or something. Gazillions of calculations a nanosecond. Plus a beautiful interface, full 3-D video, everything in English, easy to navigate, and...."

"Hacker figured it all out," said Greta. "Our Mr. Jones will be on every communications medium in every little corner of the planet. His Manifesto even will be delivered in native languages and dialects, thanks to the satellite's universal translator."

"It looks so elegant!" added Leela, who had done some mind scanning of her own. She saw the outline for the whole program via Greta's short-term memory. "So Nebula Jones will be on every kind of TV, in movie theaters and holo houses, all over the Internet, on mobile phones and wrist receivers, on every kind of hand-held device, everything wireless, on planes and trains and ships and—"

"—and even in the most remote villages in the poorest places on earth via holo projections and delivered to people who've got brain and eye implants with vid-aud receivers!" finished Jill, who had been scanning Leela. "This is amazing! And you two wrote the code to make this happen?"

"Of course we did," boasted Hacker, the former programmer. "This is nothing."

"Piece of cake," added Greta. "Which reminds me: I'm starving. Where is that waiter? We got these menus ten minutes ago!"

"I wonder if there will be any advance notice of his speech?" I wondered out loud. "Knowing Nebula Jones and his behavior patterns, he'll probably just suddenly appear on the media and start talking and you won't be able to turn him off. Do you guys think the people of Earth are ready for this? I doubt it."

I looked over at Benny, who had been watching this whole show with wide-eyed amusement. Soon, I would need to fill in the missing pieces of the puzzle. To cushion the shock. To prepare my old friend for the coming Moment of Truth.

Our waiter showed up in that moment. At least he looked like a waiter, with shiny black pants and clunky black shoes and bow tie and starched white shirt. He was tall and thin with a hint of a moustache and wore a little badge that said EDUARDO, Portugal.

"Good evening. How are you? I will be your waiter this evening. Are you ready to order? Our special tonight is Beef Wellington au jus. We also have vegetarian and vegan dishes."

It's Nebula Jones, I flashed to Leela and Jill.

Got it. Don't say anything yet, Marty. It was Leela.

Jill: *He says there will be no advance notice of his speech. He says tell your government everything, what to expect.*

What followed seemed to happen on two levels. First, Nebula Jones was feeding us —the psi trio, Leela, Jill, and I— little packets of information via the psi channel, filling in information gaps. At the same time we discussed the menu and ordered our food. I loved how my mind could absorb data from the alien and file it away while maintaining a parallel existence on the ordinary, real-time continuum.

You will need this information in the very near future to inform your comrades and to answer their questions, flashed Nebula Jones. *And of course to advance our mission.*

We ordered a very expensive bottle of Pinot Noir from California, worth every penny, but of course everything was on the house. Benny Bravo, who had been very silent but attentive during our dinner conversation, ordered two bottles of very pricey Mexican beer.

As we finished dinner, our waiter was replaced by a very efficient and slightly effeminate busboy who hovered around the table, snatching our plates as soon as we emptied them. "Feenished?" he would say, long after the plate had been confiscated. "Feenished? More *agua*?"

"Who is this dude?" complained Hacker as the busboy clumsily serviced our table.

"It's gotta be Cosmo Kincaid," I said, "here to keep an eye on us."

"Jesus," said Hacker. "He looks like he just snuck across the border."

Cosmo Kincaid did look loosely put together, squeezed into an ill-fitting modified tuxedo complete with black tie, unkempt hair, wild moustache. He wore a huge name tag that said PEDRO, Mexico City.

Benny tried to strike up a conversation in Spanish with Pedro/Cosmo, but the alien simply threw up his hands, scooped up six empty plates, and walked away, briskly.

After dinner, Leela and Jill talked about the report they were going to deliver to the State Department.

"We've decided to tell them everything, even the stuff about Nebula Jones and Big Mama and the whole thing that happened in New Mexico. Plus Jill getting kidnapped, her jump to the chopper, the spaceship that exploded, everything." Leela said this with a sigh of resignation.

"Why did the rocket explode?" asked Greta. "That fuel mix had already been tested. It should have worked."

"It was just a malfunction," answered Leela, calling on the information supplied minutes ago by Nebula Jones. "The fuel was a very volatile mix. The nuclear element made it very unstable. So...ka-boom! We're just lucky that Jill escaped it with her precious hide intact."

"So what does our government think about all this psychic stuff?" probed Hacker. "Will they believe it? That Jill could teleport from a spaceship back to the Earth? That some super-being has big plans for our planet?"

"I think Madame Secretary of State knows a lot already," offered Jill. "Except some of that stuff we talked about on the bus," she said cautiously, glancing quickly at Benny Bravo. We all knew she was talking about the black hole, a subject which Benny was not privy to. Yet. It wasn't that we didn't trust Benny; Leela didn't want to risk a leak to the public, the press, or the politicians.

"Does the president know anything?" asked Greta.

"The president has been in a secret underground bunker, along with her closest aides and her cabinet and her family since this whole crisis started months ago," said Jill. "She has been monitoring the world situation via a secure TV network and basically running the country from her bunker. My sources tell me that she has been left out of the loop on some of the major issues because the Secretary of State is on top of the big picture."

Nobody questioned Jill or her sources on this information; she sounded so authoritative that it was accepted as fact.

We finished dinner. Cosmo Kincaid, in his immigrant persona, cleared away the dishes and served us coffee. Nebula Jones, in waiter drag, came by to thank us for our business and to present us with a bill which said simply "gratis."

We returned to our suites and to our assignments. Benny elected to return to his house to watch a holo movie on his new home unit, which he had bought cheap from a looter at the beginning of the crisis. Before he left, I slipped him ten hundred dollar bills. He was still on my payroll, unofficially. Soon, money wouldn't mean much anyway. I told Benny that I would fill him in on some important details. Soon. He grinned and gave me a big hug.

I joined Leela and Jill to help them put together their report for the State Department. It was nearly midnight when we finished; we would check it over in the morning and transmit it to the Secretary, with a cc to the President of the United States.

What we *didn't* mention in the report, figuring that Nebula Jones would be covering the subject soon enough, was the imminent future of Planet Earth: To be dropped unceremoniously into a sentient black hole, and sent back into the past.

The mood in our suite was somber as we worked on the report. It felt to us like life on Earth was winding down. Together we decided—silently, in psi mode—to take a chance and go for the wormhole option. The black hole option was not for us, not for three telepaths whose psi powers might never develop on Planet Earth 2.0.

It was after midnight when we finally tumbled into bed. We three were exhausted, too tired for sex. Actually, sex seemed inappropriate. It had been a long day, a very long day. We cuddled up together, naked, in the king size bed. We played in each other's dreams. It was better than sex.

Almost.

CHAPTER THIRTY-FOUR

The Point of No Return

"Greetings, citizens of Planet Earth! Do not be alarmed. Please listen closely to what I am about to tell you. Your planet is in a great deal of difficulty right now. There is a crisis, planet-wide. This crisis only grows worse as the days and months and years go by. Soon this crisis will affect not just you and the planet you occupy, but other nearby planets and moons and suns as well.

"Something must be done. And done soon. This is an emergency situation." (Pause for effect.)

"Allow me to introduce myself. I am a visitor from far, far away. I traveled to your planet in a way that is beyond your most advanced technology and is difficult to explain. My Earth friends call me Nebula Jones. My colleague, the lady seated behind me, is called Cosmo Kincaid. We come from an organization that monitors the health of this galaxy."

"Dude's looking pretty good, eh?" said Hacker. "Not even using a teleprompter."

We had gathered at Hacker's spacious home in West Sedona to watch the show; several shows simultaneously, in fact. His huge wall unit delivered a crisp 3-D picture of the main action, the Nebula Jones speech. There were several other monitors stacked around the room, each delivering a picture, some with sound, of other locations around the world, depicting in real time the public's reaction to the alien's declaration. Large crowds were gathered in Hyde Park, London; Red Square, Moscow; Tiananmen Square, Beijing; Times Square, New York; Berlin; Paris; Delhi; Copenhagen; Oslo; Baghdad; Tokyo. All of the planet's major cities. The public was not pleased.

These transmissions were from myriad cameras on the orbiting alien satellite, delivering streaming video and still photo slideshows as it circled our planet in low Earth orbit at more than seventeen thousand miles per hour. This public reaction data was being transmitted exclusively to Hacker's receivers, thanks to a program the computer genius and Greta had quickly written and because all other communications on the planet were preempted.

"He's kinda handsome now, isn't he?" offered Jill, breaking the somber mood, referring to Nebula Jones. "In a Walter Cronkite kind of way. Seems very trustworthy."

"Love his ladyfriend, too," said Leela. "Madame Cosmo. She is so demure. In an early Hillary Clinton kind of way. Powerful, yet controlled."

"Drag queen," muttered Hacker. "The bitch is a friggin' drag queen."

Nebula Jones had morphed into yet another persona, a tall, distinguished gentleman with graying hair; he wore a pinstripe suit and a stylish red power tie. Cosmo Kincaid, who we had seen previously as a white dove and a Mexican busboy, had morphed into a woman, wearing a modest gray pantsuit with a white scarf at the throat, short brown hair, low heels. Hands folded primly in her lap, she stared intently at her fellow alien, Nancy Reagan style.

"The number one problem on the Earth today is too many people," continued Nebula Jones. "Your planet's resources are vanishing fast, and yet the people of Earth continue to produce new people, babies, at astounding rates, sometimes in competitions between the races and the religions. Your oceans are dying; drinkable water is nonexistent in many places; millions, maybe billions of your people are starving or malnourished; your air and water grow ever more toxic.

"Earthlings! Wake up! You have all been poisoned by your priests and politicians, by your childish religions, by your corrupt leaders, by your dishonest media! You are obsessed with killing each other. You have not advanced beyond the tribal rituals and practices of your distant ancestors. At this moment several neighboring nations are at war with each other. Some of those nations possess nuclear weapons. One nuclear weapon has already been fired and several more are just on the verge of being delivered by ballistic missiles."

"Wow. Sounds like ol' Nebby is just getting warmed up," said Leela.

"Yeah, this is one hell of a scolding for the human race," added Jill.

"Fine, but where does he go from here?" I asked. "Do you think all those peasants in all those desperate villages in Africa and India and China and Mexico know what the hell he's talking about? Can they relate to global warming or rising ocean levels or hybrid cars? Get serious!"

"Hey, guys, check out these other monitors," said Hacker. "Use your wireless headphones for the sound. You can dial in lots of channels from the headset. Check it out, there are riots breaking out all over the place. People are freaking out. I was afraid of this."

"The Earth has reached a point of no return," continued the alien, oblivious to the chaos erupting around the planet. We had no idea where he was transmitting from; he could have been on his orbiting satellite, he could have been on the moon, or he could have been in a suite at the Holiday Inn in Scottsdale. "The damage done to your planet by humans is irreversible. Already the fruits of your ignorance and greed and selfishness are obvious. Already super tornadoes and hurricanes and ultra-violent earthquakes and volcanoes are devastating your planet and killing and uprooting millions of people. This is just the beginning."

"Jesus," said Hacker, "why don't we just cash in our chips and go live on that nice Black Swan space station? I hear there are a lot of vacancies there now."

"Check the monitors," I said, "speaking of Jesus. People in America are out in the streets, dancing and crying and begging for the Rapture to begin."

"Because of the violent and suicidal nature of the human race," continued the alien, "and because of the certainty of global thermonuclear war on Planet Earth, and this war's effect on neighboring celestial bodies, it is necessary for my associates and myself to make some, ah, technical adjustments to the Earth's, uh, trajectory."

"This is it, folks," said Greta fearfully. "I wonder how far he's going to go with it. I don't think those peasant farmers in China are going to like the idea of being dropped into a black hole. All they're worried about is the rice crop surviving the coming typhoons. The greed-pigs of Wall Street probably won't like the idea either."

"Howzat?" asked Benny Bravo, who had been silent up to now. "Drop who into what black hole?"

"There is nothing to fear," said the alien in a reassuring voice. "You will not feel a thing. Once the technical adjustments have been made, all of you will be more safe, more secure, and better off. We are giving the people of Earth a second chance. We hope you will use the opportunity to live more peaceful, more intelligent lives, and to treat your home, your planet Earth, and your fellow Earthlings, with more respect.

"For now, good night, and good luck."

The giant wall monitor went dark. In Hacker's living room, no one said a word for several minutes. Benny was the first to break the silence.

"That was pretty heavy-duty stuff, dudes and dudettes. I wonder how de peoples of Earth are gonna handle de news of a 'technical adjustment.' And de big black hole, no? What's up wid dat? Yo, Hacker, can we check out de news feeds yet?"

"Yeah, Benny, stand by. When *Señor* Alien pre-empted all of the communications on the planet, he left behind some dust on the wires and the airwaves. Okay, here's a live feed from Times Square."

Standing in front of a surging, angry, and confused mob, John Coulter, ace reporter for GSN, the Global Satellite Network, had to shout to be heard. "...and we have just witnessed one of the greatest hoaxes in human history! After pre-empting every audio and video transmission on Earth, an unknown person believed to be the head of the Black Swan Galactic organization severely chastised the human race and threatened to send us all to hell! The president says the person will be tracked down and arrested, or shot on sight if necessary. She said..."

"The head of Black Swan!" I exploded. "What kind of bullshit spin is that? And they say it's a hoax?!"

"That's the bullshit media," said Hacker. "Look at these headlines on the Web." He punched up the Google headlines and they filled his giant video monitor, even more stark and frightening because of the scale.

HOAX! Stunt reminds analysts of Orson Welles' Martians scare in 1938

Head of Black Swan Galactic punks the world with fake dire warning

U.S. president dispatches troops, FBI to find alien terrorist

"So our friend Mr. Jones is a terrorist and a wanted man!" said Leela. "And an *alien* terrorist at that! I hope he knows what he's doing. And that he's got a good hideout."

"And I hope *you* have a good hideout, my friends," said a disembodied voice. It was the voice of Nebula Jones' latest incarnation, the dapper gentleman who had just informed the world of the changes to come. And then the alien himself appeared in the middle of Hacker's living room, tall and stately in his pinstripe suit, looking like he had just stepped out of the TV studio.

"It's the alien!" gasped Greta.

"Holy shit!" bellowed Hacker.

"*Mierda*! No fucking way!" exclaimed Benny Bravo.

"Relax, kids, it's just a hologram," said Leela. "Pretty good one, too, but the image is a little frayed around the edges. Take a closer look."

Jill and I also knew it at about the same time. We had scanned the image of the alien and found it had no substance. Nevertheless, the alien—his holo image, anyway—was there for a good reason.

"*Qué la chinga, hombre*!" said Benny Bravo, talking directly at the holo image. "What you mean, our 'hideout,' *Señor* Alien?"

"Please listen carefully, my human friends," said the image of Nebula Jones calmly. "The, ah, unexpected has happened. There has been a leak. Somehow the information about the black hole has reached the top levels of your American government. They are very upset about it. In fact, they are mobilizing right now to find all of you and bring you to CIA headquarters to question you about my whereabouts. They are pre-pared to use enhanced interrogation techniques—as you would say, *torture*—and drugs, if necessary, to extract the information they seek."

We were all aghast. After getting over the initial shock, we started firing questions at the holo image of Nebula Jones. Benny Bravo was the most perplexed of us all, since he was just now learning of the black hole adventure to come. We had withheld the infor-mation from him to prevent a leak—he might have been picked up by the cops and subjected to the latest "truth" techniques. That hadn't happened. Obviously, the leak had come from somewhere else.

"What is the source of the leak?" I asked. Not that it mattered. A leak is a leak. And we all seemed to be in imminent danger of being dragged into a mess that was not of our making.

"I suspect that it was the three Dakinis traveling in the front of our bus," said the alien in his holo form. "Although they were in a trance, their subconscious minds absorbed some of our conversation about the sentient black hole. After they were taken into cus-tody at the Black Swan ranch, they were turned over to your government's interrogation specialists. Eventu-ally they were given powerful truth drugs to find out what was stored in their minds. The rest, as they say, is history."

"Please tell us, Mr. Jones, how you know what went on in the president's totally secure conference room in her underground bunker," asked Jill. "How the decision was made to hunt us down and probe around in our minds."

Jill was sarcastic but polite, but I knew that she was seething beneath the surface. As was I. And Leela. None of us felt like being fugitives, on the run from the United States government. Which seemed to be our immediate future.

"You have heard of the fly on the wall?" asked the alien. "Cosmo Kincaid managed to dispatch one of his toys to the underground conference room. It was in the form of a small insect, nearly invisible, but equipped with an audio recording and transmitting device. Thus, I know exactly what was said in that room and by whom. Your American secretary of defense is quite the belligerent fellow, is he not? His solution to the black hole question was to deliver nuclear warheads via ballistic missiles to all of America's enemies. And to any other nation that might represent a threat to America's dominance."

"What is the fucking black hole question, *amigos?*" demanded Benny Bravo. He was growing increasingly paranoid. "Just what the fuck are you talking about?"

Benny had a right to know, but not at that moment. "Later, Benny," I said. "I'll tell you everything in a little while. Let's figure out how we're gonna get out of here, if our government plans to hunt us down like escaped convicts."

Hacker, of course, was furious. He was practically foaming at the mouth. "You effin' alien asshole! How could you have fucked this up so badly? You and your stupid computer models! What have you done? How are you gonna get us out of this?"

"Please relax, Mr. Hacker. You certainly have some anger issues. Right now, great focus is needed. Listen to me. In less than twenty-four hours, our sentient black hole will be at its closest possible distance to earth. At that moment, I will send a signal to activate the program that will, in effect, drop Planet Earth into the black hole. This action will take place from the highest point in the state of Arizona, the top of your Mount Humphries."

"Yes, but—" began Leela, but the alien cut her off.

"I would like all of you to be with me at the critical moment, the Singularity. It will be an amazing experience, a front row seat in the history of your planet. Three of you will be with me: Miss Greta, Mr. Hack, Mr. Bravo.

"The other three have chosen a different path: to jump approximately one thousand or so years into an unknown future, via wormhole. You are the gamblers. Hopefully, when we reach the event horizon, the outer edge of the black hole, a wormhole will be created. You three, Jill, Leela, Marty, will step into a portal and travel through the wormhole into the next millennium."

"But how do we get—" said Jill, before Nebula Jones interrupted again. A sense of urgency filled the room.

"No more questions, please," said Nebula Jones. "Sitting behind this house right now is a small aircraft which will deliver the six of you to the nearby village of Flagstaff. It is a kind of helicopter, which runs on electricity and is virtually silent and invisible to radar and other detection devices. It seats six humans and one small pilot. The aircraft will deliver you to the Lowell Observatory in Flagstaff, where you can watch for the imminent arrival of our black hole, although it is basically invisible. You will see its approach through the powerful Lowell telescopes as a timewave moving through space."

"But—" I began. I wanted to know where we would have dinner and spend the night and sleep. Out of old habits, old insecurities, I guess.

"We have friends at Lowell who are waiting to greet you. You will be provided with sleeping quarters and you can even order pizza, if you wish." I was sure the alien had chuckled briefly with this statement, having obviously read my thoughts.

"The next morning the aircraft will deliver you to the peak of Mount Humphries, which is just outside of Flagstaff. There I will meet you and if you have any last-minute questions, and if there is time to spare, I will be happy to answer them. When you arrive at Lowell, a counseling session with Miss Kincaid will be available."

"*Señor* Alien, *por favor*," protested Benny Bravo. "I need to go home and get my toothbrush, my leather jacket, my, you know, my drugs. A change of clothes. Some condoms. You know."

"There is no time to get anything," said the holo image of Nebula Jones. "You all must board the aircraft within five minutes or the authorities will capture you. They are on the way here now. Once at Lowell, everything you need will be provided. All you need for the Singularity is the clothes on your backs. Now, go."

The holographic image of the alien disappeared abruptly. Without a word, we dashed outside to Hacker's spacious back yard. Our escape vehicle was parked there, humming quietly, bathed in an eerie green glow. It looked like a sleek, futuristic, silver helicopter. Both side doors were open. It had two rows of three seats each, plus a miniature pilot's seat, which was occupied by a small-scale version of "Miss Kincaid." We piled in wordlessly, Leela and Jill and I in the front row and Hacker and Greta and Benny in the back row.

We all tingled with the excitement of the moment. I could feel our friends in the back seat, hearts pounding, minds racing. Leela and Jill were meditating, in a state of no-mind. I had trouble quieting my own busy mind. The doors slid shut. The aircraft shot straight up into the air and whooshed off silently toward Flagstaff, twenty-six miles away by car, probably ten minutes away in our silver spaceship. The floor of the craft was transparent and we could see the lights of Sedona below, slowly receding into the darkness.

We all figured that in a minute or two Hacker's house would be swarming with troops and police and snarling dogs and men in suits, looking for us or evidence of where we might be.

Too late. We were gone. Real, real gone.

CHAPTER THIRTY-FIVE

Transition

It was early evening when our silver helicraft landed silently on the leafy grounds of Lowell Observatory, located on a hilltop overlooking Flagstaff on a street called Mars Hill Road. The observatory's mission: to seek out new galaxies, new star systems, new planets that might be teeming with life. The planet Pluto was discovered by an astronomer from Lowell in 1930. Now, the campus where we landed was primarily for tourists. The best telescopes were kept at a research facility on a mesa twenty miles away.

No complaints from our little group, however. We were all glad to find a sanctuary where we could rest and prepare ourselves for the upcoming events which would change the course of, what...everything? The observatory had been closed for weeks, but two staff members were on hand to help us find our way around. Nebula Jones had made sure we were well taken care of. Even the observatory's most awesome instrument of celestial exploration, the ninety-six inch Perkins telescope, somehow had been moved from the mesa to the Mars Hill campus so we could watch the approach of our sentient black hole.

"I suggest you wait awhile, until the skies are totally dark," suggested Annie, one of our caretakers. "Then maybe you can see the waves in space created by your so-called black hole." She said this with a smug smile that suggested she didn't believe a word of it.

"So-called?" I said. "I know black holes are invisible, but—"

Hold it right there, Marty, flashed Leela. *She doesn't know about the sentient black hole, or what's going to happen to Planet Earth. She and her fellow caretaker think we are just special guests of somebody important. Nebula Jones has probably planted some fake data in their minds.*

They had installed us in two of the residential cabins on the Lowell campus, segregated by our destinations: Hacker, Greta, and Benny, destined to be sent back in time with the rest of humanity; and Leela, Jill, and I, ready to be launched into the future via wormhole. While Annie and her partner Stella prepared dinner for us, Cosmo Kincaid, who had morphed into a sexy blonde wearing a short skirt, black stockings, and low-cut top, led us to a meeting room in the main hall.

Cosmo sat in a leather armchair and crossed her shapely legs. "The room is clean of bugs," she said in a surprisingly deep voice. "Now, this is a Q and A session as well as a therapy session. If any of you have any questions about what is going to happen to Planet Earth, or any anxieties, doubts, misgivings, what have you, about where you are going, now is the time to address those issues. Yes, Mr. Hack?"

"Yeah, I've got a question, Ms. Kincaid." He laid heavily on the "Ms.," making it resonate like an insect sound. "What guarantee do we have that this is gonna work? I mean, a real black hole absorbs light and everything else and nothing ever comes out. What will happen to all the sentient beings on Earth? All the matter, all the—"

"The fundamental law of conservation of information states that no information can be lost," said Cosmo. "It only changes form. Look at all life forms on Earth as information. Nothing will be lost, including your minds, your memories, your individual storehouses of information and knowledge. Except, of course, the period between the Singularity and the moment in Earth year nineteen ninety when you resume your lives in the past. That time period will simply be deleted. Does that make sense?"

Hacker shook his head in a definite NO. Greta was crying softly, tears running down her cheeks. Benny Bravo looked out the window. He might have been in a state of shock, or maybe he still didn't get what was about to happen to the human race. Leela and Jill and I were all tuned in to fantasies about what our future would be like.

"Okay, look at it another way. Matter never disappears, it is transformed into energy. All of you, all life forms, will be transformed into pure light beings for a nanosecond or two while Uncle Albert—that's what we call our sentient black hole— processes the data and adjusts the space-time continuum. You will then be restored to your human form at the designated point in time, in the past, as decided by our supercomputer. None of you will have any idea that this has taken place. You will simply continue your lives as if nothing has happened."

I tried scanning the mind of Ms. Kincaid; there was nothing there—no thoughts, no memories, no cerebral cortex. In other words, no mind. I felt Jill and Leela probing around in the alien's skull. We looked at each other and nodded. There were no secrets lurking in that pretty blond head that would affect our future.

"I've heard that wormholes don't really exist, that they are just theoretical algorithms," said Jill, sounding brilliant. "Have you ever used one for a jump into the future?"

"Only once," said Cosmo Kincaid. "But allow me to quote your NASA on the subject: 'A wormhole is a theoretical opening in space-time that one could use to travel to far away places very quickly.' In other words, a wormhole acts as a shortcut or tunnel through space and time. You see—"

"That's just great," interrupted Jill, irritated and impatient. "But you didn't answer my question. Can it really work? Can the wormhole really take us into the future? And what about your 'only once?' What happened on that one?"

"Ah, that one," sighed the alien. "A very lovely couple, humanoids from a planet orbiting the star KY Cigni, a beautiful green planet similar to Earth called Sigma Six. Unfortunately, we weren't prepared for the consequences, so the subjects were instantly inciner-ated by the radiation passing through the throat of the wormhole.

"We have learned from that experience, so now we are only allowing entities such as yourself, and Mr. and Mrs. Powers, entities who possess psychic abilities and can form an electromagnetic field to protect you from radiation, to attempt to pass through our wormholes."

"Attempt...?" said Leela. "*Attempt* to pass, you said. This wormhole business is sounding riskier by the min-ute. By the way, if we make it through the radiation and pass through the wormhole, what kind of future are we getting into?"

"The future has infinite possibilities, as you know," said the alien. "There are many variables; there are no guarantees about which future or futures you may encounter. You will basically be traveling via the Tenth Dimension, where all possibilities are contained. We hope you will land somewhere around the year three thousand on Planet Earth. However, the outcome for you is entirely unpredictable."

"Whoa, whoa, whoa!" Benny Bravo finally spoke up, panic in his voice, his kitschy accent gone. Ear-lier, Benny had received a crash course in black holes from Hacker. He had also learned from Greta the alien plan to send the Earth and its residents back in time to save, potentially, the entire Milky Way galaxy. On these matters he was at least philosophical, although he did have trouble accepting the Tiffany Tattlebaum linchpin thesis.

"Whoa, *Señorita* Alien!" he cried. "What happens to all the shit that happened between Tiffany what's-'er-name doin' her thing in the White House and right now? Do we have to do it again, the same shit? What kinda changes we gotta go through? How can one *zoftig shaineh maidel* make so much difference? Maybe you could arrange that I could *shtup* her in the next life?"

"One thing at a time, please, Mr. Bravo," said Cosmo Kincaid patiently. "First, none of you will remember this time or any of the time after Miss Tattlebaum's White House adventures. All of history will be changed. For one thing, in the next version of Planet Earth, you will have a different president in the year 2000. This will have a huge impact. There will be no terrorist attack on the United States. There will be no needless wars. The global environmental disaster will be avoided, as will the global economic collapse. And so on and so forth. The human race will be given a second chance.

"For most of your species, your day-to-day lives will not change much from what has already taken place. Except the Earth will be a more people-friendly place. A sort of calm will settle over your planet. Ancient tribal rivalries and feuds will be resolved. Greed will be scorned. Precious resources will be shared. Anxieties will dissipate. More people will meditate and renounce your planet's childish, toxic religions.

"In short, the people of Earth will be more relaxed and more tolerant of others and more loving. Most importantly, the looming ecocide will be avoided." She paused and looked around at our little group. "Any more questions?"

"That's a pretty optimistic forecast, Miss Kincaid," I said, "given humanity's past performance and our basic human nature."

"Yah," growled Hacker, "it's a bunch of bullshit, all right. Humans have to eventually fuck everything up, no matter how good they've got it. Do a quick study of our history, Ms. Kincaid, then get real."

Our Q&A session was devolving into a bickerfest, so I popped a question to bring us back to the present. "This is kind of a change of subject, Cosmo, but can you tell us what happened to the rest of the Black Swan organization? And also, what has happened, and what will happen, to Big Mama Lakshmi...."

"Black Swan has been effectively closed down. All of its leaders, and most of its operatives around the world, as well as the members of The Brotherhood, the enforcement arm, all are in custody. The Black Swan space station has been disabled; its occupants will join the rest of humanity in your transition.

"Lakshmi is presently in a psychiatric hospital lockup ward in Santa Fe, having completely lost touch with reality. She has also suffered some organ failure since I withdrew my presence from her body. What of her future? Her life in the new version of Planet Earth could take totally different twists and turns. She might be a Catholic nun the next time around. Or a house-wife. She might have a career at Wal-Mart."

Cosmo Kincaid looked around again, scanning our faces. Now silence filled the small, stuffy room. There was nothing left to say. Hacker and Greta closed their eyes, acceptance of the situation settling their minds. Benny covered his face with his hands, sobbing softly. Leela, Jill, and I were wild with excitement, although we kept it a secret out of respect for our friends. The future! Our three minds locked together in a kind of cerebral orgasm, triggering cascades of endorphins and sending gallons of dopamine to our brains' pleasure centers. We grinned lopsided, stony grins at each other.

"Your dinner will be served in just a minute or two," said Cosmo Kincaid. "After that we can all try to track Uncle Albert with the Perkins telescope. Uncle Albert arrives at eight a.m., so you will be awakened at dawn and picked up by our helicraft at seven-thirty a.m. Nebula Jones will meet you at the top of Mount Humphries minutes later.

"The top of the mountain is very rocky and contains many boulders, but there is a small cleared area where you will assemble and prepare for your transition. On this clearing Nebula Jones will create two portals: one, leading to the black hole, for those going back to the past; the other, leading to the wormhole, for those going to the future. I suggest you get a good night's sleep. Special music has been provided in each cabin to help you achieve a restful and peaceful slumber."

Our dinners were great, prepared to order for each of us. Hacker looked like a condemned man enjoying his last meal. Benny had matzo ball soup spiked with salsa. Greta picked at her cobb salad. My two psi girl-friends and I, all vegans by now, feasted on our Tofu Wellington dish, topped off with a fine white wine from the South of France. Celebration was in the air—for the three of us, at least. We looked forward to the new adventure with wild anticipation.

Somehow we managed to sleep, naked, curled up in a tight little ball, with lucky me in the middle.

The alien helicraft was right on time next morning. The six of us piled in, sleepily, each with our own suite of thoughts, feelings, visions, memories, and expecta-tions. The sky was filled with dark storm clouds, the chill morning air nipping at our faces. We arrived at the top of the mountain in less than five minutes after a breathtaking ride over a forest of pines and rocky out-croppings. Cosmo Kincaid, our pilot, dressed in a fash-ionable ski outfit, left immediately in the helicraft after dropping us off on the mountaintop.

The wind howled around us as we stood in the clear-ing waiting for Nebula Jones to show up. The summit of Mt. Humphreys is the tallest point in Arizona at 12,600 feet. It was cold up there, and we were underdressed in our clothing issue, dark sweatpants and red sweatshirts,

Suddenly Nebula Jones materialized on the clear-ing. He looked much different than the last time we saw him as a holographic image; now he was wearing, instead of a pinstripe suit and red tie, a shimmering silver one-piece spacesuit. He greeted us with a nod, and then started talking as if he was in the middle of a lecture.

"...So you see, although the idea of a black hole is based on Einstein's general relativity theory, he didn't really believe they could exist. He himself said black holes were too weird to be real. What we are waiting for up here is what we call a sentient black hole, but in reality it is an A.I. construct that we use to keep order in the cosmos. We can control it remotely. At its core is a huge microprocessor which will make the necessary spacetime adjustments once your Earth is dropped into it. Surrounding its mass is a—"

"What on earth is...that?" sputtered Greta, pointing to the west and jumping up and down with fear and excitement.

Off in the distance, at the far edge of the horizon, was a spectral vision: a huge, black, circular cloud, spinning madly like the eye of a hurricane, passing in and out of existence. It was fast approaching our little *pied-à-terre.*

"That, my friends," said a grinning Nebula Jones, "is Uncle Albert on his way to our rendezvous. You can't really see the black hole itself because light cannot escape its gravitational pull. In the vastness of space it is invisible to the eye. What you are seeing now is merely refracted light from the background of mountains and green valley below—the outline of Uncle Albert."

"Does it have consciousness?" I asked.

"Does it have a soul?" asked Greta.

"It has consciousness in the same way an android has consciousness. It does not have feelings. And no, it does not have a soul. It is a super-intelligent entity that does what we tell it to do. We feed it the necessary algorithms to achieve our goals. In this case, the recycling of your Earth and all of its inhabitants. Except for these three," he said, indicating me and my two gal pals.

"Now then," he continued, professorially, "surrounding the black hole is a region of space called an event horizon. In a natural black hole, this is the point of no return. Once something enters the event horizon, the pull of gravity is so strong that nothing, not even light, can break free. For Uncle Albert, the event horizon is merely a device that will translate every living thing on the planet into beams of pure light."

"Yeah, yeah, we heard that before, Mr. Jones," said Hacker, who had been strangely quiet up to this point. "But what will this thing look like up close? Just what are we jumping into?"

"When Uncle Albert arrives, for a second or two it will look like a giant spinning vortex. Its event horizon will look like a rainbow. But all of this will happen very fast. You will feel nothing if you follow my instructions. Simply walk through the portal, which I will create for you at the appropriate time, the three of you together. Take a deep breath and keep walking. Next thing you know, it will be the year 1990 and your lives will go right on as if nothing had happened."

"What about us wormhole people?" asked Jill. "What are we supposed to do?"

"Same thing, Miss Appleton. "I will create your portal, and you and Marty and Leela will walk through it together. The only difference is, you three will create your electromagnetic force field *before* you walk through. Otherwise you will be, as they say on Earth, toast. The wormhole should appear a split second after the black hole appears. It will look like a long, rounded passageway. A tunnel. It will probably be alive with brilliant white light and throbbing with an electrical charge. It will be silent. It will be very, very hot."

"You have said the wormhole is theoretical, Mr. Jones, and used qualifiers like 'should' and 'might' and 'maybe.' What if the wormhole doesn't work? What will happen to us?" This was Leela's question, valid and frightening as hell.

"If it doesn't work, Ms. Powers, then you and your companions will be thrown into a state of non-existence. You will be trapped forever between dimensions, beyond the space-time continuum, conscious of your surroundings but unable to escape. Each of you will be alone, but surrounded by the voices and images of all humans who have ever lived and died on Planet Earth. It will not be pleasant. We will be unable to help you."

"Good lord," said Leela.

"Holy shit," said I.

"Hey, let's be positive about this," said Jill. "It's gonna work. I'm sure of it."

"If any of you wormhole people want to change your mind and go through the other portal, now is the time to decide. Uncle Albert is very close. The time is T minus two minutes. Time to say goodbye."

None of us wormhole people were about to change our minds. All six of us in our little group hugged amid tears and pounding hearts. Hacker and I had a mighty, masculine bear hug, wordless, but with a depth of silent understanding I had never felt before with my old friend. Benny was beautiful and crying, but he sucked it up and we had great hugs. Then we six all huddled together, hugging and kissing and whispering soft words of encouragement.

We all felt it. This was an ultimate moment, a moment of absolute truth, like staring Death in the face as the void opens up below. Into the Great Unknown. Beyond the Beyond.

"T minus ten seconds," shouted the alien. "Assume your positions, please."

Two portals formed. They looked like fragile doorways of light. Uncle Albert was very close to our mountaintop. The vortex was spinning madly. The rainbow-hued event horizon sparkled and glittered.

"Black hole people, go now!"

Hacker, Greta, and Benny Bravo walked through their portal and disappeared. Uncle Albert disappeared. A long, seemingly endless passageway appeared beyond our portal. It was bathed in a deep golden light.

"Force field! Psychics! Now!" shouted Nebula Jones. "Through the portal, quickly!"

It all happened very fast.

I love you guys, I flashed to my two psychic lovers, as I added my juice to the electromagnetic shield that would protect us from deadly radiation.

The force field was in place. We walked through the portal shoulder to shoulder, firmly holding hands.

It worked!

Didn't it...?

EPILOGUE

Riding the Space/Time Express

"Anybody know what the hell is happening?"

It is Jill's voice, tempered with just a touch of shrill, knifing through our cramped little space. I know for sure we are in a tall cylinder, a lift of some kind, and whooshing through space at an incredible speed. The darkness is total. I reach out and grab a handful of rounded female butt cheek with each hand, holding on for dear life.

"Hey, it's too tight in here for grabass, Marty!" scolds Leela.

"Ouch! Not so hard, Marty," complains Jill.

The lift stops. A transparent door slides open silently and we quickly step out onto a platform, Leela leading the way. It is very bright. I focus my eyes quickly and scan the landscape. The land looks completely flat and barren, devoid of vegetation, hills, mountains, roads. Devoid of anything that reminds one of life. It is absolutely silent; even the air feels empty.

Empty, except for the domes. They are everywhere, sprouting like mutant mushrooms, scattered hither and yon as if some giant god threw a bunch of marbles out into an empty landscape.

411

"So this is what it's like in the thirty-first century," says Jill. "Pretty strange."

"Agreed," I say, "but this could just be the reception station. Maybe the rest of the world now is all green and futuristic and sleek and everyone loves one another."

"One thing's for sure, we're not in Arizona anymore," says Leela. "And I've got more news for you. I just did a quick remote viewing, and everything within about a thousand kilo radius looks like this. Could be the entire planet. And no people. Nothing moving."

"Think, guys," I say, noting a tingle of panic starting to creep up my spine, "how did we get here? What's the last thing you remember?"

"We step into the wormhole together," says Jill, slowly, remembering, "and it gets very bright and hot, but we have our force field in place, our shield, so we don't get fried, and we get sucked into some kind of whirling vortex and then you are grabbing my butt in the elevator and we land here. It must have taken about a nanosecond."

"Something really strange is going on here," says Leela somberly. "I'm starting to wonder if maybe those freakin' aliens sent us to an alternate universe, either by mistake or on purpose. Or we are stuck between dimensions in some cosmic graveyard."

"Or maybe—" says Jill, then stops, her head pitched forward as if she is seeing some apparition off in the haze. Jill has great eyesight *and* remote vision. She sees objects before anyone else. "I think we have company, guys."

A humanoid figure is moving toward us very quickly, a walkway unfurling before it as it moves. It stands before us, studying us. We are looking at a young man, late twenties, unblinking blue eyes, wearing what appears to be a basketball player's uniform: baggy shorts, tennis or some sport shoes, tank top. There is a big red number 23 on the front of his black tank top. He looks human, but he is definitely missing a human vibe.

Leela, Jill, and I all do a quick scan of his brain. All we see are tiny mazes of wire and receptors. Sparks fly around the inside of his skull as electrical activity lights up the cranium. There is no visible mind, no memories. Databases are there, but inaccessible.

"You are carbon-based humans, yes? From the Early Days. Circa Earthyear two thousand one hundred, is that correct?" His voice is young and strong, the words are crisp and clear, spoken without intonation.

"Is this Earth?" I say in a rush to learn the awful truth.

"This is Terra," says our visitor, "what you called Earth and some called Gaia, third planet from the star." Big outbreath from the three of us.

"And the year is…is…" stammers Jill, hand covering her mouth, afraid to find out.

"The year is, well, I would call this New Year five twenty-one. Actually, we restarted the calendar when we reached one million. So the actual date right now, based on your old Earth calendar, is one million, three hundred five thousand, five hundred twenty-one."

We three gasp, almost in unison. "One million plus!" says Leela angrily. "We were supposed to go a thousand years into the future. Instead we went more than a million! Those freakin' orbs really screwed us up! Now what?"

"I assume you are talking about the entities your people called Nebula Jones and Cosmo Kincaid. They were sent to Terra to avert the so-called Terran Tragedy, which they achieved with the Singularity, but which tragedy was merely postponed and occurred anyway in 2030. Quite an event, according to the Archive."

"Creeps. With their manifesto and their computer models. Bunch o' nonsense. What happened to 'em?" This is Jill.

"The Council decided they had made too many errors and they were retired in Earth year six thousand four hundred and one. Actually they were converted to galactic dust and sent into the cosmic slipstream."

"Serves 'em right," I grumble. "Actually, too little too late, if ya ask me. By the way, what's your name? Do you have a name?"

"Jordan is my name. I am of a race of android, a synthetic life form, that has occupied Terra for many millennia. Our only mission, our only purpose, is to serve humans. Unfortunately, until now, there has not been a human presence on Terra for one million, three hundred five—"

"Okay, okay, Jordan, we know the stats by now." Jill is speaking. Impatiently. "But what are all these domes? Where are all the people?"

"This is what is left of Terra. Much has changed in the last million or so Earth years. These domes are indestructible, impervious to weather or geologic shifts or cometary intrusions or super weapons. Humans lived in these domes and in underground cities until, well, a long time ago. Now the domes sit idle, waiting for evolution to bring new humans. That should occur within the next twenty million years. Perhaps thirty million. When the oceans return, perhaps."

I look at my two lady loves with resignation. "Looks like we might be stuck here for a few million years, girls. This ain't exactly party town. Maybe we could settle into a nice dome, rent some furniture, and play Adam and Eve and Eve."

"You are not stuck here, my friends. Far from it. In fact, you are more free than you could ever imagine. Soon I will show you how to break through the space-time continuum. But first, it is vital that you view the Archive of Human History. This will give you a context for your time-traveling adventures. Follow me."

An elevator appears out of nowhere and a white door slides open. We all step in. The lift is pure white and seems to move at supersonic speed. Is it going up, down, or sideways? In seconds the thing stops and opens into a bare room. Leela, Jill, and I slip into comfortable seats and our new friend Jordan turns on a holo projector. We witness what no human has ever witnessed before: the whole of human history. Correction: Human history from the moment of the Singularity.

"You carbon-based bipeds already know human history up to that moment. No need to waste your time with that. We will begin with the moment after the Singularity, when the black hole operation has been completed. It is Earthyear 1990, a relatively peaceful time, except for the occasional outbreak of war and genocide." Gruesome holos follow, showing bombs exploding, bodies being ripped apart, mass executions, women crying.

"Jordan, if you don't mind," I interrupt, "could you fast-forward a little? Okay, ladies?" They both nod in agreement.

"And is there a restaurant anywhere on this godfor-saken planet?" asks Jill, in all seriousness. "A take-out place, by any chance? I'm hungry."

"There is no food on Terra at this time," says our synthetic life form. "However, in less than twenty-four hours I could create a nourishment replicator for you. Would that suffice?"

"Pass," says Jill. "I've got some trail mix in my pocket. That'll have to do. Onward, Sir Jordan! And please go fast. Our puny human brains can handle it."

And so it begins, our fast-motion history lesson.

At first, everything went according to the plan laid out by the orbs' computer models: a different U.S. president, relative peace and prosperity, the Internet, terrorism tamed, climate change addressed worldwide, a new spirit of cooperation. However, in just a few years, everything changed, quickly. Water shortages became acute; famine, starvation, tribal warfare, the usual. Gla-ciers melting. Temperatures rising. Political upheaval. Nuclear saber-rattling.

[Wolfgang von Neumann didn't become Wolfgang Maximus the next time around, or the leader of a deadly enterprise called Black Swan Galactic. He did become a highly respected quantum physicist who developed the world's most dangerous weapon, the fission-plasma bomb, and shortly after its first test destroyed Somalia, he went mad and spent the rest of his life in a psycho ward.]

By 2020, the world had run out of oil. By 2025, global economic meltdown. In 2028, a plague took out half the planet's population of ten billion. In 2030, Nuclear War One. Planet Earth didn't implode and go nova, as the aliens predicted, but the surface of the planet became nearly uninhabitable for hundreds of years due to radiation poisoning. Most of humanity moved underground or into the first dome cities.

It got worse. By Earthyear 2050 climate change became irreversible, and Mother Earth got her revenge. Coastal cities around the planet were drowned. Food and water were scarce or poisoned. Most wildlife had died out. By Earthyear 2150 humanity was finished. Only a few hardy survivors rooted around in the ruins. The game was over.

"Stop the holo! Stop the holo!" I find myself yelling. "Is this it? Is this what becomes of our species? This is pathetic! Didn't humanity ever reach the stars?"

"The stars, no. The manned journey to the fourth planet, the one you call Mars, ended in disaster. For millennia your Mother Earth healed herself, and by around Earthyear 10,000, visitors from a faraway star established a colony on Terra. They were humanoid and benign. The planet was green again, the oceans clean and flourishing. Tectonic events had rearranged the continents."

"Can we watch this in holo?" asks Leela. "This sounds encouraging."

We watch, in horror. The visitors cloned new humans from bits of DNA salvaged from the ruins. Within two hundred years the humans killed off the humanoid colonists. Around Earthyear 11,000 occurred Nuclear War Two. Jordan speeds up the holo. The same pattern repeats itself at least half a dozen times. Around the holo depiction of Nuclear War Seven, three hundred thousand years on, we three carbon-based types stand up.

"Enough, enough!" begs Jill. "Turn it off! Jordan, please tell us how to get out of here. Our minds are as one on this, right friends?" Leela and I agree.

"You said something about showing us how to break through the space-time continuum," says Leela. "Now would be a good time for that, eh?"

"Is there anything we can do to change this whole sorry human history?" I ask our guide. "I know the future isn't set in stone."

"I hear the future has infinite possibilities," adds Jill, getting freaked out, her face reddening. "And that one person can change the course of history. A Buddha. An awakened one. C'mon, dude, Sir Jordan, give us a break here! Humanity is better than this!"

"Come with me," says Jordan, declining to answer our desperate questions. "I will show you how to bend time, how to leap beyond the stars, how to soar beyond eternity itself."

"Nice words, my man, but can you show us how to alter the Earth's miserable trajectory?" I plead. "Can you show us how to explore other stars, other galaxies, other dimensions?"

"Cool it, Marty, 'cause we are back at the original lift that brought us here." Leela talking. "Listen to the man. He's got a plan. The only plan."

"This is the vehicle you came in," Jordan explains patiently, indicating the cylinder. "You call it a wormhole. I call it the Express. It is a kind of time tunnel. You can use it to go back and forth in time as you wish. The only exception is, you can't go back before your birth moment. Because before that moment you didn't exist. Otherwise, you can go anywhere on the Express."

"Wait a minute," I say, skeptical, "isn't time travel a one-way trip? Only into the future?"

"That is merely some nonsense from a science-fiction writer. You can go forward, you can go backward. There are no controls in the vehicle, except your minds. Simply decide where you want to go, and what date. Make sure you are of one mind. Otherwise your atoms could be scattered to the far edges of the Universe."

"Jeez," says Jill. "That means we three have to be in total agreement as to our destination. That could be a tall order."

"Try it," says the synthetic life form. "You'll like it."

We step into the Express. "Bye-bye, Jordan!" we say in unison. "Have a nice epoch!" says Jill.

The door slides shut.

"Where shall we go?" I ask my ladies, cautiously.

"Anyplace there's a vegetarian restaurant...and a restroom," offers Jill.

"I got it," says Leela. "Let's go to Sedona, Arizona, USA, Third Eye Coffee Shop, Earthyear 2012."

"That works for me!" I sing out.

"Me too!" cries Jill.

"Marty, please press your third eye. I have a feeling that's our Go button," says Leela.

I press: a feeling of expansion inside my skull; a sudden rush of energy inside the cylinder.

Leela laughs. "That's it! Away we go!"

WHOOOOOSH

THE END